The Urbana Free Library

To renew: call 217-367-4057
or go to "*urbanafreelibrary.org*"
and select "Renew/Request Items"

8-12

	DATE DUE	
SEP 15 2012		
OCT 13 2012		

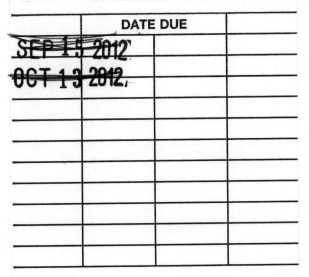

Beyond the
Ties of Blood

Beyond the Ties of Blood

A Novel

Florencia Mallon

PEGASUS BOOKS
NEW YORK

BEYOND THE TIES OF BLOOD

Pegasus Books LLC
80 Broad Street, 5th Floor
New York, NY 10004

Copyright © 2012 Florencia Mallon

First Pegasus Books edition June 2012

Interior design by Maria Fernandez

Library of Congress Cataloging-in-Publication Data is available.

ISBN: 978-1-60598-328-8

10 9 8 7 6 5 4 3 2 1

Printed in the United States of America
Distributed by W. W. Norton & Company

For my sister, Ignacia Schweda

and

For my parents, Ignacia Bernales Mallon and Richard D. Mallon

Beyond the
Ties of Blood

PART I

PART 1

I

Bearing Witness

Boston, 1990

The longest and hottest August drought ever recorded in Boston had seared the summer leaves from the trees, giving the city an eerie, bombed-out feeling. As Eugenia made her way up the stairs of the newly renovated journalism building at Carmichael College, she mopped the sweat streaming down both sides of her face. Looking down at the tissue in her hand, she saw thick streaks of mascara. She could only imagine what her face looked like, so she swung by the bathroom to repair the damage.

She gazed at herself in the mirror and wiped the remaining smudges off her face. Her light brown curls, combed into even ringlets little more than an hour ago, were now a mass of sweaty frizz. She took a wide-toothed comb from her bag, wetted it under the faucet, and began disentangling the thicket piece by piece. After repairing the curls, careful to tuck the occasional silvery corkscrew underneath the brown ones, out of sight if not out of mind, she put away her comb.

Then her eyes focused on her pinstriped blouse with the long sleeves, its even pattern smeared with sweat. Why couldn't she just wear a different top, at least until the weather cooled off? But the minute she unbuttoned the sleeves and pulled them up above her elbows, the same old shudder went through her and she knew she could not. Purple scars went up both arms like malevolent snakes. Over the years she had gotten to know them by heart, their distinct textures and shades, each of them a different length and height. But she had never been able to share their presence with anyone, or explain why they would forever mark her. And then that Chilean lawyer from the new Truth Commission had called, intensifying the old memories that had already been stirred up in the dust storm of transition and media attention as the dictatorship was ending in her native land. She had gone backwards, as if no time had passed since her arrest. She started waking up in the middle of the night with a huge weight pushing down on her chest, making it hard to breathe. Still dreaming, she felt men attach prods to her arms, nipples, and toes, then shoot her body full of electricity. She relived the burning sensation for a few seconds, but then she felt herself lifted out of her body, as if she were flying. Looking down, she saw faceless figures holding her down, forcing her down. Then she would always wake up. She began pulling palmfuls of hair out of the drain every time she took a shower.

Eugenia brought her sleeves back down, buttoned them securely at the wrists, and walked out into the hallway. Her sandals chirped softly on the newly renovated stone floor, and the old-world elegance of the walnut paneling on the walls contrasted starkly with the acrid smell of new paint. So much of the building was like this now, Eugenia thought. In her own office, the tall windows and old-fashioned high ceilings made the new linoleum floor with the fake parquet design seem garish. But she was definitely grateful for the recently installed central air conditioning. Bad with the good, I suppose, she mused to herself.

She opened the heavy oak door of the Journalism department. Mary Jean, the secretary, looked up from her computer at the front desk and smiled. An older woman with a helmet of grey hair, Mary Jean had developed an almost maternal attachment to Eugenia over the past several years. At least once a week she'd put a clipping in Eugenia's mailbox from a women's magazine containing a recipe for a new casserole or an article on the mothering of teenagers.

"Hello, Eugenia," Mary Jean said. She pronounced it "Ewe-gee-neea." "There's a foreign airmail envelope in your box that arrived yesterday."

At first Eugenia had considered getting Mary Jean to pronounce her name in a more recognizable Spanish-language way. If I see this person every day, she'd thought, and she keeps track of my mail and gives me advice on cooking and childrearing, then at least she can pronounce my name right. "Eh like in 'best'," she heard herself say. "Then ooh, heh (the E is like 'best' again), neeah. Eh-ooh-heh-neeah." But then she'd remember her struggles with her journalism students, who couldn't pronounce her last name, Aldunate, to save their skins. Finally she'd just accepted being called "Professor A." And so, she decided, "Ewegeeneea" it would remain, even though she cringed a bit inside every time she heard it.

It was more than just an issue of pronunciation, however. This had been the story of the whole five years since she had moved to the United States from her original exile in Mexico. Every time someone addressed her by this strange sounding name, a chasm opened between her experience, her culture, her life, and the world around her. When people commented that, with her light brown curly hair and blue eyes, she certainly didn't look Latin, at first she had tried to explain that not all Latins looked alike, that color was a question of social class, and that most Latins in the United States were economic refugees rather than political refugees like her. When she repeatedly received confused and disinterested looks in return, she finally gave up. After every interaction that involved her name or her coloring, a wave of longing would come over her, and for a moment she was sure she would die if she didn't see the sun set over the Pacific Ocean, the brilliant blue of the Chilean sky, or the alabaster majesty of the Andes on a winter morning. But she also knew that she lived in a way that would have been impossible in Chile. Her sister Irene, who had been in Boston a lot longer than she had, lived openly with her girlfriend Amanda. Neither sister felt the pressure to find a man (with the right last name, of course) and have the abundant grandchildren that would have sealed their mother's prestige among her friends.

Yet they were still bound to their world of origin with invisible strings. Irene returned to Chile every year to spend her Christmas break, which was during the Chilean summer, at their family's country house. Last year, Amanda had complained about being left alone over the holidays once again. Every year when Irene got back, she reported to Eugenia that although their mother knew that, as a political exile, her other daughter could not return, she still complained bitterly about being abandoned. And even though Eugenia knew it was silly, she always felt guilty.

She tried to raise her daughter differently. She wanted to give Laura enough room to develop freely, without the burden of constant judgment. So she let her stay out late and go to parties at a much earlier age than she had ever done herself. Then she saw bruises on her daughter's neck. Only fifteen, and already making out with boys! But when she remembered her mother's clinging, spying, and wheedling, she bit her tongue. Still, she was never sure she was doing the right thing. She felt that chasm again, between how she and her sister had grown up and what seemed normal in her daughter's world.

Eugenia opened her mailbox and took out the thick envelope with red and white stripes along the edges. Across the front was her name and university address in a spiky, self-assured script that was unfamiliar to her. Looking up at the return address she saw, in official-looking cursive, the name and address of the new Truth Commission in Santiago. Above it, almost on the fold of the envelope itself, was written in the same unusual script of the address: I. Pérez. Ah, yes. Ignacio Pérez. That was the name of the lawyer who had called her the other day. Ripping open the envelope with trembling hands, she found a series of documents which she presumed were sent to all potential witnesses. A small handwritten note was attached in identical spiky handwriting. "These are the basic rules of testifying," it said. "Look them over carefully, and if you feel you cannot follow the guidelines, please write to me at the Commission. Otherwise, I suggest you begin trying to remember things in systematic order, perhaps through a journal. We have found with other witnesses we have contacted that this helps a lot. Unless I hear from you otherwise, I will see you in about three months—Ignacio."

Eugenia knew it would be hard to understand the bureaucratic language in the rules, but Irene had worked in the human rights movement and could help her figure it out. She put the sheets back in the envelope, returned it to her mailbox, and retraced her steps out of the building. She took the brick pathway diagonally across the quadrangle to the student grocery store, where she picked out a blank book with lined pages, a pack of Gauloises cigarettes, and a large, fresh orange. Then she went back to her office, locked the door behind her, and sat down at her desk. She lit a black tobacco cigarette, peeled the orange, and closed her eyes. Manuel's scent surrounded her, and for a moment he was in the room. With all the lights off in her office except the desk lamp and no classes or office hours to get in the way, she opened her new journal and allowed herself to remember.

Santiago, 1971

She careened off the bus at the Plaza Baquedano, trying unsuccessfully to straighten her brown leather jacket in the crush of college students. Once the herd had stampeded by, she stood for a moment on her own, facing the statue, and wondered how in the world she would find Sergio in this crowd. Already the tide of humanity swelled in all directions. Jostled back and forth by a new wave of dark-haired demonstrators, she felt her right ankle give way as the thin heel of her boot caught the edge of a cobblestone, pushing her down on one knee. Another young woman stopped to help her up, then strode off on sturdy hiking boots, hands free of bags or packages.

As she watched the other girl disappear into the crowd, Eugenia realized she was overdressed yet again. She was trying so hard to fit in. She'd found her bomber-style jacket at one of the secondhand stores that were sprouting up all over the neighborhood near her university, filling the demand among her classmates for more worn-in, hippie styles. With the slightly faded jeans and black turtleneck she was sure she'd hit the right note. But the boots were still too fancy, and they weren't good on the uneven cobblestones.

She wished for the hundredth time that Sergio had been willing to agree on a place to meet. It'll be easy, he'd assured her vaguely. Not that many people will show up before the afternoon. She had to admit he'd been more and more evasive lately. She'd lost count of the number of times he had kept her waiting for more than an hour. True, it was barely ten in the morning and they'd agreed to meet at ten thirty, but it was an unusually hot fall day and the place was overflowing. She could already feel a thin rivulet of sweat dripping down the middle of her back. All around her the scent of young, unwashed bodies—musky underarms combined with the stench of days-old socks—mingled with cheap black tobacco and the occasional forbidden sweetness of marijuana.

From the corner of her eye she caught the fluttering of a red and black revolutionary flag hanging from the nose of the Baquedano statue's horse. Ironic, she thought, that General Manuel

Baquedano, whom she knew from her history textbooks as yet another generic nineteenth-century military hero from the War of the Pacific, should have his horse insulted in this way. This brought her attention more fully to the center of the plaza and to the three young men who seemed to be leading the chants. As she looked, two of them, sporting Che Guevara–like berets, descended the stairs of the monument and fanned out among the masses, holding bundles above their heads that looked like leaflets to give out. The single figure left at the top of the stairs held a megaphone in his right hand while his left fist waved in the air with each chant. As he climbed further up to the base of the statue, the crowd roared with approval. He turned his back on her to whip up enthusiasm on the other side of the plaza, and a blaze of light hurtled through his red curls. Ricocheting through the crowd, it shone directly in her eyes.

She stood waiting near the statue, shifting her weight from right to left, feeling the edge of her left boot rub sharply against her instep, hoping Sergio would show up quickly and end her humiliation. Instead, a group of folk singers in black ponchos moved forward and set up their microphones against the side of the statue. As they took out their *bombos* and guitars and began their first set, the red-haired student put down his megaphone and limped slowly down the stairs. He collapsed against the wrought-iron fence at the bottom, supporting his weight on his lower back. Eugenia moved closer.

"Excuse me," she said. "*Compañero.*"

He pushed his shoulders back as he straightened up. "*Compañera.*"

She shifted her weight back from left to right, trying to take the pressure off her left instep. She cleared her throat. "I couldn't help noticing, you were leading the crowd from up there, so I thought I . . ."

9

He leaned slightly sideways, right elbow resting casually on the fence.

"It's just that . . . I was supposed to . . . Do you know Sergio Undurraga?" she finally blurted out.

He sat down on the ledge of the closest flower bed, shoulders hunched forward once again. "Look, *compañera*, everyone knows Sergio. But he's not here yet."

She held out her right hand. "Eugenia Aldunate. It's just that he was supposed to meet me here at ten-thirty."

"Manuel Bronstein," he answered, standing up once again. He took Eugenia's hand in his much larger one. "No offense, *compañera*, but anyone who knows Sergio knows he won't be here until at least one o'clock, longer if he runs into a cute pair of legs along the way."

She jerked her hand from his grasp and turned to go.

"Wait! I'm sorry, I didn't mean . . ."

She stopped, her back still toward him. "Oh yes you did. Do I look that stupid?"

He hurried after her and grabbed her shoulder. "No, I'm sorry, I really am. Look, truth is . . . well, we're from different groups, different campuses . . . you know . . . opposite sides of the river . . ."

She turned to look at him, and his hand fell slowly to his side.

"Okay, look. I'm just angry because me and the guys from the University of Chile, we're always the ones left holding the bag. The guys from the Socialist Youth at the Catholic University claim to be such radicals, but they can't get up before noon."

They were standing about fifty feet from the plaza's southern edge. The crowd had thinned out around them as people pressed in to try and get a glimpse of the singers. Eugenia felt the full weight of the sun bearing down on her head. As she reached up a hand to wipe the sweat gathering at the top of her eyebrows, she noticed a line of smaller, coiled-up ringlets along Manuel's forehead. His abundant red hair and beard would not have been unusual at the Catholic University, where many of the upper-class students were light-skinned, even blond, but they did stand out in the more working-class crowd at the University of Chile. And his eyes, she noticed, were a stormy shade of grey. Still, his hair was slightly ragged along the edges, a clear sign he didn't have the money for a professional haircut. She brought her hand down and looked away.

"It's kinda hot, isn't it," he said, looking down at his watch. "I don't come back on for another hour and a half or so. You want to find a cold drink somewhere?"

Without waiting for an answer, he put his hand under her elbow and led her off toward the line of juice shops that hugged the sidewalk along Providencia Avenue. Eugenia let herself be carried along. He stopped at the third one down from the corner and claimed a table under the red awning. After pulling out a chair for her, he went inside. When he emerged a few minutes later, he sat down next to her, stretched his long legs under the table so that his boots peeked out the other side, and smiled.

"I hope you don't mind, but I went ahead and ordered for both of us. I know the guy behind the counter, and he makes a mean grape juice. It's fresh, and don't worry, he boils the water." He laughed. "I learned the hard way, believe me. Several cases of the runs before I figured out that a lot of the guys around here must use sewer water in their drinks."

A young man in a white waiter's jacket stained with what looked like the remains of strawberry juice put two tall glasses down in front of them, thick white straws floating diagonally across their rims. Eugenia's mother had always warned her about drinking water at restaurants closer to downtown, fearing that the water supply outside the more upscale neighborhoods could not be trusted. She was grateful for the reassurance and took a sip of the cold liquid. It was delicious.

"So how is it you know Sergio, anyway?" Manuel asked. "Is he your boyfriend?"

She allowed herself to focus on his unkempt hair and beard, the smells of sweat and unwashed clothes mixing with black tobacco and, under it all, a surprising aroma of oranges. Although he acted so cocky and sure of himself, there was a vulnerability to him that gathered in his grey eyes, the set of his shoulders, even the angle of his dirty beret. So this was what a revolutionary student was supposed to look like, she thought. Not like Sergio, with his expensive haircut, custom-made clothes, and imported cigarettes.

"You're awfully nosy for someone I barely know," she said, bristling a little in spite of herself.

He chuckled. "Could be." The loud slurping of his straw against the bottom of the glass made clear he had finished his juice in less than a minute.

"You were pretty thirsty, too. How could you finish it so quickly when you talk so much?"

Manuel leaned back in his chair. "Okay. Look, Eugenia. It's just that Sergio isn't a very nice guy, in my opinion. And he's not dependable. You seem like a nice enough person, but I just don't think he's being square with you, especially if he said to meet you at ten thirty and . . ." he looked at his watch. "It's already twelve, which by the way means I need to pay up and go."

He bolted up from his seat and disappeared back into the shop. When he reemerged a couple of minutes later, he threw some coins on the table and put out a hand to help Eugenia up, surprising her with the gentlemanly gesture.

"Thanks, but I'm not done yet. Let me just sit here and finish my juice. When you're done up there, I'll find you near the statue if I'm still around. You're easy to spot with your red hair. And Manuel"—she added as he turned to go—"thanks for the drink."

He turned back and nodded slightly in her direction, then turned again and disappeared into the crowd. Minutes later, she could see the blaze of his hair as he began to climb the stairs, megaphone in hand.

Eugenia sat at the table alone, nursing her sore left foot. She finished her drink slowly, enjoying the coolness of the liquid and the shade. Her foot felt a lot better after a while, though she came to realize how foolish she'd been to wear these boots to a demonstration. She got up from the table and began to walk back toward the plaza. She jumped when she felt a hand grab her arm, and for an instant she thought she was being robbed.

"Hey! Where've you been? I've been looking all over!" It was Sergio. He leaned down to kiss her cheek. "Man, what a crowd. Stinks to high heaven around here."

"You really must've been held up." Eugenia looked at her watch. "I got so hot waiting around that I decided to have a drink."

"Have to be careful around here, babe. The hygiene isn't quite what you're used to in your neighborhood, you know."

"It's okay. I had a good guide. He knows the places around here." She met Sergio's quizzical gaze and continued. "It's that guy up there with the megaphone."

"Manuel Bronstein from the University of Chile?" Sergio spluttered. "You know who he is? He's one of the top guys in the Revolutionary Left! He's from the south, Temuco I think. Word is that he had to come up here because the cops were after him. Not the kind of guy you want to invite to your house for dinner, little girl! Family's been in the country one, maybe two generations, no land to speak of. Man, I can just see your mama's face when he gets to the door, red beard and all, reeking of black tobacco and garlic, nicotine stains on his broken fingernails. Believe me, *doña* Isabel would faint at the sight."

Eugenia straightened up to her full height and wrenched her elbow free. "You can say whatever you want, but there's a few things

I know for sure, without your help. He was here early. He and his friends did all the work to get things going. He was thoughtful enough to see I was hot. He offered me a juice, making sure we went to the place that boiled its water. By the time you showed up, you were two hours late, as usual. And even if your imported Marlboros smell a lot better than his black tobacco, the stench of your patronizing attitude makes me want to throw up!" She turned and headed for the plaza, surprised at her own assertiveness and at how happy she felt that it was finally over with Sergio. It had been a long time in coming, but it took that drink with Manuel for her to finally realize it for herself.

The minute Eugenia stepped off the curb onto the cobblestones of the roundabout, she felt herself swept up and carried off by the whirlpool of humanity that now filled the whole area from the plaza to the river. As long as she relaxed into the current, she discovered, everything was fine. She felt herself carried along in the general direction of the statue. At one point she managed to look back and saw Sergio's well-groomed head bobbing along.

The ebb and flow of the crowd carried her closer to the statue, then further away. After several tries she found herself at the very edge of the swell as it reached the wrought-iron gate, and somehow pulled herself free by holding on to the rail. Sergio, still a good ten feet behind, was carried off into the center of the eddy once again. She saw him turn to look at her, and then he disappeared into the mass of berets, bandanas, and tousled locks. She sat down by a bed of sad petunias and considered her next move.

"Well. I didn't expect to see you here again so soon." Manuel was standing next to her, trying to wipe the streams of sweat with a grimy handkerchief. His face was haggard, and he walked with a slight limp. He managed a crooked smile. Her eyes filled with tears.

"What's the matter?" he asked. He fumbled through the pockets of his jeans and pulled out another handkerchief, slightly cleaner than the first one. He sat down next to her and pressed it into her hand. "What happened? Are you hurt?"

She shook her head and opened her mouth to say something, but no words came out. After taking a few deep breaths she tried again. "I . . . I'm all right. It's just that Sergio . . ."

"I saw him in the crowd, but he was being carried in the other direction. Did he find you?"

Eugenia nodded, blowing her nose into his handkerchief. "Yeah, he found me. Acted like everything was my fault. Said some pretty mean things. So I told him to get lost."

He put his arm around her shoulders for a moment. "It isn't like I didn't warn you."

"Yeah, I guess now I can see better what you meant." She turned toward him. He took his arm off her shoulders and stood up, still looking down at her.

"I'm sorry he was such an asshole. I have a last shift now before the folk singers come back up for their final set. Will you be all right here by yourself for a while? After that we can go if you want, maybe get a sandwich and some coffee."

She nodded, surprised at how very much she actually wanted to wait for him. After putting a hand on her shoulder for a second, he grabbed the megaphone and left. Sitting by herself, she wondered for a moment if it was a good idea to go out with him. After all, at least according to Sergio, Manuel was from the provinces, the son of immigrants, and a member of the most radical and dangerous leftist organization. Even she, who didn't follow politics that much, knew that they supported armed revolution and did not form a part of Salvador Allende's leftist government. Yet there was something about him. Was it his gentlemanly ways, paying for her drink, offering to help her up? Was it the contradiction between his arrogant attitude and the vulnerable glimmer she'd detected in his grey eyes? Or it could be a lot simpler. Maybe she'd finally had it with being the good daughter, especially since her mother's meddlesome matchmaking had gotten her involved with Sergio.

The first few hours of the demonstration had been more political, a generally supportive celebration of Allende's first six months in office. Speakers had praised the speeding up of land distribution to the poor in the countryside and his generally pro-worker policies. The rest of the day turned into a youth festival, with folk music and dancing. When the folk singers began their last set with a ballad, Eugenia found herself humming along, reaching down deep inside her memories for a familiar melody and harmony. Next they played several of Violeta Parra's more well-known protest songs, including "Long Live the Students," which still brought cheers and clapping from the tired, thinning crowd. Her favorite, though, was "Volver a los 17," a song she knew by heart. It was an ode to love and how it could make anyone young and happy again. Sergio said it was sappy, but it always made her cry. And from the reaction of the crowd she wasn't the only one. They finished up with a long medley of Víctor Jara songs, anchored by "I Remember You, Amanda," another sappy one, according to Sergio. But she loved this one, too, especially the part where Amanda waits at the gate of the factory for her lover, an idealistic guerrilla leader, only to learn he had been killed in the mountains. And that last line, it somehow always punched her in the stomach: "Many did not return, including Manuel . . ." Now that last line had a new meaning.

"Hi. Sorry it took so long." Even though the folk singers had ended their set, she had been so deep into the mood of the music that she jumped, and it took her a minute to return to the present. He was sitting next to her. "So I guess I made a liar out of Víctor Jara, huh?"

"What?"

"Well, you know, the part about many of them not returning, including Manuel. But I did return. Manuel is back."

"It's not really a joke in the song, you know. It's really sad. She's waiting at the gate, and he doesn't come back, because . . ."

"I've heard the song before. It isn't as if . . . Is something wrong?" he asked upon seeing her clouded expression.

She was silent for a moment, looking out over the few remaining people, mostly couples holding hands or hugging in the slanting afternoon light. "I don't know," she sighed, trying to get a grip on herself. "Sergio always made fun of me for liking that song. He said it was mushy."

Manuel leaned his elbow on her shoulder and left it there, a surprisingly intimate gesture, considering that they had just met. They sat for a while, watching the weeping willows in the *parque forestal* take on the apricot hues of the approaching dusk. To their right the traces of snow on the Andes mountains glowed against the fading sky. Manuel took his arm down and let his hand rest for a moment on hers.

"Are you hungry? We can go back to that same place. They make a mean steak-and-avocado sandwich. And their espresso isn't half bad." He didn't wait for an answer, but pulled her up to a standing position, took her hand in his, and began walking. Once again she was caught off guard by his dominant manner, so soon after he had seemed so gentle and nurturing, but decided not to resist.

They sat at their same table. The young man who had served them before came out, carrying a pad and pencil. He'd changed his stained jacket and was wearing a navy blue one. "What'll it be, *compadre*?" he asked.

"Bring us a couple of your steak-and-avocado sandwiches, no mayo, and a couple of espressos. Make the lady's a *cortado*, you know, the way you add just a touch of steamed milk . . ."

"Coming right up, *compañero*." The waiter gave Manuel a mock salute.

"What made you think I wanted a *cortado*?"

"Didn't you?"

"Well, yeah, but . . ."

"So then?"

"Well, you can't always make assumptions about people."

"Why not, if I'm right?"

Eugenia sat back in her chair and snorted. "How can you know you're right if you don't listen to the other person?"

Manuel chuckled. "Now *you're* right, little one," he answered, reaching for her hand.

"Don't call me 'little one.'" She yanked her hand away. "It's so patronizing." And it was what Sergio always called her. She was done with that, now.

The waiter arrived with the sandwiches and the coffee. Napkins, silverware, and sugar materialized from the neighboring table. Manuel piled four teaspoons into his small cup.

"Let me just hazard a guess," he said after he'd taken a bite of his sandwich and washed it down with the sweet black liquid. "This isn't really about me."

She was silent, chewing on the slightly stringy steak, savoring the combination of flavors with the salted avocado. The espresso's slightly burnt undertaste was heightened by the frothy milk. "Let's just forget it, okay?"

"Fine with me, but only if you're willing to share a bottle of red wine. These guys have a really good Santa Rita, and they sell it cheap." He motioned over the waiter. "The Santa Rita Tres Medallas, please, *garzón*," he joked.

The thick, cherry-toned Cabernet was like a soft blanket against the evening chill. Manuel ordered another bottle when they finished the first one, and pretty soon they were sitting very close together, her head on his shoulder, both smoking black tobacco cigarettes.

"I don't know what I'm going to do when I get home," she said, the unfamiliar roughness of the cigarette stinging her tongue slightly. "My mother will smell the black tobacco a mile away." She took another puff anyway, savoring the peppery aftertaste.

"One possible solution is that you don't go home till it wears off." He was now running his free hand through her soft ringlets.

"Somehow, I think not going home at all isn't going to solve the problem," she said, nudging him away playfully.

"You can't blame a guy for trying." He let go of her hair and his hand dropped slightly to her jaw line, gently bringing her head closer. They kissed. The hairs of his beard were surprisingly soft, and he tasted of burnt oranges. Her cigarette lay abandoned in the ashtray.

"So what do you think we should do?" he asked finally, his voice hoarse.

"I don't know. But one thing is clear: Sergio is going to find a way to tell her."

Manuel sighed and his chair scraped loudly as he pulled back, fumbling in the crushed pack for another cigarette. "What do you mean?"

"Well, he's my mama's favorite. From 'a good family.' They have land right next to ours. He's not very happy right now, I'm sure of it, and he's going to find a way to get back at me. What better way than to tell my mother about you?"

Removing the cigarette from the pack and scrabbling around in the matchbox helped him regain his composure. She wasn't exactly sure what had upset him most, her suggestion that he wasn't from a good family, or her bringing up Sergio. After lighting it and blowing out a cloud of smoke, his voice had recovered its ironic tinge. "No offense, but what were you doing with him anyway?"

"Our families saw each other every summer vacation since I can remember; he was the handsome older boy next door. When I started at the Catholic University this year, his mama said to watch out for me. It felt like everything was already decided, you know? He's a big-time leader, all my girlfriends were jealous. I don't know."

"Tell me the truth. Did you know he was running around on you?"

"It's not like I thought about it consciously, but when you said that before, I wasn't surprised, just offended that you'd said it to me. I guess I didn't want to admit it to myself, and hearing it from someone else set me off."

"You're right, I was acting like . . ."

"It's okay. Never mind."

Manuel stubbed out his cigarette and stood up, pulling her up and into his arms. His kiss was deeper, longer. She felt the tingle on the inside of her lips move down her body until it became a weakness in her knees. When it was over, she leaned into him, resting her head against the middle of his chest.

"I live right here, just on the other side of the river," he whispered. "Come back with me for a few minutes, then I'll find you a taxi."

They walked across the plaza and through the park, stopping to kiss again under a weeping willow. As they strolled across the bridge, their arms around each other, the Mapocho River caught the reflection of the rising moon.

On the other side of the river, Manuel put a key in the lock of a tiny door next to a dry cleaning shop. They climbed up a flight of dark, narrow stairs. Inside the apartment, he turned and crushed her in his arms, not even bothering to close the door at first. His lips left a line of fire along the curve of her right breast, fire spreading, gathering, knotting. Soon they were lying on his unmade bed, his large hands hot on her bare skin, not able finally to get close enough, soon enough, they were still too far apart, and then the pain. She gasped and drew back.

"What in the hell . . . ?" His voice was suddenly very far away. And then so was he. She sat up. "You hadn't . . . he hadn't . . . why in hell didn't you say something?" He'd bolted up from the bed and was already zipping up his pants. Then he began pacing back and forth. She was silent at first.

"What's the matter?" she finally asked.

"Why in hell didn't you say something?"

"You mean because I'm a virgin?"

"Well, yeah . . ."

"Why wouldn't I be?"

"It's 1971! Come on!"

She began picking up her clothes. No matter how hard she tried, she'd never be part of this radical crowd. Her eyes filled with tears, and she wasn't sure if it was from anger or from shame. What was the point, anyway? But then he sat down on the bed next to her.

"Wait a minute, stop." He took both of her hands in his. "Look at me. Just a moment." She refused to look up, not wanting him to see the tears. She focused on trying to zip up her boots.

"I'm sorry," he said. "To be honest, it was quite a surprise."

"I know, I should have said something, but . . . well, it happened kind of fast, I'd never let Sergio go that far. I don't know, I didn't want to stop, I . . ." She stood up and walked to the window, finally able to zip up her jeans and put her jacket back on. She stood by the window looking out at the moonlit street, the leaves of early fall swirling in eddies across the abandoned cobblestones. She rested her forehead on the pane.

"I didn't want to stop, either." He was standing right behind her, running a hand along her neck. She melted back into him, then turned into his embrace. He drew away first. "But it won't be like this. Not the first time. Let's find you a taxi."

Boston, 1990

Had she fallen in love with Manuel because he hadn't been willing to take advantage of her virginity? The more she wrote in her journal, the more Eugenia realized that her love for Manuel had also been a way to escape the grip of her mother's neediness and smothering ideas about social class and codes of behavior. She'd forgotten how tied up Sergio had been in her own family's drama, and to her mother's desire to hold on to her after Irene had left.

Her parents had fought all the time when she was younger. She awakened sometimes in the middle of the night to hear muffled arguments. Afterwards, her mother's sobbing could go on for hours. Somehow she'd felt responsible, she realized now. She tried so hard to be the good daughter who didn't cause her mother more problems than she already had, especially since Irene had always gotten along better with Papa. At the very least she could be her mother's favorite. On the farm in the summer or on vacation, it was always her sister who volunteered to go out with Papa on horseback, the two of them galloping off in the early morning and not heard from again until after dark, when they returned covered with dirt, several recently killed rabbits dangling from their saddles. When the really difficult times began in the marriage, Irene usually sided with Papa, leaving Eugenia to defend Mama.

She'd pieced the story together bit by bit. Her mother's family, from the Chilean landowning elite, had come into hard times while Mama was growing up, a product, she now knew, of the falling prices for agricultural goods. Her papa, a chemical engineer, was from a family that had made a lot of money in the textile industry and, after they got married, he used his own money to bring Mama's family's farm back from the brink of bankruptcy.

For a while things seemed to go well, and she remembered golden summers and family vacations as she was growing up, long, lazy afternoons spent at the river that ran through their property, picnics full of laughter and playfulness in which Mama and Papa seemed only to have eyes for each other.

But no amount of profit or prosperity could make up for Papa's inferior pedigree in the eyes of Mama's kin, despite all he had done for them. His family tree just wasn't as prestigious as theirs, and money made in industry, no matter how long it had been in his family, was considered boorish. That such vulgar wealth had saved them from ruin only added to their resentment. With time, even she, still a young girl, had begun to detect the edge in her grandparents' comments. When she was entering adolescence—or was it simply that she noticed it then for the first time?—Papa reached his breaking point. He began coming home late almost every night, missing dinner. Sometimes he didn't come home at all. She knew now that he had begun seeing other women, though at the time what she noticed most was Mama's tears at the dinner table, or the late-night arguments. Of course, at the time she could not have understood that, in addition to being angry that he was being unfaithful, Mama was also upset because she was unable to choose her husband over her family.

When Papa finally fell in love with someone else, he packed up his bags and left. It seemed the woman really loved him, too, since she accepted him with nothing, no hope for a new marriage or a legitimate family. There would be no formal separation; Mama's family simply would not hear of it. So after pumping a great deal of his own resources into her family's farm, he left with nothing more than his clothes and his engineering connections. The moment he shut the front gate on his way out of the house, Mama retreated into the bedroom and closed the door. Aside from trips to the bathroom, she stayed in the room, blinds drawn, for six months. She opened the door to accept the tray of food their maid Teresa put there, on the floor, three times a day. Shortly afterward, the tray would be back outside the door, plates empty, ready for Teresa to pick up and return to the kitchen.

As Irene spent more and more time out with her friends, Eugenia had nowhere else to go. She would help Teresa in the kitchen, or read books in the living room. She knew that Irene also talked to Papa almost every day, since she heard the phone ring and occasionally picked up the other receiver in time to overhear snatches of their whispered conversations. Irene was more like their father in so many ways, from horseback riding to her stellar grades in chemistry. Eugenia, on the other hand, had no one to turn to, her father having abandoned her and Mama barricaded in her room. She became obsessed with the short stories of Borges, and devoured García Márquez's *Cien años de soledad* when it first came out. Although she knew she could not write fiction, she began to dream about becoming a journalist.

By the time Mama emerged from her room, her hair had turned completely white. Her friends urged her to dye it back to its original color, but she refused, wearing it proudly, it seemed, as a badge of her suffering. Upon her reentry into the world, she spent most of her time keeping track of her daughters' movements, at precisely the moment in their lives when they needed more independence. When they got home from school, she had tea with sandwiches waiting for them at the table, and then required that they sit down and tell her every detail of their day.

"Where are you going now, Irene?" she asked every afternoon when Irene would get up from the table to change out of her uniform, substituting the pleated plaid skirt, white blouse with tie, navy blue sweater, and beige knee socks for the blue jeans that were becoming more popular among the girls their age.

"I'm meeting some friends downtown, Mamita," her older sister answered, in that excessively patient tone so typical of late adolescence.

"What about your homework? You can't let your studies slide now, you know, less than a year before the academic aptitude test."

"I don't have any."

"That's not possible, *hijita*, you're in eleventh grade now, there's always homework in eleventh grade."

"Mamita." Irene's tone would become tight. "If I've told you once, I've told you a hundred times. I'm in the advanced science program. I have time in the early mornings, when I'm watching the experiments in the lab. Why do you think I'm out of the house by seven, usually before you even come out of your room?"

"Don't use that tone of voice with me, young lady. I only have your best interests in mind. God knows how hard it's been for me, and you just don't . . ."

That was always the moment when Irene would slam out of the dining room, and Eugenia would hear her steps going up the stairs. And that would be the cue for Mama to turn her attention to the younger daughter, who sat there wishing she were on her way out the door just like Irene.

"Chenyita," she wheedled, using her pet name for Eugenia, "are you going to change into more comfortable clothes and begin your homework? I can have Teresa bring you a cup of hot tea with milk in a little while, when you're ready to take a break." Eugenia would trudge up the stairs, ever the dutiful daughter, unable to slam the door and follow in Irene's footsteps.

It was a year later, about halfway through her last year in high school, that Irene dropped a bomb at the dinner table.

"Mamita," she said casually during dessert one evening, "I've decided to apply to the Massachusetts Institute of Technology, in the United States, for their degree program in chemistry.

My teacher this year, Mr. Roberts, thinks I'm talented enough to get in."

Mama choked on her baked apple. "What? *Hijita*, what in heaven's name are you talking about?"

"Just what I said. I'm applying to MIT."

"But . . . but . . . isn't that very expensive? With your papa gone now, we don't have that kind of money, especially not in dollars, why . . ."

"I talked to Papa about it last week. He knows some people in the chemical industry who are looking to train new scientists. He thinks they're offering scholarships. The best ones pay for everything, and maybe I can . . ."

"You talked to your father? Before you talked to me?"

"Mama, the point is that I can get my education paid for, and . . ."

Mama got up from the table and slammed out of the dining room. Although Eugenia knew that Irene continued to speak with Papa on the phone several times a week, she also knew that her sister had been careful to do so when Mama was not home.

Things moved quickly in Irene's life after that. She put in all the application papers in September, and graduated with high honors in December when the school year ended in the southern hemisphere. By April of the following year she had her acceptance and she boarded the plane for Boston in late June. Though Mama had given her a special goodbye gift, an expensive Spanish–English dictionary for scientists, she refused to go to the airport. "What for," she sighed. "Her father's been behind this all the way, I know it. He wants to take my daughter away from me." So Eugenia, Papa, and his new wife went instead. Eugenia still remembered the last-minute flash of panic in her sister's eyes, the slightly too tight hug before she hefted her knapsack onto her back at the gate.

Left alone with Mama in her last two years of high school, Eugenia was placed under the microscope. Mama wouldn't make the same mistakes and lose her, too. "You need to find a nice young man, Chenyita," Mama repeated over and over, "someone from our own circle who will understand you, a young man who's been brought up right and who will know how to respect and appreciate you." Three months after Irene's departure, during their stay at the farm over the national independence holiday, her mother announced she had found the solution to their problem.

"Of course, *hijita*, I don't know how I didn't think of it before. I just had tea over at our neighbors'. Their son Sergio is home from the Catholic University, where he's studying sociology. He's such a handsome, polite young man. You know him, don't you, Chenyita?"

Eugenia had often seen Sergio, several years older than she, during summer vacations. He wore his blond hair a bit long and was constantly brushing it out of his eyes. He paraded around with a pack of boys his age that came with him for the summer. They spent their days hunting, fishing, and riding horseback through the valley, and she'd see them ride past her family's house in the afternoons when they returned from the day's excursion. On weekends they rode their horses into town and got drunk at the local tavern. The girl who came in on weekends to help in the kitchen told Eugenia that they spent their time putting the moves on the local girls, and that Sergio always scored with one of them. "It's his green eyes," she insisted. Eugenia knew that Sergio's blond hair and green eyes marked him as upper-class. The younger local girls, brought up on pulp novels and soap operas, always dreamed about falling in love with and marrying a rich young landowner. And the fact that he wore his hair long, almost hippie-like, only made him more attractive in a vaguely exotic sort of way.

"Oh, come on, Mamita," Eugenia answered uneasily. "He's at least three years older than I am. Besides, why would he be interested in me? He has friends his own age."

"That may be, *hijita*, but he's come alone this vacation. I just invited them to dinner for tonight. They'll be over in an hour, so why don't you take a bath and put on something nice."

They were there at eight, and for the first time in a long time her mother made her signature pisco sours. There was something about Sergio, Eugenia thought, and it didn't only affect the local girls. She, too, found his long blond hair and green eyes quite arousing. He'd obviously been brought up to speed on their mothers' plotting, because he spent the cocktail hour looking her over even as the conversation was mainly between the older adults. When they sat at the table her mother put the two of them next to each other. By the time dessert came Sergio had placed his leg up against hers and was rubbing back and forth very lightly. She had found it hard to concentrate on the conversation, but maybe it was the three glasses of wine she had drunk on top of the pisco sour.

They didn't become a couple, not really. They lived too far away from each other in the city and Sergio was already in college. But whenever they were at the farm at the same time, he came over and took her out horseback riding. They always ended up in the forest. After they kissed for a while among the eucalyptus trees, the crushed leaves under their bodies filling the air with their pungent sharpness, she would suddenly sit up and call an end to the session. Sergio seemed willing to accept this, perhaps because their families knew each other. She wasn't like the little country girls he could have behind the bushes any Saturday night. In fact, Eugenia grew convinced that he found her especially interesting precisely because she would not accept his advances. She began to look forward to their outings.

When she got to the university, things changed. They were all hippies in those days, no matter what their social class, confronting the system, going to demonstrations, smoking marijuana. She was pretty sure he'd told all his friends they were having sex, and he started pressuring her to finally prove her love for him, as he put it. It was after one particularly ugly scene at a party, when he'd been drunk and had tried to force her upstairs, that he began arriving hours late for their dates. Her refusal had been public that time, she now realized, and that had been unforgivable because it made a fool out of him in front of his friends. But when she went to the demonstration that morning, she thought she still wanted to reconcile.

As she wrote in her journal on a daily basis in the peace and quiet of the summer break, Eugenia thought back to an especially warm afternoon at her family's farm, when she and Sergio had gone riding after a large barbecue punctuated by red wine. The head servants had killed and cut up a steer and a sheep, and placed the pieces on the old grill over a pit of hot coals. Gathered under the weeping willow tree in the back, the two families had feasted on the juicy, smoky meat with potatoes also roasted on the grill, and a salad made of tomatoes, onion, and cilantro. After several bottles of Chilean Cabernet, they had also savored a meringue cake with wild strawberries her mother had made. Then the stable hand had prepared two horses, one for Sergio and one for Eugenia. They rode off, Eugenia having to hold on more carefully because of her tipsy state.

When they were hidden away in their usual spot in the forest, he began to undress her. She could tell he had been with lots of girls. He knew just where to touch her. Inside her blouse, moving lightly over her nipples, then down her belly. She felt an urgent warmth and opened her legs, wishing his hand in, pushing hard against him. But then he unzipped his fly. She tried to get up but he pinned her down. After struggling for a few minutes, she managed to bring her knee up and score a direct hit between his legs. He doubled over in pain, and she was able to stand up and rearrange her clothes, even get back on her horse before he recovered.

"Quite the tiger," he said when he was finally able to get up. "But it's all show, little one. You're as frigid as the Andes in winter."

At the university, surrounded by girls in faded jeans who wore tight blouses with no bras and thought nothing of making the first move, she'd begun to fear he was right. What was wrong with her? Why couldn't she, too, be a modern girl? When she hadn't wanted to stop with Manuel, she felt immense relief. But, she realized, in order to be absolutely sure, she actually had to sleep with someone. Even more important to her, however, was the fact that someone had to desire her enough to try again. By the time Manuel called, almost a week after they'd said good-bye, she could barely breathe from waiting.

Santiago, 1971

She had the chauffeur drop her off on the other side of the plaza, closer to the river. She waved good-bye and walked in the opposite direction, toward downtown, until she saw him turn and drive back up Providencia Avenue toward the mountains. Then she walked southeast across the plaza toward the line of sandwich shops. Almost immediately she saw him, sitting under the awning at the same table.

"Hello."

He looked up from his book at the sound of her voice. "Well. That was quick."

"Mama was in a good mood and sent Jacinto in the car to drop me off."

"A chauffeur and everything. I didn't realize I'd made it into the jet set." He stood up and came around the table, taking her in his arms. He was so full of bravado, trying to be cool. His familiar scent, burnt oranges with a touch of black tobacco, enveloped her, but she pulled away before he kissed her and sat down.

"I know you resent Sergio and the other guys from the Catholic University, but I'm not part of their group," she said, smarting a bit from his remark about the chauffeur.

"I know. I'm sorry. I didn't mean it that way; it was a lame attempt at a joke. It's just that . . . it's like I'm onstage and the script in my hand is for a different play." He walked back to his chair and sat down. When he looked at her, his grey eyes dared her to leave and begged her to stay, all at the same time.

"I have no idea what comes next, either," she said.

"Okay, let's just worry about right now. Are you hungry? Do you want some wine?"

He ordered steak-and-avocado sandwiches and a bottle of Santa Rita Cabernet. "The phone book had five whole pages of Aldunates," he said. "I didn't know what I was going to do if I got to the end and hadn't found you." He reached out and covered her hand with one of his. With his other hand he took out a pack of cigarettes and offered her one. When she said no, he shook one free for himself, and then had to use both hands to strike the match.

Their sandwiches came, warm juicy steaks with freshly mashed and salted avocado. He put out his cigarette and they ate in silence. They were well into their second glass of wine before she spoke again.

"It's official now, me and Sergio broke up. Mama's really shaken up about it."

He took another swallow of wine, and it ended in a cough. "How's that?"

"Well, the two days after, you know . . . well, Sergio called, I forget, maybe a total of eight times. Each time my mother tried to get me to pick up. He was so sorry, she said, all that kind of stuff.

But I said no. I guess by the time I'd refused to pick up for two days running, he decided there was nothing to lose. He told Mama he'd gotten angry because you were trying to pick me up."

"And?"

"I denied it. But his calls stopped then. So I guess it's official."

They ate for a while, and then Manuel put down his knife and fork. "My chauffeur comment, I—"

"Forget it. You don't have to explain."

"But I want to. The thing is—"

"I know exactly what you're going to say and . . ."

"No you don't! My family had one in Temuco, and—"

"What?"

"There, you see? You didn't know. After my father made a lot of money in the baking business and we moved into this fancy house, they put me in a horrible private school and kept sending their new chauffeur to pick me up, and—"

"Wait a minute, you're going awfully fast. So you come from the south, and your father has a bakery."

"Okay," he said, after taking another sip of wine. "I was born in Temuco, you know, in the south. My dad had immigrated from Germany around World War II, first to Argentina and then to Temuco where he opened a bakery business. It kept him really busy, I hardly ever saw him, but he made a lot of money. They still live in Temuco, although I came north to Santiago to the university."

"It's funny," she said. "When Sergio told me you were from Temuco, and your family hadn't been in Chile long, I just assumed . . ."

"I get that a lot. People here in Santiago assume I must be poor. But there's a lot of rich immigrants in the south, especially Germans, you know. A lot of them came at the beginning of the century, when the Chilean army took the land away from the Mapuche Indians and gave it to the German colonists."

"But why are you angry at your dad? Did he take land away from the Indians?"

"Well, no. But he was never home. My mom raised me, basically, and I spent a lot of time with her mom and dad, Grandma Myriam and Grandpa David, who were immigrants from Russia. They had a tailor shop, and they lived very simply. My grandpa had been a socialist back in Odessa, before the Russian Revolution, and I looked up to him, I guess, as a father figure. The longer we lived in the big house, and they had me in that awful school . . . I don't know. Sometimes I wished I was poor."

She stood for a moment and dragged her chair closer to his, pulling her place mat, food, and wine along with her. After sitting back down she put her right arm through his left, leaning into his side. "I'm getting cold," she said. He leaned over, put his right hand under her chin, and brought her face up to kiss her.

"So your grandpa David made you a socialist," she said after she caught her breath.

His right index finger traced a corkscrew in the hair along her left temple. "Well, maybe. Not exactly. It was more the times, what everyone else was doing, wanting to fit in at first. But when so many homeless families began invading municipal lands on the outskirts of the city, guys not much older than me, with kids, their wives already missing teeth, without a roof over their heads, I really woke up to the reality of poverty. Somehow, helping them under cover of night, building shacks before the sun came up, getting the government to agree to build them houses, it seemed like I could make a difference. It seemed so much more important than the stupid classes I had in school, or the disgusting amount of money my father made."

"Sergio said you came to Santiago running from the police."

He poured them each a last glass of wine and called the waiter over. "Another bottle, please, *compadre*. Surprisingly, he's almost right. I got into a disagreement with the socialists over the land invasions and joined the Revolutionary Left organization. Then me and one of my buddies ended up running from the cops and actually got shot at. So technically, it's true. After that point, my organization pulled me out, then I got a high score on the university aptitude test, and here I am."

The waiter appeared with the new bottle, uncorked it, and left it on the table. Eugenia ran her hand along the side of Manuel's face, rubbing her thumb back and forth across his cheek right above the line of his beard. "So you're a member of the Revolutionary Left," she said. "Does that mean you carry a gun?"

Manuel laughed softly and caressed the side of her neck, then pushed lower past the neckline of her denim shirt until he heard her sharp intake of breath. "No," he said softly. "The Revolutionary Left fights with actions, not with guns." Their kiss deepened, and they were unable to find a way to get close enough with the chairs in the way. He stood up, fumbling in his pocket for some bills, tossed enough on the table and picked up the recently opened wine bottle.

"I have two glasses in my room," he said, offering his free hand to help her up.

They walked across the bridge in the glimmer of the late-afternoon sun. The two blocks took a long time because they kept stopping. Once inside his room, he closed the door, put the bottle down on the table near the makeshift kitchen, and began rummaging through the cupboard for the glasses. He took out a couple of candles, lighting them and using their own wax to set them in two ashtrays. Then he put out two glasses and filled them with wine. They sat down together in the candlelight.

"Looks like you're more prepared for romance now," she said.

He stood up, refilled their glasses and carried them over to the night table. He placed the candles next to the glasses. They cast a warm blush across the wall and onto the pillows of the bed. He came back one last time, pulling her up and folding her into his arms.

"Yes," he whispered into her ear. "This is much better."

They lay down together in the reflected glow of flame and sunset. He peeled back her clothes, revealing golden highlights along the curves of her breasts. By the time he entered her and she felt the pain, she was no longer afraid; and he stopped and waited, lips grazing her ears and neck, until she began to move. Then they moved together, and she felt his sharp release but he kept moving, and she tried to wait, not to let it come, but it did. For a long time they lay side by side in the flickering dusk.

As darkness began to gather around them, he sat up, reaching to the night stand for a cigarette. "It's after eight," he said as he blew out the first mouthful of smoke and offered her a puff.

She inhaled deeply, letting the fragrant black tobacco smoke out through her nose before handing it back. "What happens now?" she asked.

"Well, you could take a shower, and then we could find a taxi."

"That's not what I meant."

"What, then?"

"I've never done this before. But it feels like we should know what comes next."

"It depends."

"On what?"

"On what you want."

"I don't know what I want."

"Well, then we don't know what happens next. The old problem of the script," he said.

She turned over with her back to him. "Don't make jokes." Her voice was muffled by the pillow.

"It's not a joke," he said, putting out the cigarette. He ran an arm under her neck and shoulders and pulled her gently back toward him so that her head was on his chest. "It's kind of new for me, too."

"Come on. Even I know that's not true."

"No, no, I'm serious. For one thing, I've never been anyone's first before. All the other girls . . . well, mainly they've been older, but . . . I don't know, it was different this time."

"How so?"

"Well, one way to put it might be that I've never made love before. Until now what I've done is have sex."

"I might be inexperienced, but I'm not stupid," she said into the hair on his chest. "We did have sex."

His laughter had a rich rumble to it, a tremor from deep inside that came up slowly to the surface. Her head bobbed up and down slightly. "Who's joking now?" he asked. "Give me a break, Eugenia. What I'm trying to tell you is . . . well . . . it's possible that I could end up falling in love with you."

"That settles it, then," she said. "What happens now is that we fall in love."

Boston, 1990

Several weeks after she had begun writing in her journal, she accepted an appointment with a student who wanted to talk to her. Though Eugenia wasn't teaching, the student had been in her class the previous semester, was the daughter of Guatemalan exiles, and spoke Spanish. She had introduced herself as Elena Manríquez and emphasized she was interested in learning more about culturally sensitive reporting. Her eyes sparkled as she sat in Eugenia's office, and she seemed ready to write down anything Eugenia said.

"I've been doing research in Mexican newspapers," Elena said. "I ran across your article on the leader of the human rights group in Mexico, and then some of your portraits of survivors of the 1985 earthquake. I must confess, Professor Aldunate, I just don't know how you do it."

The first thing that crossed Eugenia's mind was that this student, a native Spanish speaker, was the only one who had known how to pronounce her name. But the young woman was looking at her expectantly, waiting for an answer.

"I'm sorry, Elena," she said, "I'm not sure I understand what you mean."

Elena looked puzzled for a moment. "You know," she finally answered, "how it is you get these women to talk to you so openly, from the heart. I've been reading a lot of politically committed journalism from the early-to-mid eighties. But there's something different about your work, a spark, like empathy, or maybe vision. I don't know. Somehow, you get women to talk to you like a friend instead of a journalist or interrogator. Do you have a particular strategy, a method, that you can share with me?"

Eugenia leaned back in her chair. Elena's long dark hair was pulled into a ponytail on her neck, showing off large silver earrings. She was dressed in jeans and a Guatemalan textile shirt, and wore no makeup. Eugenia felt a tightness in her chest as she realized she did not know what to say. She had to clear her throat several times before she felt she could answer.

"I must confess, Elena, that I'm really not sure," she began, her voice sticking slightly along her tongue. "I've never asked myself this question. Excuse me just a second." She picked up the earthenware mug she kept filled with water on her desk and took a long swallow. "Once or twice I've wondered about the connection, though," she continued in what felt like a more normal tone. "I have to say that the only thing that occurs to me might seem a bit obvious. I'm sure you know that I was arrested in Chile after the coup and spent some time in jail. My daughter's father was disappeared by the military. Perhaps it's just this commonality of experience that generates a natural empathy."

For a while Elena just sat there looking at Eugenia, a puzzled, vaguely disappointed look on her face. "But Professor Aldunate," she said, almost apologetically, "in class you always tell us that being a good cross-cultural reporter doesn't require that you have the same experience as the people you write about. Why, last semester you said that if this were necessary, there would be no point in communicating beyond our own culture. You said that—"

"I'm sorry, Elena." Eugenia cut her off, standing up and looking at her watch. "I have another appointment right now that I can't miss. This is really fascinating, and I hope we can continue the conversation another day. My apologies."

After she closed the door behind the retreating student, Eugenia returned to her chair and sat down. Her mouth felt very dry. She reached for her water and found that her hands were trembling as she brought the mug to her mouth. After taking a couple of shaky swallows she put it back on her desk, stood up, and walked across the room. She turned off the lights, locked the door, and went back to her chair.

Santiago, 1971

After they made love, Eugenia began spending more and more time at Manuel's apartment. The new socialist government was in its honeymoon period, and so were they. She no longer felt like such an impostor in the radical crowd. Not that she really understood the politics, and she didn't join a student organization. But the fact that they were a couple somehow made everything better. When she saw those radical hippie girls with the see-through blouses and no bra, she no longer felt inferior, because everyone could see Manuel had chosen her.

Irene came back from Boston and took up a research position at the University of Chile, renting an apartment downtown near her lab. Although their mother was disappointed at not having Irene back in the house, Eugenia found that Irene's apartment provided a good excuse when she decided to stay over with Manuel. She was gripped by an irresistible urge to redecorate his one-room flat, and when she did not have classes she roamed the secondhand stores and flea markets looking for suitable items.

She managed to make the most of the space available, sprucing up his old couch with a batik bedspread she bought from a young girl with henna-tinted braids at an open-air market downtown. A week later she went back and bought a second one, using it to make curtains for the one large window facing the street. But she was proudest of the Andean rug in earthen shades that matched the brick-colored lines in the batiks, which she bought secondhand along with a small battered coffee table that she sanded and refinished by hand. By the time the cold of winter took hold of the city in the second half of June, she had created a small, warm oasis where she and Manuel could hide out and make love under warm quilts.

"You've really made some changes in this apartment," he said one afternoon when they were sitting at the kitchen table drinking tea and eating fresh rolls from the corner bakery.

"What's the matter, don't you like them?"

"Sure," he said after a pause. "You've put a lot of work into them, and I like the fact you want to make us a comfortable place to live."

"But?"

He ran a finger along the edge of his mug. "I don't know," he said. "It's just that the place feels really different."

"Isn't change good sometimes?"

"Yeah. But don't get me wrong. Especially when you put up the curtains, you made me think of my mother."

Eugenia stood up from the table and walked over to the window framed by the offending curtains. She looked out at the tree that was now completely denuded of leaves.

"Now you're mad," he said. She was silent. "I told you not to get me wrong," he continued. "But quite frankly, I don't think the time and money you've been spending on this is really worth it. There are a lot of other things to be done right now that are more important."

She turned to look at him. "That might be," she said. "But I'm not an activist. All I wanted to do was to make us more comfortable. I haven't spent a lot of money, and even if I had, it's mine, not yours."

He stood up and came over to her, trying to put his arms around her. She pulled away. "Okay," he said. "I get it. I'm sorry."

Though she knew Manuel was with the Revolutionary Left, and there were nights when he didn't come home until very late, reeking of cheap wine, Eugenia hadn't wanted to get involved. Though sometimes she wondered what he was doing late at night, why he came home drunk, mainly she'd seen his politics as through a veil, vague outlines and figures with a certain mystery to them that she had never been able to figure out. That changed one night in July, right before winter vacation. She'd been feeling guilty about not going to the country house with her mother over the upcoming break, so she'd gone home to spend the weekend with her. When they got into a fight, she had decided to go back to the apartment and surprise Manuel.

She could hear the noise from the ground floor as soon as she let herself in. She climbed the stairs. When she opened the door the stench of sweat, black tobacco, and cheap wine was like an uppercut to the jaw. She stood there for a moment. The floor of their one-room apartment, newly swept only a few hours before, was now covered with crumpled pieces of paper and overflowing ashtrays. The ashes and cigarette butts that could no longer fit in the containers were being kicked around by muddy hiking boots as scruffy, long-haired young men moved between the kitchen and her coffee table. Whenever they passed over her Andean rug they ground a fresh mixture of mud and cigarette ash deeper into its formerly brick-colored pattern. The batik spread on the couch had been crumpled into a corner.

They didn't notice her at first. Then a shout went up. "Hey! Manuel!" He looked up and came running to the door.

"*Mi amor*. Weren't you going to—"

"We got into a fight, so I thought I'd come back and surprise you. Looks like I was very successful."

"We needed to get out an emergency leaflet, and since you weren't going to . . . Just give me about five minutes. I'll clear them out, and then I can clean up and . . ."

"Don't worry. It'll take a lot longer than that for the stink to clear out. I'll go stay at my sister's."

She called her mother from Irene's downtown apartment and said her plans had changed. She would go to the country for winter vacation. She returned in time for classes and continued sleeping on the couch in Irene's living room. She was unable to return to the one-room place where they had fallen in love and that she had spent months making comfortable and pleasant. She could not fully explain her sense of betrayal, but she felt as if Manuel himself had caused each ash stain on the carpet for which she had scoured the secondhand stores, each scuff on the coffee table she had refinished by hand. For the first time she could see clearly that what mattered most to her was not as important to him. She felt a stab of pain every time it occurred to her that his politics were more important to him than she was.

On the Friday of the first full week of classes, she got back to Irene's to find Manuel sitting on the front steps of the building. He looked like he hadn't slept in days, and he gave off an odor of stale wine. When he saw her, he stood with difficulty, swaying slightly. He was drunk.

"Please. *Mi amor.* Just listen for a moment. Please."

She stopped, but kept her distance.

"I'm sorry. I've cleaned the whole place up, kept the windows open, aired it out. I promise they won't come over again. I'm so sorry. Please come back, I . . ." He took a step toward her, but she stepped back. He stopped. "Eugenia," he said, the roughness of tears palpable in his voice. "I love you. I don't know what I'd do without you. Please come back." Then he sat back down on the steps, his head in his hands. And he began to sob.

She wasn't entirely sure why she'd gone back. Had it been that vulnerable streak of his, that from the first time at the Plaza Baquedano had mixed with the hint of danger emanating from the Revolutionary Left? Was it the smell of burnt oranges and black tobacco? What he knew how to do with his fingers, his lips? How every nerve ending in her body stood up, when he simply walked into the room? Until she met Manuel, she hadn't known what real pleasure felt like. But part of it, too, was the allure of the prohibited, her knowledge of how shocked her mother would be if she found out. And she had to admit how good it felt that, out of all the girls, the leader of the Revolutionary Left had chosen her.

Whatever it was, her decision had sealed her fate. After that, their story accelerated along with the political events in Chile. As the economic crisis got worse and the government still refused to send in police against demonstrators taking over farms and factories, the right-wing opposition got more and more militant. At first it was mainly landowners in the countryside whose farms were being taken over by peasants or expropriated by the agrarian reform. Then factory owners and other members of the investing classes got involved. They were encouraged by the women from the upper class who went out into the streets, banging on pots to protest the shortages of goods.

When the neighbors complained about Manuel's radical politics, they were evicted from their apartment. The polarization between the Allende government with its working-class, radical student, and peasant support, and the right-wing opposition with its coalition of urban and rural upper classes, only got worse through 1972 and the first months of 1973. As strikes and street demonstrations spread, the Allende government lost the support of the middle classes and of their political party, the Christian Democrats. By June of 1973, the smell of tear gas was constantly in the air.

Manuel and Eugenia took to skipping classes at their respective universities. The professors weren't there half the time, anyway. Somehow, Eugenia decided, they'd probably known that their days together were numbered. They drank coffee in bed for hours in their new third-floor walk-up, the slanting sun of winter tracing highlights in Manuel's red beard. What she remembered most about those days, what had made her happy, was the feel of Manuel's red locks between her fingers, the smell of freshly ground coffee at the small Italian shop on the corner, the little pot of English ivy on the windowsill that thrived in spite of their neglect.

Even as they lingered longer in bed in the mornings, Manuel still went out in the afternoons to help build the school at the site of a new working-class community at the edge of town. He dismissed her worries about his safety, even though the more conservative upper-class students at the Catholic University, the supposedly apolitical ones who had never joined a political party or student organization before, now began arming themselves to fight the Revolutionary Left. Rumor had it that they were collaborating with the new fascist group known as New Fatherland, the one that had been started by angry landowners from the south of the country.

She knew that students like Sergio, who had been in the Socialist Party, were not willing to join in, but there were still a lot of these conservative hotheads at the Catholic University.

Her fears became all too real the night his jaw was broken in the fight with the right-wing thugs. She'd waited up for hours, and when he finally made it home, his friend Hernán almost carrying him up the stairs, she foolishly expected him to say he would give up politics. But he just stayed in bed, groggy on pain medication, and she fed him soup and mashed potatoes.

He was all right by the time of winter vacation. He took to sitting around the apartment, looking thinner and more haggard, and sometimes he opened a bottle of wine at lunch and kept drinking it through the day. The government had taken over her family's farm in the agrarian reform, so her mother had insisted they spend the break together in the north and she couldn't think of a convincing excuse. Besides, after all the time she spent helping him get back on his feet, she felt as if she owed her mama at least this one holiday. And maybe, just maybe, she needed to remind him that she wouldn't always be waiting around, her hands clenching a cold mug of tea, no matter what he did.

She returned at the beginning of August, a little more than a month before the military overthrew the government for good. A week or so after her return, they were evicted once again. The only room they could find was a ragged little dump behind a gas station. Three weeks later, right after the military coup, the Revolutionary Left put out a statement calling for armed resistance. Even she knew what a joke that was, a few cornered guys with pistols facing the tanks and planes of the armed forces. She'd heard the planes bombing the Presidential Palace the day of the coup, and rumor had it that they'd bombed some of the working-class neighborhoods, too. But the statement meant that the military would target all members of his organization, and that made him a marked man.

She was the only one who could walk to the corner store two blocks away to buy bread, coffee, and the two horrible newspapers whose publication the junta still allowed. Every morning, when she returned, she put the coffee and sandwiches on the table and they ate in silence. Then he turned to the last page in each newspaper to check for names he knew on the lists of those arrested. As she sat there, looking at him run his finger down the list, stopping every now and then, closing his eyes or shaking his head, she wanted to ask him what they were going to do, but she found she couldn't ask the question out loud. She hoped she'd be able to at some point, but they ran out of time.

They were still finishing up their sandwiches late on a Sunday morning when the crash of the front door startled her so badly that she spilled her coffee. The thought that she must get up had not even formed completely in her head before she felt a fist hit her face and she was down on the floor. Looking up through the red haze of pain, all she could see was an olive-colored form. Then the sharp stab along her side when he kicked her. She closed her eyes, wetness spreading across her cheeks.

They left her alone after that, focusing on Manuel. She was afraid to open her eyes. She heard, again and again, the hard thud of military boots hitting human flesh, his grunts and moans mixing with the curses of his attackers, all of it punctuated by the sound of glass shattering against the floor. When they finally hauled her up, they tied a blindfold over her eyes and half-dragged, half-carried her out into a waiting car. She was thrown into the back, her head hitting the door on the opposite side.

After they were picked up, Eugenia realized her mistake in taking him back. She was in love with him, but he loved politics. That's why she ended up on that metal frame, the electricity crashing through her until all she wanted was to die. To escape the searing pain. She couldn't tell them anything because she really didn't know anything. She just happened to be in love with a political leader. And then that horrible day, when they took her into the room where they had him and she saw how badly they had tortured him. She was sure the only reason they brought them together was to taunt him one last time. She knew that, after that moment, he'd be gone. She wasn't sure what was worse, having lost him, or seeing him again, in the state he was in, right before losing him forever.

But then she became aware she was pregnant. The sickness started coming every morning, and pretty soon it was clear that she wasn't just suffering delayed effects from the beatings and electric shock. Her breasts got large, and her stomach grew round and full. When the young girl with whom she had shared a cell was released from Villa Gardenia and let Irene know where she was, her sister moved heaven and earth to get her out. Eugenia remembered the cold wetness of the winter morning when she was transported to the Mexican embassy in the old VW van that smelled of gasoline. She shivered all the way, nauseous from the fumes, her swelling belly making it hard to get in and out of the back seat where they'd put her. Irene had been waiting at the embassy gate with a large poncho to drape over her shoulders.

Even after they took her to the embassy, she had to wait until the Chilean government accepted the Mexican request for political asylum. She took to strolling back and forth among the tables of exiles waiting to leave the country, watching their endless chess games, their disputes over a hand of bridge. Irene came every day, bringing treats to still her cravings, new clothes as her belly got larger. Yet every day, when she woke up, she wondered how things could just go on as normal. There were people dying, she thought, being tortured, beaten, and killed all around them. She didn't even want to think about how much Mama must have suffered, her daughter disappeared and tortured, and now, pregnant, about to go into exile. And people were arguing over cards? Every time the baby kicked she felt like the ultimate, and most banal, symbol of how life goes on, even in the midst of tragedy and grief. Her baby was a flower growing on earth made spongy with human blood.

The contractions began one evening while she was still waiting for approval from the Chilean government. After all, there weren't that many countries that, like Mexico, were still accepting exiles. The large number of petitions made the wait so much longer. Canada had filled its quota, and the United States accepted no one. She had never really had Manuel, but now she would have his child. Irene was there, too, when Laura was born, the first person to hold her, tears streaming down her cheeks. Because Laura was born in the embassy, she was a Mexican citizen. In any case, Chile wouldn't want her, the child of two subversives, one of them gone and the other damaged beyond repair. Her birth certificate read: "Laura Bronstein Aldunate, born on Mexican soil, Mexican embassy, Santiago, Chile, September 16, 1974." Only later, after they'd lived in Mexico for several years, did the full irony of that date strike Eugenia. Her daughter had been born on Mexican Independence Day.

Mexico City, 1974

A month later, she and Laura were booked on a flight to Mexico City, where they were picked up at dawn by representatives of the Revolutionary Left exile organization. The young man who drove the tattered station wagon into which they put her two small bags still sported the large, dark moustache and long hair that had been marks of Revolutionary Left militants. His voice took on a hushed, awestruck tone when he spoke about Manuel.

"You were there, *compañera*," he said respectfully, "so I don't have to tell you how much he suffered. But one of our guys who was also in there with him, and got out by some miracle, he said that *compañero* Bronstein became a legend in the torture camp. They tortured him every day in Villa Gardenia, *compañera*, for hours and hours. And he never said a word. Not one. Here in Mexico, *compañera*, well . . . we consider him a hero."

As the widow and child of a hero, she and Laura were given a place to live and she was put into contact with several newspapers, where she learned slowly but surely to be a journalist. She had always loved reading and had dreamed of becoming a journalist, and this was a way for her to take her mind off Manuel. And Mama. Even Papa. Loved ones she would never see again. By focusing on the stories of others, she didn't have to think about her own.

Slowly they settled into a life in Mexico City. They moved to a small second-floor apartment in Coyoacán, a southern neighborhood full of artists and cobblestone streets. A bougainvillea grew up the side of the balcony, spreading its luxuriant purple blossoms along the edge of the wrought-iron railing. On her third birthday, Eugenia bought Laura a small stuffed porcupine made of pink velvet. They called him Paco. A Zapotec woman from Oaxaca, not more than eighteen years old, helped in the kitchen, washed and ironed their clothes, and took care of Laura when Eugenia had to go in to the office at the newspaper.

Mostly Eugenia wrote at home, clacking out articles on a small Olivetti portable typewriter. Over time, her byline, which at first had felt like charity from the exile community, developed a prestige of its own. The change came after she landed an exclusive interview with the mother of a young leftist disappeared by Mexican authorities the same year she and Laura arrived in Mexico. Hundreds of letters poured in at her newspaper, lavishing praise. From that moment, her editor always sent her when a story had to do with human rights. Between her arrival in Mexico City in 1974 and the beginning of the 1980s, the horrors of military massacres in Nicaragua, Guatemala, and El Salvador—not even to mention Chile and Argentina—kept her very busy.

As the widow of a revolutionary hero and an expert on human rights, Eugenia could not shake the feeling that she was an impostor. After all, she had never done anything truly revolutionary herself, except be in love with Manuel. And what had made Manuel such a hero, anyway? She pretended to know, but she really had no idea. He hadn't talked under torture, everyone kept repeating. Not a word, they said in awestruck whispers. What she never mentioned was that she, too, had never said a word. But that was because she had nothing to say. And it didn't matter to the soldiers. They tied her down and sent electric currents through her anyway, until welts formed on her burning flesh that would mark her forever.

Whenever these thoughts came into her head, Eugenia locked herself in the bathroom and took off her blouse. In the mirror she looked at the purple marks on her arms, the scars from where the electricity had seared her skin. She ran an index finger over each one, felt the raised edges, the points at each end that were still slightly tender to the touch, even after several years. More than anything else, she thought, these made her an expert on human rights. The nightmares did too, full of nameless and faceless beings who did horrible things to her. Things she still managed to suppress during her waking hours.

The first night that Laura brought her the blanket, then the glass of water after another one of her night terrors in 1984, Eugenia felt happy that her daughter wanted to take care of her. In fact, Laura used the same words to comfort her mother after her nightmare that Eugenia had used a few weeks before when their roles had been reversed and Laura had been sick. If only Eugenia had been able to comfort her mother back when Papa left, but Mama had locked her door during the time she was ill. Then she and Laura had talked about Manuel. For the first time, Eugenia realized, she was able to tell Laura about their daily life together, things she thought about constantly but had never been able to share with her daughter before. Now that Laura was ten, perhaps it was easier for her to understand.

She wondered if Laura had seen the scars on her arms that night. She'd been wearing a sleeveless nightgown. When Laura didn't say anything, Eugenia relaxed. But when it happened again, Eugenia bought a new wardrobe of nightgowns, all with long sleeves. They were especially useful after the earthquake, when she found she could not sleep at all.

�֍

One September morning in 1985, Eugenia woke to the worst earthquake she had ever experienced. By the time she became conscious, her bed was on the opposite side of the room from where she'd fallen asleep and the walls were changing shape. She was unable to stand until the first shock passed, and found Laura crying under her bed.

For weeks Eugenia roamed the apartment at night. Laura took to sleeping in Eugenia's bed, Paco the porcupine clutched to her chest. Sometimes, just the regular breathing of her daughter next to her calmed her enough so that she could doze off for a while. But then she would wake up again. In the early mornings, with slivers of almost-sun peeking in through the drawn curtains, she spent hours watching her daughter sleep. The straight jet-black hair, the long raven lashes that fluttered against her cheeks as she dreamed. She did not look like Manuel. She tried to put them side by side in her mind's eye, and found that the minute one of them came into focus, the other disappeared. It was almost as if the presence of one was conditional on the absence of the other. Again and again, in the apologetic light of early dawn, she tried to hold both together in her mind. When she finally gave up, only Manuel stood there, his red hair glowing. She shook her head back and forth to get rid of him and reached out and gently moved a finger across her daughter's right cheekbone, imprinted now with the folds of the pillow.

She called her sister, who now had a job as an associate chemist at a lab at MIT, and said she could no longer stay in Mexico. Irene called back a week later to tell her about the fellowship being advertised at Carmichael College, which was also in Boston. They were looking for someone with experience in cross-cultural reporting who could also teach a class to undergraduate majors. Her ten years of experience as a journalist in Mexico impressed the search committee, and somehow the school administration convinced the Immigration and Naturalization Service that no one else could do the job.

Boston, 1990

As she sat in her darkened office, Eugenia realized how out of place she'd felt in Mexico. Everyone presumed she shared Manuel's political values, his passionate sense of justice. But beyond her own vague belief that the poor should have access to land, a place to live, basic rights, things like that, she had no idea what he really stood for. His romantic revolutionary figure hovered over every conversation she had with Chilean exiles, and she had to pretend she knew his politics. While others went on and on in hushed tones, all she could remember was him crying on the steps of Irene's apartment, or his body doubled over in the torture camp.

Her early journalistic forays had an almost desperate quality to them. Why had the poor been so important to him? Why had he been so passionate about it all? The interview with the human rights leader had been a stroke of luck. She could definitely understand the other woman's loss, that sense of seeing her loved one through a veil, not quite able to make out what he believed in and what it meant.

Through her interviews, she realized, she had tried to make sense of her own loss. What was so important, so powerful, so overwhelmingly just, that he'd had no choice but to abandon her? Perhaps her grief, her desire for Manuel, her sense of being left alone—these were the things people connected to. But how could she say these things to her students? No, she had to forge a different explanation to satisfy the motivated ones like Elena, who came asking uncomfortable questions. Elena had been the first one to really put her on the spot, and she had not been prepared. How ironic that she had played the culture card, the unique experience card, so completely contradictory to everything she had ever taught them. But how ironic, too, that the truth was exactly the opposite. It was her hunger to know something she didn't know, her desperation to explain something that had no explanation, that made her interviews stand out. A hunger, a desire, so intense that it was almost sexual.

Even now, just thinking about it, her body awakened to a desperation she hadn't felt for a long time. She'd spent fifteen years as the widow of a revolutionary hero, tending his flame, but she was an impostor! Aside from sexual pleasure, all they'd really had together was a mutual desire for romantic love. Sure, she raised his daughter to know his sacrifice, but it was all a story she concocted to prevent people from knowing the truth. And that was why she trembled now in her darkened office. It wasn't the air conditioning. It wasn't even the memories, or her inability to answer her student's simple question. She was afraid she would finally be revealed as the liar she really was.

❧

The doorbell rang about nine in the morning, an hour after Laura had left for school, in a greater hurry than usual because it was the first week, still gobbling down her breakfast on her way out the door. The temperature had shot up again on Monday, threatening the hundred-degree mark by ten in the morning and making it hard to remember that school had already started. Ignacio Pérez had called the night before when he got to Boston, and she was expecting him any moment. Eugenia did not have class that day, so she had been taking advantage of the time to continue writing in her journal. In this latest entry she was focusing on the coup itself, on what had happened immediately afterward.

She pictured herself and Manuel in that last one-room apartment. She remembered the morning the soldiers burst in. The crash of the door, pulled halfway off its hinges, mixed with the downstairs buzzer, wrenching her back into the moment. Eugenia jumped. It took her a split second to separate the past from the present. She pressed down the button on the intercom.

"Hello?"

"Eugenia? It's Ignacio Pérez."

"Oh. Hi, Ignacio. Just push on the door when you hear it buzz."

Almost immediately she heard his quick steps taking the stairs two at a time, all the way to the third floor. She opened the door before he could knock, and found a young man with black hair and blue eyes. His hair was very straight and he wore it relatively short, except for a single lock that hung over his right eye, almost like a curtain meant to screen out the sorrow in his stare. That deep-rooted suffering was the only thing about Ignacio Pérez that made him look older than twenty-three. Perhaps for that reason he dressed formally, in a full summer suit and, despite the heat, a dark blue tie with wine-colored stripes. He was sweating and his face was flushed. Eugenia felt an almost maternal concern.

"Please come in, Ignacio. It's so hot out there, and I'm sorry that I don't have air conditioning. Sit down, and let me get you a glass of cold water. Or would you prefer iced tea, or mineral water?"

Eugenia busied herself in the kitchen preparing two glasses of mineral water with ice and lemon. She brought them out to the living room, opened a small drawer on the bottom of her coffee table, and took out two coasters. She placed everything on the table and looked up. Suddenly she did not feel ready to proceed.

"I'm sorry," she said, "but are you hungry?" Her voice sounded as if she'd had to force it around several jagged roadblocks in her throat. "I have some grapes in the kitchen, I . . ."

She let her sentence trail off, and went back into the kitchen. She took the grapes out of the refrigerator and washed them under running water in the sink, then put them in a large yellow bowl. She brought it out to the living room and placed it on a small mat next to the glasses. She took a seat in the armchair facing the sofa. She felt short of breath. The heat was becoming oppressive. Ignacio cleared his throat.

"Well. Eugenia. We have a protocol we follow in all our interviews. I hope you don't mind, but I must summarize what I already said to you over the phone several months ago, as well as some of the material in the documents I sent you in the mail." Ignacio cleared his throat again before proceeding. Then his voice took on an official, routine, almost sing-song quality.

"We need your help in the case of Manuel Bronstein Weisz, whose disappearance we believe to have been politically motivated. His mother, Sara Weisz, who now lives in Santiago, was the first person to come before the Commission when we began our interviews. She had been contacted by an ex-member of the secret police who said that you had arrived in Villa Gardenia with her son. As a founding member of the Committee of Relatives of the Detained and Disappeared, she used her contacts and tracked you to Boston. I am here in her name to request your help in confirming the abduction of Manuel Bronstein Weisz.

"And one more thing, if you'll permit me. The Commission has defined its work essentially as establishing and confirming, through reliable data and testimony, the human-rights abuses suffered by the executed and disappeared and their families. It is not our mission at this time to document the experiences of people like yourself, survivors of prison and torture. Personally, however, I feel you must have the opportunity to give testimony in as detailed a fashion as you wish, and will not stop you if you include your own experiences."

When Ignacio finally stopped talking, a deep silence settled between them and their eyes locked. Eugenia realized that, ironically enough, his official, vaguely formulaic intonation had calmed her down. It suggested a larger, almost paternal authority, a newly empathetic government hovering over his shoulder that now wished to listen to its citizens. And she knew then that this was the way she could make a difference, not only for Manuel and his parents, but for herself and Laura. No matter how limited her understanding of his politics, she was the only one who'd been there and survived, the only one who could tell this story.

Ignacio took a small portable cassette recorder out of his pocket. When he pointed to it, Eugenia nodded. She began talking as soon as he pressed the RECORD button, raggedly at first, then slowly gaining resonance and power until her words were like a wave that, after spending many years on the high seas, suddenly rushed toward the shore.

"They caught us in our last apartment in Santiago, the tiny one we'd moved to after Manuel's last eviction. It was October 7, 1973. It was a clear and luminous morning, a bit chilly, a typical spring morning in Santiago. Like every day since the coup, I'd gone out as soon as the curfew lifted to buy food, coffee, and newspapers. It was amazing how soon after the coup the shops were full to bursting with exactly the items that had been impossible to find before. I remember thinking, over and over, how right people had been to accuse shopkeepers of hoarding. To this day I don't know whether I was followed that morning or not. I probably was, because they couldn't have arrived more than twenty minutes after I got back from the store.

"I imagine you must already know, more or less, what happened next. They burst in while we were having coffee. You know what that was like, don't you? They broke everything, threw us to the ground. They beat us for the mere pleasure of it, because once we realized what was happening we didn't put up any resistance. They put a blindfold over my eyes and tied my hands behind me. Then they shoved me into a car and threw me in the back, on the floor. I don't know for sure what they did with Manuel, but I imagine it was pretty much the same. They must have put each of us in a different vehicle.

"They kept me blindfolded for a long while. Perhaps they didn't want me to know where they were taking me, but for someone who'd grown up in Santiago it wasn't too hard to guess. There was a small uncovered place near the corner of my left eye, and every now and then I managed to make out something familiar. I could tell that we reached the outskirts of town, what I later understood was Villa Gardenia. But maybe the reason they blindfolded me was so I couldn't identify those who tortured me. Especially those who gave me the shocks. Because in the following weeks, torture—and the fear of torture—became my new world . . ."

Eugenia took the glass of mineral water in her hands, trying not to spill any even though she was shaking violently. After several large swallows she took a deep breath, put the glass back down on the coffee table, and continued.

"The last time I saw him, they brought him into the room where they'd been torturing me. At first all I noticed was that the electricity stopped. I felt tired, thirsty, relieved. I don't know. Truth is, I was so tired, so run down, everything hurt. At least now I don't remember exactly what I felt. It's even possible I didn't know it at the time.

"There came a moment when I realized that there were more people in the room than before, and they had removed my hood. I looked up. There he was. I think they'd broken his right arm, because it was sort of hanging at this weird angle. His face was so swollen, Ignacio, that the only way I recognized him was by his long, curly red hair. The left side of his face was more than double its normal size. His beard was caked with blood, and the pieces of his face you could see, you can't imagine the color, between red, purple, green, blue . . .

"When I first noticed him, he was sitting with his head hanging down, as if his neck didn't have the strength to hold it up. At the precise moment I looked up at him, his guard hit him with his rifle butt. 'There's your whore,' he growled. Manuel looked up then and saw me. That's when I saw the blood caked all over his face. One of his eyes was swollen shut.

"I think I actually felt, more than saw, him look at me. Something passed between us, as if he were trying to talk to me. I tried to talk to him the same way, without words, to tell him not to worry about me, that I was hurting too, but that I could stand it, and that I loved him. To this day I'm convinced he understood me. His head went back down, almost with relief, it seemed. And I'm glad. I'm happy that I saw him then, that we could look at each other and speak without words. Because what happened afterward . . . of course I couldn't know for sure until later, until I got out. When I reached Mexico, in fact, that's when they told me he'd disappeared. That he'd never said a word, even under the worst torture. In the eyes of his organization, this made him a hero. But I knew when I saw him, that it was right before . . . why else would they bring us together, and mock us that way? That's what has haunted me all these years, given me nightmares, pulled my hair out by the roots . . ."

With that, Eugenia lost control. She began to sob, deeply, with her head between her hands. After turning off the tape recorder, Ignacio hesitated for a moment. Then he walked over to her, to the large armchair where she was sitting, and put his arms around her. Sitting on the arm rest and cradling her head under his jaw, he rocked gently back and forth and let her cry a long time on the shoulder of his previously well-pressed summer suit.

II

Taking a Stand

He must have dozed off for a moment. As he startled awake, the pain was a rusty knife gouging through the top of his right shoulder. He tried to move away from it, but then it started down his right side, into his hip. He found that if he lay quietly, as still as he could, it returned to his shoulder and seemed to calm down just a bit.

As always happened in the dank, windowless cell, Manuel felt the sun begin to rise, a slight warming of the air around him. He thought back—had it been yesterday?—to the moment they brought him into the room where Eugenia was, where he managed to look at her with his one good eye. Her face was purple and swollen, dirty tear tracks down her cheeks, and she sat bent over, trying not to put weight on any sore part of her body. The beatings hadn't left her much chance of finding a comfortable position. And what else had they done to her?

How stupid he'd been, and how arrogant. She'd never been much of an activist. When did he expect to inform the soldiers she wasn't involved? Before they beat him senseless? After they shocked him unconscious with bolts of electricity? They would release her then, of course. We apologize for the confusion, we only meant to torture your boyfriend.

But still he managed to look at her, somehow to will her eyes to meet his one open one. And with all his remaining strength he tried to talk through his pain and hers, brain to brain, blood to blood. I'm sorry, he shouted inside his head. Whatever they've done to you, whatever happens, I'll always love you. The uselessness of his words had echoed through his heart. Now, in the early dawn, in the dark closeness of his cell, the echoes returned.

When had his ideals turned into this?

Temuco, 1963

The late-model Oldsmobile sedan gleamed navy blue in the mid-afternoon sun. Manuel circled the back end of the car on his way to the driver's side. The driver's door swung open just before he reached it and a tall man stood at attention before him. The chauffeur must have been tracking him in the rearview mirror.

"*Niño* Manuel," he said, "please step back on the curb. I'll open the back door for you."

Manuel stepped back onto the sidewalk. After the chauffeur opened the back door of the car, he waited politely for a minute or so, then spoke again in a carefully burnished baritone.

"You can get in now, *niño* Manuel."

"No, Francisco, that won't be necessary. I'm going to my grand-parents' shop again. In fact, you can tell Papa I won't be needing the car at all this week."

Nodding politely, no change of expression on his face, Francisco walked around to his own side and got in, started the car, and pulled away from the curb. Manuel watched him disappear around the corner.

He turned and walked a block in the opposite direction, past the intricate wrought-iron gate that framed the tasteful entrance to his school, past the queue of chauffeur-driven cars waiting to pick up his schoolmates, past the sugar-sweet aromas that emanated from the rose garden hidden behind the school wall. As he turned left at the corner and began the five-block hike to the city's main avenue, he recalled yet again how dramatically his life had changed since they'd moved to their new house.

He'd spent the first decade of his life on a tiny street a block long that ran diagonally between two small parks, right off the main boulevard in Temuco's oldest immigrant neighborhood. The chubby, ruddy-faced woman who cleaned, washed, and cooked for them during the day would go home when his mama came back for tea. Mama would read him stories or trot behind him in the park as he learned to ride a tricycle, then a bicycle, by himself. Papa was even busier at his bakeries on weekends, so when it was sunny Mama would take him to the park that overlooked the city and they'd have lunch in the small sandwich shop and she'd buy him an apricot ice cream for dessert. On rainy weekends they'd visit her parents at their tailor shop, but Mama and Grandma Myriam would usually get into a fight. Almost always it was about the same thing, why didn't his papa come over too, why didn't he spend time with his family, why was he always at the bakery. When Grandma made some comment about how making money wasn't the most important thing in the world, the visit would end suddenly as his mother took him by the arm, putting his wet overcoat back on, the drops of rain from the umbrellas pelting him on the nose as she opened them back up on the way out the door.

One day, about a month short of his tenth birthday, Manuel was out in the park when his mama came home. He ran up to her, his brand-new friend in tow. "Mama," he asked, "can Marcelo have tea with us?" Mama had looked the other boy up and down, her glance lingering over his scuffed shoes, the hole in his sweater right below the left elbow, the old dirt and snot stains on his cheeks.

"Not today, Manuelito," she'd said after a short silence. "Maybe another day."

There'd never been another day. He'd asked her about it a couple of times, but her answer was always vague, and she always managed to change the subject. When he'd wanted to invite Marcelo to his birthday party, Mama had murmured something about "keeping it in the family." They celebrated with Mama and Papa, Grandma Myriam and Grandpa David. Several weeks later, he'd come home from the park to find both parents at home, a special teatime snack ready, their faces shining with anticipation. His mama gave him a hug, and Papa beamed encouragement from his place at the head of the table.

"Manuelito dear, we have some wonderful news," she began. "We've found a wonderful new house, it's at least three times bigger than this one, you'll have your own room, study and bathroom, almost like your own apartment. The yard is huge, you won't even have to go out to the park to ride your bike."

"Yes," his papa chimed in, the remnants of his childhood German still echoing in his accent, "the yard, it is so large, you can invite all the children in the neighborhood over, they all fit to play soccer, we build the goal posts if you want."

"And Manuelito," his mother added, "we'll be so near that wonderful new school I've been wanting for you, and they give preference to people in the neighborhood, so yesterday when I went by and explained about our new house the headmistress went right ahead and signed your acceptance papers, and . . ." She petered off in mid-sentence as she got a glimpse of his shocked face. "What's the matter, niñito?"

"But I don't want to move. I'm happy here—" His papa had cut him off.

"It is better in the new house. Many children live on the street, from families more like us. In school, too. You'll be happier there." Manuel knew that Papa meant it as a promise, but it had sounded like an order.

And so Manuel had begun attending Temuco's newest and most expensive private school, with a reputation for progressive learning methods. It was so different from his other school, a public one that welcomed all the children who had lived nearby, no matter how much money their parents made. The children of all the best families, the ones whose parents had the largest farms and the biggest lumber mills, went to this new school. They all lived in the same neighborhood, too, the one with streets named after European countries. Like all the other mothers in her new social circle, Sara Weisz de Bronstein was now too busy with her charity work and her Tuesday canasta games to pick her son up from school or take him to the park; but unlike the other children, he refused to be picked up by his father's new chauffeur-driven car.

He crossed the avenue into the downtown district and continued along the edge of the tree-lined plaza. A block further on, tucked between a large button store and a newly remodeled grocery right across from the Central Market, was his grandparents' tailor shop. He knew they had opened the shop when they moved to Temuco from further north, where his grandpa had managed a farm after they had come over from Russia. Even before he opened the door, he caught a wisp of cinnamon and knew his grandma was baking *rugelach* in the wood-burning oven. As soon as she heard the clinking of the small bell nailed to the door's upper corner, she emerged from the back, wiping her hands on her large flowered apron.

"Oh good, Manolito, it's you. Come, you should taste the surprise I have for you."

She'd started calling him Manolito because she'd taken a liking to the Spanish bullfighter of the same name, the one whose picture hung on the ancient, dust-covered calendar on the wall. As far as Manuel could tell, she'd never seen a bullfight, nor did she want to. But there was something about the figure of Manolito, his impossibly thin waist, the way his matador cap sat jauntily on the edge of his forehead, that made her happy. And so the calendar had hung there, gathering its yearly layer of dust, from as far back as he could remember. The first time, on a visit to the tailor shop, that it had been him and his mama who'd gotten into a fight, Grandma had told him he was acting like a bullfighter, waving a red cape in front of his mother's eyes. "Now I have another reason for the nickname, Manolito," she'd chuckled gently the next time he visited on his own.

As he made his way back toward the kitchen, his mouth watering in anticipation of the snail-shaped *rugelach*, their brown cinnamon and sugar syrup trapped between layers of crisp, warm dough, he saw Grandpa David stooped over the foot-powered sewing machine, a single electric bulb hanging above his head. He had his half-moon glasses all the way at the tip of his nose, concentrating on the collar of what looked like a dress shirt. His curly red hair, liberally sprinkled with white and grey, rose to several points along his forehead. Manuel knew he'd been pulling at it as he worked. He put his hand on his grandpa's shoulder for a moment.

"Hi, Grandpa. You going to have tea with us?"

It took Grandpa a full minute to come back into the room from wherever his head had been while sewing. "Ah. Manolito. *Rugelach*. Yes. Just a moment."

Manuel gave his grandpa's shoulder a squeeze and continued toward the kitchen. For just a second, it crossed his mind that it was taking Grandpa longer every day to focus on the things going on around him. But then Grandma placed a mug of sweet, warm tea with milk and a plate of *rugelach* on the table and all concerns were swept away.

A full twenty minutes later, Grandpa emerged from his sewing room. Grandma Myriam had served him some tea, then put it back on the stove, served him some cookies, then put the tray back in the oven, at least three times. She had gotten up a fourth time before her husband had finally appeared at the door.

"*Ach*, David, another minute and I come get you. You take so long. What is happening to you these days, you take so long?"

A puzzled glimmer passed through Grandpa's grey eyes, then he realized he still had his reading glasses on so he took them off, folded them, and tried to put them in his pocket. He missed twice before he finally managed to tuck them in safely. He smiled down at his wife, putting his large arm around her shoulders.

"Ah, my soft little peach, you get impatient in your old age."

Grandma Myriam relaxed into his arm. When she spoke again, all irritation was gone, replaced by a warm sweetness that matched the cookies she was taking from the oven.

"Such a charmer. Sit down while I pour your tea."

About halfway through his plate of *rugelach*, when he tried to pick up his mug to wash down a mouthful of sugared cinnamon, Grandpa David's hand collapsed and the mug fell to the floor, pieces scattering in all directions. Manuel and Grandma looked up in alarm, and Manuel began cleaning up the pieces of the broken cup. A disoriented look in his eyes, Grandpa tried to pick up one of the remaining cookies. But he had lost all function in his right arm. Manuel sat down next to him and handed him the cookie, but Grandpa's fingers could not close around it. Looking up, Manuel caught Grandma's gaze and saw his own panic reflected in her eyes.

Within a month, Grandpa David had taken to his bed, stricken by a mysterious disease that ate away his muscles and turned him into a tiny, wizened fraction of his former self. Though business petered out as people learned of *don* David's condition, Grandma insisted on keeping the tailor shop open every day. Except for the stray shirt or jacket that needed mending, which she would then see to herself, she spent her time in the back room, next to the wood-burning stove, stirring simmering soups that wafted rosemary and basil into the shop's increasingly stale air. Every day, once he got home from school, after drinking his hot, sugared tea with milk and eating the snack his grandma had prepared, Manuel restocked the woodpile next to the stove with small dry logs that kept the fire going. Then, in the late afternoon, rain or shine, he helped Grandma Myriam lug the pots filled with soup and tea out the back door and through the alleyway that connected the shop to the family residence.

When they reached his grandparents' living quarters, they entered through a battered wooden door into a narrow passageway. Their footsteps echoed briefly in the dark hall, which quickly opened up onto a spacious, sunny garden planted with geraniums and orange trees. A line of tall doors with shutters bordered the garden along its eastern side, and together they opened the third door from the right. On a sunny day they left it open as they fed Grandpa, because Manuel thought the sunlight might keep the old man from shrinking further down into the furrows of the mattress. He wondered, too, why his mama didn't come to visit her father. Grandma and Grandpa needed her so much more now, and she never came by. It wasn't as if she was spending so much time with Papa, who was always at his bakery, anyway.

Every couple of visits Manuel bent down, putting his hand on Grandpa David's forehead, the skin so transparent that he could almost see the blood course slowly through the veins. He tried to persuade Grandpa to eat a roll or two by waving a piece in front of his face and holding the bony fingers that peeked out from under the embroidered coverlet, wondering how the capable hands he'd seen darting over seams and collars, tucking and folding in rhythm with the sewing machine, could so quickly have become skeleton's claws. When Manuel succeeded in feeding his grandpa, even though the old man could no longer talk, a small spark lit up in the back of his grey eyes, and for a second there was a return pressure on his hand. Manuel moved closer, thinking that the remains of the man he'd known only a few months before might still be in there somewhere.

"Grandpa . . ."

But Grandma inevitably cut him off.

"Manolito, what good this does you? He's gone, you know. My husband the big charmer, he helps everyone, supports everyone. No matter the worker who needs to sew up his only pair of pants, or the high society lady who comes in with her piece of imported silk. He treats them all the same. But now he's gone and left me. He's not in there, you know. And that's why we can't stay longer today. Must open the shop. Otherwise what do *we* eat?"

Although he knew his papa was paying most of the bills these days, Manuel didn't correct his grandma but helped her carry the empty pots back through the alley in the opposite direction. He'd settle in to do his homework and, if he was lucky, Grandma would give up waiting for customers and sit down at the kitchen table with him. Every now and then she remembered a story about Grandpa and smiled with pleasure, a delicate patchwork of wrinkles deepening around her green eyes, her sun-freckled skin tightening slightly across her cheeks. Then she put down her mending, refilled their cups, tucked a stray white curl back into the bun atop her head, and painted a picture with her words. Sometimes the glittering images carried them well beyond nightfall.

"You know, Manolito, your grandpa and I, we meet and fall in love in the fog. We're both from Odessa. Your grandpa gets caught up in the workers' movement back then, and the Czar's police, the

Cossacks, they take his papa away. I lose my family, too, in the troubles in the city, but we both make it to Istanbul. One night, when it's very foggy and I have just arrived, I'm sitting on a bench near the port, under a streetlight. I'm all alone, someone stole my money, and I'm very sad. I'm crying. To make myself feel better, I begin singing *Oseh Shalom*, the shabbat song I always sing at home with my family.

"Then a young man dressed in grimy, fishy clothes walks up to me speaking Yiddish. It's your grandpa! 'My mama used to sing that song to us on Friday nights,' he says. 'I hadn't heard it in a long time.' I must look scared, because he says, 'I'm sorry, I didn't mean to frighten you. I was around the corner, and I thought I heard angels singing.'

"He has nice grey eyes and a red beard, and he's puffing on a pipe. This reminds me of my papa's pipe tobacco, and I start crying again. But when I stop, I look up at him and smile, and he smiles back.

"'Did you just arrive?' he asks. I nod. 'Do you have money? A place to stay?' My eyes fill with tears, but I don't start crying again. I shake my head. 'Are you mute?' he asks, grinning, and I smile back. 'No,' I say. 'Besides, you heard me sing already.' He laughs at that and, after a few seconds, I laugh too."

But Manuel's favorite story was about how they had ended up in Chile.

"We get married in Istanbul, Manolito. Somehow we find a rabbi in the dirty slum near the port and your grandpa's two friends from the Ukraine, Jews like us, are the witnesses. We make plans to go to Palestine together. But weeks pass, and only two ships come through port going to Palestine, each with room for only one passenger. David's friends leave, and we promise to meet in Jerusalem. Three weeks later, still no ships have room for two, so we think maybe if we go west, deeper into Europe, we have better luck. After many days—on foot, mostly, though once or twice a cart gives us a ride—we reach Trieste. The last man who picks us up says there are ships to everywhere from Trieste.

"There are plenty of ships, but also plenty of people waiting for them. It takes us a week to understand how the lines work. Most people are going to America, so at first we think it will be easy. But soon we realize almost no ships are going to Palestine, and the few that are, don't have space!

"One morning I notice a man in a brown suit going up and down the lines I know are for America. Mainly the men he talks to shake their heads and he goes on down the line. Sometimes, when they talk longer, the man takes a big piece of paper out of his small bag, opens it up, and points at something. Then whoever he's talking to shakes his head, and the brown suit keeps going. Finally, after everyone in the lines for America has said no, the man looks at our line. He comes right to us, though we're not at the front. As he gets closer, I notice he smells of lime.

"First he speaks in languages we can't understand. When David tries to answer in Russian, the brown suit shakes his head. Finally we figure out that if the brown suit speaks in German and David answers in Yiddish, we can more or less understand each other.

"'Where is it you're trying to go?' the man asks.

"'Palestine,' David answers.

"'You willing to go somewhere else?' David looks over at me and I nod.

"'Yes,' he says. 'Me and my wife want to be together, and to have steady work.'

"'You heard of Chile?' the man asks. We shake our heads. 'You know how to read?'

"We nod, and the man takes out the same piece of paper he was showing people in the other line. It's a big map of the world. 'This is Chile,' he says, pointing to a long, yellow strip running down one side of South America. With his finger he traces it down, down, down, to a place with a strange name: Angol. 'A man named Fernando Larraín just bought a big property right around here,' he says. 'He needs a couple he can trust to run the farm. You know how to read, so learning Spanish will be easy. You worked in agriculture?'

"Our eyes meet, and with just a glimmer passing between us, we agree to lie. We nod. The man nods back and smiles. He points to the top of the hill, far away from the port, where the fancy hotels are. 'Then it's settled,' he says. 'Come with me and we'll sign the contract.'"

❧

One night when Manuel came home, having missed dinner yet again, Mama was sitting alone in the living room, reading a book. Aside from the lamplight framing her in the chair, the house was dark. The glasses on her nose made her look like Grandpa David, although the black curls in her hair, punctuated by a few grey exclamation points, were more like Grandma's. So was her height as she stood to face him, her hands and feet quite small. He noticed as he got close that he had to look down now to see into her eyes, and that deep lines marked their outer corners. The nails on the right hand she passed shakily through her hair were chewed down to the skin.

"Well, I guess she must prepare something pretty delicious back there in that tiny, smoke-filled kitchen, something you could never get in this house. Otherwise I might get to see you now and then." She tossed the book on the coffee table for emphasis. "Besides, you never let us know if you're eating here or not. I keep waiting for you, and you've made it so clear to Francisco that he's not to pick you up. So I never know what you're doing, where you are . . ."

Manuel felt a familiar wave of anger welling up from his stomach and tried to control the tone of his voice when he answered.

"That's not true. You just don't want me over there. But Grandpa David keeps getting worse, and Grandma insists on keeping the shop open, and *someone* has to help her."

"Your papa and I hired a nurse a while back, you know. Who else do you think bathes him and keeps him clean?"

"I can't believe that's all you think it is, Mama. Grandma's alone now! You haven't even been over there recently! You haven't even *seen* him! Does it ever occur to you to do anything besides pay the bills?"

His mama pulled herself up taller than her five feet two inches, reached up with both arms, and grabbed him by the collar of his shirt, pulling him down so that they were face to face. He struggled to keep his balance and not fall against her. Her brown eyes, suddenly as dark as charcoal, blazed as she spat out the words.

"How *dare* you, *niñito*! Do you even have a clue about what it was like to grow up in that house, never knowing what he'd do next? One week it was a group of Indians with no land, the next a pile of factory workers on strike. The nights he didn't come home, us not knowing, and he was locked up in a local jail somewhere. Your grandma crying her eyes out, yet every time he came back, he hardly had his coat off before she'd forgive him. Except now he can't come back, and who do you think is left to clean up the mess? At least now somebody can pay the bills, which is more than I could say for them when I was growing up!

"Of course you don't know what that's like. You've always known where your papa is, working himself to the bone for you! Your papa doesn't bring home a flock of dirty peasants and railroad workers, stinking of garlic and wine, to mend their pants and fill their heads full of garbage! You've never opened the door and had a bill collector spit in your face! Believe me, you don't have a clue!"

Manuel slammed his book bag down on the floor of the hall and ran up the stairs to his room. It seemed that every time he saw his mother these days, it ended in a shouting match. He'd become the bullfighter. Manolito. But at least this one was his mother's fault. Grandma Myriam had told him all about their lives, the adventures they'd had before coming to Temuco. Grandpa David wasn't the kind of man his mother said he was. He had been kind to everyone, looked out for everyone. And besides, the old peasants and railroad workers who still brought their dirty pants in for mending didn't smell of garlic or wine. All he could smell in the tailor shop was the cinnamon in the *rugelach*, basil and rosemary in the soup, and oranges in his grandma's hair.

When his grandpa finally died, Manuel was about to enter high school. They took the plain pine coffin to the Jewish cemetery on a gloomy winter day, in a cart drawn by a bony nag of a horse. A crowd of mud-spattered workers and peasants followed them, hats in their callused hands while the rain ran down their faces. Manuel stood in the rain as they lowered the coffin into the ground. Alongside many of the more modestly dressed people present, he took his turn with the shovel and heaved three muddy mounds of dirt into the grave. So did his mama and papa, but when they all said *Kaddish*, it was Grandma Myriam's hand he held, listening to her sobs, holding her up. And he held her all the way back to the tailor shop, where she heated water for tea as they all dried their coats and hats before the fire, the smell of wet wool swirling with the pungent tea leaves as they steeped. After they drank a cup of tea, warmed their hands and feet, and waited for the storm to calm, Mama and Papa hugged Grandma and left. Only then did he ask the question that had been inside his brain all day.

"Why were all those poor people there, Grandma?"

When Grandma answered, her splintered voice came from a bone-tired place inside her he had never heard before.

"It's been so long now, since your grandpa took care of us. All those old peasants and workers, he took care of them, too, Manolito.

Sure, he mends their pants and shirts, but he also tried to mend their lives. He helped them write letters to the government, asking for land, for jobs. He helped organize unions and traveled to tiny villages to help the Indians fight the big landowners who moved the fences on them and took away their homes. He got in trouble, too, like he did back in Odessa when he and his papa organized the workers. But no matter how much I begged him, he didn't stop. Those old men, they remember the meetings every Sunday night in the sewing room."

Temuco, 1967

Manuel entered high school a few months after his grandpa died. The times were beginning to change, and he often wondered what Grandpa David would have thought about the Cuban Revolution, the young guerrillas in Peru, Colombia, Guatemala, and Nicaragua, the student demonstrations in Mexico, or even in the United States against the Vietnam War. Would he have remembered Odessa? Or the Sunday night meetings in the sewing room? It seemed there'd always been landless people, poor or homeless families, unemployed or dispossessed like the frayed and mud-spattered old codgers who had stood by his side and shoveled earth into his grandpa's grave. But now, somehow, it seemed different. It was the young who were in the lead, marching, mobilizing, standing up for everyone's rights. And it was happening all over the world. The young Cubans— Fidel, Che, Camilo—they hadn't looked that much older than he was now when they'd marched into Havana less than a decade before. And then there were the wars in Algeria and Vietnam, not even to mention the struggles for independence in other parts of Africa or Asia. He looked carefully at the grainy pictures of the young, bearded Cuban revolutionaries in the radical newspapers and leftist magazines his older classmates were passing around in school. "Young idealists cheered by the masses," read one caption. "When the young *barbudos* entered Havana, they changed the world," proclaimed another. And Manuel saw the truth of these statements reflected all around him. Why, even in his school, some of the students in the higher grades were singing new songs on their guitars, sitting in the plazas on weekends and debating the future.

One Sunday, when his mama was out somewhere and he was alone in the house, he took a walk in the warm afternoon sunlight. Without really thinking about it, he ended up at the plaza next to his school. As he drew close to the statue in the garden near the middle of the park, he heard someone calling his name.

"Hey, Manuel! *Compañero!*"

It was one of the guys from the twelfth-grade class, tall and gangly, with a German last name and a long blond mane. He was sitting on a bench next to a bed of petunias, smoking a cigarette, a black beret perched rakishly on the side of his head. Manuel could see he was trying to look like Che Guevara, but the peach fuzz along his chin that was imitating a beard only made him look younger, and vaguely clownish. Still, Manuel knew him as the leader of the most radical student faction, a charismatic speaker who'd earned the admiration of most leftists at the school. The classmates Manuel envied most, the ones who never tripped over chair legs or bumped into desks, spoke admiringly, almost in hushed tones, about this guy. Once, when he'd been walking unnoticed behind a group of popular twelfth-grade girls, he'd heard this guy's name come up in conversation. The girls had giggled, breathless, as if they were talking about a movie star.

Manuel approached the bench and sat down on the other side.

"Hey, Ricardo. How come you're by yourself? Where are the rest of the *compañeros*?"

"They're on their way. We have important plans for this afternoon. Wanna join us?"

"What's up?"

Ricardo leaned back on the bench, letting the cigarette smoke out through his nose.

"We're starting a student group affiliated with the Socialist Party. This guy who's big in the Temuco branch is meeting us at the tea house across the street in an hour. You interested?"

The socialist from the Temuco branch, a university student dressed in blue jeans, hiking boots, and an olive-green shirt that looked like he'd gotten it off a *barbudo* marching into Havana, had treated them all to mugs of tea and black tobacco cigarettes. Though Manuel had coughed a bit at first, he'd actually taken a liking to the sweet, acrid taste of the cigarette and how it mixed with the black, unsweetened tea. For hours the university student had talked about changes in the world, students marching, oppressed people rising up to throw off their chains. It was their moral obligation, he said, to join the others fighting for world justice. Then, as the late-afternoon sun angled through the dusty windows, scattering luminescent patterns along the black tile floor, he pushed his guerrilla cap off his forehead and reached into his olive-colored pack.

"Here, little *compañeros*, I have one last present for you." He took out a bundle of small mimeographed booklets and passed them around. "There's enough for everyone. Just one apiece, though; I need to save the extras for other interested people."

Manuel picked up his and examined the cover page. An amateurish drawing of a pair of hands breaking the chain between the manacles attached to the wrists covered the majority of the space. Below the drawing were stenciled the words "Workers of the world, unite! You have nothing to lose but your chains!" Above the picture, in larger block letters, was the title: *The Communist Manifesto*. He looked up as the organizer began talking again.

"This is where it all started, little *compañeros*. Karl Marx and Friedrich Engels wrote this more than a hundred years ago. It has inspired the poor and dispossessed across the world. We are all part of this world-historical movement for socialism, justice, and equality. We must all contribute our little grain of sand.

"Even though we support the principles of the *Manifesto*, we have big differences with the Communist Party. You'll soon learn why, but for now, just read this pamphlet over. It will help to read it several times, maybe discuss it in your group. Its principles of equality and solidarity are the principles we socialists live by. They're your principles now, too."

Why do the Socialists and Communists have differences? Manuel suddenly wanted to ask. Had this world-historical movement been going on the whole time since this document was written over a century before? How come there still wasn't more equality and solidarity? But as he got ready to open his mouth, the college student got up from his chair and, after straightening his cap and picking up his pack, began shaking everyone's hands on his way out the door.

"All right, little *compañeros*. Welcome to the Young Socialists. I'm late for my next meeting, so I gotta run. I'll be in touch with Ricardo in a couple of weeks to see how you're doing."

The door closed softly behind him. A long silence settled into the glittering dusk of the room. Then the new socialists filed quietly out into the cold of the rising moon.

Manuel was always in a rush after that, and enfolded in a cloud of black tobacco smoke. His mama complained about the smell, and she still nagged him about how he was never home for dinner. But he was too busy to be Manolito the bullfighter anymore. There were leaflets to write and hand out, statements to mimeograph, meetings to attend. They argued late into the night. What position should the Young Socialists take on the Vietnam War? The kidnaping of the American ambassador by urban guerrillas in Brazil? The Mexican student movement? The massacre at Tlatelolco? What about the limitations of the Chilean Agrarian Reform law? And should the police evict the homeless families that were taking over Temuco's municipal land and building shacks on it? Every day there was a new issue, a new statement to make, a new leaflet to explain the historical context for their position.

But he also had to admit, while combing himself just so in the mirror one morning, that even as he tried to look like Che Guevara, in the end he looked most like Grandpa David, red hair and all. He couldn't go to the shop that often anymore. There were too many demonstrations to attend and pamphlets to distribute. He drank his tea unsweetened now. Sometimes, when he dropped by on a Friday, he only had time to give his grandma a quick hug. She stopped baking *rugelach*. Now that he didn't come by that much, she told him, she just wasn't strong enough to haul the wood and start the oven in the back. All she could do was cook soup on the new gas-powered stove his mama had brought in. When he remembered, he took her a tray of good European pastries from his papa's bakery on the other side of town.

One Friday, Grandma asked him to clean out the sewing room in the back. "Since David got ill, I haven't touched it," she said. "Can't look at it. Full of ghosts."

Full of dust is more like it, he thought. He took a broom and dustpan and began in the corners farthest from the old sewing machine, working his way toward the center of the back wall. He borrowed a fruit crate from the grocery store next door and gathered up the junk and old clothes lying in mounds along the sides. Once he was done picking up all the junk and had given the whole room an initial sweeping, he began again from the same corners, washing the floor with soap and water. Making his way toward the middle of the room again, he scrubbed and scraped first, then used the cloth he kept wetting in the bucket to finish picking up the grime. After rinsing the brush and cloth out, he moved to a new position. During one of the moves, he happened to look up and his eyes fell upon a small, dusty, forgotten book jammed in between wall and table, right behind the sewing machine.

Brush, cloth, and bucket forgotten behind him, he stood up and moved closer. Giant dustballs flew up as he struggled to dislodge it, but it seemed glued to the spot. Coughing and sneezing, he pulled at it for a while, but his fingers kept slipping on the accumulated dust. Finally it burst free, and when his eyes stopped running he used the brush to get some of the settled grime off the cover, enough to glimpse the familiar title. It was different from his own thumbed-through, well-worn copy, but it was the *Communist Manifesto* without a doubt. The design was from an earlier time and it looked like it was written in German, not Spanish. He could just make out the title cobbling together familiar letters. The authors' names were the same in any language, Karl Marx and Friedrich Engels. Grandpa's original copy, from Odessa, all those years ago. So this was what the world–historical movement for socialism looked like.

At least that's what he told Armando, the Young Socialist from the university, when he came by the school to leave off a fresh bundle of leaflets. Armando seemed impressed when Manuel showed him the booklet. He held it gingerly.

"Wow," he said. "This was behind the old man's sewing machine? What did you say his name was?"

"David Weisz. He was my grandfather."

"Wow. I don't know the name, little *compañero*, but that doesn't mean anything. I'm not originally from here, you know. I'll ask some of the old guys at party headquarters if they ever heard of him. This is quite a family heirloom, my friend."

Armando reported back on his next weekly visit. "There's one old guy who knew your grandpa," he said. "They worked together further north a long time ago. Says your grandpa had just been thrown off a farm he was in charge of, because he sided with the little guy. Mainly he remembered the stories your grandpa told him about the workers' movement in Russia. They set up a group together in a town named Angol, where it seems David Weisz had a dry-goods store.

"Back then, there was no Socialist or Communist Party in Chile. The old Democratic party had the only credible organization, so they started talking with the bigwigs in the local branch. But they got frustrated pretty quickly. Seems there was a feud with the anarchists in the coal mines, and folks spent their time infighting instead of working for the small fry who needed them most. Not long after, your grandpa sold his store and moved to Temuco to open a tailor shop, so the two guys lost touch. But you come from good stock, my friend."

He wanted to tell Grandma Myriam about the old codger in Armando's central office. But when he dropped by for tea the following Friday, the shop was closed. In panic, he stumbled back through the alleyway and pounded on the old door of the Weisz residence. He thanked the nurse who opened the door and ran down the hallway into the patio full of orange trees. She was sitting in her wicker rocking chair, a shawl over her legs, warming herself and napping in the afternoon sun. It was the first time he had truly noticed how she much she had aged since Grandpa David's death.

After that, he tried to stop by every day and help her drink her soup. She talked about Moldavanka, her old neighborhood in Odessa, and how she knew everyone from the boys who shined shoes to the shaggy man who pushed his cart down the street, calling on his whistle for the ladies to bring out their kitchen knives to be sharpened. "*Ach*, Manolito," she repeated over and over, "sometimes, when Temuco smells of wet smoke, I think I'm back in Odessa."

✧

By the beginning of twelfth grade, Manuel was chain-smoking black tobacco cigarettes, the unfiltered kind. He grew his beard long to match his hair, and found that his thick red curls made him look very revolutionary. The popular girls at his school gathered in groups near him, giggling and whispering among themselves when he passed by. Occasionally, before or after class as they all milled around near the school building or along the exit gate, he singled one of them out. He would greet her by name as he came up close to her, leaning slightly sideways with his right arm against the wall or fence behind her in an inviting, yet casual, pose. He relished her quick intake of breath as he brushed lightly against her, the way his belly burned in response.

"I could have any of them," he boasted one day to Armando, by now a perpetual student at the university, like many other activists. "It's amazing what a bit of revolutionary beard, plus the smell of black tobacco, can do."

"You're right, little *compañero*," Armando answered. "But why do you want one of those bourgeois greenhorns? They're so boring, and still wet behind the ears. The revolutionary *compañeras* at the university, they're the ticket. All grown up, you can talk politics with them. Plus they've already been broken in, if you know what I mean. No complications, no crying to mama. They can teach you a trick or two between the sheets. I'll take you over there one of these days. They'll really lust after that red-haired Che Guevara look of yours."

Yet when Armando invited him to a university party a couple of months later, Manuel begged off. He wasn't exactly sure why, but the whole socialist youth scene was beginning to get on his nerves. It had been so exciting at first, fitting in with the popular crowd. Girls he'd never dreamed would give him a second look said hello to him in that breathless way of theirs. But then he started to notice that some of his *compañeros*, like Ricardo, seemed to be in it only for the girls. And as the presidential campaign began to heat up and Salvador Allende, the old-time socialist with the horn-rimmed glasses, began to catch people's imaginations, it seemed to

Manuel that a lot more was at stake than intellectual posturing and seducing women.

At first he was hesitant about this guy, this Allende. He was such a stereotypical politician, with his fancy suits and silk ties, giving inspirational speeches in the same old pompous language they had all heard time and time again. But the more Manuel saw him on TV, wading into crowds, jacket off, shirtsleeves rolled up, tie long gone, the more he began to think that, maybe, this time might be different. He wondered if the guy had more to him than his image. If he would really live up to his rhetoric.

"I know the Socialists signed on to the Popular Unity platform, and our demands about land reform and workers' rights are in there," he told Armando one afternoon when they were sitting in the old tea house near his school. "But I don't see how he's gonna get it all done. I think maybe he's been in the system too long." A heavy winter rain was pounding up against the windows. Clouds of pungent cigarette smoke surrounded their table, refracting the light from the antique standing lamps.

"I know he's an old-style politician," Armando admitted, "and he's been at it thirty years. Can't even remember the times he's run for president. But he's a member of our party, *compañero*. And the way we see it at the Temuco office is, if he wins, it's not the end of the struggle. But it'll make it a little easier, that's what we think, to have someone from our organization in the presidential palace."

Manuel shifted in his seat and poured himself another bit of tea from the pot that sat on the warmer in the middle of the table. He lit another cigarette from the end of the one he'd been smoking and leaned back in his chair, letting the smoke out through his nose. "How much longer do people have to wait for what belongs to them?" he asked. "You think just another election will make the difference for them? The guy's not suddenly gonna turn into a *barbudo*, like the bearded revolutionaries who marched into Havana, if he gets to the presidential palace. You can bet on that."

Armando sat forward, and as he continued talking he began tapping his open hand on the table for emphasis with every phrase.

"Come on, *compañero*. You know how these things work. Is there another candidate who can get elected who would be better for us? The people are going to vote for him, even some of the Christian Democrats whose party is now in power. They promised so much after winning the last election, unions for the workers, land reform for the peasants. And then they couldn't deliver even half of it! People started demanding more, and they still are! And once our candidate's in the presidential palace, that's when we strike, *compañero*. That's when things heat up, mark my words."

Salvador Allende was elected in September, a month and a half into the second semester of Manuel's senior year. He joined Armando in the street celebrations, thousands upon thousands of people with horns and drums, clapping and singing through the center of Temuco. As the two of them were carried away in the human crush and adrenaline rush, Manuel wished Grandpa David had lived long enough to see this, getting one of your own elected president, and peacefully at that. He knew this had not happened to the workers' movement in Odessa—or any other place, for that matter.

It was easy to believe that things would be different, and by the end of the evening Manuel was sure of it. Armando took him to a party at someone's house. They were playing the Rolling Stones on a scratchy record player, and Manuel began to dance with a tall university girl, long black hair in a loose braid down her back. She was not wearing a bra, and when they danced close he could feel her nipples against him through his cotton shirt. She'd been drinking. When the music stopped at the end of the record, she took his hand and led him toward the back of the apartment. They found an empty room and lay down on the bed.

He lost his virginity to a dark-haired revolutionary beauty, on the same night his country elected a socialist president. If that isn't poetic justice, I don't know what is, he told his friends, though he left out the part about it being his first time. Besides, he added, when I asked her for her name she refused. We will always remember this night, she whispered. Let's not mess it up with names. Okay. So that last part was an exaggeration. Afterwards, while smoking the best cigarette he'd ever had, he asked her name. But she shook her head, said something about free love, revolutionary sex, no strings. He couldn't quite remember. But it sounded better when he told it the other way.

❦

Late on a spring evening, when the newly-elected socialist was just getting settled in his office at the Moneda, Manuel was up studying for his academic aptitude test. A series of clicks sounded against the window of his room. His parents were asleep, but he quickly opened the window and leaned out, finger to his lips. It was Armando. Manuel motioned him around to the kitchen door and tiptoed down the stairs. They whispered in the soft spring air.

"What's up, *compañero*? I wasn't expecting you to show up tonight. Weren't we supposed to meet tomorrow?"

"This is different. Come with me right now, I'll explain on the way. You'll need a sleeping bag, a flashlight maybe, a good supply of cigarettes, a little cash. Oh, and just in case, your identity card."

The mention of the identity card set off an adrenaline rush. He would only need it if he were arrested, so this could only mean one thing. Some kind of illegal action.

"Wait here. I'll be right back."

He ran up the stairs as quietly as he could. Hands shaking, he groped around for his wallet and took out his identity card and a couple small bills. He put them in the pocket of his jeans before placing the wallet on his night table. Then he jammed two packs of cigarettes, some matches, and his keys into his jacket, grabbed a flashlight, his sleeping bag, and his beret, and hurried back down the stairs. He joined Armando outside the kitchen, fumbling for his keys to relock the door. They moved quietly through the still, moonlit night. Neither of them spoke until they were a block from the house.

"So where's the takeover tonight?" Manuel asked. Armando laughed softly.

"You definitely got the message, *compañero*. It's that group we've been talking to, about twenty families right now, nobody can find a place to live they can afford, even now after Allende's election. They're taking over that stretch of municipal land on the southern edge of the city, by the river, and asked us to help."

They walked along deserted streets. The moon's incandescent light guided them as surely as the sun. It took them a good half hour to reach the site. A group of people were huddled by the river, the men in felt hats and ponchos, the women in shawls with babies swaddled under them. Large quantities of cardboard, wood, and corrugated tin sheets lay in piles off to one side. When Manuel got close, the ragged filth of their poverty, mixed with the smell of fear rising from their bodies, was like a slap to the face. He had never seen this kind of need up close, and he was pretty sure Armando hadn't either. One of the men recognized Armando and came forward, a tentative grin on his face. They shook hands.

"*Buenas noches, compañero* Roberto. Nice night for a takeover." Armando's tone was light, in an effort to put the other man at ease. "Where do you want us?"

Deep lines marked Roberto's forehead and cheeks, standing out as shadows in the moonlight. As his grin expanded, Manuel could see he was missing one of his front teeth. He smelled of cheap tobacco and unwashed feet. "Wherever you can see best, *compañero*."

He spoke rapidly, with the rasping rhythm of the poor. He gestured north, back toward the center of town: "If the cops come, it'll be from over there."

"Are you sure you want both of us to stand guard, *compañero?*" Manuel asked. "Couldn't you use some help with the shacks while we're at it?"

Roberto's eyelids came down slightly, guarding his eyes. He turned to look at the group of men behind him. They all shook their heads. He moved back to join the men, and they conferred in whispers, voices rising and falling. Manuel could make out an occasional phrase, like "how can we know" and "we didn't agree." At one point he thought he heard "rich kids" or something like it. Then Roberto was back, his accent even choppier than before. "Thanks, *compañeros*, but me and the others, we know what to do. Quicker this way than teaching you now, at the last minute."

Armando and Manuel set up camp where they could see the main street, sitting on their folded sleeping bags and lighting cigarettes. Manuel couldn't shake the feeling that they weren't welcome. The men and older boys began lifting beams of wood and pounding them together with hammer and nail, and pretty soon several uneven shacks were gleaming in the night. Not that he could have helped much anyway, Manuel thought, since he'd never even held a hammer before. All the repairs at home had been done by hired hands. But it still felt like they were being excluded.

"Weren't any other guys from the Temuco office going to join us?" Manuel lit his second cigarette and offered the match to his friend.

"Good question, *compadre*. And I thought we were actually gonna help them build their shacks. But something changed at the last minute, I don't know what."

Suddenly, Armando poked Manuel in the leg. "Over there, walking along the sidewalk to our right, a block and a half up. You see him?"

Manuel made out a single shadow moving quickly between the patches of shade cast by the moon through the trees that lined the avenue.

"Yeah. But he's alone. You think it's the cops?"

"Dunno. But go tell Roberto. We need to keep an eye on him."

Manuel ran over to the work crew and tapped the leader on the shoulder.

"There's a guy. Only one. Coming up the street, about a block away."

The men stopped working and formed a wall, their women and children behind them. Manuel went back and stood next to Armando. When the guy was even with the two of them, they shone their flashlights in his face, blinding him momentarily. Then Armando heaved a sigh of relief in the shape of a name.

"Mario. What the hell?"

The man lowered his hands from his eyes when they turned off their flashlights. Manuel recognized him as one of the leaders from the central office.

"Glad I caught up with you, Armando. We can't stay here. We're not helping with this action anymore. Decision came down from the top."

"What the—what the hell are you talking about?" Armando spluttered in disbelief.

"We can't. Seems these guys have been talking with the Revolutionary Left. They got help from them and didn't tell us. We can't work on an action when the Revolutionary Left is involved, you know that. They're not part of the coalition. Decision came down from Santiago."

"That's news to us, *compañero*." Roberto talked straight at Mario, rasping ironically over every word. "So we're not all working together now? One group's not in the government, and so you can't help us out? Seems being in the government has made you just another bureaucrat."

Even Mario was embarrassed into silence for a moment. He grabbed Armando by the arm and walked him out of earshot. The two gestured wildly back and forth for a few minutes, a passionate pantomime Manuel could not understand. Then Armando came back.

"I'm really sorry, *compañero*," he said, a hand on Roberto's shoulder. "Problem with party discipline. Sometimes the guys giving the orders have been sitting at their desks too long."

Motioning to Manuel with his head, Armando picked up his things. As he began to walk with Mario toward town, he looked back and noticed Manuel wasn't following. After gesturing once more and receiving a shaken head in response, Armando shrugged his shoulders and fell into step behind Mario. They disappeared up the street.

For a moment Manuel just watched them go. He remembered Allende on the campaign trail, wading into crowds of people very much like these *compañeros*. Then the huge celebrations in Temuco with drum and horn, so many people believing that things could be different. But no one could be Che Guevara from the presidential palace, even if it was the poor who had put him in the Moneda in the first place. Well, he thought, then I guess it's up to us to remind him that it's about more than political parties, and who is in or out of the coalition.

"Well, *compañero*," Manuel said, turning back to face Roberto. "I think I'll be looking for a new organization come daybreak. Seems I've just been kicked out of the Socialist Party. You willing to lend me a hammer and some nails? I promise not to do too much damage."

Roberto looked Manuel up and down, then handed him some tools and went back to work. When the sun came up, a small settlement had appeared on the bank of the river, Chilean flags fluttering from every tin roof. As he looked out across those rooftops, Manuel felt a rush of blood to the head, a burning pleasure that made his fingertips tingle. So this was what the world-historical movement for socialism felt like.

He got home at eight-thirty that morning. His mama was sitting at the dining room table drinking a cup of tea, still in her nightgown and robe. The smudges under her eyes suggested she'd been up a good part of the night. When she saw him, tears of relief ran down her cheeks, but her voice was anything but grateful.

"You thankless, selfish brute. How dare you?" He stopped dead in his tracks and just looked at her.

"Where have you been? I was up at one in the morning and noticed a light on in your room. Your wallet was on the night table, but when I looked inside your identity card was missing. Where in the hell have you been?"

He didn't know what to say. But she didn't leave him much room to talk in any case.

"Your papa went off at five in the morning, as usual, not knowing if you were alive or dead. Do you have even a scrap of human consideration left in your body?"

He thought of all the ways he might answer that question. That all the people he'd been with since last night thought he was pretty considerate, seeing as he had just risked arrest and personal injury to help folks like them who needed a roof over their heads. That all he ever felt he really needed in his life . . . but she was talking still.

". . . I've been through all this once before, up all night with mugs of tea going cold on the table, not knowing if someone is alive or dead. Once is enough. I saw the book out in your room, looks like you were studying for the aptitude test. If you can concentrate long enough to get a good score, maybe you can go to Concepción, or even to Santiago. That'll be better, you won't have to bother about us anymore." Her voice broke on the last phrase, but she pushed away his attempt to hug her and walked quickly upstairs.

His last two months of school were a blur of meetings, leaflets, and demonstrations. He became quite a specialist in the Revolutionary Left's urban takeovers since that fateful night with Roberto, and quickly became an ace with a hammer and nails. The mayor of Temuco, a member of Allende's governing coalition, refused to send the police against the poor, and the takeovers multiplied. His skills were in great demand every day, and his reputation spread.

This was also true with the ladies, he found. Maybe it was the risk, the scent of danger. Or maybe the women were just wilder, freer, in the Revolutionary Left. Like Erminda, thirty, maybe thirty-five, with a four-year-old son. She'd had several *compañeros*, and wasn't sure who was her son Camilo's father. But it didn't matter, because everyone in the organization was his parent. We don't own our kids, she said; it's a collective project. This was a new concept for Manuel. He couldn't help but compare Erminda to his mama, so protecting and enveloping. But he learned more from Erminda in bed than about parenting. Sometimes he wondered if he was falling in love. But they both slept with other people, because love, too, as Erminda reminded him, was a collective project.

As things heated up in the first few weeks of January, after his graduation from high school, the police began cracking down on illegal takeovers and arresting more people, targeting the actions and actors of the Revolutionary Left and their allies among the poor. One night in a small town west of Temuco, he and Roberto, together again for another takeover, were shot at by a group of cops on the payroll of the local landowner. They ran across a field through a cloud of bullets, jumped in the river, and swam to the other side. As they climbed out, shivering, on the other bank, Roberto's raspy voice trembled with cold and fright.

"Too close for comfort, *compañero*."

Manuel's voice was also a bit shaky. "No kidding, *compadre*. What the hell went wrong?"

"Who the hell knows. But I bet someone had a loose mouth on this one."

When the Revolutionary Left investigated the case, they found that one of the peasants involved in the action had told his wife, a marketwoman in Temuco. After that, they all agreed, there were a hundred different ways the information could have gotten to the police, since the cops had many friends and connections at the central market. A friend of the Revolutionary Left who worked in police headquarters also let them know that everyone was looking for Manuel, especially after that last adventure. The red hair and beard made him stand out like a sore thumb, even at night. When the leadership decided to pull him out, he couldn't decide if he was mainly disappointed at not being allowed to participate in more actions, or proud that he had become so notorious.

That next week he got the results of his academic aptitude test. He'd scored high enough that he could attend school wherever he wanted. Everyone in his group agreed that Santiago would be the best choice. The University of Chile could not be beat, they all said. It was the public university that had the largest radical student population. Of course, if he'd consulted his mother, she would have picked the Catholic University, the most prestigious private school. But he agreed with the Revolutionary Left. He'd be a big asset to them at the University of Chile.

Classes started at the beginning of March, so he only had a couple of weeks to prepare the move. There were books, documents, and Revolutionary Left position papers to transport. He packed a suitcase of clothes, taking special care with his berets. The hardest thing was to say good-bye to Erminda. Two nights before he left, they stayed awake until dawn. Between bouts of passion, they talked about the future, the new society that was taking shape, and all the work to be done. She said he was lucky to be going to Santiago, the hub of the student movement.

His mama and papa had been watching him pack, but he just left them a note with an address where he could be reached. He did stop to see his grandma one last time on his way to the train station, Grandpa's copy of the *Communist Manifesto* folded carefully into the deepest corner of his knapsack. He sat in the orange-scented patio for a long time, holding her hand as she dozed. When she opened her eyes, he told her he was going to Santiago. "My friends tell me I have no other choice," he explained. "I've been helping people, Grandma, just like Grandpa. So the police aren't happy with me. Maybe in Santiago I won't stand out quite as much, with all my red, curly hair and a name like Bronstein."

His grandma coughed and sat up straight, and her hand suddenly became a small, tight claw inside his much larger one. Her eyes darkened, then filled with tears. "*Ach*, Manolito," she quavered. "But they always found your grandpa."

Santiago, 1971

The three young men walked across the bridge and crossed the *parque forestal*, blocks of trees and lawns and wrought-iron benches along the edge of the Mapocho River. They reached the Plaza Baquedano, a large disk surrounded by an ornate black metal fence. The roundabout that surrounded it reconnected to the east and west with Santiago's main avenue, cobblestones glistening with dew. Manuel looked up at the rider on horseback that graced the center, so much like every other heroic figure in every other park in the city. What made this statue different was that it stood at the pinnacle of a set of stairs rising majestically from the eastern side of the disk.

After setting his knapsack against the black fence, Manuel opened it and took out the leaflets they'd brought to pass out. Hernán and Carlos, other new members of the Revolutionary Left at the University, ran up the stairs and out onto the base of the statue, scaling the front legs of the horse all the way to its neck. They unfurled their red and black revolutionary flag, hanging it over the ears and down the animal's nose. As his friends climbed back down, the flag began to flutter lightly in the breeze, serving as a signal that the demonstration was about to begin.

"Hey, Manuel. What's the deal with the guys from the Catholic University?" Hernán was standing at his elbow.

"Your guess is as good as mine, *compadre*. One thing we know for sure. Those manicured mama's boys aren't about to appear anytime soon."

"No kidding," Hernán snorted, lighting a black tobacco cigarette and trying to anchor his beret more firmly on the nest of unruly chocolate-colored straw that sprung out in all directions from his scalp. He offered Manuel a cigarette, brought out a box of wooden matches, and cupped his hands around his friend's to protect the flame. "Especially that Sergio what's-his-name. Real piece of work, that guy."

"No argument here." Manuel blew out a cloud of smoke. "But we have to work with them anyway, at least for now. They have a big following, and besides, with the Left in power we have to play nice." The two leaned on the fence, right hiking boots over left. "Good news is," Manuel continued, "we get the place to ourselves for a while. We set the tone, and when they get here, they won't be able to take over." He slapped his friend on the back and they both got back up, preparing to turn on the megaphone and begin warming up the crowd.

"The early bird gets the worm, my friend."

❧

Manuel put down the megaphone and limped slowly down the stairs, the last of the adrenaline draining from his limbs. No matter how many times he led a demonstration, the feeling was still the same. It began to build slowly, as the growing throng answered his chants, and then he was riding on the crest of the collective roar, controlling its ups and downs yet being controlled by it. And then, once it was over, the quick collapse, his body a punctured balloon.

"Excuse me. *Compañero.*" She was standing right in front of him. She was trying hard to look like she belonged, with the black turtleneck, faded jeans, and worn-in leather jacket. But the shiny, pointed boots, lost look, and expensive haircut screamed upper-class.

"*Compañera.*" He tried to straighten up, his arms and legs resisting as if he were a puppet with broken strings.

She seemed nervous, shifting her weight from right to left on those ridiculous boots. "Sorry to disturb you, but . . ." she cleared her throat. Her eyes were almost turquoise. He felt a familiar warmth rising through his legs. He leaned slightly sideways, right elbow on the fence, and noticed a small rivulet of sweat inching its way down her left temple. "Do you know Sergio Undurraga?" she finally blurted out.

He crumpled back down, the promise of sexual adventure collapsing around him. She held out a small, square-fingered right hand. "Eugenia Aldunate. It's just that he was supposed to meet me here at ten-thirty."

"Manuel Bronstein." He shook her hand briefly. Even he, freshly arrived from the provinces, knew her name had a pedigree.

There were a couple of Aldunates at the University of Chile, from branches of the family that had ended up on the skids. It wasn't unusual for this to happen in huge clans like the Aldunates, which had a bit of everything. Yet the Aldunates he'd met at the university, who didn't have the money for a decent lunch at the subsidized student cafeteria, still looked down on those like him whose last names marked them as recent immigrants. He looked her over once again. She didn't look like her branch had done any suffering lately.

Annoyed by what she represented, he made some reference to how Sergio was always chasing skirts. She'd been angry, of course, but in the midst of it all she managed to exude strength and a surprising dignity. And she didn't just walk away. He had to admit that most girls, no matter what social class they were from, wouldn't have pulled off such dignity after some random stranger told them their boyfriend was cheating on them. So he offered to buy her a juice and they talked for a while.

When it came time to go back to the demonstration, he was pretty sure that nothing else would come of it. She'd find Sergio, they'd make nice, and off she'd go. Even as she played at being radical, she was so much like the girls at his fancy high school in Temuco. She and Sergio deserved each other. And yet. Was it the turquoise eyes? Was it that dignified attitude, not letting him get away with anything?

In the end, the truth was probably a lot simpler. Ever since he'd gotten to Santiago, he'd felt like one of his legs had grown longer than the other. He was constantly tripping over himself with the girls. The minute he said he was from Temuco, they'd get this strange look in their eyes, a cross between pity and disdain. This was especially true of the more political girls, who in Temuco had fallen over each other trying to get close to him. Ironic. So what was it with Santiago chicks? Maybe he'd have to settle for a greener upper-class one, more like the girls at his school.

When he finally got Eugenia back to his apartment, it took him forever to get the key in the lock. After they climbed up the stairs he pulled her into his room and pressed her belly and thighs into him. He unzipped her jacket and pulled the turtleneck up over her head. He fumbled with the hooks on her bra, the girls he'd been with before never wore them. But then it was off, her breasts free, their large dark nipples rising up against his tongue. Only then did he see the door was still open, and managed to slam it with one kick. He turned and swept her onto his bed, removing her jeans. His large hands took off her panties and spread her thighs, her thick, musky scent inviting him in. Then she gasped and drew back.

Armando had been right. These bourgois greenhorns were something else. She was crying. Yet when she spoke her voice was as dignified as if she had just accepted a cup of tea. Again he was off balance. What was it about this girl?

⟡

In the first few days after the fiasco with Eugenia, Manuel spent more and more time at the café. He hadn't been going to many of his classes anyway, but as he sat drinking red wine by himself, hours would go by and he started missing political meetings. After his buddies came by his apartment one morning to find him lying in bed, Manuel turned to the "A's" in the telephone book, wondering idly how many Aldunates would be listed. As he thumbed through, his eyebrows slowly went up. One . . . two . . . three . . . five whole pages. Just out of curiosity, he told himself, to see what would happen, he started dialing from the top of the list, calling a few names a day.

What he mainly got was irritation. Wrong number! No Eugenia here! Occasionally the person on the other end stopped for a second, then said, wait, I'll get her. But then the voice on the other end clearly was not hers, and he would hang up. On the fourth day, twelve names in, he hit pay dirt.

"Aldunate residence." He could tell it was a maid.

"*Buenas tardes,*" he began.

"*Buenas tardes,*" she answered.

"Is Eugenia there?"

"May I ask who's calling?"

"I'm a classmate of hers at the university, I sit behind her in one of her classes. I seem to have misplaced my notebook, and I need the homework for tomorrow."

"*Niña* Eugenia is doing her homework right now. May I tell her your name?"

"I'm in her grammar class. I'm not even sure she'll remember me by name."

"All right, young man," the maid answered. "I'll go see if *niña* Eugenia is willing to talk to you."

For a long time he waited. If it hadn't been for the sound of the maid's retreating footsteps, he would have been sure she'd hung up on him. Then—

"Hello?"

"You're exactly the twelfth Aldunate in the phone book. I've been calling four a day."

"I can't talk very long right now."

"I've missed you, too."

"No, Manuel, you don't understand, I—"

"It's okay. I think we should meet, at the same place at the Plaza Baquedano. I can be there in fifteen minutes."

"You know it'll take me longer, plus it's getting late already, I don't know if—"

"It's only five in the afternoon. You can tell your mom that I'm a stupid classmate who needs your help. Play up your generous side."

"Mama just got back from shopping. If she's willing to have the chauffeur drop me off, I can be there in twenty-five minutes. If I'm not there by six, it means I couldn't get away."

"I'll wait till six-fifteen. And Eugenia?"

"Yeah?"

"If you don't make it, I won't call you again. But you know where to find me."

She did make it, and he'd waited until she arrived before he started drinking. He needed to be in control, he'd decided. And this time they made love. It was the first time he'd called it making love instead of having sex. She made fun of him for that. Not that he'd admit it to anyone else, but maybe that was part of why he fell for her. It was nice to be teased. The Revolutionary Left girls might be freer spirits than Eugenia, but they definitely took themselves a lot more seriously. After she lost her virginity, he was sure she'd be fishing for declarations of undying love, when am I going to see you again, that kind of stuff. Instead, she made fun of him. And when he got her clothes off, she put the Revolutionary Left girls to shame.

❧

August gave way to September, and Allende approached the first-year anniversary of his election. Cherry and apple blossoms bloomed merrily against an incandescent blue sky, and the Mapocho River swelled with the early melting snows of the Andes. The mood in the city was also springlike. People who didn't know each other smiled in greeting on the streets and buses.

"The shops are full and prices are so low," Eugenia said one day when she came back to Manuel's place with a beef tongue for dinner. "Everyone has plenty of money in their pockets."

Most weeks, Eugenia stayed downtown several times, saying she was sleeping at her sister's apartment. Manuel's organization had brought in another activist to help with the land takeovers along the edges of the city, and they managed leisurely meals most evenings she stayed over. Sometimes they'd invite Irene and her friend Gabriela and share the preparations of a chicken or lamb shank stew served with fresh bread from the corner bakery. It was the most domestic Manuel had been since David died.

But spring was short, and things heated up everywhere as summer approached. With the Christmas holidays around the corner, the right-wing newspapers began to carry horror stories about the lack of basic goods, such as toilet paper, oil, and soap. Mainly it was propaganda, of course, an attempt to whip up a fear of shortages. One headline after another screamed about children not getting toys that year and that it was Allende and his government's fault. In the week before Christmas, the rumored scarcity of flour, sugar, and eggs sent everyone into the stores to stock up, and thus real shortages did develop.

"When I was home last week, I told my mother that hoarding had actually created shortages where none existed before," Eugenia commented shortly after the New Year. "But she asked me when I'd become such a leftist, and accused me of thinking the government was doing a good job."

"Did you say that was exactly what you thought?" Manuel asked, laughing.

"I don't think that would've gone over very well," Eugenia said. "She had a group of her friends over, and they were clearly plotting something. They would go quiet when Teresa or I walked into the room. They'd start talking again when we left. Only yesterday did I finally figure out what that was about."

Eugenia was referring to the demonstration that had marched on the presidential palace, a crowd of mainly upper-class women who had banged on empty pots to dramatize the shortages.

"Mama was in on it, I'm sure of it," she said.

Manuel smiled. "If my mother were in Santiago, I'm sure that's exactly what she'd be doing too," he said. "It's the class struggle. It's supposed to deepen now, you know. It isn't often that the workers have the upper hand." And people like Eugenia's and Manuel's mothers couldn't stand it.

But they began to wonder if the workers really did have the upper hand. As summer faded into the Chilean fall and winter of 1972, the lines to buy bread, milk, oil, and soap, while everywhere, were still the longest in the working-class neighborhoods. Inflation kept getting worse, and it was clear that supplies of basic goods could not keep up with the new demand caused by workers' increasing incomes.

"It's ridiculous," Gabriela said one day when they were eating stew at Irene's apartment, the half-chicken they'd begged through Manuel's contacts in the Revolutionary Left cut up into tiny pieces among the four of them. "My mama says she doesn't know how she's gonna make it to the end of the month. Prices keep going up, and even if Papa's getting paid better than ever before, it doesn't go half as far."

Eugenia and Manuel began to see the wear and tear on people's bodies, the way they walked, the glassy stares in their eyes. There was a tightness, a tension right below the surface. In restaurants, on street corners and buses, the slightest misunderstanding would lead immediately to a shouting match, even to physical confrontation, especially when the people involved were from different social classes.

One afternoon in August, when the rains were hard and cold, Manuel and Eugenia came running up the stairs to the apartment, shaking the water from their umbrellas and laughing. They stopped short at the sight of the landlady, a brawny, square-bodied woman with worn hands and missing teeth.

"*Buenas tardes*," she said, her stance squared off like a boxer's.

"*Buenas tardes, señora*," Manuel answered respectfully. "It's really cold and wet today."

She nodded in agreement, then stiffly in Eugenia's general direction, before passing him a slim envelope. "I'm sorry, but I need the apartment for someone else. You'll have to be out by Monday."

"But *señora*, according to the law you must give people a month's notice, I can't find something by—"

She cut him off abruptly with a chop of her hand in the air. "This isn't about the law. Some of the people who come up to see you, well . . . the neighbors are complaining." She rushed down the stairs and out the door, not seeming to mind the downpour as she hurried across the street.

Manuel stood still for a moment, staring at the envelope in his hand. Shaking his head, he took out the key and opened the door. They started the heater in silence and put a kettle of water on for tea. Manuel put the tea leaves to steep in the pot and walked slowly over to where Eugenia was setting out the bread and jam, her face clouded.

"People are getting scared," he said.

"What do you mean?" Eugenia asked, although the undertone to her voice hinted that she probably suspected.

"Well, you know the stories coming out in the opposition papers. That the Left is organizing a coup in order to get rid of Congress and the right wing. That we're planning another Cuba."

They sat down at the kitchen table. Eugenia put some jam on a piece of bread and stirred some sugar into her tea. "That's not what she said. What about the time I came back unexpectedly last month? All those dirty, rowdy guys, smoking black tobacco and drinking cheap wine. It was a mess! You don't think the neighbors could hear you?"

They were quiet for a while, neither of them wanting to remember that moment in too much detail. When Manuel spoke, his voice was low.

"You're right, *mi amor*. But we're part of the world-historical struggle for socialism. We can't just give up because a landlady gets scared. Everyone has to do their part."

"I know," Eugenia answered softly. "But I would be willing to wager a lot of money that the world struggle for socialism will not repay your loyalty by finding you a new place to live."

❦

Classes started late in the fall of Allende's third year in office. A confrontation between right-wing and left-wing students closed down the Catholic University at the beginning of the semester, and the leftist majority at the University of Chile went out on strike in solidarity with their comrades. As a result, both institutions called a delay in the start of classes until the end of April. Manuel had managed to find a new apartment, a third-floor walk-up composed of a single room with a tiny sink and gas-powered hotplate. The bathroom was out in the hall, and there wasn't space for their couch or coffee table. Eugenia had been angry, but they'd made up and she was staying over again most nights.

The first Tuesday in June began normally enough. Eugenia's class didn't start until ten, so they lingered longer in bed, drinking coffee. By the time he got to the new shantytown along the eastern side of the city, the one taking shape from the takeover the week before, it was close to eleven.

"Manolito!" The creases along Sonia's cheeks folded together into pleats as she smiled, opening the door to her shack and inviting him in. She was from Temuco, too, and he'd told her about his grandma's pet name for him. "Sit down! A *mate* tea will help warm you up, then you can go to the construction, help the *compañeros* build the school." Between the *mates* and the homemade bread Sonia took out of the wood-burning oven in her potbellied stove, he didn't make it to the construction site until noon. He settled into the hard rhythm of the work, and the hours passed quickly. The next thing Manuel knew, it was close to six.

"Shit. I'm gonna be late again," he told Hernán, his buddy from the Revolutionary Left who'd been working next to him. "Eugenia's already been on my case about this, but I can't help it, the buses are damn full this time of day and—"

A shout went up from the guard on duty. They always had a guard at the new shantytowns, especially in this part of town where the neighbors were notoriously hostile.

"*Momios*! At two o'clock!"

All the men working on the school stood up in unison, looking around for sticks of wood just in case. It was hard to tell who was coming and how many through the late afternoon light. As they marched through the empty field, dust billowed up around them, forming a curtain that caught the flat undertones of the setting sun. Besides, *momios* was a pretty general term, meaning conservatives, people opposed to the government, anyone who seemed even remotely upper-class.

These *momios* were goons from the New Fatherland, the fascist political party that formed as soon as Allende got elected. As things had heated up over the previous six months, their influence had spread to the more upper-class, right-wing student groups at the Catholic University. Rumor had it that they were behind the recent wave of confrontations there, and responsible for the increasing violence on the streets. This group looked pretty young, probably all university students, and there were lots of them. The yells and blows, the dust. The taste of blood between his lips. His fall to earth was in slow motion, only one thought sharp in his mind: how'd the son of a bitch get ahold of my hammer?

He woke to Sonia's worried face as she placed another cold rag on his cheek. "I think the cheekbone's broken," she whispered.

"It's very swollen." And then the pain nearly made him pass out again.

By the time he was revived enough to try standing, Hernán at his side to keep him from falling, it was pitch black outside. Fortified by several *mates* laced with cheap pisco, he was able to walk, if a bit wobbly, with Hernán's help. They made it to the bus stop, and the fresh air helped him walk straighter. Hernán stayed with him till his stop, and continued to prop him up as they walked the three blocks to his building. Making it up to his apartment was definitely a stretch. Hernán was staggering under his weight by the last flight of stairs. But Eugenia must have heard them, because the door was open by the time they reached it.

It all came back at him in her gasp—his swollen face caked with blood, the haggard look on Hernán's face. "Oh, God," was all she said. Then she had him by the waist, taking over from his friend, her sobs stabbing through his temples. Behind her, he just made out Irene and Gabriela, sitting at the table, leaping to their feet as he stumbled in.

It took Manuel's cheekbone a full month to heal. A friend of Irene's at the University of Chile Medical School saw him for free and gave him pain medication that made him useless to his comrades at the land takeovers.

"Don't worry about it, *compadre*," Hernán told him during a visit in the middle of June. "There's not much we can do there anymore, there aren't enough of us. The party's pulling us from all those resettlement projects anyway. We gotta concentrate on the New Fatherland goons. They're getting bolder all the time, you know, and they're even trying to recruit at the University of Chile now. They're like sharks that smell blood in the water. We have to defend ourselves every day on the streets." No kidding, Manuel thought to himself.

As his comrades got more and more involved in street fighting, Manuel had trouble seeing the connection to the rights they were supposed to be defending. He was reminded of his high school friends in Temuco, who had seemed more interested in sex than in justice. In this case, they seemed more interested in the confrontation itself. True, the images on television, with most reporters and stations in opposition to the government, were sensationalist and put the Revolutionary Left in the worst possible light. Yet too often his *compañeros* just seemed to enjoy the violent rush of the moment, the thrill for blood. He moved further and further into the background, his injury the excuse and Eugenia his refuge. They talked late into the night about the solidarity that had seemed so palpable even a few short months before. He could still trace its shape between her shoulder blades and along the moonlit curve of her back.

When she left for winter vacation in the second half of July, he tried to contact his old comrades. Two weeks earlier, when on television he'd seen the stray tank make its way toward the presidential palace, it had seemed comical at first. But most of the news reports had not taken it so lightly. For the first time there was open talk of a military coup. It was general knowledge that the Air Force was in favor of military action, but the head of the Army still supported the constitution and the Allende government. It all depended on the Christian Democrats, reporters said. At first they had supported democracy, even though the elected president was a socialist. But when the shortages began to alienate the middle class, they began to waver, and the Christian Democratic party had taken the lead in Congress in opposing government reforms. If they were willing to ally with the right wing, things would come to a head very quickly. But then the commander of the Army, who still wanted to abide by the Chilean constitution, bowed to right-wing pressure and resigned. General Augusto Pinochet, whose political position was not well understood, took his place. Manuel started to worry and wonder what plans his comrades in the Revolutionary

Left were making to address all this. He might disagree with how they had been acting, but if push came to shove he would stand up with them and be counted.

Carlos was the only one he could find shortly after Pinochet became head of the Army, because he was still living with his parents. There was surprise in his friend's eyes when he answered the makeshift bell attached to the metal gate outside the small one-story dwelling.

"Manuel! What's up, man? I thought you were long gone by now."

"What's that supposed to mean? You know I broke my cheek-bone in that fight after the takeover, *compadre*. Pain meds turned me into a zombie. Pretty much recovered now, though."

"No, man, it's just that . . . well . . ." Carlos fumbled with the bolt on the gate. He could not meet Manuel's eyes. The silence between them was broken only by the clicks of the metal bolt and the shuffling of Carlos's uneasy feet. Suddenly Manuel understood.

"Did you get instructions about me from the local committee?"

Carlos's shoulders crumpled, and he stopped fiddling with the bolt. Finally he looked up and met Manuel's eyes. "Look, *compadre*, it wasn't my idea. If it were me . . . well, you know, we've been together for years. But that new guy, the one the central committee sent in, he said your girlfriend was a *momia*. That we couldn't trust you anymore, and that you were no longer part of the organization."

"The central committee sent someone in?"

Carlos nodded, then hung his head. "It's over, man. Word came down from the top. There's gonna be a military coup, and we're gonna resist, arms in hand. The armed struggle, *compadre*. Can't afford any weak links."

Weak links. The full irony of Carlos's words didn't hit him until much later. When Eugenia got back from vacation, a last eviction at the beginning of September forced them into a small, grimy room behind a gas station that didn't even have a kitchen. That was the first time he'd benefited from his infamous *momia* girlfriend, and the account she kept at the national bank. At least she had money in there to pay for their meals.

On September 11, 1973, after the four branches of the armed forces united to bring down Allende's government and formed a military junta, the Revolutionary Left issued the call they all knew was coming. No one had the right to seek political asylum in the embassies. They all had to participate in armed resistance against the dictatorship. Manuel knew that, in the last desperate days before the coup, not even the rest of his own organization would have known that he had been expelled from the Revolutionary Left. That meant that Military Intelligence, no matter how many comrades they arrested and tortured, would not know, either, and even if they had, they probably wouldn't have cared. As a result he couldn't even risk showing himself at the door. Eugenia was the one who went out every morning to get some food and coffee and bring back the newspapers so he could see what new lies were being published that day. He found that in the tabloid, toward the back of the second section, they would list some of the people who had been arrested. Although the Army, the Navy, the Air Force, and the Military Police each had a separate listing, all were full of names he recognized, guys in the second or third tier of the Revolutionary Left.

"Why haven't your buddies gotten in touch?" Eugenia asked one morning, about a week after the coup. "Weren't you guys supposed to have a resistance plan or something?" They were sitting at the rickety table toward the back of the room, far from the danger of the windows. Manuel put down the paper he'd been reading and shook his head.

"I only wish. Most guys I knew have been falling pretty quickly. In fact, this morning I just read the names of a couple of guys in my cell."

"So you're next?" The question was a choppy uptake of breath. Manuel let out a sarcastic chuckle.

"Don't think so. Remember what I told you when you got back from vacation. These guys were playing cops and robbers, decided I was a security risk, and cut me from the group. Funny how these things work, don't you think? Their stupidity may have saved my life."

But he had been the stupid one. Two weeks later, the goons had followed Eugenia back to the room. How'd they know? The light bulb went on that first night in the torture camp, when they put him in the same cell with Carlos. By that time there wasn't much anyone could do for Carlos, but Manuel was sure his friend recognized him. A look of horror crossed his face when the guards tossed Manuel in. And through the night, as Manuel heard death slowly seep into his friend's deep, jagged hacks, he also heard something else.

"So—sooo—sorrrr—y . . . y . . . y . . ."

At that point, fresh off the street, Manuel realized they were playing games with him. Making sure he saw Carlos die. Making sure he connected the dots: Carlos, who knew Eugenia . . . At least he'd had the presence of mind to figure it out before Carlos died. To realize that anyone who is being tortured to death might say anything, to make the pain stop. After all, what had everyone in the Revolutionary Left always said? After an arrest, no one is responsible for what they know for more than twenty-four hours.

How innocent they'd all been, and how short-sighted. Everyone was a weak link once the pain started. And the goons weren't just picking up the revolutionaries. So that first night, before they could begin to wear him down, he resolved he would not say a word. No matter what. He would prove that bureaucratic lightweight from the Central Committee wrong. He would not be a weak link. Sure, in part it was his revenge on the Revolutionary Left, not that they'd ever know. But it was also because he felt responsible for Eugenia's arrest. Not that she'd ever know, either, but there wasn't anything else he could do.

He found it wasn't quite as hard as he had feared. One of the worst moments had been in the car on the way to the torture camp, lying on the floor in the back, hooded, dizzy from the beatings to his head, his ribs screaming from where they had kicked him around on the floor of their room. The fear he felt then, of what they might do to him, was even worse than what they did. When they broke his arm, or gouged up his eye, or shot him full of electricity, as long as he split himself from his body, looked down from near the ceiling at that poor bastard with the red hair shaking and moaning, he could keep his mouth shut.

Yesterday, though, when they brought Eugenia in, and he saw the horror in her eyes at what he must look like. It was like a mirror being put up to his own face. And when he saw the shape she was in, he almost lost it then. But with his next breath, and with immense relief, he realized he'd reached the end of the line. Why else would they bring them face to face? What hurt most was not knowing what would happen to her.

Now, back in his cell, he longed for an open window to let in the day's first light, perhaps a warm breeze to halt the shriveling in his bones. He pictured his grandpa running to the port in Odessa, jamming the *Communist Manifesto* into his pocket. His mama, hunched over a mug of tea grown cold from waiting, but was it him or his grandpa she was waiting for? His grandma, crying on his mama's shoulder when Grandpa went missing during a strike. Yet when she turned her head, it was Eugenia. As he heard the boots stop outside the door to his cell, he knew they'd come to get him for the last time. He gathered up the torn pieces of his family's suffering into the agony of his own wounds, sat up straight, and waited.

III

Disappeared

Sara was always happiest on Friday nights, when they celebrated *shabbat*. The fragrance of brisket and *challah* wafted through the house, and Mama sang songs and told stories from her childhood. Sara's favorite story was about Istanbul, when her papa had heard her mama singing *Oseh Shalom*. They were both from Odessa, but had never met before. Mama was from a merchant family, and their house was made of stone with geranium pots on the stairs and an orange tree in the back. Papa was a tailor's son, and they'd lived in a neighborhood near the port. Tell me again, Sara would beg almost every Friday night. Tell me about how you fell in love. But her parents never mentioned why they had ended up in Istanbul in the first place, or why they'd left Angol, the first place they'd lived in Chile, and moved to Temuco, where she had been born.

When Sara turned six, her parents placed her in the local German school, the only one that did not require a baptismal certificate. Her classmates were the children of German colonists, most of whom had arrived in southern Chile a generation before as the frontier was opening up. She was the only Jew, and the only one whose parents were not wealthy merchants or landowners.

As she learned to read and write, she also began to decipher new tensions in her house. After he closed the shop and sat down to dinner with them, her papa would go out and not come back until very late. She'd awaken in the middle of the night to arguments, even hear her mama crying. Every now and then she'd find pieces of paper lying about in the corners of the shop, and when she picked them up the ink would rub off on her hands. They were hard to understand, but as she got better at reading she began to get a feel for what they contained. It was something about poor people, working people who didn't get paid what they deserved. Somehow, she knew that these papers were a part of what made Mama cry.

When she was ten, Sara woke one morning to find her mama in her bathrobe sitting at the kitchen table. It looked like she had been up all night.

"Mama! What's the matter?"

"Ay, Sarita, your papa. . . ."

"What? Where is he?"

"I don't know where he is. I knew it would come to this, I just knew it."

"What are you talking about? Has he left us?"

"What? Oh, no, not that, he'll be back."

"Then what happened?"

Mama only sighed.

Sara did not go to school that day. She brewed chamomile tea, helped her mother make a soup for their lunch, and walked to the corner to buy bread. They sat at the kitchen table for hours, talking. Sara learned about the troubles in Odessa, back when Mama and Papa were young. She learned how some people just hated the Jews, and blamed them for everything. She learned that a group of these people had run through the Jewish neighborhood, breaking into people's houses and killing them, for no reason except that they were Jews. They had broken into her mama's house and killed her whole family, including her twin baby sister and brother. Mama was the only one who survived because she hid in the attic. Papa, too, had been left alone after his father died in the workers' rebellion near the port.

Sara began to understand that her mama and papa came from very different families. Mama's family had money, but Papa's did not. Papa's family was socialist, Mama explained, and this meant that he was always defending the poor. Which was not a bad thing, she said, but sometimes they seemed more important to him than his own family. In fact, Mama said, when they had traveled from Europe to Chile on a ship, stuck in the third-class cargo hold filled with dirty, smelly people, Papa had criticized her for complaining about them. It wasn't their fault that they were smelly, he'd said. They were poor and had never known anything different.

Mama also told Sara about the farm near Angol where they had lived when they first got to Chile. It was in the south of the country, too, but further north than Temuco. They had been hired as managers, but when the landowner built a fence to keep squatters off his property the surrounding farmers got angry because he blocked the road they used to get their goods to market. One night, when the farmers burned down the gate in protest, her papa had helped them. Then the landowner had fired her papa, and they had been evicted. That's when Mama finally stood up to him, telling him he had to stop getting involved in politics if they were going to have a family.

"So, are you going to say something to him again?" Sara asked when her mama was done. It was the middle of the afternoon and they were drinking yet another mug of tea. Mama placed her mug on the table, then looked down at her hands.

"Ay, Sarita," she sighed, "what is there to say? Will I leave him if he doesn't stop? Where would we go? What would we do? And it isn't like I haven't tried before."

At that moment Sara decided that she would talk to her papa, stand up for her mama. But by the time her papa came home late that night, giving off a strange scent that, over the years, she learned to recognize as jail smell, she didn't know what to say to him. So she didn't say anything. And her mama just melted into his arms. All it took was one "my little peach," and everything was forgiven. Over the years, Sara would grow to hate that phrase.

1940

Papa was always involved in workers' politics, and Sara finally lost count of the nights he didn't come home. But the worst was the time he went into the countryside to help landless Mapuche peasants. There was an electricity in the air then, and people were marching through the streets of Temuco, gathering in the main plaza every afternoon. In the two years since he'd been elected, the new president had been changing things, and people were expecting more. You could just see it in the headlines of the newspapers the boys hawked on street corners.

Times like these, when people got their hopes up, they were always the worst, Mama said. When that had happened before in Angol town, where they'd opened the dry-goods store after they were thrown off the big farm, the police got it into their heads that Papa was to blame. Mama still remembered coming into their store to find everything turned upside down, bags of flour, rice, and sugar torn open, their contents spread across the floor and ruined, because the police had raided them during the night looking for who knew what. But even Mama had to admit that, in the end, the worst of the worst was the time when Papa helped the poor

Mapuche peasants invade the land the big farmer had taken from them so many years before.

It was November, and the days were getting longer. The sun still came up timidly, covered in fog, and the fragrance of burning wood still lingered over the shivering city in the early hours of the day. But in the countryside the wheat nursed its spiky golden crown, turning eagerly toward the light, while potato plants hugged the sides of the rolling hills and sent out blue and white flowers that trumpeted the approaching harvest. In the countryside during this time of plenty, it was only natural for peasants to think about what they had lost, how the big landowners had moved in with their thugs and torched their parents' houses, the smell of their burned belongings lingering in the air for days.

At least that was what her papa told Sara before he left for the countryside. There was a small community of Mapuche Indians, he said, near a big river that fed the Pacific Ocean. The Mapuche were an indigenous people, he explained, which meant they had been there first, before anyone else. All the land had been theirs, and when the Spanish first arrived, they'd fought to defend it. But fifty years ago, the Chilean army had finally defeated them. Like most Mapuche, this community got a small land grant from the government. It hadn't been much, but at first it was enough to raise their families, plant crops, and keep a few sheep. Then a big landowner appeared one day and said that half their land was his. His gunmen moved the fence, then burned the houses inside his new claim.

Like many Mapuche communities, they'd been fighting in the courts for years, trying to get their land back. Papa had helped them find a lawyer, and they actually won their case. But the big land-owner took it to the higher court and it got stuck there, gathering dust and cobwebs, because that judge was the landowner's friend. When the new president was elected and people said he would give the land back to the poor, Papa's friends were happy. But several years went by, and the president did nothing. So Papa agreed to help them; and one morning before the fog burned off, he put on his hat and jacket, hugged Mama, and left.

The next morning, Papa was in the newspaper. The reason Sara bought a copy from the boy in the market was that Papa's wide-brimmed hat and beard were unmistakable on the front page. "Police called in to protect farmer," blared the headline. When the Indians had invaded a German farmer's land during the night, the newspaper story said, among the people arrested was a "known communist agitator" by the name of David Weisz. Sara wasn't sure what that meant, but she knew it was not a compliment.

That afternoon, three scraggly men came into the tailor shop. Sara had stayed home from school to help her mother. Besides, she knew that with her papa in the paper invading a German farmer's land, she would not be welcome in school for a while. She wondered, as she looked the men over, whether they were communists, too. "*Buenos días,*" she said. "Can I help you?"

The tallest one of the three, whose clothes looked a little cleaner, moved closer to the counter. "*Buenos días, niña,*" he answered. "We're looking for *señora* Weisz. Is she here?"

"What is this about?"

"Actually, we'd like to tell the *señora* ourselves if you don't mind."

"If this is about David Weisz, I'm his daughter."

"Is your mama here?"

"She's sleeping. She was up half the night when Papa didn't come home. I'd rather not wake her."

The man's shoulders slumped slightly. "Well then, *niñita,* let me write a name down for you." Sara handed him a piece of paper and a pencil, and after smoothing the paper on the counter's wooden surface next to the old cash register, the man began to write. "This is the lawyer who has agreed to defend your father in court," he explained. "His case will be heard the day after tomorrow. Your mama should go to this man's office, at the address I'm writing here, later this afternoon if possible. Please give this paper to your mama when she gets up."

For about a month Papa stayed in jail while the lawyer fought to get him out. There were stories in the newspaper and pictures of Papa being brought in handcuffs before the judge, looking thinner and thinner every day. Mama tried to get in to see him and take him some food, but the police refused. Sara did not go back to school, and at night the only way her mama could sleep was if Sara made her some chamomile tea and then rubbed her back for hours.

When she thought back to those days, what Sara remembered most was the fragrance of chamomile and how it combined with the smell of newsprint on her hands from reading the latest about her father. Only after workers and peasants held a large demonstration in the central plaza calling for Papa's release did the judge finally hear his case. The following day, as she was adding chamomile flowers to the boiling water for tea, Sara looked up to see her father standing in the doorway. He was so thin that his clothes hung on his body, and there were deep circles under his eyes. As she stepped forward into his open arms, the sweet chamomile wafted up and mixed with the sour jail smell coming off Papa's clothes. It was so much stronger than before, because he had been in jail for so long without washing. Never again would Sara be able to smell chamomile tea without feeling sick.

Yet if it hadn't been for Papa's jailhouse adventure, Sara had to admit, Antonia Painemal, the young Mapuche girl, would never have come to live with them. Tonia, as they called her, was not from the community fighting the German farmer. Her mother, who was, had followed Mapuche custom and gone to live in her husband's community. It was Tonia's grandparents, old friends and comrades of David Weisz, who had asked him to take Tonia in.

Although they were the same age, Tonia was a full head taller and much stronger than Sara. At first it was hard to communicate because Tonia didn't speak good Spanish, and the Weisz family could not speak the Mapuche language. When Sara mentioned this to Tonia years later, and said they had been like immigrants trying to communicate with each other, Tonia corrected her. "I was the only one there who wasn't an immigrant," she said.

Sara wasn't sure she liked Tonia at first. The house was small, so she ended up having to share her bedroom with her. And she didn't even know how to use a knife and fork properly. Then, a few days after Tonia came to live with them, Sara found her coming into the shop from the garden in the back.

"What were you doing?" she asked, using her hands to try and mimic her question. Tonia looked puzzled for a moment, then made the motion of lifting her skirt and squatting down.

"Pee," she said.

"Where?" Sara asked.

Instead of answering, Tonia took her hand and led her into the back garden, to a corner under the orange tree. She pointed to a wet spot, and laughed softly. "There," she said.

In the unexpected intimacy of that moment, for the first time Sara saw things from Tonia's point of view. She knew the Mapuche were poor; her papa had told her that. But now she realized they must not have bathrooms. Torn from her family, stuck in a strange place, Tonia had never used a toilet before.

Sara brought Tonia back into the house and opened the door to the bathroom that was next to the kitchen. She walked in, made the motion of lifting her skirt and pulling down her underwear, and sat on the toilet seat. After making the motions of using toilet paper, she stood up, mimicked lifting up her underwear and smoothing down her skirt, and flushed. "There," she said. "Bathroom."

From then on they could talk about anything. As Tonia learned more Spanish and Sara a few words in the Mapuche language, they gradually stopped having to act things out. They understood each other so well that, as time went by and they grew older, sometimes they did not have to use words in either language.

When Sara finally returned to the German school, Tonia stayed at the tailor shop and helped out with the sweeping and cooking. At the end of her first week, when every day she came back to the shop to find her friend working, Sara decided to ask her papa about it. After changing out of her uniform, she went into his sewing room and stood near his pedal machine. He was concentrating so hard that at first he didn't notice her.

"Papa," she said softly. Startled, he looked up at her over his half-moon glasses. His red hair was standing on end.

"Oh. Sarita. I didn't hear you come in."

Sara moved closer, putting her hand on his shoulder. She gave him a quick kiss on the cheek, at the edge of where his beard began. "Papa," she said, "I was wondering. Why doesn't Tonia go to school?"

Papa took off his glasses and rubbed his eyes. "Well, Sarita," he began, "you must know that Tonia can't go to your school. They don't accept Mapuches there."

"I know, Papa, they hardly accept me because I'm Jewish. But there's lots of other schools in Temuco."

"You're right, sweetness. But Tonia never went to school before, and I don't think her parents want her to."

"Why not?"

"Well, it's hard to explain, and I don't understand it completely myself. You remember when we talked, before I went to help the community with the land invasion, about what had happened to the

Mapuche? They're a proud people, Sarita, and they still remember when they were independent. Tonia's grandparents, their generation . . . well, they grew up before the Chileans conquered them. They have a different way of explaining the world, and they taught this to their children and their children's children. Especially to the girls, because when they grow up they teach the next generation. The Mapuche don't want their children learning foreign things."

"But Papa, she's living here now. That's foreign."

"You're right, Sarita. And to be honest, I'm teaching her things."

"Like what?"

"Sewing. How to use my machine. But I'm also teaching her to read."

"That's good, Papa. She should know how to read. But now I'm even more confused than before."

"Why is that?"

"Well, if her parents don't want her to learn foreign things, why didn't they just keep her at home? Why did they send her to Temuco?"

"A very good question, Sarita. I'm not really sure, but I think it was because she got very sick." He then turned back to his machine, signaling to Sara that the conversation was over.

As time passed, the reason behind Tonia's presence in their house remained a mystery. Sara tried to bring it up once or twice, but Tonia would always change the subject. And then there were the dreams. Some nights Tonia churned up the sheets and moaned, talking in gibberish, screaming or roaring once in a while and waking Sara up over and over. The mornings after were the hardest, and during the day at school Sara could barely keep her head up off her desk.

One night, Tonia seemed in great pain. She was not thrashing or screaming, just moaning and crying quietly. Sara went over to her and placed a hand on her shoulder. "Tonia," she whispered. "Are you all right? Please wake up."

Tonia's dark brown eyes fluttered open. "Sara," she breathed. Sara took her hand.

"Are you all right?" she asked, smoothing the other girl's sweat-drenched hair back from her forehead. "You don't seem to have a fever."

Tonia closed her eyes and let out a sigh. "I'm not ill," she said. "At least not that you can cure."

"What do you mean?"

"It's a Mapuche thing. Sometimes, when a person has the gift, or the mark, a spirit comes to live inside her head."

"How come? What does that mean?"

"Ay, Sarita, the mark . . . it never goes away. My mama tried everything, but nothing worked. That's why she sent me here, to get away from *Kuku*, but she still comes to me in dreams."

"Who, your mama?"

"No, *Kuku*, my grandmother. She was a great *machi* and it's her spirit. Mama said that *Kuku* died of grief after the Chileans took away our land. Now *Kuku* comes to me at night and scolds me for running away."

"What's a *machi*?"

"It's someone who can hear the spirit world. My mama said *Kuku* wanted to give me her spirit and make me a *machi*, but it was too hard. An old man in our community with grizzly hair is a *machi* and offered to teach me, but he charged a lot of money my parents didn't have."

"So that's why they sent you here?"

"Yes. But *Kuku* found me."

"So what do we do now?"

"Please don't tell anyone, Sara. I don't want to go home."

"But are you going to be all right?"

"As long as I don't get sick, I'll be all right. Sometimes, when the *machi* spirit gets really angry, it makes you sick. For now, though, it's all right. Just don't tell anyone, okay?"

The secret made them closer, because now they shared something no one else knew. They were like sisters, Tonia said, under the skin. The sister neither of them had.

⋈

When the war heated up in Europe, many Germans in Temuco went public with their support for Hitler. From one day to the next, the girls at school began to laugh at Sara, insult her, push her into walls. "Jew," they whispered under their breath, and then crinkled up their noses as if she smelled bad. One day she tried fighting back, but the teacher sent her to the headmistress, saying it was her fault. The old, fat principal, the ruddy web of capillaries on her nose and cheeks clashing with the sky-blue color of her eyes, shook her three chins in disgust.

"Our school is built on tolerance," she said in her heavy German accent, "but even reasonable people have limits. I know about your parents, their Jewish Communist ways; but you can't bring that in here. You will not talk back to the other girls, insulting their beliefs. You will do your work quietly and respectfully. Remember that you are in this school exclusively thanks to our generosity and good will."

That was the same day she'd taken her special doll to school in her bookbag. At the end of the day, when she put on her coat, her doll's newly bald head peeked out from the top of her bag and she could see the star of David carved into her scalp. "Jew," they spat at her. Somewhere deep inside she felt something break.

After she got home and closed the door to her room, she could not come back out. Her mama and papa knocked. What happened, they asked. Are you sick? But she couldn't answer them. Her mama finally opened the door and came in.

"What happened, *m'hijita?*" she asked, placing her hand on Sara's back. But Sara could only lie there, on her stomach. Although she felt the tears wetting the pillow, she wasn't sobbing. She felt paralyzed. She couldn't say or do a thing. She could see the pieces of herself laid out on the bed, in the wrong order. She couldn't put them back together.

After waiting for an answer, and gently rubbing a hand back and forth across her shoulders, Mama finally left the room, closing the door gently. Sara could hear Mama and Papa whispering on the other side, then their footsteps retreating. After the door opened again and Tonia came in, Sara realized that they had gone to ask her for help.

Only Tonia understood. Sara didn't say anything to her, not a word. But when Tonia put her hands on Sara, she knew. When she rubbed softly at the knot under her shoulder blades, then moved her large hands up to massage her scalp, could Tonia feel the Star of David that was carved there? Every night, after Mama and Papa went to bed, Tonia ran her large hands from Sara's head, along her shoulders and down her spine, kneading out the pieces of her sorrow and putting her back together. Then she was able to sleep. She didn't know how many days had passed when she finally opened the door. In a few weeks she was even able to go back to school.

When she came home that first day, Tonia was at the counter of the tailor shop.

"Everything go all right?" she asked.

Sara nodded. "But it's so strange," she said. "It's like everyone else belongs to a different country, and I'm a foreigner there. When they look at me the expression on their faces makes me feel like the old prejudice about Jews is true, and I must have horns growing out of my head."

"I know what you mean," Tonia said. "I feel like that all the time when I leave the shop. People look at me in the street like I don't belong."

"Why do you think that is?"

"In my case it's because I'm Mapuche. I do look different, and besides, my mama keeps sending me these clothes to wear that make it even more obvious." Tonia laughed, looking down at her colorful apron, her hand reaching up to check the kerchief she wore over her long braids.

"And in my case," Sara said, "it's because I'm Jewish."

"Do you look different, too?"

"Well, I'm shorter and darker than the other girls. Although, looking at my papa, it's clear that not all Jews are short and dark."

"But the other girls at the school won't think about that."

"Why not?"

"When people see you're different, they don't think about you in the same way. They don't care."

After that it was easier for Sara to get up in the morning and face the German girls at school. She knew her sister would be waiting for her at home. Tonia's love was the amulet she needed to protect herself. Together they were safe on an island in the middle of a dangerous sea.

The year they turned fifteen, Tonia got sick. At first her dreams got longer and more frequent, but pretty soon she began running a fever and refusing to eat. Mama tried the home remedies she remembered from Odessa, chicken soup, plus various concoctions with raw eggs that turned Sara's stomach. Even her papa's old friend Dr. González, who had delivered her, came by to help. But nothing, not even cold baths, brought the fever down. And there was nothing they could do for the chills, the dreams, the crackling of her bones.

"There's nothing else, *compadre*," Sara overheard Dr. González whisper to her father outside the door one day. "I think it's time you took her home." When her papa hired a truck for the journey back to Tonia's community, Sara sat for a long while next to the bed, holding her hand.

"I'm sorry, *lamien*," she said, using the Mapuche word for sister. "I broke my promise."

Tonia looked at her with fever-shimmering eyes. "Oh no you didn't," she croaked. "I said only if I didn't get sick, remember? *Kuku* just got too angry."

Papa came in and wrapped Tonia up in a large blanket. Sara watched through the blur of her tears as he picked her up in his arms like a small puppy. She'd been ill so long in their house that she was nothing but skin and bones.

A gash opened up in Sara's life then, a before-and-after that would not heal. She refused to go back to school. Without Tonia's comforting presence, her mind sometimes traveled to a parallel world where angry spirits shrunk loved ones to a third of their original size. In this world, Jews got their heads shaved and stars of David carved into their scalps. Being a Jew meant that the pieces of your being got separated from one another, sent to different locations as soap, lamp shades, or gold fillings taken from your teeth. Being a Jew meant that your family was killed for no reason except that they were Jews. Her mama and papa's migration through Istanbul, their foggy story of love and survival, lost any vestige of romance in the world unfolding before her. Her mama, huddled in the Istanbul fog, was nothing more than her family's only survivor from the Odessa pogrom. Her papa, no longer a dashing, pipe-smoking suitor who swept her mama off her feet, was a scared working-class kid alone in the world. This harsh world had always been there, Sara realized, and it spared no one.

1948

When Samuel first came into the tailor shop, a shy, plump, slightly greasy young man, Sara took pity on his desire for her. He smelled of the yeast he used in his bake shop. After putting the offending item of clothing on the counter between them, he would take a thick roll of bills out of the right pocket of his pants and, not able to look her in the face while he talked, whisper what he needed: a button replaced, a seam repaired. Then he threw the money down on the counter and ran out of the store. Sometimes she ran after him, in his yeasty wake, just to return the extra money he left among the folds of his clothes. But he was long gone, surprisingly swift for such a pudgy creature.

It took him a long time to gather up his courage to ask her out, and even then he stammered so hard she could barely understand him. It took him so long to get the words out, it was as if the weekend went by while she was waiting. He couldn't look her in the face but stood staring down at his hands, the left one still clutching the shirt he'd brought in that day, the wad of bills glistening with sweat in his right fist. She put her hand over his fist and waited for him to look up. The minutes dragged by. Finally his gaze came up slowly, fear vibrating in the green irises of his eyes. She waited just a second for their eyes to lock. "I'm free on Sunday right after lunch," she said. "I love to walk in the park and eat peanuts."

Sara lost count of how many little triangular cones of peanuts he bought her Sunday after Sunday as they walked, in silence, around the plaza. Candied ones, salted ones. A fine haze of sweat would gather across Samuel's forehead, and somehow that endeared him to her. For weeks he barely opened his mouth. She occasionally made a comment about the weather, the hard work at the shop, how good the peanuts were. Anything to break the silence. He would nod gratefully, there would be an audible intake of breath, as if he were about to answer. Then nothing. Each week as she waited for him to arrive, she wondered what the point was. But then she counted the number of Jewish families in Temuco, added up the ones with young men more or less her age, and came to the unavoidable conclusion. If she wanted to marry, he was her only hope.

One Sunday evening when he brought her home, she took his hand. "Shmuel," she said, using his Hebrew name. "Let's do something different next weekend. Why don't you come by on Saturday night, after the end of *shabbat*, and we can go out and have a *schnapps*. It isn't as if we're little kids, you know. Maybe we can even go to a movie." He seemed startled. But he said yes.

The following Saturday, right after sunset, they took a walk to the river. A four-piece band with an asthmatic accordion was playing waltzes and polkas. Several older German couples were turning stiffly on the wooden boards that served as a makeshift dance floor. The remaining dusky light glittered in the beads of sweat on the bald pates of the men. They stood watching, and Samuel was silent as usual. But she noticed that, in spite of himself, he would tap his right foot when an especially lively number came along.

Suddenly the band seemed to come alive and launched into the new tango that was on all the radio stations. She was utterly amazed when Shmuel took her hand and led her gently out onto the floorboards. He swept her up into his arms, pressed his slightly sweaty cheek to hers, and carried her off in the wave of his smooth steps. She closed her eyes, letting him guide her; they dipped and turned for what seemed like hours and she did not stumble even once. She only opened her eyes when she realized they were back on the grass by the side of the bandstand. He was looking down at her, a smile playing along the edges of his lips.

"Where did you learn to do that?" she asked. His smile opened up and took over his entire face. He was almost handsome then, his green eyes sparkling.

"When I left Germany I lived in Argentina for seven years before coming to Temuco. The bakery business, it was too cut-throat, and I had no entry capital, so first I made some money bartending at a tango bar. Sometimes they needed an extra man to dance. I found I have a knack for it."

They danced several more sets, wrapped in a silken cloud softened even further by several glasses of wine. She was sorry when the moon began to set, and the band packed up its gear. They walked back through the deserted streets, arm in arm, her head resting on his shoulder. "So," she asked, looking up at him, "how did you end up in Argentina?" He stopped and let go of her arm. "What's wrong?" she asked. His face closed up, harsh and jagged. He didn't say anything for a long time and just kept staring at her, his eyes suddenly flat. His right hand, claw-like now, clutched her left elbow. They walked in silence to her door. He didn't even say goodnight.

For several weeks he did not return to the tailor shop. What had happened to him that he had reacted in such a way? True, he wasn't her knight in shining armor, and maybe she should be glad he was gone. But as time went by she realized she missed him. Why had he been so upset when she'd asked him about leaving Germany? Finally she decided to ask her father about it.

"Papa," she asked, putting her hand on his shoulder as he worked at his pedal-powered sewing machine. "Was there something that happened to Jews in Germany before the camps?"

As usual it took her father a few minutes to react. She could see he was working on an especially demanding design. "Germany? Well, I'm not sure exactly, but as soon as the Nazis came to power, you know they weren't kind to the Jews." He took off his sewing glasses and turned around to look at her. "Why do you ask?"

"Well, it's just that . . . Shmuel immigrated to Argentina before the war, and I think something pretty terrible must have happened to make him leave Germany."

"Well, then, why don't you go to the library and look in the European history books? Maybe you'll find something there. Or if not, maybe the old newspapers."

She went to the library every day after they closed the shop and finally, in a new European history book they'd recently received at the Temuco library, she found a short paragraph. "On November 9-10, 1938," she read, "throughout Germany almost every window in every synagogue and Jewish-owned business was shattered. In German, *Kristallnacht* means night of broken glass. Ninety-one Jews died and thirty thousand were arrested and sent to concentration camps. Survivors tried to leave the country, but only the lucky few made it out." Sara shut the book. That must have been it, she realized; the dates worked with when he arrived in Argentina. Shmuel was one of the few who got out alive.

One Thursday right after lunch, he walked in and stood at the counter. His eyes were a muddy shade of grey, and under them his lack of sleep had gathered in smudges of soot. He had no clothes to put on the counter, no wad of bills. He just stood there and looked straight into her eyes. He still smelled of yeast.

"I know about *Kristallnacht*," she whispered. "Your family . . . you were the only one who got out." His eyes closed. "My mama and papa," she continued softly, "they were the only ones, too. From Odessa." He opened his eyes, then his mouth. But nothing came out. She reached a hand across the counter, but he turned away. He stood, his back to her, for a moment. Then he walked out.

When he came back a month later, he placed a small, worn velvet box on the counter between them. She opened it to find a diamond ring. It had been recently cleaned and polished, but the setting was antique. Though he never said anything, over the years she grew convinced that it had belonged to his mother, perhaps even his grandmother. She pictured him smuggling the box out in the pocket of his pants.

They were married the following week in a civil ceremony, her parents the only witnesses. Mama and Papa never took a shine to him, she was never sure why not. Maybe it was because they saw her Shmooti, as she took to calling him, the way she'd first seen him, plump and sweaty, shy and needy. They'd never seen him dance tango. Sara had been sure that, after that first magical tango evening, and especially after she told him about her mama and papa, he'd slowly open up to her. The more he's in love, she'd thought, the more we live together, the more he'll want to tell me. Over the years she'd come to realize what a worn and weary masquerade that was. She lost count of the number of women she met who fell in love with the ideal man into whom they hoped to turn their husband. She, too, hadn't married Shmooti the man, but the smooth tango dancer who would surely become the man she'd imagined. And they stayed together, she'd come to understand, largely on the strength of her imagination.

When she lay awake in the night, listening to the keening and rumbling of his frequent nightmares, she imagined the scene of his dream by focusing on his movements. She watched him as he turned and groaned in his sleep, protecting his head with his arms from what must have been the soldiers' kicks when they broke into his family's house and shop. She began to imagine the other side of his reactions, to visualize a *pas de deux* in his lonely, frightened movements. To every protective move Shmooti made, she added the opposite aggression, until she pieced together a narrative of a battle to the death. It was a battle she relived, almost on a nightly basis, in her matrimonial bed. It was a battle scripted only on one side, to which she added her own stage directions.

When she first got pregnant with Manuel, Shmooti was angry. "Why bring a child into this crazy world," he muttered over and over. Once the baby started kicking, though, he was transformed. He could sit for hours with his hand on her belly, waiting for the next punch. Then his eyes would light up. "He has quite a step," he'd say. "Either a soccer player or a tango dancer. We'll see." And when Manuel was born, Shmooti just melted. Never a day would go by that he wouldn't come home with a gift for the baby, if only a ball or a small stuffed bear.

The circumcision was a struggle. "I know your parents want the *bris*," Shmooti grumbled, "but I'm not religious. What's there to be religious about? We do nothing but suffer for our religion, day in and day out, for thousands of years. Enough is enough." In the end he relented. "All right," he sighed. "But just the *bris*. No religion, no Bar Mitzvah." And that was that. They drank wine and ate *rugelach* at her parents' house.

Shmooti and Manuel were fine together, as long as Manuel could be consoled with a stuffed bear. But as he grew older Manuel didn't like soccer, or tangos. He wanted his papa to explain the world to him. Where had Papa come from, that he had an accent? But Shmooti had been silent too long. He no longer had a voice to talk about the past.

"Mama, what's Jewish?" Manuel asked one afternoon, when he was eight years old and they were still in the old house. Sara's hand froze on the handle of the teapot as she was serving him the tea with warm milk he always had when he got home from school.

"Why do you ask, *m'hijo*?"

"Because at school another boy said I was, and the teacher told him it wasn't nice to say that."

Sara struggled for an answer. "Well," she tried, "being Jewish is a religion, a different kind from Catholic or Protestant, which are the two religions that most of your schoolmates are."

"But we don't go to any church, Mama. What religion doesn't have a church?"

"Jews do have a church, except it's called a synagogue. But Papa Shmooti doesn't like to keep the traditions."

"What are traditions?" He stumbled a bit over the word.

"They're things you do to remember who you are, like when Grandma and Grandpa light candles on Friday nights when we're there, or Grandma bakes *rugelach*."

"Those are Jewish traditions?"

"Yes, *m'hijito*. They are."

"Then I guess I'm Jewish, Mama, because I like those traditions."

When Manuel was eleven, the Bronsteins moved into their fancy new house. It was about a year later that Manuel had it out with his papa. It began routinely enough, with yet another fight about soccer. Sara could follow it easily from the other room where she was measuring the windows for new curtains. Shmooti wanted Manuel to invite the neighborhood kids over for a game, but Manuel didn't like soccer, and he didn't like the kids on the block. But at some point the tone changed and their voices rose. Manuel's was the loudest.

"You can't tell me what to do, Papa! What do you know about my life, you're never here, always at that stupid shop of yours!"

"We live here now, so why not make friends? You're not the best soccer player, but with a ball and a field you get people to come."

"I don't want them here! They're stupid, snotty rich kids! All they can talk about is how much money their papas make!"

"You don't think you're a rich kid?"

"How do I even know *what* I am? You never talk to me about your family, where I come from! You always leave or change the subject!"

And then it was over, and Sara heard the door close as Shmooti walked out. He stayed overnight at the bakery for three days.

After that Manuel spent less and less time at home. Every day, he stayed longer at the tailor shop with his grandparents. He stopped talking to his father, and avoided being around in those few short hours in the early morning or evening when Shmooti wasn't either asleep or at the bakery. The less she saw her son, the more Sara worked to fit into her new neighborhood. She imagined him sitting at her mama's kitchen table, hungrily consuming the stories of her parents' heroic and romantic migration along with the *rugelach* and hot tea with milk. After Papa passed away, Manuel began to stay out later, and she knew he wasn't with his grandma. One day she woke to the realization that he was almost a grown man, and she had no idea who he really was.

1973

Sara's mother Myriam died the first Tuesday in September, exactly a week before the military coup, while the fog still hung milky white over the rooftops of Temuco. The knock on her door came at that moment before dawn, when the sun hesitates just long enough behind the mountains so time stands still and you see the world in two dimensions. "In keeping with Jewish law, we buried her right away. It's what she wanted, so there's no point in your coming back right now," Sara wrote Manuel that very evening. "We placed her next to your grandpa in a plain pine coffin, just like his. The day was sunny, quite a contrast with his funeral," she continued. "And by this point no peasants showed up, hats in hand, the water streaming down their faces. I don't know if they, too, have died, or just got so old that they forgot."

As time went on, Sara grew increasingly glad that her mother had died before the coup. Not that Sara wasn't happy when the military first stepped in. The demonstrations stopped and people weren't afraid any more. Her friends all talked about not having to sleep with revolvers under their pillows anymore when they went out to their farms in the countryside, and about how much more respectful their servants were now. Occasionally Sara wondered what had happened to Tonia, and to her community, with the coup. She knew that the Mapuche had benefited from the land reform, but the military had begun taking it all back. Sometimes she yearned to see her Mapuche sister again, but they had lost touch. How could she look for Tonia now?

When the junta issued its communiqué explaining how the previous government had stolen all the country's wealth, and asked everyone to contribute what they could to a new national fund to save Chile, her neighbors had stood in line to contribute jewels and heirlooms. She had even donated the pearl necklace Shmooti had given her on their fifteenth wedding anniversary. And it wasn't just the rich ladies from her neighborhood standing in that line. She'd seen humble women donating their wedding rings, or taking their one pair of pearls from their ears to put into the donation basket at the bank.

But when a number of Sara's canasta friends got together and wrote a letter of congratulations to the military intendant, at the last minute, she wasn't sure why, she decided not to sign. Of course, if she'd known then what she learned later, she'd have had plenty of reasons not to sign. But she didn't know. Only later would she understand the immensity of her ignorance, and the uselessness of her regret.

So it was good that her mother died before the Army took over the city. "All that yelling and banging," her mama had said when the street demonstrations got bad toward the end. "It's like Odessa in 1905, it scares me."

"She died peacefully, sitting in her orange grove in her wicker rocking chair, smelling of cinnamon," Sara wrote in her note to Manuel. "Don't come back now, there's no point. Just come back for summer vacation." But the note returned two weeks later, unfamiliar writing across the front, saying he'd moved and left no new address. By then the military had just taken power, but Sara thought nothing of it, at least not until about a month later, when she began to worry just a little. Not that Manuel was a good correspondent before, but at least every time he'd moved he sent them his new address. And these were not normal times. At least he could send a few lines, she thought, just to tell me he's all right.

By December, three months after the military took power, she was beginning to worry a lot. "I'll go to Santiago," she told Shmooti, "to his old place, or maybe to the university where he was studying. Someone will know where he is. Just to make sure," she added quickly. "I'm sure it's nothing, but it's been too long and classes are about to end."

When she got to Santiago, she learned the university had been closed with the coup. She rented a room in a *pension* near downtown and made the rounds to all the addresses on the tattered envelopes she'd brought with her, from one of his old lodgings to the next, from rooming house to apartment building to hole in the wall above a dry cleaner's. She said his name out loud but all she got in return was a door slammed in her face. By the time she arrived at the place from which she'd gotten the returned letter, she was crying.

The woman who opened the door took pity on her and invited her in for a cup of tea. "Ah yes, the red-haired young man," she said as they were sitting in the living room in the gathering dusk. "I remember sending you that note back, he'd just moved out the week before. But *señora*, I need to warn you. Everyone here knew he was a revolutionary. Chances are the soldiers picked him up pretty early. It's too late to check the morgues, that's what people did last month and the month before. Go to the police stations, maybe there's a record somewhere. But be careful. The secret police have eyes and ears everywhere in Santiago."

Sara spent weeks going from one police station to the next, but there was no trace of Manuel. She wrote to Schmooti every night, short notes that said almost nothing because there was no news. She never got an answer, and sometimes she wondered whether he even read them. But what could he say to the same message, over and over? What could he say to the fact that she could not find their son?

What she did find was other women, the same women at every one of the stations she visited. They, too, were looking. As they began to recognize each other they began to move together from one place to the next, a wave of grieving humanity, finding wordless comfort in each other's presence. When there were no more police stations, they went together to the Archdiocese, and the lawyers who worked there helped them fill out writs of habeas corpus. Together they waited for news sitting on long wooden benches. They didn't find their loved ones, but they found each other.

One night, after an especially frustrating day of waiting, Sara could not sleep. Not that she'd been sleeping that well before, but now she couldn't stop thinking about the woman who had sat next to her on the bench that day. They were about the same age, but the other woman looked twenty years older. She had lost her daughter and husband. She spoke of them in such loving terms, without even a tinge of resentment. Sara couldn't help but compare herself to this woman. Even as she grieved his loss, why did she still feel such anger toward Manuel?

Finally she gave up and sat in the rumpled old armchair in her darkened room, images of her son floating, gleaming on the wall. When he'd refused a ride from their new chauffeur and she'd seen him that one time, crossing the plaza, a frail kid bent under the weight of his books, walking to Mama and Papa's tailor shop. Or when Papa died, and she'd watched him hold Mama up at the graveside, then take his turn with the shovel, heaving a slab of mud into the pit where Papa lay. Or when he'd started to shave, and she saw Papa's same red beard take shape on his chin. There was something hovering right beyond her understanding, in a corner of the room she couldn't reach. Did it have something to do with the first time he'd suddenly hung up the phone when she walked into the room, or was it the first time he'd looked at her with his grey eyes so full of anger? Hate? Disappointment?

Then he started smoking, unfiltered black tobacco cigarettes whose bitter, acrid scent hung in his closet and in every corner of his room. He'd been coming home late for a long time, helping out with her papa and then, even after his death, staying to have dinner with her mama. But when he started coming home so late that she no longer waited for him, still she could not fall asleep until she heard his heavy steps on the stairs. Once, when she went to the bathroom after she heard him close his bedroom door, she caught a whiff of cheap booze. Even worse was the day that, as she tried to tidy up his room before the maid could wax the floor, his overstuffed backpack fell over and a small, slim book fell out. *The Communist Manifesto.*

Was it Papa's copy, passed on to him when Papa died? She never knew. She remembered the weekly meetings Papa had in the sewing room. Crowds of shaggy men with fetid feet sitting on the floor under the single lightbulb, Papa slapping that small book against his trundle machine for emphasis.

She'd lost Manuel at least once already, long before this unbearable loss. But when? The answer to that question was hidden in the furthest corner of the room, too dark and distant in the middle of the night, gone before first light nudged its way past the venetian blinds. Was it that horrible night, when he didn't come home at all? The dawn breaking over her mug of tea grown cold on the table. She should have seen it coming, of course. But the finality of it was so sudden, so terrifying. When he came back, Shmooti was off to work already, not even knowing if his son was alive.

Manuel's face that morning, his baggy, sleep-deprived, yet somehow exhilarated eyes staring at her from above his unshaven, hollowed cheeks, suddenly materialized in the dark corner of her rented room. That exhilaration. She'd seen it once before, when he was very small and they still lived in the tiny house in the working-class neighborhood. It was the same exhilaration in his eyes when he'd brought that little boy home, the one with the torn sweater who kept wiping his nose on his sleeve and only succeeded in crusting more snot on his cheeks. She had turned that little boy away and refused to let him stay over and play. Thinking back on it now, she wasn't exactly sure why. Had she been afraid that Manuel would prefer the poor the same way her Papa had? Or did she fear he would be hurt, like she had been, when social differences had torn her best friend from her? Not that it had helped at all since shortly after that, they had moved. Manuel had lost his friend anyway, and as far as she knew, he'd never had another one. Come to think of it, neither had she.

After he didn't come home that night, when she read the newspapers the next couple of months, she followed the trail of a shadowy red-bearded young agitator who was reported at scene after scene of land takeovers, where poor families with snotty-nosed kids got a chance to build themselves a home. She'd been so angry because he was acting just like Papa. It came back to her then, the mix of chamomile and jail smell, and she'd felt sick. Like her father, he was a mystery. What made these poor, destitute, smelly people more important than his own family? But his only childhood friend had been one of those snotty-nosed kids. Had he been trying to make his own small childhood loss into a human connection by supporting the struggles of people like his friend? Had Papa been compensating for a personal loss as well, the death of his father in Odessa in 1905? Now she would never know for sure, about either of them.

That first night Manuel hadn't come home she'd focused on her own fears, and her mama's from all those years ago. Even now she could not entirely forgive him for what he'd done. When he finally appeared she'd told him he was no longer welcome in their house. Later that summer, he'd left the note on the table with an address in Santiago: "I'm going to enroll at the University of Chile."

That had been the final resolution of the story. But the climax, she realized now, the point at which everything changed forever, had come that earlier morning when he returned from being out all night and she had told him to leave. "I'm sorry," she whispered to the image of his face, his stubbly cheeks, his gleaming eyes, right before they faded from the room.

❦

As soon as Santiago's shops opened the next morning, she sent Shmooti a telegram that said, simply, "Come. I think we made a big mistake."

"We lost him a long time ago," Sara told her rumpled, sleep-deprived Shmooti as soon as he got off the train from Temuco. "But if we're lucky, maybe we have a chance to get him back."

At first Shmooti didn't know what she meant. They spent several weeks walking the streets of Santiago, through the warm late-summer light. They walked under the weeping willows of the *parque forestal*, next to the drought-shrunken Mapocho River, and sat on a wrought-iron bench near a bridge that, for some reason, day after day, they knew how to find.

"How can we get him back if he's missing?" Shmooti asked over and over. "You know how to find him then?"

In trying to answer his question, Sara also grew to understand more fully the meaning of what she had said. "I don't think I meant just finding him physically," she began late one afternoon, when they were sitting on their favorite bench, the last rays of sunlight playing along the few thirsty rivulets of water left in the riverbed.

"What then?"

"I'm not entirely sure, but maybe find him spiritually, what he was thinking, what inspired him to do what he did."

"Now, Sarita, I'm completely confused. We don't find his body, but we get inside his head?"

"I know it sounds silly. But I've been thinking about how losing his father made my papa want to help others, while losing her family made Mama live in constant fear. And Manuel, when we moved into our big house he went to the tailor shop and followed in Papa's footsteps.

"And you know what? Shmooti, you and I . . . well, like my mama, we've put a lot of effort into not losing. A lot of good it's done us. So maybe now I need to be more like my papa."

Shmooti picked up a flat stone from the path and threw it at the absent river. It clattered through the boulders that framed the Mapocho along the other side. The power behind the throw surprised Sara, and she looked up into his face. It was closed, almost as tight as that time when she'd asked him how he made it to Argentina. When he spoke, his tone was as flat as the stone.

"So you think he's dead."

Sara picked up a short branch that had broken off the neighboring willow tree and, for a long time, concentrated on picking its tiny leaves off the stem, dropping them on the path in front of them, and then grinding them into the dirt with her shoe.

"I don't know," she finally whispered. Then more firmly, after a short pause. "I've been making the rounds—the morgues, the police stations, finally the Archdiocese—for three months now. All these other women, they're doing the same thing. We've all lost loved ones; no one knows where they are. The junta refuses to answer our questions. Of course we all want to believe that our loved ones are alive, in some jail somewhere, their papers misplaced, maybe on purpose. We all want to believe that someday they'll be returned to us alive. But Shmooti, don't you think we need to prepare for the worst?"

He picked up another stone and threw it, even harder. It echoed through the rocks for a long time.

"Well then, what's the point? You did what can be done already. Maybe we should just go home."

Sara let go of the branch and reached for her husband's hand. Slowly she traced its outline, up from the wrist and along the thumb, then along the top of each finger, and down to the wrist on the other side. When she spoke her voice was very soft.

"My darling. After we went dancing for the first time, you disappeared for a month and I thought everything was over. Then you came back, and we got married. For a long time I was sure you would tell me more about your life, that slowly we would share our sadness. But you never did. And I accepted this, without words, I now think because maybe I, too, was more comfortable not thinking too deeply.

"But things have changed now, at least for me. You say we should go home. But where is home now, my Shmooti? Temuco? All that's there is your business, and a very large and very empty house. At least in Santiago I feel closer to Manuel. I think, maybe, he was happiest here. I want to make Santiago my home, and I want to make my loss into something useful. I want to stand with the other women and demand that the generals answer for our loved ones.

"You don't have to do what I do, my darling. But I would be very happy if you would be willing to live with me here. And maybe, just maybe, even if we don't find him physically, we can find a way to understand."

Samuel Bronstein and Sara Weisz de Bronstein sold the bakeries in Temuco and moved to Santiago. They bought a small Mediterranean house in a new development along the eastern edge of the city. The house was surrounded by a stucco wall with planted geraniums along the top, and the wrought-iron gate opened into a small front yard framed by cypress trees. In the center was a patio with a fountain, and an avocado and three orange trees. On a clear day, they could sit in their living room and see the mountains.

Samuel began a bakery in the same neighborhood, and together they joined a synagogue in the older, more established part of town. Samuel became a sustaining member of the congregation. "My papa was a cantor in his temple back in Germany," he told the younger Jews of the community, every *shabbat* and twice on holidays. "It never pays to forget where you come from. I learn this the hard way."

Sara became a founding member of the Committee of Relatives of the Detained and Disappeared, and together she and the women like her with whom she had first begun her search looked for their sons and daughters. Their mingled yearnings for relatives still alive caused their dreams to fly like doves, bringing back their loved ones' hopes for a better world in the lattice of their wings. They also grieved together whenever someone's relative was confirmed dead.

1979

In late January, in the early morning before the summer heat covered Santiago like a thick blanket, Sara heard a knock on the door of the Committee's office. She had already been working for several hours, trying to catch up on the paperwork connected to the recent discovery of bodies at the lime ovens of Lonquén. When the remains of several peasants had been identified and traced to their disappearances while in custody of the military, the case had become an international event for the human-rights movement. The Committee had been helping provide the necessary documentation.

She stood, stretching her shoulders and neck as she made her way down the hall. She opened the large wooden door to find a tall Mapuche woman in typical dress, a flowered apron tied over her *chamal* and her hair drawn back under a kerchief. The woman looked to be about Sara's own age. They stared at each other for a moment, and Sara felt an electric current moving up her spine, lifting the soft, curly hairs along the nape of her neck.

"Can I help you?" she asked, her voice barely a whisper.

"Sara Weisz?"

Sara felt the electricity buzzing along her temples, then a dark current of fear. "How do you know my name?"

"Sara, it's me, Antonia Painemal. Tonia. Remember?"

The current became a bright white light. Tears coursed down Sara's cheeks. "Tonia? From Temuco?"

"Sara, I saw you in this magazine." Tonia held up the issue of the Catholic Church bulletin, *Solidarity,* that had reported on Lonquén. "The picture around your neck, he looks just like *don* David. It is how I recognized you. Is he your son? Because Sara, I lost my Renato, too. And Sara, remember when you were hurting? Back when we were girls? And I would rub your back to help you sleep? Sara, I need you now. Please. I must help my Renato rest in peace."

Sara opened her arms. Tonia's *chamal* smelled of burnt wood, and the large, hard muscles of her back were familiar to the touch. It was Sara's turn now to rub along them, kneading out the knots of loss she found there, tears streaming down her face.

For several months, until she found a relative in a downtown neighborhood of Santiago who was willing to take her in, Tonia stayed with Sara and Samuel. In the kitchen after Shmooti went to the bakery, or at the offices of the Committee where Sara began to teach her about the work they were doing, Tonia would take a hollowed-out gourd, silver straw, and *mate* tea leaves from the small bag she carried under her apron. After heating some water on the stove, she pressed *mate* into the gourd and shared the tea with her friend. There was something about sharing a *mate* brew, Sara realized, that made conversation flow more easily.

Slowly Sara learned what had happened to Tonia after she'd gone back to her community. Accepting the inevitable, her parents had apprenticed her to the old *machi*. It had not been easy, and for years Tonia struggled to tame the anger and the visions her grandmother sent her. But she learned to ride the whirlwinds of the spirit world and, through her dreams, to see things others could not see. She finished her education and married a man from a nearby community. According to Mapuche custom, she had gone to live with him. Their son Renato had been adopted after he was abandoned at their doorstep, but he had become so much a part of their lives that, when he disappeared, Tonia's husband died of grief.

"You know, Sarita," Tonia said one day, "I didn't want to have my own child because I worried about *Kuku*'s spirit claiming her, too. You remember what that was like for me, and I wanted to spare my child the suffering. But that would have been easier. After the coup Renato suffered so much, and in my dreams I saw it all. In my dreams I could see what was happening, but I couldn't change it. It would be better not to see, Sarita, because even *machis* can't control the powers of the universe."

1989

On a warm September morning, Sara left the Committee's offices in the Archdiocese and walked down the stairs to the first floor. After sixteen years of fear, repression, and frustration, it seemed almost unreal that the Chilean people were finally preparing for the first open elections. Through her work in the human-rights movement, Sara had always known there was opposition to Pinochet, to the repression and the harsh measures of the dictatorship, but for a long time it had seemed impossible that things would ever change. Then, six years ago in May of 1983, the copper workers' union had called for a general strike against the military regime. To everyone's amazement, the country had exploded. True, it had taken six more years of violence, death, and the inevitable divisions within the opposition to finally reach a compromise. The Chilean people went to the polls in a plebiscite, voting yes or no on whether General Pinochet should remain in power. When the results were announced the next morning, the "no" vote had carried. The street celebrations that followed reminded Sara of what had happened after Allende was elected president nearly twenty years before.

As Sara walked out of the building onto the street, a man walked up to her smoking a cigarette. She was afraid of him at first, because he walked nervously, constantly looking over his shoulder, and his unshaven face and deep bags under the eyes suggested desperation, perhaps some kind of addiction to drugs or alcohol. But when they came face to face, her fear vanished as she looked into his eyes. Between the slate background and the light blue specks she read the sadness of the world. It was a look she had seen many times in the eyes of her friends and co-workers on the Committee.

The man was a taxi driver; she never learned his real name. He'd been drafted into the Army in 1973, shortly before the coup. When his superiors discovered how intelligent he was, they moved him to the secret police. He'd worked in Villa Gardenia, one of the worst torture camps. He said he had information about Manuel. He swore he'd seen her son, but didn't feel safe telling her anything more in the street. He promised to meet her on the North-South highway, at a stop south of Santiago, the following Saturday at eight in the morning. She said she'd bring her husband, and he agreed.

The man told his story at a nameless stop along the North-South highway. As the sun began to burn off the morning fog, Sara could hear the birds chirping between the roars of the trucks speeding by. Crying openly, he explained he couldn't live through another September without doing something.

"I know I'll never forget," he said. "I feared too much for my own life. A friend of mine who got drafted with me was shot trying to defend an innocent man, and I watched him die. I was too afraid to do the same. That's why I'm here, talking to you, and my friend is not. At least something good should come of my cowardice. Maybe that way I will be able to forgive myself someday.

"I remember your son Manuel Bronstein very well, because he was the only prisoner during my time at Villa Gardenia who never said a word. The guards talked about him constantly, they just couldn't believe it. He was brought to Villa Gardenia in October of 1973.

"The guards also talked about the woman who was arrested with him. Her name was Eugenia Aldunate. I remember this, she was very beautiful, with curly brown hair. Her name marked her as being from an upper-class family. Everyone wondered what she was doing there. The only explanation, the guards decided, was that she and Manuel were lovers. Soon it was clear she was pregnant. She saw him right before he disappeared. She was freed later, directly into the Mexican embassy. "

Sara and Samuel were surprised at how much they'd still hoped to find Manuel alive. Through her work on the Committee, Sara had seen these attacks of grief, held people's hands through them, every time a death had been confirmed. But neither she nor Samuel thought the same thing would happen to them. They'd assumed they understood the situation too well. But like everyone else, they had to grieve the death of their illusions.

"He was so young," Shmooti repeated over and over as they drove home from the North-South highway. "He needed more time. We needed more time. Sure, we make mistakes. But we needed time to tell him we were sorry." The problem was, they'd only discovered their mistakes because he'd disappeared. Sara knew that was the hitch in Shmooti's logic, the persistent mirage of a way out. The disappearance itself sometimes felt less painful than the bottomless what-ifs.

When they got home, they closed all the curtains and turned on no lights. They put on slippers instead of shoes. Sara covered the mirrors with dark shawls. It wasn't until they'd each brought an empty orange crate into the living room to sit on that their eyes met, brimming over with recognition. Shivah. It was time to mourn. They did not move for two days, even when the phone began to ring at persistent intervals.

On the third day, Tonia knocked on the door. "What is it, Sara?" she asked. "How come you haven't been to the office? How come you don't answer the phone?"

"An ex-guard from Villa Gardenia saw him, Tonia. He saw Manuel. He said Manuel disappeared from there. Everyone at the Committee knows what that means, we've seen too many of these cases already. He's dead."

Tonia came over and sat next to her on the crate, putting her large hand on Sara's back.

"This darkness, I've seen it before. It's dangerous. It's how my Florindo died after Renato . . ."

"No, Tonia. It's Shivah. Jewish mourning."

"My people say that everyone's tears help to send the deceased over the river to the other side, so they don't get lost and keep wandering among the living. Will my tears help Manuel?"

"That's not the Jewish way."

"Then I will stay a while. And you will need to eat."

Organized by Tonia, the women of the Committee began coming by in twos or threes. After Sara and Shmooti missed two *shabbats* in a row, people from the synagogue began coming by as well. Once a day, Sara and Shmooti would get up and brush their teeth. Occasionally they would take a shower. After the first seven nights, they began sleeping in their own bed. But they kept the vigil going. When they finally thought to ask what day it was, they discovered they'd been sitting Shivah on the orange crates, the house dark yet full of people, conversation, and the fragrance of food, for three months. Shmooti's hair and beard made him look like Moses.

"Sara," he asked when she teased him about his scraggly appearance, "did you ever sit Shivah for your mama and papa, or they for their parents?"

"Mama and Papa couldn't," she said. "I didn't."

Shmooti nodded. "I couldn't either." After a pause, he continued, his voice raspy. "So the twelve weeks, they will just have to be enough for everyone."

They opened the curtains then, uncovered the mirrors, and cleaned the house. Freshly showered and shampooed, Shmooti with a new haircut and shave, they began to use the networks of the Committee and quite a bit of their own money to track their son's lover. She was the only link left, and besides, the ex-guard had said she was pregnant. Might there be a grandchild? By April of the next year, shortly after Patricio Aylwin was elected the first civilian president, to general rejoicing, and almost immediately announced the creation of the Truth Commission, they'd traced Eugenia to Boston.

When Sara Weisz and Samuel Bronstein appeared before the Commission to request an investigation into the disappearance of their son Manuel, they walked into an office with high ceilings, as cold as midnight. Sara held on tight to the hand of a young lawyer with large, sad eyes who had stepped forward to greet her. Shivering in the chill that rose from the floorboards, she looked straight into the mournful depths of the young lawyer's gaze.

"Young man," she said. "A crucial witness in my son's case lives in Boston, in the United States. Please find her and bring her back."

In the first week of September, once the winter's hard frost had melted and the sun began to warm the soil, Sara and Samuel replanted geraniums on the stucco walls of their house. They began sitting out on the patio over the noon hour, when the sun was warmest and the newly forming orange blossoms sent a tentative fragrance out toward the snow-capped mountains. That same week, during the worst September heat wave Boston had ever seen, the young lawyer with the sad eyes rang the doorbell of Eugenia Aldunate's apartment.

IV

Displaced

Boston, 1990

Eugenia called very early one morning in May. Irene was sitting in her yellow kitchen, watching the rising summer sun turn the linoleum a luminous shade of gold. Her coffee maker had beeped and she had just finished filling her mug. This was her favorite time of the day, when no one else was up. She could sit quietly, comfortable in her own skin, sheltered by the warmth of her own house.

"Nenita? Did I wake you?"

"Chenyita? No, don't worry; I'm already drinking my first cup of coffee. But what is it? You wouldn't call at this hour unless it was important."

"Yeah, usually I'm not even up. But I couldn't sleep. Listen, I just got a call yesterday from a Chilean lawyer, from that Truth Commission that got set up recently. Remember the article I showed you in the *New York Times*? It's supposed to investigate all the people who were disappeared, and although I don't count because I'm still alive, at least it's a start and—"

"Whoa, wait a minute; you're going a hundred miles an hour. What does all this have to do with you? Who's this lawyer? What did he want?"

"It turns out that Manuel's parents have been very active in the Committee of Relatives, and they brought the first case before the Commission. They've named me as a witness, and I'm really the only person who can swear to having seen him in Villa Gardenia, in the shape he was in, right before he disappeared, so—"

"Chenyita." Irene's voice took on a hard yet patient edge. "What did the lawyer want?"

"He's coming to interview me in about three months. Depending on the results, the Commission might have funds to fly me back to testify."

"And Laura?"

"There's no point in saying anything to her now. With her starting high school and all, it might be a good moment to take a break. If things go well, I'm sure the Commission will be happy to fly her back with me. And she has always wanted to see Chile. Of course she doesn't remember anything; only what she's read in books. But maybe this will help her find a place where she can fit in. She can even meet her paternal grandparents . . ."

Eugenia's voice trailed off. There was a long silence, punctuated only by the exhale from her cigarette.

"Is there something you want me to do?" Irene asked.

"I don't know. It depends. But since you were there so much longer and saw the dictatorship with your own eyes . . . I don't know. All I saw, really, was Villa Gardenia and then the Mexican embassy. But you. You lived through so much more of it than I did."

"Chenyita, all I did was answer phones and drive cars. You, on the other hand . . ."

"But you were in the human-rights movement. You understand them better. Me, I . . ." Eugenia coughed.

"Well, look," Irene said after a pause. "You know I'm here to help. Just don't promise anything or sign anything without consulting me, okay?"

⚭

After she hung up the phone, Irene poured her second mug of coffee and settled back into her chair at the kitchen table. But her early-morning mood was gone. She hated to think about it this way, but every time she began to settle down, her sister had a crisis. First it had been the earthquake, and now the transition and the Truth Commission. Ever since the coup, she'd been there for her sister, and that wasn't going to change. But now her own memories of those days paraded, uninvited, across the linoleum floor.

July 1971

It had been nearly two months since Irene had returned from Boston. She had always planned to complete her degree in organic chemistry at MIT before deciding whether to return to her native land or try to get a job in the United States. But then she began to get wind of the changes going on. Increasingly curious, she took a year's leave and accepted a job as an assistant research chemist at the University of Chile. In preparation for her return, she wrote her mother that she was homesick and wanted to get her foot in the door of the Chilean academic system. She wrote Eugenia separately and said she was also coming back because she needed to see for herself what Chile looked like, with all the changes that were in the air.

She knew there would be fences to mend with Mama, given how she'd left the country three years before. They'd exchanged letters, but there was always a cold and distant tone to her mother's communications. And when the reality of her new job had sunk in and she was assigned the late shift at the lab three nights a week, she'd had to rent an apartment downtown. That set Mama off and they began having the same old fights.

Two weeks later, when she was almost settled into her apartment, she had stayed later than usual at the lab. She'd been so involved in her work that she hadn't heard the footsteps in the hall. She jumped when the door opened suddenly.

"What the—?!"

"Oh, I'm sorry. I didn't realize someone else was here." The other woman was wearing blue jeans under her lab coat and her hair was long and very dark, pulled back in a doubled-over ponytail and held in a leather clasp with a wooden needle threaded through it. Her eyes were large and round and brown, framed by thick, straight lashes. As she moved closer, Irene caught a breath of sandalwood perfume and an undercurrent of cigarettes.

"Hello," Irene said. "I didn't know anyone else had been assigned to this shift. By the way, I'm Irene." She held out her hand.

"I'm Gabriela," the other woman said, smiling. Her hand was slightly smaller, and it was warm and dry to the touch. "I'm the technician here, and I don't always have a set schedule. I was a bit behind, so I thought I'd come in and catch up on some maintenance I've been putting off. At this hour it's easier because there's less going on."

"I agree. It's very peaceful."

They worked in cordial silence for a while. But Irene was acutely aware of Gabriela's presence, every movement or cough. And whenever Gabriela moved from one side of the room to the other, a wave of smoky sandalwood tickled Irene's nostrils.

Irene finished checking the last set of measurements and looked at her watch. Three-thirty. It was probably time to call it a night.

She got up from the stool where she had been sitting and stretched, yawning lightly. Gabriela was on the other side of the room.

"Well," Irene said, "I think I'm done for today." Gabriela looked up from the centrifuge she had been recalibrating.

"I'm almost done, too," she said. "Do you live nearby?"

"In fact I do. I rented an apartment up the main avenue a few blocks from here."

"Wow. You're so lucky. I still live at home with my family, and when I come in at this time I often end up waiting until the morning rush hour before catching the bus home. It feels safer that way, and I discovered there's a small room at the back with a cot."

"You're welcome to come back to my apartment with me and wait until a safer hour. I'm always too keyed up to sleep for a while, anyway. We could have a cup of tea or something. And I have a couch in the living room that must be more comfortable than that cot."

"That sounds great," Gabriela said. "Just give me a couple of minutes."

They walked out together into the quiet of the early morning. Except for the occasional taxi that blinked its headlights at them to see if they wanted a ride, the streets were deserted. Arms folded across their chests to try to keep warm, they hurried the short distance to Irene's building. They rode up the elevator to the fifth floor, and Irene opened the door.

"Come on in," she said. "I'll start the space heater, and the living room should be warm in no time." She turned the switch to start the flow of gas and placed a lighted match next to the wick to get it going. "Take off your coat and make yourself comfortable. It'll just take a minute to warm up some water for tea."

Gabriela took her coat off and settled into the sofa, taking a pack of cigarettes and a book of matches from the inside pocket of her bag. In addition to her jeans and black boots, she was wearing a form-fitting turtleneck sweater the color of nutmeg. Her breasts were small and round and high, and the nipples stood out with the cold. She crossed her legs.

"A cup of tea will hit the spot," she said. "It always seems to be coldest in the early morning. By the way, is it all right if I smoke?"

Irene brought out an ashtray and took her coat and Gabriela's to the hall closet. She hung them up and went into the kitchen. Her hands were trembling slightly and it took two matches to light the stove. She filled the kettle and put it on the flame. As she riffled around in the cupboard above the counter, she was surprised at the strength of her attraction. It hadn't occurred to her that this would happen in Chile, where, in spite of the socialist government, people still seemed so straitlaced and repressed.

"Is Earl Grey all right?" she called.

"Sounds perfect," Gabriela answered.

Irene took the tin down and pressed some leaves into the teapot. By then the kettle was boiling, and she filled the pot with hot water. Placing the rest of what they needed on a tray, she picked it up and walked back out into the living room.

"Mmmmm. That smells so good," Gabriela said. "And you must have read my mind. I love Earl Grey with milk, and I have a real sweet tooth."

Irene set the tray down on the coffee table and sat on the couch, with what she hoped was a safe distance between them. For a while they were busy pouring, spooning in sugar, and stirring.

"This is perfect," Gabriela said, leaning forward to put her cigarette out in the ashtray. "Thanks so much."

They were silent for a while. The milk and sugar warmed Irene's belly, but she was also conscious of the knot of arousal gathering inside. Before she'd gone to study in the States she'd had a group of friends, mainly from the advanced science program. She remembered one of them, a boy on her same schedule, and their occasional trysts in the back of the science lab in the early mornings before the teacher got there. During her years at MIT, there had been several clumsy classmates who'd taken her to the movies and tried to make out in the back row. At the beginning of her third year she'd met another woman, on an exchange from nearby Wellesley College. They'd been friends for a while, and in the free spirit of the time, they'd experimented with something more. Irene had been fascinated by the softness of her friend's hands, and how they felt along her skin. Although the relationship did not last for more than a few months, Irene had found women more interesting after that. She'd learned to read the codes, to get a sense for who was open to a relationship, and yet often it was still the other woman who had made the first move.

Trying not to be too obvious, she glanced at Gabriela. They were probably about the same age, their early-to-mid-twenties, but she was pretty sure that Gabriela hadn't gone to the university. Her reference to taking the bus to her family's house, when combined with her olive skin and black hair, suggested to Irene that she was from a working-class family.

"I'm sorry, Irene," Gabriela said, interrupting her thoughts. "I really need to go to the bathroom. Can you show me which door it is, please?"

After escorting her guest to the bathroom and making sure there was soap and fresh towels, Irene sat back down on the couch. Whatever the political changes going on in Chile, she thought, it was clear that the sexual atmosphere hadn't opened up enough for her to feel comfortable making the first move. When Gabriela got back from the bathroom, she would suggest that it was time to try to get a bit of sleep. She'd bring out some blankets and a pillow, and that would be that.

"That's much better," Gabriela said as she approached the couch and sat down. Was it Irene's imagination, or did she sit a bit closer?

Gabriela turned to face her, bringing one leg up just a little on the couch in order to find a more comfortable position. In addition to the touch of sandalwood that floated across her face, Irene smelled something muskier and more pungent.

"Would you like another cup?" Gabriela asked. "Let me serve it this time." She stood and came around the table, picking up the teapot. They both reached for Irene's cup at the same time, and their hands met. At first, neither of them moved. Then Gabriela put down the teapot. Still sitting and without looking up, Irene moved her thumb lightly, back and forth, across the top of Gabriela's index finger. When Gabriela pulled away, Irene felt a flash of panic. Had she misinterpreted? But Gabriela knelt by the side of the coffee table, bringing her face even with Irene's. Their eyes met, and it was Gabriela who reached out, stroking Irene's cheek, her lips grazing Irene's nose and chin before settling gently, yet more firmly, upon her mouth. Irene tasted the bittersweetness of tobacco.

⚬

By the end of July, when winter had Santiago in its dank and frigid grip, Gabriela was staying over whenever she worked late at the lab, and also on weekends. One Sunday, after it stopped raining, they decided to take a walk. Heading east, then north, they reached the willow-lined pathways of the *parque forestal*. Although it was Sunday, the recent cold rains had emptied it out and they were alone. After walking a bit, they found a secluded corner behind the generous branches of an old weeping willow and sat down, their arms around each other. In that deserted corner, the rays of the sun an afterthought following the hard rain of early afternoon, they felt secure and anonymous enough to kiss. Irene closed her eyes.

"Irene!?"

They jumped apart. When Irene focused her eyes, she saw Eugenia, holding the hand of a long-haired, red-bearded young man who looked like he'd just stepped off the plane from Cuba. For a while no one spoke. Irene recovered first.

"Well," she said, casting an eye toward Eugenia's companion, "it seems we've both been keeping secrets from Mamita.

"Gabriela," she continued, "this is my sister, Eugenia." She looked back at the revolutionary poster child. "And who is this?"

Eugenia gave Gabriela an awkward kiss on the cheek, then took the young man's hand. "This is Manuel," she said. Irene and Manuel touched cheeks. In the silence that followed, the rush of the swollen river was distinctly audible in the background.

"Well, *compañeras*," Manuel said, "let me suggest that we adjourn to Eugenia's and my favorite restaurant, for a bottle of red wine. My treat."

They sat inside, at the table nearest the small gas heater. They didn't have to fight for the choice location, because no one else was there. It was clear that Manuel and Eugenia were regulars, because the waiter brought them a bottle of Santa Rita without even being asked, uncorked it, and poured out four small glasses. "Anything to eat, *compadre*?" he asked Manuel. They all shook their heads in unison, then nursed their wine in silence. Manuel passed around a pack of black tobacco cigarettes, and the sharp fragrance filled the air as Eugenia and Gabriela joined him. The gas heater hissed quietly in the corner near them, casting a copper glow across the marble tabletop.

"Eugenia tells me you're a chemist," Manuel said to Irene, breaking the silence at last.

"I guess you could say that," she answered. "Though I don't have a degree yet."

"And you, Gabriela?" Manuel asked after a few more minutes had passed.

"We met at the lab," Irene answered quickly. "Gabriela is a lab technician."

The hissing heater, the light clicks of the wine glasses against the table, only deepened the hush that settled upon them after that. Finally the waiter approached to remove the empty wine bottle. "Do you want another, *compadre*?" he asked. Looking around the table, Manuel nodded. Once the waiter brought the bottle and refilled the glasses, Manuel raised his. "Here's to all of us. Anybody want a sandwich? I'm treating." Eugenia and Manuel ordered their usual steak and avocado, but Irene and Gabriela preferred ham and cheese. The familiar routine of ordering helped ease the initial awkwardness that still hovered in the air.

About halfway through her sandwich and three quarters done with the second bottle of wine, Eugenia looked at her sister. "When you rented an apartment," she said, "I guess I believed you when you said it was because of your work." She looked briefly in Gabriela's direction.

"Hold on a minute," Irene said. "The experiments actually do have to be checked at two in the morning, at least three times a week. Besides, there's no reason that I couldn't keep my relationship a secret from Mama, just like you are. In fact, it would be a whole lot easier, because I could say we were just friends."

"Well," Eugenia said, "I'd hoped that when you got back we'd be able to distract the police together, if you know what I mean. But now I'm the one running interference again, just like in the old days, and I don't like it. Before, when Mama and Papa had their huge crisis, you were just waltzing along in your own life, and then you left, and who do you think had to pick up the pieces . . ." Eugenia caught herself and sat back, taking a deep breath. Manuel and Gabriela were moving their heads back and forth as if following a tennis match. Eugenia's hand trembled as she lifted her glass to her lips to drink the last remaining drops of the Santa Rita.

"I think that's enough wine for now," Manuel said. "Let's have some hot tea. *Compadre!* A pot of black tea and four cups, please! Bring some hot milk, too!"

They busied themselves with the pouring, adding milk and sugar cubes, stirring, sipping. Everyone but Irene lit up another cigarette. It was raining again outside, though more gently than earlier in the day, and the drops slanting against the window combined with the occasional sputter of the heater to throw a blanket of syncopation over the group's jangled nerves.

"Maybe it's not my place to get involved," Gabriela suggested eventually. "Irene and I have known each other less than a month. I don't know what it's been like in your family. But I have a sister. She's the next one younger than me, and we've been like twins all our lives, only eleven months apart. We were always finishing each other's sentences. In high school we covered for each other, you know? When we started hanging out with guys, or smoking behind the school, or taking our first drink, it was like we were figuring everything out together.

"But in my last year of high school, there was this girl from the neighborhood. She was a year older, had started at the teachers' college and was still living at home with her parents. We started talking one day at the local store, and one thing led to another. Long story short, my sister caught us one Sunday in the park, pretty much like what just happened today. I'm not sure she's over it yet, and it's been three years. And with me going to technical school, then getting this job . . . well, I don't think our relationship will ever be the same. Sure, she's been cool about keeping the secret, she's loyal to me and everything, but we'll never be as close again.

"Running into each other the way we did today, none of us planned it. So maybe we should just be a little patient with each other."

Manuel had been listening intently, his head cocked sideways, left index finger rubbing the edge of his teacup. When he finally spoke, his voice was coarse. "Maybe you'll think this is stupid," he began, "but listening to all three of you I'm feeling pretty jealous, to tell the truth. No, wait!" He lifted his hand as all three seemed poised to answer at the same time. "I don't mean to say it's been easy for you, no. But you're all talking about having somebody to share the family stuff with. Sure, maybe you'd like things to be different, for the other one to understand you better, support you better, who knows? But at least you have someone." He took a sip of his tea.

"I grew up an only child. Whenever there was conflict, I was the only one who stood there and took it, or dished it out sometimes. The big arguments were always my mom and me. We haven't seen each other since I came to Santiago. I write her now and then, and she writes me back, but I don't know when, if ever, we'll get past it. At least you, *compañeras*, can run interference for each other. That's the point of having a brother or a sister, it seems to me. And it's easier for me to see it, maybe, because I never had anyone."

September 11, 1973

Irene didn't know what woke her at first. The room was still dark, though she could see threads of light through the slats in the venetian blinds. Turning on her side, she saw the numbers glowing on the clock. A few minutes after eleven. Oh, yes. Tuesday. She and Gabriela had stayed in the lab until close to three in the morning. Turning onto her back, she stretched slightly. This was definitely the nicest morning of the week, when they were able to drink coffee in bed, get up when they wanted, and relax over a late lunch.

She turned in the other direction and found Gabriela's back, the skin so soft. Irene allowed her hand to linger, tracing the tight curve along the side, over the small mole parallel with the ribs, down to the waist. She nuzzled Gabriela's shoulder, taking in the musky fragrance of sandalwood and tobacco. It was still so new to her, this deep connection, this predictable familiarity. Every morning reaching out, just in case. And every morning thinking, good. She's still here.

But there was something different. Silence. Eleven o'clock in the morning, their apartment overlooking the main avenue downtown. Even though they were on the fifth floor, by this point on a weekday morning there was at least the muffled sound of traffic on the street below. Was it the silence that had awakened her?

And then she heard it, the sibilant scream of jet engines. So close to downtown? She jumped up and, pulling on her bathrobe, went running out to the living room balcony in time to see the next Hawker buzzing by, so close she could almost touch it. Immediately a loud boom, and a cloud of smoke rose a few blocks away. And she knew. After all the waiting, the denial that it could happen in Chile, the pressure from right-wing parties, the military was overthrowing Allende. They were bombing the Moneda.

She ran back into the bedroom and turned on the radio. Though she kept moving the dial, all she could find was military music. Gabriela stirred.

"What's going on, Nenita, let me sleep, okay, I—" Suddenly she was wide awake. "What in the hell?"

"It's happening, it's finally happening. They're bombing the presidential palace, the jets are coming in right over our building."

At that instant, Irene's constant moving of the radio dial paid off. It was Allende's voice. "Surely this will be the last time I will address you . . ." Irene turned on the bedside lamp. The two women sat on their bed, holding hands, then putting their arms around each other, as they listened to their president say good-bye through the crackling static and the occasional screech and boom until, finally, he was done.

They sat quietly, each feeling the other's tears on her neck. For several months now, street fights between Allende's supporters and the increasingly confident right wing had become a daily routine. Then, a few weeks before, organized women of the Right had roamed through the city, scattering chicken feed at the doors of all the top Army generals, symbolically taunting them to take action against the government. Days later, the commander-in-chief of the army, the last holdout known for his democratic leanings, had resigned.

After a few more jets shrieked down over their building, delivering their murderous message a few blocks away, an eerie silence settled over downtown Santiago. No cars or buses, no voices seeping in from the street. Then Gabriela tensed and sat up straight.

"Ay! Papa! I have to call home! He had orders from the union!"

"Gabita, the phones won't be working."

"Have to try! Maybe I'll be lucky . . ." Her voice faded away as she ran into the living room to pick up the phone. Then, after a few seconds: "Hello, Mamita, it's—yes, we heard him. And Papa? Oh, no, and when did he—do you think you'll—yes, we'll be here. No, when he finished we—yes, you're right, we'll put on one of the other stations, at least we'll—yes. And Mamita? If you hear anything, anything at all about Papa, you call right away. Promise? Yes, *mi amor*, me too. I'll tell her."

When Gabriela got back to the bedroom she collapsed against Irene.

"Where'd he go?"

"Just as I thought, he went to union headquarters. He left hours ago. Mamita was beside herself! At least she has sense enough to know there's no point to going out looking for him."

"What do you think we should do?"

"You heard me. There's really nothing we can do right now."

"So I guess all we can do is wait."

"That's right, Nenita. But what about Eugenia and Manuel? And your mother?"

"At their new place where they had to move last week, they don't have a phone. So I think it's best to wait and see what they're saying on the radio. Depends on whether they let us out on the streets, plus I don't want to lead any spies directly to Manuel. I guess I really don't know what to do. As for Mamita, I'm sure she'll be fine, since this is what she's been wanting all along. But I'll give her a call since the phones are working, just to make sure."

After Irene got through to *doña* Isabel and made sure everything was fine, there was really nothing else they could do. On the radio, everyone was being ordered to stay home. Anyone on the street would be considered a subversive, the announcers insisted. After three o'clock in the afternoon, they would be shot on sight. Luckily, they had just done some grocery shopping a couple of days before.

They showered and dressed, then made some coffee. They raised all the blinds in the apartment and spent time on the balcony, looking out at the smoke that hung, shroud-like, over the presidential palace. The mist settled grey and heavy upon the street, its humidity gathering like tears on the sidewalks. Even after the fog dispersed, the plumes spreading out from the palace, rancid with electric smoke, obscured the sun and made it hard to breathe. Every now and then a jeep full of soldiers zoomed down the avenue, and occasionally they heard gunfire, shouts, or screams. Radio and television spewed military music, punctuated by orders of the day. Occasionally lists of names were read, people who were supposed to give themselves up immediately to the authorities. There was no sunset that day, only a sudden falling from ash to black.

Sometime after dark, when they had forced themselves to sit down and eat a little bread and cheese and were finishing a bottle of red wine left over from the weekend, the phone rang. Gabriela answered.

"Mamita? What—oh, thank God! When did he—yes, all right. No, of course not. And Mamita, please, just listen a moment. Yes. He shouldn't step out anymore now, okay? What? You're right, it's hard to believe that Papa would ever say anything like that. But I think he's right, Mamita, and I think maybe you should think about joining him. Yes. Well, at least it's something to think about. And don't worry, me and Nenita, we'll talk to Dr. McKinley and see what he says. Yes. I'll call you back when I have some news. I'm not sure, but probably not before tomorrow afternoon."

"Sounds like good news," Irene said when Gabriela came back into the kitchen.

"Papi walked in half an hour ago. He got to about two blocks from union headquarters and saw a military truck speeding off in the other direction. There were people in the back, with soldiers guarding them. He got the message and ducked into a side street. He's been hiding in the shadows since then. I can't believe how lucky he was."

"What was that about talking to McKinley?"

"Seems Papi's had enough. He doesn't want to live in a country where soldiers can do what he saw in the streets today. He says he wants to get out. I said we'd talk to Dr. McKinley about the Canadian embassy."

❧

As soon as the curfew lifted, Irene and Gabriela went to the lab. Dr. McKinley was talking excitedly on the phone. After he hung up, he came over to them, giving them each a hug.

"Am I glad to see you're all right," he said in his slightly accented Spanish. "The phones have been ringing off the hooks. Because I'm Canadian, everyone thinks I can help them get out of the country. I was worried that all the experiments would fail due to lack of attention."

Gabriela looked down at her hands, smiling ruefully. "I should have known," she said.

"What do you mean?"

"Well, Dr. McKinley, my papa . . . he was in a union, you know? He tried to get there yesterday, but thankfully turned back in time. He's at home now, and when my mama called yesterday, well . . . they were hoping you could help get him into the Canadian embassy. But I can see now that—"

"Wait a minute, *hija*." Dr. McKinley's voice turned deeper, more determined. He put his large, beefy hand on her shoulder. "Of course I'll help your papa. I do have contacts in the embassy, and I am helping people. My God, I can't believe even the few things I've seen right around here, just looking out the windows! But I hope you understand that it's easier right now to get foreigners out than Chileans. He'll have to wait his turn and, by the way, we have to be very careful what we say when we talk on the phone, all right?"

The phone began ringing again, and as he went to answer it he spoke to them over his shoulder. "Could you just check that the experiments are all right? Between that and the phones, I think we will have our work cut out for us over the next few days!"

By the end of the week they had worked out a routine. In the mornings, while one of them tended the experiments, the other one would help Dr. McKinley make phone calls to his contacts in the Canadian embassy. The lines were so busy that it took hours to get through, and someone had to be constantly redialing the numbers. There were so many people seeking asylum that even when they got through, they would have to wait, sometimes several days, for Dr. McKinley's friend to call back and tell them, in code, what to do next.

In the afternoons, before the curfew began, Gabriela would go home to her family and check on her father. She tried to assure her increasingly anxious parents that yes, they were in the asylum queue, and would be notified when their turn came. Irene would drop by her mother's house. One day, when she arrived for tea, her mother told her that Eugenia had called.

"Where is she?" Irene asked. "Is she safe?"

"Ay, Nenita, who knows. I knew, of course, that before the military takeover she was living with someone. I always suspected the worst. And now it's been confirmed."

"And how's that?"

"Well, she said she's fine. I'm glad about that, of course. But she said she couldn't come home now, that she had to help a friend. It's her boyfriend, right? He must be running from the police. Do you know this boy?"

Irene refilled her cup of tea. "I've met him. Don't make him out to be a criminal, because he's not. Now, with what's going on, who knows what the Army is doing to people!"

"Don't start with that, my dear, because I won't have it. Whatever they're doing, it must be for good reason. Things were completely out of hand here by the end, so don't try to justify—"

"Did Chenyita say where she was living?"

"Are you kidding? I was lucky to hear from her at all! How did this happen to her? She'd always been such a good girl . . . I just don't understand what's happening in this country."

For several days after that, Irene wondered if she should go by the room she knew they'd rented a few days before the coup, just to see if they were all right, to make sure everything looked normal. On the second-week anniversary of the coup, after finishing at the lab, she finally decided she would.

She got off the bus at a stop two blocks further up from the gas station where their room was located. It was about three in the afternoon. She sat down on a bench at the stop for a few minutes, trying to figure out her plan. Then she saw Eugenia walking toward the gas station, carrying what looked like a bag of food. Of course. They had mentioned they really didn't have a kitchen. She got up quickly and crossed the street.

"Chenyita," she said softly, falling into step with her on the block before the gas station.

"Oh! Nenita!" Her sister jumped, then seemed to want to hug her, but managed to control herself and keep walking. "I'm sorry," she said, looking straight ahead. "I can't call attention to myself."

"Wait a minute," Irene said, "just stop walking for a minute. Are you all right?"

Eugenia stopped at the corner of her block and stood, looking back and forth across the street, as if she were trying to decide whether or not to cross. "Yes," she said. "At least for the moment. Manuel's holed up in the room. Some of his *compañeros* have already been taken, according to the tabloids, but he may be lucky. You know when he broke his cheekbone? The distance he took from the group then may have helped him. At least we're hoping it will."

"But what are you going to do in the long run? Living in this room, eating out of paper bags, maybe for a month or so, but then what?"

Eugenia shook her head and turned to go. "Can't think that far ahead," she whispered. In the brief moment she met her sister's eyes, Irene saw nothing but the grey of a tomb.

✢

The day after Irene saw Eugenia, the Canadian embassy called with the news that Gabriela's father was next in line for asylum. One of the human-rights networks that had developed clandestinely over the previous weeks was in charge of getting refugees into the embassy, and Gabriela took one of its members to visit her family and work through the details of exile.

"They're happy but nervous," Gabriela reported when she got back to the apartment. "The woman who came to the house with me explained that only Papa would go through the embassy. The rest of us can just go to the airport and meet him there. They'll arrange visas to Canada, and have a place for us in Toronto."

"Us?" Irene asked. "Since when are they us?"

They were finishing dinner. Gabriela stood up and took the plates to the sink. She busied herself washing and rinsing, then drying, then putting everything away. Irene stood next to the table, watching silently.

"Since when is it us with them?" she asked again when Gabriela was done and had lit a cigarette. "For a while now, when I've heard the word us, it's meant you and me."

Still standing by the sink, Gabriela smoked quietly for a while. After putting out the cigarette in some cold water from the sink, she threw the butt in the trash, walked over, and took Irene's hand. She brought Irene's arm around her own waist and held on tightly.

"It's still you and me, Nenita," she whispered. The exhale of breath tickled the right side of Irene's collarbone, and the smell of fresh smoke filled her nose.

"Then I don't get it," Irene said.

"I don't have to tell you that Chile's changed," Gabriela said, pulling away.

"But what does that have to do with us?"

"It's not something you'll have noticed, Nenita, because it won't happen to you. But now, people with my coloring, my background, we're suspect. We have working-class written all over us."

"But your job is safe, so is your life with me. Dr. McKinley and I, we'd protect you if something were ever to—"

"I know that, *mi amor.*"

"Then why?"

"It's the weirdest thing. During the last government, there was so much talk about class struggle and everything, yet I felt class differences didn't matter as much. I could be where I wanted, do what I wanted. Now, that doesn't seem possible. And the idea of not seeing my family, any part of my family, for who knows how long? It's just unbearable."

"And me? What about me?"

"If I really had a choice, Nenita, I'd always choose you. But whatever changes were going on in Chile, however much my family was a part of them, you and I could never really be open about our relationship."

"I can understand that with my mother. But your mama and papa, they were always so accepting."

"They like you a lot, and I think deep down, even though they'd never say so openly, they know we're living together. But now it's different. They're leaving the country, and they may never come back. If you were a man, if I were about to get married, have children . . . they might accept that. But if I stayed behind because of you, they would never speak to me again."

A week later, Gabriela and her family left the country. Under the circumstances, Irene did not go to the airport to say good-bye. They stood in the foyer, right inside the door to their building, holding hands and waiting for the taxi.

"I'll look for a job in Toronto, too, you'll see."

"Don't, Nenita."

"I speak good English, and with my MIT background . . ."

"Don't."

"You'll barely have unpacked your bag and gotten settled, when the phone will ring, and . . ."

The horn of the taxi sounded. Gabriela turned and, for a long minute, took Irene's face in her hands. She gave her a quick kiss on the lips, bent down to pick up her bag, and slammed out the door. Like a fist, a smoky wave of sandalwood hit Irene full in the face. For a very, very long time Irene would dream of that last look, the sadness and loss in Gabriela's eyes. And she would know that only part of it was for her.

⋯

On the Sunday afternoon after Gabriela left, unable to bear the emptiness of her apartment, Irene took the same bus over to Eugenia's neighborhood. It was about one-thirty, when she and Gabriela were usually having a late lunch, laughing over glasses of red wine. The minute she got off the bus, she knew something was wrong. Staying on the opposite side of the street, she walked back until she was even with the gas station and looked across, behind the pumps. The door to the room was hanging crazily, like an arm broken at the elbow, halfway off its hinges.

She ran across the street. Inside, a table and two chairs were lying on their sides. A small unmade bed against the wall had collapsed in on itself, a body with a broken spine. The two cupboards over the sink lay open, doors torn completely off their hinges, their dishes and glasses, shards now, scattered on the cement floor.

She stepped into the room. The smell of fear floated, feather-like, across her face. They were taken, she thought, and leaned dizzily against the wall.

"What do you think you're doing?"

She looked up and tried to focus. A balding, middle-aged man in overalls, the kind used by mechanics, was staring at her, arms folded angrily across his barrel chest.

"What happened?" Her lips felt swollen shut. "Do you know what happened?"

"What does it matter to you?"

"Are you the owner?"

"Who's asking?"

"The young woman who was living here, the one with the turquoise eyes?"

"What about her?"

"She's my sister."

The man crumpled. "The soldiers came not more than an hour ago," he said softly. "I'd be careful if I were you. No sense in going around yelling, getting yourself into trouble. Think of your mother. At least she still has you."

Irene could not bring herself to go back to her apartment. She imagined her first loss, that spiky, ugly thing that had already unpacked its bag and made a bed for itself in the middle of her living room, making room on the floor for this second one. She decided instead that, before the curfew began, she would take a taxi to her mother's house. Besides, she realized, *doña* Isabel was entitled to know. Think of your mother, the man had said.

She let herself in, using the keys to the gate and the front door that she had kept from when she was a teenager. Her mother was sitting in the living room watching television.

"Irene! What are you doing here, I wasn't expecting you, is—" *Doña* Isabel's voice trailed off when she got a look at her daughter's face. She opened her arms and Irene fell into them, surprising them both with her sobs.

"It's Chenyita, isn't it," *doña* Isabel said once Irene started to calm down. "She's gone, isn't she?" Irene nodded. "That revolutionary boyfriend of hers, is he gone, too?"

Irene sat up. "They're both gone. I went by their room. The soldiers came this morning."

"I knew it! I knew that horrible bastard would get her killed! What came over her? What in the hell came over her?"

"Now, Mamita, it's not their fault, they—"

"Don't start with that now! Who was he? Was he the one Sergio told me about, who flirted with her at that demonstration? Was he that criminal from the south who came to Santiago running from the police? You met him, Irene, you tell me! How in God's name could Chenyita fall for someone like that? How could she?"

The sun rose and set, then rose again, and still they sat in the living room. They did not open the curtains. They did not eat. Irene watched her mother stand and pace, then sit and pound her fist against the sofa, then stand and pace again. The same questions, over and over, with the short ones providing the drumbeat: What came over her? Who was he? How could she? She did not really want an answer, it was her way of grieving. All Irene could do was listen, and compare her image of Manuel, the idealistic and scruffy refugee from a wealthy family, to her mother's diabolical leftist, complete with fangs, claws, and tail.

✠

After Eugenia and Manuel disappeared, a dark curtain fell across Irene's life. She continued working in the lab, but found it harder and harder to return each day to her apartment. Sitting at her kitchen table, she would suddenly remember an evening when she and Gabriela, Manuel, and Eugenia sat laughing over glasses of wine. If she took a cup of tea into the living room, she pictured the first night with Gabriela. Although she now visited her mother regularly, their inevitable political fights made it hard to imagine that she could ever move back in.

The only thing that kept her sane was driving for the group that made asylum runs to the Canadian embassy. When there was a "delivery" to make, as they called it, Irene drove a late-model sedan. She varied the color and make to prevent easy identification. Sometimes she used Dr. McKinley's dark blue Cadillac, sometimes a car belonging to a sympathetic colleague. She even persuaded her mother's chauffeur to lend her the family car every now and then.

The person seeking asylum hid in the trunk of the car, under some blankets and what hopefully looked like random disorder. It was easier, they found, for a younger woman, nicely dressed, to get through the numerous patrols that surrounded each embassy, so it was Irene who made most of the "deliveries." She took a foreign man with her, often Dr. McKinley, and if the military police stopped them he pretended not to speak Spanish and showed his Canadian passport. She smiled and translated, saying she was taking her husband to the embassy to renew his visa.

When they arrived at the embassy they both got out, speaking English, and looked to see if the front door was slightly cracked open. If it was, they opened the trunk, arguing about something or other as couples do, and quickly pulled out the "delivery," who ran for the door. At first, before the military police near the embassy had been tipped off to expect such maneuvers, they could get the person inside, slam the trunk back down and take off, before anyone noticed. The more people sought asylum, and the more the Canadian embassy got a reputation for accepting refugees, the harder it was to use the front door. They were restricted to clandestine operations, mostly after curfew, in which several strong men would throw the "delivery" over the wall.

Irene liked the nights with no moon or an overcast sky. She had grown up in Santiago and knew her curves by touch, almost like a lover. On dark nights, she moved from memory, guided by little more than her intuition. It was on nights like these that she could meet the city on equal terms, grabbing this sudden stranger by her murky throat, wringing revenge for the loss of the two women she loved most in the world. It was on these nights that she felt she could face down the evil dictator, and win.

Two separate times, after they had successfully made over-the-wall deliveries, Irene had to drive like mad when they were sighted by patrols. Her knowledge of Santiago was a godsend, as was her experience driving the back roads and hairpin curves near her family farm. The first time, she escaped the soldiers by driving off the street into a plaza, swerving to avoid the benches, then out on the other end onto a side street. The second time, she crossed the Mapocho River and drove deep into the Bellavista neighborhood, pulling up between two other cars in an alleyway and turning off the lights.

After that, Dr. McKinley said she could not continue. He worried that she had been identified. He and the others also began to suspect that she was enjoying the chase too much. On the last occasion, one of them said, she seemed to wait around a little longer than necessary, as if she wanted to be seen. So they insisted she stop driving the cars. They couldn't afford to have the whole operation broken apart, so they put her on desk duty, keeping track of new requests and trying to persuade the embassies to increase their quotas.

By that point, the lease had come due on her apartment. She moved back in with her mother, where she was a great deal safer and more secure. No one would suspect that she was using her mother's phone to arrange the escape of so-called subversives, and even though she was pretty sure her mother knew about it, they never discussed it.

One day at the beginning of April, when as usual she answered the phone sitting in the study she'd set up on the second floor of her mother's house, the voice on the other end was so soft that she could barely understand what the woman was saying.

"Hello? Is this the Aldunate residence?"

"Yes?" People looking to leave the country usually asked for "*la señora* Irene," so she was on her guard at this unfamiliar salutation.

"Could I speak with Irene, please?"

"Who's calling?"

"I'm sorry, *señora*, but I would like to identify myself to Irene."

"And why is that?"

"Let's just say I have news about someone she's been worrying about for a long time."

Had something happened to Gabriela? "I'm Irene," she said. There was a sigh of relief on the other end of the phone.

"Good. Irene, all I can say right now is that I have news about your sister. There's a juice place near the Plaza Baquedano, she said you'd know which one. Tomorrow at three P.M."

The next afternoon, at a table under the awning of Eugenia and Manuel's favorite place, Irene sat with a short, beige-colored young woman with brown curly hair who could not have been older than nineteen. From her, Irene learned that her sister had been taken to one of Santiago's worst torture camps, Villa Gardenia.

"I was a prisoner there too," the woman said. She unbuttoned the cuffs of her blouse, rolling up the sleeves to show the purple marks of electricity. "I wasn't an important catch. Not even my boyfriend, who was their target, was really involved in anything. They let me go, finally, into my parents' custody, but only if I left the country. I leave for Sweden this Friday.

"I saw your sister. We were in the same cell for a couple of nights right before I was released. They had moved her into a different part of the camp, because she's pregnant. She's been badly tortured, but she's alive. She said to call and tell you she's alive."

Boston, 1986

Irene sat in her kitchen in the early-morning sun. She had grown to love this old house, its large, pockmarked eaves hanging, like protective arms, over the flowerbeds on both sides. The first summer, she'd sat out on the small porch and tried to make sense of the growth that appeared, like magic, from the soil. Were these weeds to pull out? Perennials she should nurture? The gardening book she'd bought had insisted that when faced with an old garden, you needed to let a year go by before you could tell what you would want to keep and what you needed to pull out. She had come to believe that it was good advice for her life too.

Irene had been back in Boston for about four years before she'd finally decided to settle down and buy a house. After Eugenia's exile from Chile, she had allowed the frenetic routine of the Chilean human-rights community to take over her life. She continued helping exiles leave the country, but the work became increasingly bureaucratic. Finally, as the dictatorship got ready to legitimize itself and its new constitution at the polls, she decided she'd had enough.

On the spur of the moment, she wrote her old professor at MIT and asked if she might go back to finish her degree. She started again in January of 1981, almost ten years after she'd gone back to Chile. Enough had changed in her field that she needed two and a half years to finish, but her professor was sufficiently impressed with her past work and her story to offer her a full-time assistantship in his lab when she was done.

Two years later and less than three months after Irene had moved into her house, the earthquake hit Mexico City. Eugenia called in a panic, and it had seemed the most natural thing in the world for Irene to look around the Boston area for anything that might bring her sister and niece closer. At her suggestion Eugenia had applied for a fellowship in multicultural reporting at Carmichael College. When Eugenia got it, Irene invited them to move in with her. But she'd forgotten about the schools, which were important for Laura. So finally she'd found them an apartment just over the line into the Brookline school district.

Toward the end of October, with Eugenia settled into her office and Laura finally placed in school, they had planned a belated party for Laura's twelfth birthday. Irene and Eugenia bought a cake for a family celebration and, after some hesitation, Irene invited her new girlfriend Amanda. They drank cider with the cake and drove out into the countryside for a pumpkin. When Irene had explained to Laura that they must hollow it out and carve a scary face on the front, Amanda offered to help. The result was an intricate design with curlicues for eyebrows and individual teeth in the smile, and Laura had insisted it seemed happy rather than scary. But Irene thought it looked absolutely fantastic with a burning candle inside for Halloween.

Maybe it had been the pumpkin, or perhaps she'd finally been ready to focus on the present. About six months after their excursion into the fall-dappled countryside, Irene asked Amanda to move in with her. They spent several early-spring Saturdays plying the antique sales in the small towns around Boston. Amanda insisted that a Victorian house deserved a few authentic pieces to show it off. And she was willing to pay for these expensive adventures out of her own pocket.

It was not a smoldering, sandalwood-tinged kind of longing. But as time went on, Irene felt anchored and secure, and in a different, perhaps more nostalgic way, deeply in love. They were both on the threshold of their forties, and she found on Amanda's lightly wrinkled skin, in the warm pockets behind her ears, along her neck and in the folds of her arms, a scent of lilac that spoke of home. On Sundays, when they cooked and baked together in the kitchen, the fragrance of warm bread and roast and pie held them together in a soft embrace.

But just as Irene was beginning to feel settled, another embrace, that of her family and her homeland, turned into a vise once again. Demonstrations against the Chilean dictatorship had begun the same month she had finally graduated from MIT, but it took several years for the crisis to become so large that the Boston newspapers, and even the local television stations, began reporting on it regularly. By the time she and Amanda had moved in together, there was talk of a plebiscite to decide whether or not Augusto Pinochet would remain in power.

The phone rang one Saturday morning, just as Irene and Amanda were finishing breakfast. Amanda answered.

"Oh, hi, Eugenia. Yes, she's right here. I'll put her on." Irene took the phone from Amanda's hand and sat back down at the kitchen table.

"Hi, Chenyita," she said. "Are you ready for Laura's birthday lunch today?" It was shortly before Laura's fourteenth birthday, and just a couple of weeks shy of the Chilean plebiscite. Eugenia had managed to change her fellowship into a temporary teaching position, renewable on a yearly basis because her courses were so popular and no one else could teach them.

"Hi, Nenita," Eugenia said. "I am, though that's not what I'm calling about. You'll never guess what just happened. They called me from Eyewitness News. They want to do an in-depth interview with me about Chile."

"Wow. Do you think it's a good idea?"

"I don't know. Just last week, some of my worst nightmares came back."

"And?"

"Well, if the nightmares are back anyway, maybe doing something useful, like helping people here understand some of the background . . . I don't know . . ."

"So when do they want to interview you?"

"This afternoon, on their weekend program."

"Oh, my God."

"Exactly. So could I ask you and Amanda to pick up Laura and Marcie from the movie at the mall?"

"Of course, sweetie. But isn't this kind of short notice? Don't you think that—?"

"I mentioned that. But they're right. It's short notice, but that's how breaking news is. I should know that, as a reporter, don't you think?"

"I'm not worried about you as a reporter, Chenyita."

"I know. But I think I have to do this."

So Irene and Amanda picked Laura and her friend Marcie up at the mall in the old blue Saab they'd recently bought. What no one had predicted was that, on the television sets prominently displayed in the windows of the electronics store they'd passed on their way out, Laura and Marcie had seen Eugenia being interviewed. And that was only the beginning.

When elections were held in Chile in December of the following year, the opposition candidate won. Irene and Eugenia stayed up all night, watching the television coverage at Eugenia's apartment. Amanda had stayed with them until midnight, then driven the Saab back to the house. When it became clear that the candidate of the democratic coalition was going to beat the right-wing candidate supported by Pinochet, they broke open the bottle of champagne. They hugged and wept for hours, still unable to believe that Chile's seventeen-year dictatorship was really coming to an end.

The following May, her sister received the phone call from that Truth Commission lawyer. The nightmares came back, the sleeplessness. The more her sister wrote in the notebook Ignacio Pérez had suggested, the worse things seem to get. Those early-morning phone calls, always at the moment when Irene was settling into her day, also turned her world upside down. But nothing had prepared her for the call she got the morning after Ignacio interviewed Eugenia. The minute she heard her sister's voice, Irene knew she was crying.

"Chenyita! Are you all right? What happened? Is there anything I can do?"

"Not at the moment." A short pause and a deep intake of breath as Eugenia composed herself. Then she continued, her voice less ragged. "It looks like the Commission wants to fly me and Laura back, sometime in the next few months. Laura's not happy about it, and she made a bit of a scene with Ignacio last night. But depending on what happens, I might need a lot of help."

"And why is that?"

"Well, Nenita . . . I've been wondering, you know? And it kept me up all night. It might be time to go back for good."

V

Exile

Even before the door closed on Ignacio Pérez's elegant figure, Laura knew they were going back to Chile. She felt that same burning sensation deep in her chest she had felt years before when her mother had moved them to Boston, and that sense of resigning yourself to the inevitable that had been a part of her life for as long as she could remember. What made it even worse was that her mother had no idea what she had done. This had always been the case, Laura knew. And she didn't know what was worse: that her mother kept doing the same thing to her, or that her mother had no idea she was doing it. So she locked herself in her room, took out Paco the pink porcupine, lay down on her bed, and closed her eyes.

Mexico City, 1977
Laura's first memory was of standing on the balcony of their apartment in Coyoacán, the edge of the wrought iron railing barely below eye level. She moved down into the corner, straining her

hand between the bars to reach the bougainvillea's lush purple blossoms that seemed slightly out of her reach. Ah, success. And all at once, the vague disappointment at how quickly the flower fell apart between her probing fingers, leaving only a small reddish stain along her palm; and then the whoosh of Inocencia, her sandals flapping against her brown heels, tongue clacking disapprovingly as she swooped Laura up in her arms.

"Ay, *niñita*! What if you fell and your mama came back from the newspaper and found you in broken pieces on the sidewalk! Ay, *Dios*, I can't get anything done around here when you go off like this."

When Laura behaved and played quietly with her toys, Inocencia would bustle around between the kitchen and the backstairs laundry, cooking fragrant soups and breads, beating clothes against the large stone that served as a washboard before rinsing and hanging them on the line. There, pinned between two wooden clothespins that stood up like horns, the blouses and skirts and slacks would swing gently in rhythm with Mexico City's light breezes. Sometimes, when she ironed in the early afternoon sun, Inocencia would sing songs in her native language, and the round, soft tones of her voice enveloped Laura like a warm blanket.

On days when Mama stayed home, Laura would hear the clack-clack of her typewriter in the small room at the back of their second-floor apartment. Rather than live in that room, in a more traditional arrangement, Inocencia insisted that she preferred to make the one-hour commute daily in each direction to the southern edge of the city, because on the land her brother-in-law had inherited from his family, she could keep chickens and grow herbs in a small plot they gave her by the side of the house. It worked out well for all of them, because it gave Mama a study and Inocencia could live with her family. Besides, the dishes made with the eggs and the fragrant rosemary and basil

Inocencia brought from home were delicious. And since Mama never set foot in the kitchen except to warm up the soup Inocencia left for them to eat on her day off, Laura was especially happy that Inocencia's cooking was so tasty.

When Mama worked at home, Laura was not allowed to interrupt her, whether she heard the typewriter clacking or not. Only when Inocencia announced that lunch was ready would the door to the study open, releasing the sour smell of cigarettes. Laura would run to the table, mouth watering with the expectation of a delicious chicken or squash soup and some special time with her mother. If Mama was in a good mood, she could sometimes lose track of the time and they would sit and laugh for hours. But when Mama was sad, all conversation stopped. Then Laura felt like a cloud of smog came down and draped the room in shades of grey and brown. There was nothing she could do or say that would make Mama feel better, so she would just sit and look at her mama's face: her eyes as bright as the small turquoise earrings Inocencia wore; the short curly hair that spread out like question marks from her head; and most of all her light skin, with slight wrinkles around the eyes. Sometimes Laura would tiptoe to her mama's side and reach out to touch her hair, each strand so light between her fingers, so different from the thick, black pieces she felt growing from her own head.

As Laura grew older, she began to stand in front of the mirror and compare her face, thick dark eyebrows and eyelashes, olive skin, large round dark eyes, and straight, thick, raven hair, with her mother's light looks. One day, during the early part of third grade, her friend Cecilia was standing near the gate of the playground when her mama dropped her off.

"Who was that?" Cecilia asked minutes later, while they were playing on the swings.

"What do you mean?"

"Who was that who just left you off?"

"My mama."

"She doesn't look like your mama."

"How come?"

"Well, she's so light, a *guerita*, not like you. Is your papa dark?"

Laura realized that, even if she knew a lot about her papa— that he had died in Chile before she was born, that he was from the south of the country, that he had been a hero fighting for the poor—she really had no idea what he looked like.

"Was my papa dark, like me?" she asked later that day at home.

"What?"

"Did my papa look like me? Because I don't look like you, Mama."

That expression came over Mama's face, the one she got when she would think about Papa, a combination of happy and sad that lit up her face and brought a smile to her lips, yet also filled her eyes with tears. For a few minutes she said nothing.

"Well, *hijita*," she finally said, "he didn't have your coloring. But sometimes these things skip a generation, you know."

"What was he like, Mamita? Was he tall? Did he laugh a lot? Do you have a photograph? Did he sometimes get very sad, like you?"

Mama took Laura's hand and led her over to the couch in the living room. They sat down, and Mama put her arm around Laura's shoulders and hugged her close.

"Laurita," she whispered, her voice cracking, "your papa was a wonderful man. He was so kind to everyone, and loved to laugh. He would have been such a good father if he had lived to see you. And you know, I've often thought about not having a photograph. It seems like such a silly thing now, but we were always so busy.

And we didn't have a camera. So all I have now is the picture of him in my heart."

Then her mother softly disengaged herself and, standing up from the sofa, walked slowly to her study and locked the door behind her. She didn't come out again that afternoon.

✿

One night, when Laura was ten years old, she got up to go to the bathroom. As she was heading back to bed, she heard moans coming from her mother's room. Was she sick, or in pain? She rushed over to the bed. Mama was dreaming. She took her hand.

"Mamita, Mamita, wake up. You're having a bad dream. It's okay, it's not real." This is what her mother always said to her when she had a bad dream.

Her mama woke up shivering. Laura hurried to the hall closet and, standing on tiptoe, managed to pull an extra blanket off the top shelf. She placed it on her mother's quaking shoulders, then brought her a glass of water. In a few minutes her mother began to calm down.

"It must have been awful," Laura said.

"It wasn't really scary," her mother answered. "It's just that, sometimes, I dream about your papa and then, in the dream, I know he's gone and that makes me very sad."

"What was in the dream?"

"We were sitting at a café in downtown Santiago, where we often went, having dinner. We were laughing."

"What was he eating?"

"His favorite. Steak-and-avocado sandwiches. And we were drinking wine, and after we finished the food he ordered an espresso and lit up one of his black tobacco cigarettes."

"Did he smoke a lot?"

"In those days everybody smoked. But his brand of black tobacco, it was special. Not expensive, just a distinct smell. It stuck to all his clothes. When I opened the closet in our apartment, the smell was everywhere. And it was in his hair and beard, too."

"What else did my papa smell like?"

"He smelled of oranges. I remember noticing that the first time we talked. Later I learned that his Grandma Myriam had orange trees in her patio in Temuco, and he used to visit her every day. I used to imagine that, after years and years of daily visits, the smell had stuck to him permanently. But it was probably just because he liked to eat oranges. He peeled at least one a day, and the smell just stayed on his hands."

Until that night, no matter how often Laura asked her mother questions and no matter what the question was, she had not been able to get a direct answer or a clear picture of her father. Laura had begun to think of her father as a luminous yet foggy presence, almost as if she were seeing him through a window that had steamed up from the outside. It did no good to try to wipe the glass. But that night, talking to her mother right after she woke up from a dream, cuddled up against her side as they both fell back asleep on the bed, her mama's sweet tobacco scent in her nostrils, she learned more about her papa than she had ever known before. After that, Laura learned to sleep with her door open. There were nights when she lay awake for hours, hoping to hear her mother's voice. Her sleeplessness was rewarded often enough that she slowly filled in the details of her father's form. She grew to love the middle of the night.

❦

When the horrible earthquake came, just two days after her eleventh birthday, Laura was still asleep. She'd had a bad night, coughing and wheezing; so her mother had decided to keep her home from school. By the time she awoke, she was under the bed. The drills from school, about always getting under something, seemed to have worked even in her dreams. The only thing was that the bed was on the opposite side of the room.

Her bedroom had a crack so large in one of the walls that you could see through to the street. It was three days before Inocencia came back. Although her brother-in-law's house had collapsed, everyone had gotten out safely.

Laura's mother was badly shaken. It didn't help that there was such a strong aftershock barely two days later. Mama began getting into bed with a pair of slip-on shoes right next to the night table, just in case another earthquake came. When the crack in the wall of Laura's bedroom made it unsafe to sleep there, she moved into Mama's room, and Laura could tell she was glad for the company. They shared Paco, the pink velvet porcupine that had slept with Laura since she was three years old.

Because Laura's school had been destroyed, she had nowhere to go after the quake. She accompanied her mother when, like other journalists, she roamed the city with a notebook, taking down people's stories. But there was something special about her mama, the way she interviewed people, especially women. Laura didn't quite understand how it happened, but at first a woman would be talking in that singsong voice, the one you heard on all the reports on television once the broadcasts had been restored. I have told this story a hundred times already, the voice seemed to say, and it has always been exactly the same. And then, all of a sudden, her mama would make eye contact, or she would ask a question or put her hand on the other woman's arm just so. Laura wasn't exactly sure how, but the woman's voice would change. Looking straight into her mother's turquoise eyes, the woman would talk from a deeper place, crackling at first like the stones of a falling building. Then her story would take flight into the smog-filled air.

No matter how many wonderful stories her mother gathered and then published in her newspaper, Laura could tell that the earthquake had broken something inside her. Mama began to lose weight, and big pools of soot gathered under her eyes. Finally, one morning when they had decided not to go out, Laura heard her mother on the phone from her room. She was talking to her sister Irene. She was using her sister's nickname.

"Ay, Nenita, I can't take it anymore. Every night I'm sure we're going to have another quake. I don't know why, somehow it's like the bottom of the boat turned to glass and all I can see is the dangerous ocean underneath. I need to get out of here, preferably somewhere with no history of quakes, I . . . Okay. Call me if you have any news. It's just that . . . yeah, I really don't understand it, but it just feels like it was the last straw. Yes. Thanks, *mi amor*. I love you too."

Laura knew then that it was only a matter of time before they left their apartment in Coyoacán, with Inocencia's songs and flapping sandals, the sun coming in through the windows in the afternoon, and the clothes waving merrily under their clothespin horns. She could tell that the earthquake had torn up more than the big buildings downtown and the walls of their apartment and her school. Even the bougainvillea had begun to droop, no matter how much water she took down to it. For the first time in her life, Laura understood that you couldn't be sure of anything, not the ground under your feet, or even your own mother.

After *tía* Irene called back a month later, her mother bustled around the apartment, typing things and placing them on the dining room table, stapling piles of sheets together, then putting it all in a large orange-colored envelope. When Mama noticed her observing everything from the doorway, she sat down on the couch in the living room and motioned for Laura to sit next to her.

"*M'hijita*, your *tía* called to tell me that there's a fellowship at a school near where she lives. It's in a journalism school, for people who write for newspapers, so it would be perfect for me. The applications are due next week, so I'm putting together my credentials."

"What are cred . . . en . . ." Laura's tongue seemed to stick on the word.

"That's the papers you have that show the kind of work you've done. In my case it's copies of the stories I've published, letters from my editor congratulating me on the good ones, things like that. I have everything pretty much ready now, and will send it up to the school in Boston. I'm sure there will be a lot of people applying for the fellowship, so I won't hold my breath, but it would be worse if I didn't try. And maybe my experience here writing for newspapers will make my file stand out."

"What happens if your file stands out?"

"I don't know, Laurita. Probably they'll want to talk to me, find out what I'm like. I'm sure they'll have a lot of interesting applicants."

"If they like you, does that mean we're moving?"

"It's much too early to tell, *m'hijita*. But even if this job doesn't work out, there could very well be other ones. We'd be a lot closer to *tía* Irene, wouldn't that be great? I think you should begin to think about practicing your English."

⬥

The call from Boston came at the beginning of March. Laura knew her mama had been interviewed by phone two weeks before, but her school had just opened back up so she hadn't been home. Since then they'd been working hard at school, trying to catch up on the materials from the first semester of sixth grade. Between the math and the Mexican history, Laura felt her head spinning every night as she tried to finish her homework.

Her mama took the call in her bedroom with the door closed. Laura could hear only the cadences of her mother's voice, its rise and fall with the moods of the conversation. But then there was a loud shriek, and the door flew open as her mother came barreling out into the living room, then into her bedroom.

"Laurita! I got the fellowship!!" Her mama pulled her up from the bed and hugged her tight, scattering Mexican Independence heroes right and left. "I start in September, *m'hijita*! We're going to the United States!"

Laura busied herself picking up the notes for her history test. Then she looked up. Her mother was still standing there, an expectant look on her face. But she couldn't share the happiness that was burning in her mother's eyes.

"How soon do we have to move?" she asked. She gave up trying to put the papers back in chronological order through the fog that had come over her eyes and sat down. "Do we pack everything up? Can I take Paco? Will Inocencia come with us?"

Her mother sat down next to her and put an arm around her shoulders. "I'm sorry," she said. "I got so excited, I was only thinking of myself. Of course you can take Paco, but Inocencia can't come with us. We can't get her a visa. Even us, there are no guarantees we can stay once the fellowship is over."

"Then why are we going, if they might throw us out?"

"I don't think they'll throw us out, *mi amor*. Your *tía* Irene has permanent residency, and besides, the school said the teaching position can be renewed, especially if the students like my classes. So there's a good possibility we can stay for a while."

"Where will I go to school?"

"I don't know yet, but your aunt is looking into that. She says that the neighborhood schools are pretty good on the west side of the city, and she's going to try and get us an apartment in one of the neighborhoods over there."

"Will we have a bougainvillea?"

"I don't think so. The climate is very different from here. Irene says it snows a lot in the winter and for months the temperature is below freezing. That would kill a bougainvillea. But there will be other trees and other flowers. And in the fall, around your birthday, Irene says the leaves on the trees turn beautiful colors—red, orange and yellow—and then fall off. She says it's a wonderful time of the year. We'll get to see it when you turn twelve."

And they did. What *tía* Irene had not mentioned was that, after the leaves fell off, they made crispy, crunchy noises under your feet, and that the smell of burning leaves and wood was in the air. The sky was brilliant blue, and apples were red and juicy.

Boston, 1987

"Laurita, Laurita! Hurry up! You're going to miss the bus and I have a nine-thirty class!"

Laura stopped trying to get all of her long hair into the single barrette, and wrapped her ponytail up into the elastic band she always kept in the pocket of her jeans. She had to stop being tempted by these pretty barrettes, with their tortoiseshell designs and metal clasps. She knew she should always try them before buying them, because her hair was so thick, but usually the clerk in the shop told her she couldn't try one on without buying it first.

"Laurita! Hurry up! We have to go!!"

She ran down the three flights of stairs from their apartment to the entryway. Her mother was waiting, a briefcase slung over her left shoulder. The bus was coming up their street, and she had to run to catch it at the bus stop. After waving to her mother, she settled in next to the window, making sure her backpack was on the seat next to her to discourage other riders from sitting there, and looked out.

It had been over a year now since they'd moved to Boston. True to her word, *tía* Irene had found them an apartment on the third floor of an older building, with polished wood floors and leaded glass windows on the doors. Her room had a window seat that looked out over the street, which was lined with older oaks and maples. They were on the boundary between Brookline and downtown Boston, which meant that Laura could be in the Brookline public school system, but they were also quite close to her mother's job. The only problem was that being on the edge of the district meant she had a long bus trip to her school. Laura didn't really mind, though, since she could always read or think on the bus without anyone bothering her.

Because her school in Mexico had been closed for almost six months after the quake, Laura had ended up repeating the year. She'd been really upset at first, but then realized that, between learning English and trying to get accustomed to the school, it was probably okay that a lot of the material in math and science seemed really easy. Now that she was in seventh grade, it felt good to be one of the older girls in the class.

The hardest thing had been making friends. In her school in Mexico, she'd always had a couple of close friends, like Cecilia, and then a group of others who had invited her to their birthday parties. It had seemed natural. But here, in Boston, she felt like everyone just stared at her. They must have all been together since kindergarten, and there she was, the new one who stuck out. The pain in her stomach the first few times at recess was so strong, she thought she would throw up.

Laura took the book she was reading out of her backpack and placed it open on her lap, but went back to looking out the window. The leaves on the maple trees blazed orange and red. In this part of Boston, the old brownstone buildings were crowded together, like passengers on a bus with no elbow room. Some of the buildings were being refurbished, their shiny picture windows blinking out onto the street. Newly painted wrought-iron bannisters guarded the stairs that rose up from the sidewalk, and recently refinished oak doors with fancy knockers glowed copper-like in the morning sun.

Her own efforts to remake herself were almost as obvious. She'd grown her hair longer and pulled it back in a thick ponytail, using her nail scissors to cut some bangs that emphasized her large dark eyes. She combed the local stores for pairs of earrings that set off the tones of her clothes and skin. In the mornings when she looked in the mirror, she began to notice how her cheekbones stood out more if she applied just a bit of blush along the middle of her cheeks. It had taken her forever to find the right shade at the drugstore. Almost all the brands had names like peach melba or strawberry fruitcake, and when she'd bought one of those, it had made her look like a rag doll with fake pink circles on her face. Finally she realized that the shades called copper or even ebony, that looked like the oak doors of the brownstones through the little window on the front of the compact, turned the right color when she brushed them on. And a lip gloss in a similar shade looked good on her mouth.

At night, when she lay awake from habit even though she hardly ever heard her mother dreaming anymore, she would run her hands along her rapidly changing body. Some nights she could almost feel her breasts grow under her hands. Running her fingers over them, then down her belly, filled her with an almost overwhelming need for something that she could not define. Except that when she noticed a boy at school, the line of his jaw or his eyelashes or the pungent scent of his armpits, she would feel the same thing.

When she'd turned thirteen earlier in the month, she celebrated with her mother and her aunt Irene and her aunt's friend Amanda. Mama had asked if she wanted to invite any friends, but she'd said no. Who would she invite, after all? Later she remembered the conversation she'd had with one girl in her math class at the beginning of the school year. Her name was Marcie. She had carefully styled hair, wore makeup, and hung out with the popular kids. Laura envied the easy way she laughed, how comfortable she seemed talking to boys. Marcie had come up to her right before class. Her sweater and eyeshadow matched the light blue line in her plaid skirt.

"I noticed your name is Bronstein," she said. "Are you Jewish?"

"My dad was," Laura said.

"What do you mean, 'was'? Did he convert to something else?"

"No."

"What, then? As far as I know it's not something you grow out of."

"He's dead."

Marcie's rush of breath formed an "oh" that pushed her down into the seat right behind Laura. "I'm so sorry," she said. "I didn't know."

"That's okay," Laura said, softly. "He died before I was born."

Since then, she and Marcie had talked a few times. Marcie seemed fascinated by anything that had to do with Laura's father or his family.

"It's just so weird," Marcie said one day after Laura asked what was so interesting about it all. "My family, and the families of my friends. They all migrated, too, from Russia, because of the pogroms, or from Germany after Hitler came to power. But I never knew that Jews went to South America. Wow. Jews who grew up speaking Spanish. It's just I'd never thought about it. I'm sorry, it just seems so weird."

The bus pulled up to the front walk of the school and Laura joined the line exiting through the front door. She hiked her pack onto her back and slowly straightened up, heading toward the main entrance to the building.

"Laura! Hey! Laura!" It was Marcie. "Wait up!" Laura turned. Marcie was hurrying up, out of breath, wearing a red cardigan with white mother-of-pearl buttons.

"Hey," she panted when they were face to face. "Glad I caught you. Do you want to come to my house for dinner this Friday? When I told my mother your dad had been Jewish, she said I should invite you over for *shabbat* dinner. You want to come?"

Laura considered it for a moment. "Sure," she said. "But I have to ask my mother."

"Of course," Marcie answered. "My mom said it was fine if I let her know the night before. You want to just tell me in math class tomorrow?"

When she asked her mother for permission to have dinner at Marcie's house, Laura could tell Mama was happy she was making friends. Laura felt happy too, but a little nervous. Especially since she had never known her papa, or any of the Jewish traditions. Would she know what to do or how to act?

Marcie's mother picked them up at school that Friday in a shiny new sedan, the kind of car you couldn't see into because the windows were made of tinted glass. The seats still smelled of new leather as the girls got settled in the back. Looking at Mrs. Bronfman's newly styled hair and polished nails, Laura was glad her mother had insisted she dress up for the occasion.

"It's so good to meet you, Laura," Mrs. Bronfman said in a voice as polished as her nails. "Marcie has talked a lot about you over the past few weeks. I'm glad you could join us for *shabbat*."

"Thank you," Laura said. "I'm glad too."

Marcie's house was in the fancy part of Brookline, the part Laura had heard other kids refer to as "the hill." Only a full minute after entering the gravel driveway did the house appear, large and broad, picture windows spilling colored light onto the lawn and walkways. From the garage they entered a large kitchen, marble countertops on all sides, a gleaming stainless steel stove in the middle of a shiny tile floor, copper-bottomed pots hanging from hooks and shimmering softly in the warm light. Laura had only seen things like this in magazines.

"Come on in, girls," Mrs. Bronfman said. "I think you have enough time to freshen up before we light the candles."

Marcie's room was decorated in shades of pink. Ruffled curtains framed a picture window that looked out on an old maple tree, its leaves now a deep red. Laura stood for a moment in the center of the room, noting the glow of the matching furniture, the huge walk-in closet in the corner stuffed with clothes, the sound system with large speakers that dominated the other wall near the window.

"We can wash our hands in my bathroom over here," Marcie said. The bathroom, too, was all in matching pinks. Even the soap and the washcloth hanging on its own hook, right inside the alcove that contained the shower and tub, were pink. Laura's eyes met Marcie's in the mirror, and she realized she must have been staring.

"I wish I had a bathroom all to myself," she said. Marcie laughed.

"Yeah," she said. "Since it's all my own stuff, I can always tell when my mom's been snooping around, because things are in a slightly different place from where I left them. I don't think the colors I have will go with your complexion," she added, riffling through the makeup drawer, "but maybe we can go shopping tomorrow. I'm sure we can find some colors that are better for you."

The girls had tried on most of the lipstick and eyeshadow colors when Mrs. Bronfman finally called them down to dinner. The table was set formally with silverware and china, and in the middle a braided bread and two candlesticks. Mr. Bronfman was standing at the head of the table, a small skullcap perched on his head. After the introductions, Mrs. Bronfman lit the candles. They also said blessings over the bread and wine, and then sat down. A salad was served first on a small plate, and Laura wondered which fork to use for it. She followed Marcie's lead and picked up the smaller one on the outside. Once they finished the salad, she and Marcie gathered the plates and followed Mrs. Bronfman into the kitchen. A bright red-and-white apron wrapped around her waist, she was arranging a fragrant roast with baked potatoes onto a silver tray.

"Here, girls," she said. "Laura, could you please take out these steak knives? And Marcie, take your dad the carving set. You know where it is."

They sat back down and waited while Mr. Bronfman cut and served slices of pink roast for everyone. Then Mrs. Bronfman passed around a bowl with sour cream and a small dish with tiny pieces of green onion. Laura wasn't sure what to do since she'd only eaten something like that on Inocencia's *quesadillas*. Marcie noticed.

"You put the sour cream and chives inside the baked potato," she said. "It tastes pretty good, actually."

Laura watched Marcie, then carefully imitated what her friend had done. She was concentrating so hard on getting it right that at first she didn't hear Mr. Bronfman asking her a question. She jumped when Marcie elbowed her in the ribs, right below the line of the table. When she looked up Mr. Bronfman cleared his throat and tried again.

"So. Laura. Do you know what part of Russia your father's grandparents came from?"

Laura took a swallow of water before she answered. "My mother told me it was from the city where the sailors on a ship rebelled."

"Odessa!" Mr. Bronfman exclaimed, looking very pleased with himself. "Of course. It was Odessa. My mother's family was originally from there, too. Do you know what their last names were?"

"My mama has never told me that. She might know, though. I could ask."

"I would like that. My mother used to tell me so many wonderful stories about Moldavanka, her old neighborhood. Everyone was Jewish, they had their butcher and their tailor, and everyone looked out for everyone else. These days we all live so far apart.

No one can even see our house from the street. If anything were to happen to us here, it's possible we wouldn't be found for weeks. It wasn't like that in the old neighborhood, why . . ."

Laura felt Marcie kick her under the table and looked over at her. The other girl made an almost imperceptible gesture as she brought her napkin up to wipe her mouth, a finger across her throat that Laura took to mean they were about to cut it short. Then she heard Marcie's chair scraping back, and her friend stood up from the table.

"May we be excused, please? There's something I want to show Laura in my room."

"But Marcie," Mrs. Bronfman said, "we haven't even gotten to dessert. I picked up your favorite, a lemon poppyseed cake from the bakery."

Marcie moved around the table and gave her mother a hug from the back. "I need to lose five pounds to fit into that new skirt I just bought. And I'm sure Laura's pretty full, too, aren't you, Laura?"

Laura had never tried lemon poppyseed cake, and it sounded really good. But she could tell from the look Marcie was giving her that she needed to agree. She nodded. "I'm stuffed," she said. "Everything was so good."

Mr. and Mrs. Bronfman laughed. "It's all right, Laura dear," Mrs. Bronfman said. "I'll cut a piece for you to take home for you and your mother." And with that, they were free to go.

"Why did you do that?" Laura asked once they were upstairs in Marcie's room.

"I don't know. I've just heard his story about Moldavanka a zillion times. And it always ends with a long lecture about the good old days, and how everyone looked out for each other then, and weren't so individualistic, blah, blah, blah."

Laura sat down on the bed. "I wasn't bored yet," she said.

Marcie sat down next to her. "That's because you'd never heard it before," she said. After a short pause, she continued. "Does your mom repeat herself over and over like that? I don't know. My parents are getting more and more annoying all the time."

For a moment the two girls just looked at each other. Then, almost simultaneously, they burst out laughing. Two hours later, when Mrs. Bronfman came up to the room to offer Laura a ride home, they'd tried on every possible outfit in Marcie's closet, and about half of its contents were spread across the bed. The new skirt that Marcie couldn't quite close looked great on Laura, and she was now wearing it. The two girls had also decided to meet the next morning and go to the discount makeup store.

When Laura woke up the next day, at first she couldn't remember why she felt so different. She got up and went to sit in her window seat, tucking her bare feet under her to warm them in her nightgown. The leaves on the big oak tree outside her window had turned a sunburned shade of brown. And all of a sudden she knew. She had a friend.

"Laurita! Laura! Are you up?" It was her mother calling from the kitchen. She could smell the fragrance of coffee and freshly toasting bread.

"Yes, Mamita! Do I have time to take a shower before breakfast?"

"No, *m'hijita*, just come to the table in your nightgown! You can shower later!"

By the time Laura put on her slippers and padded into the kitchen, her mother was already pouring the hot milk into their coffee. The bread, toasted and buttered, was sitting on dishes in the dining area, and the orange juice was already poured.

"You got up early today," Laura said as she brought in the sugar and the salt and pepper for the fried eggs her mother was just removing from the stove.

"I woke up early and decided to get going," her mother said. "You know, Laurita, I was thinking. It's such a beautiful day today, and I don't have any emergency work to do. What if we call *tía* Irene and see if we can borrow her car? We could go out into the countryside, the leaves are so beautiful right now. And I was thinking about last year, when we went out and found that pumpkin and carved it and everything. Would you like to do that again?"

Laura chewed her bread carefully, then took a slow sip of her coffee and milk. "I'm going out with Marcie. We're meeting at the shopping center, you know, the one right on the bus line. We're going to look at makeup."

"Oh."

"Are you upset?"

"Oh, no, *hijita*, of course not. It's wonderful that you're getting to be friends."

"I'm sorry I didn't tell you last night, it's just that I was really tired and—"

"No, don't worry, *mi amor*. It's great. This way I can catch up on some work, get ahead of my classes for the week. And I might even have time to go visit Irene. No, no, don't worry."

But the more her mother protested, Laura noticed, the flatter her voice sounded.

❧

As Marcie and Laura became best friends, Laura began getting invited to parties. Since her mother didn't have a car, she was always having to bum rides from Mrs. Bronfman.

"At least I wish our moms could share more," she said one day in school. "It's not fair that your mom is always having to stay up late to go get us."

"Don't worry about it," Marcie said. "My mom really likes you. It's been a while since I had a best friend, and I think she was getting a little worried."

After that, Laura felt better about Mrs. Bronfman. She began to see, too, that even though Marcie had a lot of friends to hang out with, she didn't seem to have a lot of special ones to confide in. So it balanced out in the end. But she did occasionally worry about her mother. It was the first time she noticed that, unless *tía* Irene and Amanda came over to take her somewhere, her mother never went out. She began to wonder why her mom didn't have any friends of her own. It would certainly make her own life easier if she didn't find her mother waiting for her every time she got home, always eager to hear about how things had gone. For the first time in her life, Laura began to dread those middle-of-the-night conversations.

It was worse when she began hanging out with Jacob at parties. Everyone was pairing off, it seemed, including Marcie. At first, Laura felt the same old pain in the stomach—the sense of being the odd one out—that she'd felt when they first moved to Boston. But one night Jacob came over and asked her to slow dance. He took her hand and led her out into the open area that served as a dance floor. A lot of couples were dancing already, and once they got a little further out into the middle of the room she could see that others had begun making out on the couches, just outside the reach of the lamplight. She felt a warm yearning that made it hard to breathe. Jacob took both her hands and brought them up around his neck, then placed both of his on her waist. He put his head down onto the top of her hair and she settled into his chest.

That night when she got home, she was sure her mom would notice. What would she say in her own defense? Look, Mamita, I'm thirteen and a half. Don't you trust me? Do you think I'd do anything wrong? Everyone's doing it. Nothing sounded right. So she didn't say anything, and had a hard time meeting her mama's eyes.

After a while, she and Jacob began making out. They'd dance for a while, and then he would take her hand and lead her to a couch outside the circle of light, pulling her down onto his lap. When his lips moved along her jaw she found that, at least for a moment, she could forget where and who she was, and no longer felt out of place. But she began to worry that Mama would see the warm, burning spots he left along the sides of her neck. A couple of times she had to wear her hair down and a scarf because he'd left a bruise. A hickey, Marcie called it. Everyone got them, she said. She made it sound like it was something to be proud of.

⟡

When Laura turned fourteen, she and Marcie, Laura's mom, and Mr. and Mrs. Bronfman all got together for Saturday lunch at a local restaurant. Later that day, Marcie and Laura went out to the movies and for pizza. Just the two of them. They'd decided to go it alone, because they had both broken up with their boyfriends and were still feeling a little strange.

"I'm so glad we decided to do it this way," Marcie said when they'd finished the pizza and she was drinking her third diet soda.

"Me, too," Laura answered. "And by the way, thanks for the perfume."

Smiling, the two girls got up and took their garbage over to the bin. Laura looked at her watch, a present from her mom.

"We only have fifteen minutes until my aunt Irene picks us up," she said.

They began walking in the general direction, but the window of the electronics store caught their attention.

"That is such a cool sound system," Marcie said. "It has extra bass and you can—wait a minute!" She interrupted herself, then reached over to poke her friend in the side. "Look! Your mom's on TV!"

The two girls stared, open-mouthed. The television was tuned to the evening news on one of the local stations. With the sound turned down, they couldn't hear what people were saying, but there was Laura's mother, dressed up in a nice grey pinstripe suit, being interviewed by one of the anchors.

"Wow," Laura said. "She never told me she was gonna be on TV."

It was a long interview. Even with the sound turned down, Laura could tell that her mother was giving long answers to the questions, and at one point she even dabbed a tissue to the corners of her eyes. It seemed to be something really dramatic.

"I bet Irene'll know what's going on," she said, hurrying toward the front of the mall.

Irene and Amanda were already waiting for them in their blue Saab. Amanda rolled down the front passenger window.

"Hi, girls," she called. "Go ahead and get in the back seat. Door's open."

They climbed in. Laura scooted over, folding her legs behind her aunt's seat. "We just saw Mom on television at the electronics store," she said. "The sound was down but it looked serious. What's up with that?"

Irene didn't say anything as she took several quick turns on her way out of the parking lot. Laura had to hold on in order not to be tossed around. Her *tía* had always been a bit dramatic behind the wheel. Whenever Mama mentioned it, Irene would only laugh. "You can thank General Pinochet for that," was all she'd ever say. Now she didn't answer until they were at a red light about a block away from the mall.

"It started on Friday afternoon," she began. "With your birthday celebration and all, your mother didn't want to take attention away from you. She arranged to record the interview after your birthday lunch. They promised to give her a video copy so you could see it."

"But why did it happen in the first place? Why do the news programs want to talk to her all of a sudden?"

"Well, Laurita, it's understandable that you wouldn't have been keeping track. Your mama and I, well . . . we've been following the story for several months now, but it didn't seem necessary to call your attention to it until something had really happened."

"What are you talking about?"

"There's big changes going on in Chile, *mi amor*. At the beginning of next month there's going to be a special election, a plebiscite, to decide whether or not Chileans want Pinochet to continue as president. I think some of the debate finally ended up catching the attention of the media here in the United States. When the local news stations called around to find out who would be a good expert to interview, people recommended your mom. So she got a call."

"But why was she crying?"

"You know it's still a pretty sore subject for your mom. But I think she was also caught off guard. She called me after the recording session was over. The anchor started asking her about the Allende years, about her own experiences back then. They asked her some pretty personal questions, and at one point your mama starting talking about your papa."

"Oh, my God. Does she feel embarrassed now? Is she okay?"

"She's going to be fine, sweetie. But I think she's a little worried about what you're going to think since, being on the evening news and all, you'll probably get a lot of comments from your friends."

Laura was glad she had a chance to see the interview on video before she went back to school on Monday. It had been decided that, as part of the special birthday celebrations, Marcie would stay overnight. So when they got back to the apartment Laura, Marcie, and Eugenia, still wearing her grey suit, watched the video together.

After it was over, everyone was quiet for a while.

"So, what do you think?" her mother finally asked.

Laura looked at Marcie. Her friend was sitting on the couch, her knees up against her chest. There was a puzzled line between her eyebrows. Then Laura looked at her mom. "What was that question about torture?" she asked.

Her mom played with her hands, pulling at a piece of skin on her left thumb, before she answered. "Well, there's no reason you would know this, but the military hurt a lot of people after they arrested them."

"Like how? What did they do?"

"*M'hijita*, there's a good reason I didn't talk about it in the interview. They did some pretty awful things."

"Like what? What did they do to you?"

When her mother finally answered her voice was ragged but firm.

"Look, *mi amor*, I don't think there's any point in going into detail. Let's just say it was not pleasant, and that a lot of people suffered."

"This is why you have nightmares, isn't it," Laura said. It was more of a statement than a question.

"And what do you think, Marcie?" Laura's mother asked after a long silence.

Marcie busied herself smoothing the legs of her jeans, then folding her feet under her. "Well, Mrs. A," she began, "I thought it was kind of cool, about the two of you falling in love, and then how you ended up running from the police. I think the kids at school are gonna focus on you running from the cops." They didn't discuss the interview much more after that.

"Are you okay?" Marcie asked Laura after they'd turned out the lights and settled in for the night.

"I guess so," Laura said. "It's just a shock, you know? It never crossed my mind that my mom was tortured. I can't even really wrap my mind around that. It doesn't seem real. And then, it turns out that my parents were hippies and outlaws, and they never married. I don't know, when I think about your parents, and how they've been together so long, and . . ."

"You know what?" Marcie said. "My parents are boring. They say boring things. At least your mom is interesting."

"My mom's always been unpredictable, you know?" Laura said after a short silence. "I never know if she'll be sad, or happy. I haven't been able to figure it out my whole life. And then, out of the blue, she moved us here."

The first days after her mother's interview aired on the news, a couple of Laura's friends stopped her in the hall in school and said things like, that was your mother on television, wasn't it? I didn't realize you'd had such a hard time growing up, without a father and everything. So she began to relax. But on Friday that week, she ran into Jacob in the lunch room. Since they'd stopped hanging out at parties, he'd always just nodded his head but kept on going. This time he stopped right in front of her as she was putting her tray down on the conveyor belt.

"Wow," he said. "I didn't know your parents were radicals running from the cops. It's like a spy movie or something."

Laura kept her eyes focused on the tray, trying to look like she was being extra careful putting it down. What was she supposed to say? But he kept standing there.

"Now I understand why your last name is different from your mom's," he continued. At that Laura turned to face him.

"Actually, Jacob, I tried to explain that to you before," she said. "In Latin America a woman doesn't take her husband's last name. At most she adds it to her own. But the kids get their dad's."

"Yeah, I remember," he said. "But maybe you should've kept hers anyway since your parents were never married. And besides, you never knew him, did you?"

Laura found Marcie after school and they decided to take a walk. They talked a lot about what a bastard Jacob had been.

"I think it's because you called it off with him first," Marcie said.

At home, her mother was reading in the living room and got up to give her a hug. "What happened?" she asked as she pulled away. "I can feel your back and it's all tight."

Laura headed toward the kitchen. "It's not important," she said. "Besides, I'm hungry."

Her mother followed her into the kitchen and watched her take out some bread and put it in the toaster. She waited until Laura had taken it out, buttered it and put some jam on it, taken out a glass of juice to go with it, and sat down at the table with her snack.

"What happened?" her mother repeated.

"Mamita, I already told you, it's not important."

"Is it about my interview on TV?" Her mother put her hand on Laura's arm, preventing her from getting the toast to her mouth. "That's it, isn't it?" she said.

Laura gave up trying to eat the bread. She looked up. "It's nothing, really, it's just that—"

"What?"

"Well, there's this boy in my class, and I think he has a crush on me. He asked me out once but I said no, and I think he got angry. Today he just said some mean things."

"What did he say?"

"He'd seen you on TV. He talked about you running from the cops, and then he said that it would have been better for me to take your name instead of Papa's, because I never knew him anyway."

"Ay, Laurita." Her mother brought a chair over and sat next to her. "He doesn't have any idea what he's talking about. Some people are just ignorant, m'hijita."

Her mother offered to complain to the principal, but Laura said no. Finally her mother relented. But Laura couldn't shake the feeling that, in the end, her mother's anger was more about herself than about her daughter.

✣

After the new year, Marcie and Laura began going to parties again. Laura started talking with a new guy, Simon, who seemed to think that the stories circulating about Laura's life only made her more interesting. Mysterious, was the word he used. At first Laura felt that same old pain in the pit of her stomach, that same old awareness of being different. But unlike Jacob, Simon was actually interested in getting to know her, and they spent hours talking. Although sometimes she wondered if he even found her attractive, Laura also found that with Simon, just talking made her feel like she belonged. And she really needed that, especially since she was getting more and more worried about her mother.

Her mother was smoking more, and she was dreaming again. Mama's room began to reek of tobacco and sometimes, when Laura got back late from a party, she could hear her moaning. She'd be tempted to go in and make sure Mama was okay. But then she would wonder what would happen if, in the middle of it all, Mama would really wake up and start trying to get involved in her life again. So she didn't enter her mother's bedroom, but simply lay in bed listening to her voice until she calmed down. Even on the rare occasion when she returned at one in the morning, it would take several hours before that happened. There were times, especially toward the end of the spring, when Laura saw the sun come up before her mother was finally quiet.

It was a relief when, for her fifteenth birthday, her mother gave her a new Walkman. She had just started high school, and all the kids were getting them. She and Marcie compared favorite albums. But the best part was that when her mama dreamed, she could put on the earphones and turn up the music. The louder her mama dreamed, the more she turned it up. At first she listened mainly to the same music they played at their parties, like Michael Jackson's "Billie Jean" and "Beat It," or Madonna's "Express Yourself." Prince's "When Doves Cry" tore her heart out every time.

One day, when she was at the music store, she heard a different sound coming over the loudspeaker. It was not the kind of music her friends listened to. There was a twang to it that was almost like country music, the kind that made Marcie roll her eyes. It was mixed with some heavy rock guitar, and the combination really intrigued her even though she knew she could never share it with her best friend. The singer's voice was just a bit ragged, but the energy, the anger, she didn't know exactly what it was, but it called out to her. And then she began to listen to the words. It was something about a family, a broken home. Then the singer said he wished he knew where his father was. She walked up to the counter. The young man at the cash register had long hair and was wearing a flannel shirt. Marcie would have called him a refugee from the sixties.

"Excuse me. Can you tell me what album's playing right now?"

"It's Neil Young," he said. "His new album 'Freedom.'"

"I'd like to buy it," Laura said.

⚗

At the beginning of December, the elections heated up in Chile. Laura was not paying too much attention, though occasionally she'd catch bits of the reports on the public radio station her mother listened to. It was then that her mother's dreams turned violent. There were nights when she'd get home and her mother was moaning so loudly, she was afraid the neighbors would hear. Finally, one night when she got home to hear her mother howling, she decided it was enough. She took a glass of water in with her to her mother's bedroom and set it on the night table. She came in close to the bed and placed her hand briefly on her mother's shoulder. A sharp intake of breath, and her mother propelled herself into a sitting position. Luckily Laura managed to jump back before Mama's whirling arm hit her right in the jaw.

"Mama. Mama! Wake up!"

"Ah! What?"

"Mama, you're dreaming. You're howling so loud, you're going to wake the neighbors."

Slowly, as her mother woke up, she calmed down. Laura felt secure enough then to sit on the edge of the bed. Her mom reached out for her and put her head on Laura's shoulder.

"Ay, Laurita. I can't stand it anymore. The elections, I don't know, they've just brought all these things back, I . . ."

Laura felt strange with her mom's head on her shoulder, almost as if she were the parent.

"Is it your torture you're dreaming about? You've been so loud recently, howling and everything."

Her mother sat upright and moved away slightly.

"I don't know," she said, her face turned to the wall. "By the time I wake up, it's gone."

"Have you thought about seeing a doctor? Maybe you could get some sleeping pills or something that would make you sleep deeper and not dream so much."

Her mama didn't answer her, so Laura went back to turning up the volume on her Walkman.

⚬

In the summer of 1990, Laura and Marcie discovered the Chilean group Inti-Illimani. When Laura saw an advertisement for a concert they were giving in Boston, she asked her mother if they could go.

"Ay, Laurita, yes," Mama said, looking up from the journal she always seemed to be writing in lately. "They're wonderful. You'll love them. They'd just started out when—" She cut herself off.

"Do you want to come?" Laura asked, regretting it the moment the words were out of her mouth.

"I don't think so, *m'hijita*. The memories . . . I don't know, I think I have all I can handle right now." Laura was embarrassed at how relieved she felt.

Marcie's mother dropped them off at the theater. Laura couldn't believe the number of people there who were speaking Spanish. She linked arms with Marcie, because she could see that her friend was feeling a bit disoriented and out of place. As they pushed through the crowd to find their seats, Laura felt her chest fill with a new kind of exhilaration.

When the lights went down in the theater, the boisterous crowd was suddenly silent. All at once the curtain went up and the theater was filled with a cacophony of musical sounds. When the stage lights came up, seven men appeared. They had long hair and dark clothes, and some of them wore black ponchos. The lights at first only illuminated their craggy, serious faces, a startling contrast with the upbeat tempo of their guitars, drums, reed pipes, and other instruments. After a short hush, the audience was on its feet, cheering and clapping. One of the older members of the band, his long white mane reflecting blue and silver in the stage lights, approached the microphone. Again the crowd hushed.

"*Buenas noches.*"

The crowd responded in kind. The singer continued in Spanish.

"My apologies to the members of the audience who cannot understand me. I'm sure their friends will translate for them." He waited a minute for the translations, which could be heard as a muffled murmur through the crowd. Laura translated for Marcie.

"My *compañeros* and I are filled with hope tonight." A cheer went up from the crowd. "About six months ago, we Chileans inaugurated a civilian president for the first time in almost twenty years." Another cheer. "We are honored to pass through Boston, a city that always welcomed us warmly during our long exile, on our way back down to our country to celebrate the formation of a Truth Commission." Thunderous applause. "To mark this historic moment, we will play for you tonight a combination of some of our old favorites, with recent songs that speak directly to the situation today. We dedicate this concert to the Chilean people, and to our future as a democratic country."

They played for over two hours without a break. Occasionally they rested by playing quiet songs, and the audience sang along. Sometimes Laura sang words that she had never heard, and yet she knew them. She turned to Marcie from time to time and translated softly.

After an especially energetic version of "Samba Landó," a song about the African heritage in South America, the white-haired leader stepped again to the microphone. His hair was now plastered with sweat.

"Don't worry," he said to the hushed crowd. "We're not done yet. We'll take a short break, and then bring out a surprise guest. And after we play a couple of songs with her, we will finish with two other songs that we know you will like."

They returned fifteen minutes later with a red-haired woman whom they introduced as Holly Near. The first ballad they played, by Cuban songwriter Silvio Rodríguez, brought tears to Laura's eyes. She translated some of the words for Marcie: "I give you a song when I open a door / And you appear from the shadows / I give you a song at daybreak / When I most need your light / I give you a song when you appear, / The mystery of love, / And if you don't appear, it doesn't matter, / I give you a song."

"Why are you crying?" Marcie asked. Laura knew then that the song was about her father, his shadowy presence at daybreak when her mother woke from a dream, the mystery of her love for him.

Holly Near stayed for one more song, a version of Violeta Parra's "Thanks Be to Life," transparent as a mountain stream. Then the leader was at the microphone again.

"We want to thank you for being such a wonderful audience tonight," he said, holding up his hand to stop the applause. "You carried us on your backs when we got tired, and I think we did a bit of the same for you. But now we are really, really exhausted. So we are going to play our encore for you now, and then leave, so there's no point in trying to bring us back again. You can see my head, the sweat sticking to each blessed inch of each strand of hair, and my *compañeros* are all in the same condition. Still, one last thank-you. With your love and energy you inspire us as we return once again to our beautiful country. We will sing three songs appropriate to the occasion: '*Vuelvo*'; '*Llegó volando*'; and '*Las caídas.*'"

As Laura whispered to Marcie at the beginning of the first song, its title meant "I Return" and it was about an exile returning to Chile. That was all she could tell her, because after that she was once again carried on the crest of this strange-familiar music. But it was the last two songs that brought down the house. The first of the two was about dictatorship, not only in Chile but in all of Latin America, and it ended with the promise that the day would soon come when the people would fight back and bring a new dawn to the continent.

The last song Inti-Illimani played that night was about falling dictators: "And they'll keep falling, / there's no doubt. / Freedom works, / suffers and sweats / and finally cleans / our land / of the sterile excrement / of the little tyrant. / Oh, what a relief!"

The whole theater was on its feet when they were done. As the band filed off the stage, the audience locked arms and swung back and forth, chanting the last line of the song in Spanish, over and over, "*Ay, qué consuelo.*" Though Marcie and Laura had to leave, threading and pushing their way through the swaying crowd, it showed no signs of letting up.

⟐

Laura rushed out the door of their apartment, a piece of bagel still in her mouth, the zipper to her backpack at half-mast. She waved acknowledgment at whatever advice her mother was giving her, not interested really in knowing what it was. She hated oversleeping and having to rush for the bus. It made her feel out of control, and unable to get ready for the day. At least she didn't have to find a coat. After a short respite during the last week of vacation, the blazing temperatures of the August drought had returned for the first week of school.

She managed to catch the bus, though she had to knock on its already closed door. She settled in her usual seat, the sweat stinging her eyes. Thankfully the bus was air-conditioned. Opening her backpack all the way, she felt relieved to see that her Walkman was there, one of her favorite tapes of Inti-Illimani still in it. After she and Marcie had gotten back from their concert at the end of July, she'd started collecting their albums as quickly as money permitted. Putting on her headphones, she settled back into the cool seat and closed her eyes.

The tape had ended by the time she got to the high school, so she took off her headphones and stashed away her equipment before getting off the bus. As she stepped onto the sidewalk, Marcie came running up.

"Laura, guess what!" Her wavy light-brown hair was caught up in a high ponytail, and she was wearing a short-sleeved blouse over a halter top. "I just ran into Simon and he asked about you. He's hanging out with this guy Brandon, a transfer student from another high school, and they were wondering if we'd like to meet up after school. You think you can come? Do you have to ask your mom first?"

"I don't ask my mom anymore," Laura said. "I just tell her." But things turned out a little differently that day. When Laura called her mother from the public telephone near the school, her voice sounded strange and excited, but also like she'd been crying.

"What is it, Mamita?" Laura asked.

"No, it's fine, Laurita, go with your friends, I'll be all right."

But Laura could hear, from long experience, that her mother was not all right. She told her she'd come right home and went to find her friends. Marcie and Brandon were already talking up a storm, standing very close to each other. All three looked up when she approached, and Simon put out an arm to wrap around her shoulders.

"Sorry, guys, I can't go," Laura said. "I'll catch up with you next time."

When she reached their apartment, her mother was sitting in the armchair in the living room. Her eyes were red and swollen, but she was smiling. On the couch near her was a man Laura had never seen before. He seemed quite young, and a lock of his dark hair kept falling over one eye. He was sweating in his suit and tie, but one side of his jacket, from the collar to the shoulder, looked damper than the rest.

"Laurita," her mother said, "this is Ignacio Pérez. He's a lawyer from the Chilean Truth Commission."

Ignacio stood and walked toward her, as if to give her a peck on the cheek. Laura put out her hand. He stopped himself in time and took her hand in his. "Pleased to meet you, Laura," he said formally. Laura shook hands with him and looked back at her mother.

"*Hijita*, Ignacio came because your grandparents have brought your papa's case before the Truth Commission that has just formed in Chile. Remember when you came back from the Inti concert? They'd mentioned it and you asked me what it was? The Commission wants me to come to Chile and testify."

All of a sudden Laura felt like the ground was moving under her feet. She sat down on the other side of the couch.

"Maybe the two of us can go together, Laurita. You can meet your grandparents, see Chile . . ."

"What about school?" Laura asked. "I've just started the year."

"We can figure that out later, *hijita*. You're so good in school, I think if you miss a month, or maybe two, you'll have no trouble making it up. When we came from Mexico you adapted so fast and made good friends, and you learned English, and—"

"Mama. I lost a year."

"You know what," Ignacio said, making a move toward the door. "We can adapt to whatever the two of you decide, as long as you come down sometime in the next four months. Maybe during vacation? No, no, don't worry," he continued as Eugenia made a move to escort him down the stairs. "I know my way out. I'll call you in the morning, all right?"

As soon as the door closed behind Ignacio, her mother turned her back on her and moved into the kitchen, washing some things in the sink.

"What do you want for dinner, Laurita?" she asked when she was done.

"Nothing," Laura answered. She went to her room and closed the door, and her mother didn't even try to come and talk to her. Over the next few weeks as her mother and *tía* Irene packed up the apartment and she said goodbye to her friends, she spent a lot of time in her room listening to Neil Young's album "Freedom." She brought Paco out of retirement and cuddled him as she lay on the bed. But she found that she could no longer listen to Inti-Illimani.

PART II

PART II

VI

Testimony

The plane traveled on through an endless night sprinkled with stars. Like she had done for the previous two weeks, on the plane ride from Boston to Miami Laura had shut her mother out by putting on her earphones and turning up the volume on the Walkman. When the flight attendant requested that she turn it off for landing, Eugenia saw her chance and pulled the guidebook out of her bag.

"Laurita," she ventured, "do you want to take a look at this book? It has some really great pictures of Santiago."

Laura took the book from her mother's hands and leafed through it, carelessly at first. But she was drawn to the dramatic picture of the city at sunrise, its new skyscrapers gathered in the middle of the shot like mystical towers, the snow-covered Andes mountains glowing orange with the dawn.

"Are the mornings always like this?" she asked.

"They were when I was growing up. But now, according to your *tía* Irene, the city's grown so much that the smog often covers the mountains unless it's been raining."

"Bummer," she muttered, but kept looking through the book.

When they switched planes in Miami, Laura had kept the book in her backpack and taken it back out once they were settled in their new seats. She asked Eugenia questions about several other pictures, including the central market, the Santa Lucía hill, and the Moneda. At least she hadn't brought her Walkman back out, Eugenia thought.

After the food was served and the lights dimmed, Eugenia suggested that Laura move into the unclaimed aisle seat. They'd lifted up the armrests between the seats in their row to make Laura more comfortable, and she'd fallen into a deep sleep, her stork-like adolescent legs stretching out into the aisle, her head at an angle against Eugenia's ribs. Now Eugenia felt trapped against the window. She couldn't even go to the bathroom, she feared, without waking her daughter up.

As she sat looking at the moon's glimmering reflection on the wing outside her window, she thought back to the last two weeks of frantic preparations. As usual, Irene had been a godsend, opening up a space in the attic of her ragged old house so they could store the things they couldn't take with them.

"Once we're settled I can always ask you to send anything we need," Eugenia had said as they squeezed the last box into the corner.

"That's true," Irene answered, "but you might not need these. Especially if you decide to come back."

Eugenia had let that last remark go. She was optimistic that, maybe, Laura would feel happy in Chile. Irene just shook her head, repeating again and again that Chile had closed up like a fist under dictatorship.

"If you think our country was uptight under socialism, Chenyita," Irene had said, "you should see people now. You couldn't go back before," she added, "but I could. I know what I'm talking about." Eugenia had decided that she'd just wait and see.

Ignacio told her the country was opening back up. "It's almost like a fresh spring morning," he said, "when you open up the window in the living room. People are breathing in the fragrance of the first honeysuckle blossoms. They know democracy is on its way back."

Eugenia hoped Ignacio was right. Ever since he'd held her in his arms in her Boston apartment, the need to return had been kindled somewhere deep inside. They smoldered together now, her desire for home and maybe for Ignacio, incandescent, fusing distinct memories into a single yearning. How the Andes looked on a winter morning, covered with snow after a hard rain in the city. The weeping willows of the *parque forestal*. The look on her mother's face that misty morning as she held Laura, barely a month old, on the way to the airport. The roughness of Ignacio's linen jacket on her cheek as she sat sobbing in the armchair in her Boston living room, and the way he smelled, that mix of cologne and expensive soap. She had to admit she was attracted to him.

Was she making too much of their connection? She was pretty sure Ignacio felt it, too, but was it more than the emotional impact of having heard her story? After all, when he'd held her in Boston she had been crying because of the memories stirred back up. She was sure he didn't hold all his witnesses in his arms. But maybe it had been the intimacy of the setting rather than any personal attraction on his part. Besides, she hadn't been with anyone since Manuel, and maybe she didn't know how to read the signals anymore. She didn't know if it would feel the same between them in Chile.

In fact, she wondered if anything would feel the same. She remembered the morning the soldiers came, only a few minutes after she'd gotten back from the store. That fear, the one she'd felt bubbling up from the cracks in the sidewalk every morning since the coup, had finally pounced and grabbed her by the throat. Would it still be hiding in unexpected corners, waiting for her to pass by?

Eugenia looked down at her daughter, still sleeping soundly, her head nestled now along one side of her mother's lap. Running a light hand across Laura's forehead and brushing back a strand of hair that had wandered over one eye, she wondered what the next few weeks had in store for them. Thankful for the predictable routines of her job, her daughter's school and new friends and Irene's presence, Eugenia had begun to feel a certain sense of rootedness and belonging in Boston. True, all it took was one missed cultural cue, one mispronunciation of her name, and the old familiar longing would well up. Yet what was she longing for? The military government? Her mother's controlling attitude? Then with the transition toward democracy, the plebiscite and the elections, everything had been turned upside down once again. When the Truth Commission's invitation provided an excuse, she had been surprised at how quickly she started making plans to return for good.

Looking back on it now, Eugenia realized that she should have seen how disruptive the trip to Chile would be for Laura. When they'd moved from Mexico City to the United States, her daughter had not yet been a teenager. She'd seemed to fit in so easily, and the friendship with Marcie had been a great help. But Eugenia had forgotten about the missed school year, the early difficulties, the isolation that she and Laura had felt at first despite Irene's help. She could still remember the look on Laura's face when she'd come back to the apartment to find Ignacio. Eugenia had felt shocked at her daughter's hostility and hadn't known what to do or say, so she let Laura go to her room and hadn't tried to explain. By the next morning, she realized now, it had been too late. Laura even refused to celebrate her sixteenth birthday.

✣

"Good morning, ladies and gentlemen. This is your captain speaking." The smooth Texas drawl over the loudspeaker caused

Laura to stir, and she moved back into her own seat, still half asleep. "I hate to wake you up, but we're about an hour and a half from touchdown in Santiago. Our flight attendants will be coming through the cabin soon to serve you breakfast and pass out the forms you'll need to clear customs and immigration. So this would be a good time to stretch your legs, use the facilities if you wish, before things get busy. And thank you for flying with us."

Eugenia stood up and squeezed out into the aisle, joining the line for the bathroom that was forming at the first row of the coach cabin. As she waited, she went back over the list of verbal instructions Ignacio had given her. For now, Laura could enter on her Mexican passport, and Irene had helped her get a visa at the Mexican Consulate in Boston. Once they got their bearings, they'd decide if they wanted to go through with the paperwork it would take for Laura to apply for Chilean citizenship. As for Eugenia's situation, Ignacio had explained that the problem of returning exiles was still a work in progress, especially for those who, like her, had been classified as "subversives." Inevitably there would be some bumps in the road. They'd gone over the papers she had in her possession: her proof of exit from Chile, issued by the Mexican embassy and stamped by the military police on the way out; her exile identity papers provided by the Chilean consulate in Mexico City; her green card and employment record in the United States. For the moment Eugenia had no passport, but it would be just fine, Ignacio had assured her. With copies of her papers, the newly formed Office of Return would issue her an entry permit, and they could take it from there once she was in the country. He promised he'd be waiting at the airport.

Still, she was nervous. She remembered how she'd been treated on her way into exile. She wondered if the military police were still in charge of immigration. And would her mother be waiting at the airport too? Irene had promised to call and let her know the details of the flight. But it had been a long time, and they'd not been in close touch.

"Sorry to interrupt you again, ladies and gentlemen." That southern drawl, the vowels multisyllabic. "Those of you who have your window shades raised might've noticed that the sun's coming up. If you're on the left-hand side of the plane you'll be able to see the Andes mountains. On a personal note, though I've flown this route for years, I must admit the dawn glow on 'em still gives me a thrill. Take a look if you can."

Along with the other people in the bathroom queue, Eugenia bent down and looked across the cabin to the windows on the left side. The blush of first light shimmered salmon-hued off the snow-clad peaks. In between, the jagged, cliff-like indentations looked lilac, almost purple. Violet valleys plunged down into the clouds, drawing her into a place where only phantoms could survive. Her vision began to blur. When she finally looked up, her eyes locked with those of the man ahead of her in the line. His long, dark hair, greying now, hung in waves to his shoulders and was matched by a huge handlebar moustache. Tears were rolling down his cheeks.

"*La cordillera*. First time back?" he rasped. She nodded. "Me, too, *compañera*," he said. Swatting at his eyes with one hairy paw, he turned to open the door to the bathroom.

⌗

By the time the plane had landed and taxied to the gate, Laura was wide awake. After wolfing down her breakfast and half of Eugenia's, she'd struggled to pass her hairbrush through the sleep tangles in her thick hair. She gathered it up in the one barrette capable of holding it all and, after the plane reached the gate and the seatbelt sign was turned off, stood to rummage through the overhead compartment for her backpack and leather jacket. She struggled to squeeze her thin arms into the sleeves without hitting another passenger, then took Eugenia's bag out and passed it to her along with the guide-book she'd retrieved from the seat pocket.

"Are you sure you have everything, Laurita?" Eugenia asked as she stood up.

Laura nodded, then took and squeezed her mother's hand for a second before turning to stand in line. Eugenia's eyes filled at the unexpected gesture. Perhaps things would be all right for Laura in Chile after all.

They exited the plane into a glass-enclosed, tube-like pas-sageway. A late winter drizzle made it hard to see much, and in any case they soon entered a sanitized, fluorescent hallway. Small icons with arrows pointed them in the direction of immigration. They entered a large room with a recently waxed linoleum floor, red velvet ropes dividing the space into five separate lines, each headed toward a booth at the far end. The person sitting in each one of those booths, Eugenia realized, her stomach suddenly recast into a single burning knot, was wearing the toad-green uniform of the military police. Trying to control the violent trembling in her knees, she focused on reading the signs above each booth in an effort to choose the line that was correct for them. Two lines for Chilean citizens. Not really, at least not now. Two lines for foreign visitors. Well, not exactly. One line for foreign residents. That wasn't it, either.

"Mamita? You all right? Where are we supposed to stand?" Laura had taken her mother's clammy hand and was looking at her with concern. "What's the—"

"I'm so sorry I'm late. You wouldn't believe the traffic! I don't know what's up with Santiago, no matter what time of day or night, it just seems you can never—well. I'm here, you're here, and every-thing's going to be all right." It was Ignacio, his formal grey winter coat and dark blue tie contrasting with his impossible youthfulness. As he ran his hands through his hair in a vain effort to smooth it down, the one long black strand over his right eye stood out at an apologetic angle. Eugenia relaxed into his embrace.

"Are you all right? You seem really tired." Ignacio kept hold of her elbow as he turned to give Laura a more formal peck on the cheek.

"Well, I didn't sleep much, but that's not the problem," Eugenia answered. "It's just that the police in the booths . . . well, they look pretty much the same as when we left."

Looking up, Ignacio nodded, then turned back and led them off to the left side with a hand under each woman's elbow, stopping for a moment by the wall. "Absolutely right. But that's not where we're going. I have copies of all your documents, duly stamped. Do you have Laura's passport and visa handy?"

As Ignacio reached into the inside pocket of his coat and took out an official-looking envelope, Eugenia removed Laura's papers from her purse. Ignacio folded them into the same envelope, then escorted the two women to an exit along the left wall. He handed the envelope and his own pass to a guard standing there. The man looked through all the materials carefully and then nodded, waving them through. Before Eugenia could catch her breath, they were in the baggage area. A porter took her luggage tickets and collected their bags from the carousel. They went off to the side again, and Ignacio showed his pass to the customs guard standing there. Within minutes they were out in the greeting area where hundreds of people stood waiting for their loved ones, bouquets of roses and carnations splashing the crowd with red.

"There are a number of returnees arriving on your flight," Ignacio said, noticing Eugenia's stare. "Most of them haven't seen their family in nearly twenty years. In this group you were one of two without some kind of valid passport. The Commission is also sponsoring the other person, but I made sure I was assigned to be your welcome committee."

Eugenia looked up as Ignacio's hand tightened slightly on her arm, feeling the warmth spread up into her chest. Their eyes held for a moment. "Thank you," she said softly. "I—"

"Chenyita! Oh my God! Chenyita! Laurita!" They were enveloped in the overpowering scent of red roses combined with Chanel N° 5. It was her mother. *Doña* Isabel's milk-white hair was pulled modishly back into a french twist, the pearls in her ears matching a single, flawless string around her neck. She wore a soft cashmere jacket in a muted houndstooth pattern.

"Chenyita! I can't believe it! My God! Oh, and Laurita! Look at you! A young lady already, why the last time I . . ." Her mother interrupted herself as she looked up and caught sight of Ignacio. "*Buenos días*, young man." Her voice took on a more formal, proper tone and she looked at her daughter expectantly, her arms slowly dropping to her sides. A pile of roses now lay on the floor around their feet. Laura had managed to hold on to about half a dozen. Eugenia stepped carefully over the red-rose carpet and took Ignacio by the hand, bringing him back into the circle.

"Mamita," she said, "this is Ignacio Pérez. He's the lawyer with the Truth Commission who arranged my return. Ignacio, this is my mother, María Isabel Valenzuela de Aldunate."

"*Señora*." Ignacio took her hand formally in both of his, bowing slightly.

"A pleasure, young man," she fluttered. "Though you don't look old enough to have graduated from the university, much less to be a prominent lawyer. Pérez. And your mother's last name?"

"Mama!" Eugenia admonished.

"Don't worry, Eugenia," Ignacio chuckled. "You know, *señora*," he added smoothly, "people often comment on my youthful looks, which is why I always dress formally when I'm working. You see, I graduated from high school in 1974 at the age of sixteen, and went straight into the law program at the university. So I became a lawyer and went overseas in 1984 and took a Master's degree in human-rights law. After I returned in 1986, I joined a firm here in Santiago that had begun working with recently returned exiles, and I'd been with them for four years when I was asked to join the Commission on Truth and Reconciliation. I'm actually thirty-two years old, *señora*, and my mother's last name is Letelier."

As smoothly as he had dealt with her questions, Ignacio began collecting the red roses from the floor. Between him and Laura, they gathered them into two large bunches. After motioning to the still-waiting porter to follow them, Ignacio piled his bouquet on top of Laura's, took Eugenia's and her mother's arms and moved the group toward the street. Her face peeking out from behind the combined rose bouquets, Laura brought up the rear.

The automatic doors opened to reveal a uniformed chauffeur standing beside a late-model black sedan. Ignacio motioned to him, and gave the porter a tip while the other man hoisted the bags into the open trunk of the car.

"Wait a minute, Ignacio. Of course my daughter and granddaughter are staying with me. I thought I could just get a taxi and . . ."

Ignacio gently patted *doña* Isabel's forearm. "Of course, *señora* Isabel," he answered. "Eugenia and Laura will stay with you. But please allow me to spare you the inconvenience of a taxi. There's always a line, you know, and the rate just went up. There's no point. So once we're all comfortable and on the way out, you can just give Custodio here the address and we'll have you home as soon as possible."

In a matter of minutes everyone was settled, Ignacio in the front seat next to the driver, *doña* Isabel in the back between her daughter and granddaughter. And they were off into the drizzle and heavy morning traffic, dense smog covering the *cordillera* that only a couple of hours before had brought tears to Eugenia's eyes.

✿

The house looked just the same, though when *doña* Isabel rang the doorbell the young girl who ran out to open the dark wrought-iron gate, thin brown legs pumping quickly beneath a formal black and white maid's uniform, was unfamiliar. The maid struggled with the suitcases Custodio passed her and managed to drag them up the walk, then up the three tile stairs to the front entrance.

"Don't worry, Rosa," *doña* Isabel said after the young maid had propped up all four bags next to the door. "The gardener should be here soon. I'll ask him to carry them upstairs to the bedrooms. This is my daughter Eugenia and my granddaughter Laura," she continued. "They will be staying with me now." And to Eugenia, as if she had heard her daughter's unspoken question, "Teresa went back to her family in the South. You know, she never really was the same after you disappeared. Once we found you and Irene got you out of the country, she decided she'd had enough. She packed her bag and went home."

Eugenia went back toward the gate to say goodbye to Ignacio. As he moved forward to take her in his arms, the moist smog enveloped trees and buildings in a somber veil, suffocating all hope of sun.

"Don't worry. Everything will be fine," he whispered. "I'll let you get settled and call you tomorrow morning. If you need to talk before then, I also wrote my car phone number on the back," he said, pressing a card into her hand. With the fleeting touch of a thumb against her right cheekbone and a wave to her mother and daughter, he was gone.

Eugenia walked slowly up the steps to where Laura stood, sheltered from the rain under the ledge that overhung the front door. Luckily the entrance was large enough for her and the bags. *Doña* Isabel had just gone inside and could be heard giving orders to Rosa about lunch. Eugenia squeezed in under the overhang and put her arm around her daughter's shoulders, trying to gauge, more from touch than sight, how she was feeling. At first Laura pulled away from her, a tightness spreading through her shoulders. But when Eugenia insisted, gently rubbing her fingers over a cord of muscles gathering into a hard braid along the side of Laura's neck, her daughter relented.

"Well, then, I guess it's true," Eugenia said.

"What's that?" Laura asked.

"We're back. But as they say, you can't go home again."

Laura let her mother's fingers work on the knot along the top of her shoulder. "So this is the house where you grew up," she said.

"Yes, *m'hijita.*"

"Was it always this gloomy?"

Eugenia let the question settle between them, heavy in the damp air.

"Well, it is different when the sun is out."

"That's not what I meant."

"I know. But I'm not sure. Maybe it was after my papa, and then Irene, moved out that things changed."

"But you left, too."

"You're right. That's a triple dose, then."

"Do we have to stay here?"

"Not forever."

"But for how long?"

"I'm not sure."

"I don't like the feel of it."

"Look, I promise we won't stay longer than we have to. In the meantime, though, can you give your grandmother a chance? You're the only grandchild she has." Laura nodded slowly, as if measuring the size of the request. Then the two women turned and walked into the marble-floored front hall.

As they entered, they were caught in the middle of a frenetic wave of activity. *Doña* Isabel was running back and forth at a speed that seemed implausible for any human being. She flitted through the swinging door to the kitchen, shouting instructions to Rosa, then moved back out and into the bathroom, arranging the soap and towels, peering out the window to check for the gardener.

"Why isn't Demetrio here yet? He's usually here by eleven, and it's half past already. Do you think the traffic, or maybe the rain . . . Rosa, have we decided what to cook with the roast for lunch? Do you think some fried potatoes, or better yet, mashed? Is the avocado ripe? We could stuff it with the chicken salad I made last—" She caught herself as she turned and saw her guests. She literally skidded to a halt in front of them, her heels squeaking on the marble tiles.

"Oh. Chenyita, Laurita, you're inside. Good. It seems like it's going to keep raining. Thank goodness the bags are under the ledge. I don't know what's keeping Demetrio, but once he gets here and takes your bags up I'll show you where you're sleeping. Are you tired? Thirsty? Can I—"

Eugenia stopped her mother with a hand on the shoulder. "Mamita, there's no hurry. We're not going anywhere today, and nobody is coming here, at least that I know of. So let's just sit down for a moment in the living room, and when Demetrio gets here, maybe we can unpack before lunch. You know, I could stand a shower at some point, it's been more than twenty-four hours. And maybe a nap later, I didn't get much sleep on the plane."

As she talked, Eugenia put her arm through her mother's and the three of them moved slowly toward the living room. They crossed the deep oriental rug and sat on the tapestried old couch next to the French doors. *Doña* Isabel let out a deep breath.

"My goodness. I don't know what came over me," she said. "I guess with all the excitement . . . Laurita," she continued, reaching across her daughter to take her granddaughter's hand, "come over and sit by me. Let me get a good look at you."

Laura sat down next to her grandmother. The older woman ran her hands softly over Laura's hair, checking the texture and length of it, smoothing a rebellious strand or two off the forehead. Then she moved on to the shoulders and across the back, ending by holding the young girl's two hands in hers.

"Well, my dear, you've certainly grown into a beautiful young girl. Such long eyelashes, don't you think, Chenyita? And her eyes. Such a dark, dark brown. The hair, it's almost black, isn't it? I remember my mama talking about an aunt of hers with that dramatic Spanish coloring. The Moorish influence, no? Or maybe she takes after her father."

Laura stiffened. Eugenia stood up and moved over, sitting down on Laura's other side and freeing one of her hands from her mother's grip. "Actually not, Mamita," she said, "since her father had red curly hair and grey eyes. Maybe someone else in his family, though. I guess we'll find out pretty soon, won't we. Oh, look," she added. "There's Demetrio."

Eugenia was glad that, in the excitement that followed, her mother's attention moved away from Laura. As they clambered up the stairs behind a puffing Demetrio, *doña* Isabel made sure the right bags were in the right rooms, checked to see the water heater was on, and was then distracted by the gardener who commented that, with the rain, he wasn't sure he could be doing much outside today. "*Doña* Chelita," as he called her, disagreed, so the two of them made their way down the stairs, still arguing over what would be possible, and whether or not the rain might stop.

In the ensuing silence, Eugenia followed her daughter back to her room and watched her unzip her bags, open the closet door, and begin hanging the clothes she had brought.

"She hasn't seen you since you were a month old," she said.

Laura looked up from the sweater she was refolding. "She made me feel like a piece of meat."

"Laurita, *mi amor*, she didn't mean it. It's just that she—"

"I don't care. Even if I'm her only grandchild, there's a limit to what I can take." Laura finished folding the sweater, put it in the bottom drawer of the dresser, and began removing things from her backpack. Eugenia sat down on the end of the bed.

"I know what you mean," she said. "It's been so long that I'd almost forgotten how she can be sometimes."

"It's like passive-aggressive! She starts off so sweet and nice, and then suddenly she just takes out this knife and slashes you! Even at the airport with Ignacio, so polite and all, and in a blink of an eye she's told him he's too young to be who he says he is, and then the thing with his mother's last name, what was up with that?"

Eugenia chuckled in spite of herself. "Yeah, that was priceless. Though there's no reason you would understand that, since you haven't lived here before and I didn't teach you to behave that way. It's all about lineage, Laurita. The top families in this country have been intermarrying for generations, passing around property and political connections. Someone like your grandma keeps track of that kind of stuff. Since Ignacio's father's name, Pérez, is very common, in order to place him in her status map she had to know his mother's last name."

"Jeez. That sucks."

"No kidding. But Ignacio really had her number, didn't he? He pushed all the right buttons. Master's degree outside the country, prestigious Santiago law firm. But the kicker, Laurita, and there's no reason you should know this either, was his mother's last name. Letelier is a very aristocratic family."

⚬

Ignacio called the next morning shortly after breakfast. Eugenia took the call in her bathrobe.

"Have things calmed down a bit?" The warmth of his voice was even more relaxing than the hot steam of the shower.

"Well, not exactly. I think Laura slept well, and so did I, even though I took a nap in the afternoon yesterday. But my mother was still pretty wired at breakfast this morning."

"I think it's understandable. She hasn't seen you since—"

"I know, I know. But I'm worried about Laura. She was so distant the last couple of weeks when we were packing up, and I think she's really upset about being taken away from her life in Boston. And my mama's so nervous around her, and keeps saying just the wrong thing. I feel like I'm in a suspense film, that it's only a matter of time until either she says something totally unforgivable, or Laura announces that she hates us and is going back to the United States. And that's when I lose my daughter forever."

"I did notice how upset Laura was when you announced you were coming back to Chile. Let's give her a few days to get adjusted. In the meantime, it sounds like the two of you could use a break, and maybe your mama could, too. Why don't you and Laura come with me to my parents' house? I don't live with them anymore, but I often eat lunch there."

"I'm not so sure that's a good idea."

"Why not?"

"I don't know, it just seems . . . how often do you take single mothers and their daughters to lunch at your parents' house?"

"Never, which is exactly the point. I've been talking so much to them about you. I know they're eager to meet you."

"I just feel strange, and Laura . . . I don't want to impose on . . ."

"Nonsense. I'll send Custodio around to pick you up at one."

Ignacio's family lived on the other side of Providencia Avenue. Like in her mother's neighborhood, new stores and businesses were invading on all sides, leaving only a few residential blocks tucked in between the office buildings, boutiques, and restaurants that grew like weeds all around. Even the wrought-iron gate was similar.

After the maid had opened the gate and ushered them into the foyer, the first person to come out and greet them had to be his mother, Eugenia decided. She had dark, straight hair, and deep green eyes the color of the sea at night. Like most Chilean women of her social class, she did not look her age; although laugh lines gathered at her eyes when she smiled, there was not a single grey hair on her head.

"Mamacita, this is Eugenia Aldunate," Ignacio said. "She's the witness in the Bronstein case I was telling you about. And this is her daughter, Laura. Eugenia and Laura, this is my mother, Cecilia Letelier."

"Eugenia. May I call you Eugenia? So pleased to meet you, Ignacio has been talking so much about you. And Laura. What a beautiful young lady. I must say, Eugenia, you look much too young to have such a grown-up daughter. Please come into the living room and sit down," she continued, taking Eugenia by the elbow and moving everyone toward the French doors to her right. "We were just sitting down to have a pisco sour. Clemente!" she called toward the kitchen. "Bring out two more glasses for *el niño* Ignacio and his friend! Laura," she added, "would you like juice? Or perhaps a Coca Cola? Clemente!" she called again, not waiting for Laura's answer. "Bring a Coca Cola for the young lady!"

Ignacio's father rose from his dark velvet chair and came forward to greet them as they entered the room. As was customary in Chilean families, his name was also Ignacio. His thinning grey hair was combed straight back in the old style Eugenia remembered from her childhood, and his brown eyes were surrounded by lines both strong and tender. During the greetings she noticed that he paid careful attention to Laura.

"So Eugenia, what did you do in Boston?" Ignacio's father asked once they had all been served their drinks.

"I taught journalism at a local college, *don* Ignacio."

"That's very interesting," Ignacio's mother said. "I didn't know you were a journalist. Would I have seen your byline in any of Santiago's papers?"

"Not really. I learned the trade in exile."

"Oh." *Doña* Cecilia's voice seemed a little flat. "Did you start out in Boston?"

"No, Mexico City. I specialized in human-rights reporting."

"So you have that in common with Ignacio," his father said.

They lingered over their pisco sours and plates of *quesillo*, a fresh curd cheese with a flavor that unlocked memories of grandparents and long tile hallways. The house itself, the faded elegance of its stucco exterior and polished mahogany floors, also felt familiar. When they were called to the table, the combination of the linen tablecloth, discreetly worn along the edges, with crystal goblets, antique china, and recently polished silverware and silver serving platters, reminded Eugenia of her own family's quiet and self-confident pedigree. Because they were who they were, she realized, they did not have to replace the tablecloth.

They began with *empanadas*, the brine of the olives contrasting with the succulent sweetness of the raisins mixed in with the small chunks of beef. Then the maid brought in cold *locos* with mayonnaise, and the familiar tang of the abalone-like meat of the shellfish elicited a quiet moan at the back of Eugenia's throat.

"I didn't know you were so passionate about food," Ignacio teased.

Eugenia laughed, her mood loosened by the wine. "Only about *locos*," she said. "Laurita, have you tried them?" Laura took a bite, but did not like the taste.

"No problem," Eugenia said. "It leaves more for me."

The appetizers were followed by a tender pork loin roast with small golden potatoes, a Chilean salad of tomato, onion, and cilantro, and another bottle of rich, dark Cabernet. Then the maid passed around a tray of Chilean pastries, their sweet dough bursting with *dulce de leche*.

"I don't think I'll ever eat again," Laura moaned as the adults finished up their coffee. "I don't think there's any danger of that, Laurita," Eugenia laughed. "At your age, I suspect you'll change your mind by dinner."

"Maybe you want to walk off the meal," Ignacio's father suggested. "There's a lovely park near here that's usually abandoned, and the sun's coming out. So Laura, why don't you and I get a little fresh air?"

Ignacio decided to join Laura and his father on their walk. After seeing them off at the gate and admonishing them not to take too long, Ignacio's mother returned to the table and served Eugenia and herself snifters of cognac. By the time they were done, Eugenia had relaxed completely.

"Well, my dear, we don't need to go off on an ambitious excursion," Ignacio's mother said. "But perhaps you'd like to join me outside in the garden. I would love to show you my roses. They're my pride and joy."

They walked out onto the back patio through the tall French doors off the living room. The previous day's rain had washed away most of the smog, and the afternoon sun warmed Eugenia's shoulders. She took off her jacket and draped it over one of the patio chairs as the two of them stood looking out at the roses. It was a larger garden than Eugenia had expected, and the combination of pink, red, and apricot hues was breathtaking. Eugenia was especially drawn to one patch of flowers whose petals were light pink with darker edges.

"These are so beautiful," she said, walking closer. She touched one of the blossoms lightly.

"Thank you," *doña* Cecilia said, coming up beside her. "You know, when my grandchildren come visit, I tell them to be careful. I make up a story about a bug that lives inside the roses, a bug that loves to jump onto children and go live inside their ears." She laughed softly. "I know it's probably not a good idea to lie to children, but it protects my garden."

"How many grandchildren do you have?"

"Besides Ignacio, I have a daughter and a son. Both of them are married. My daughter has two children, a girl who's five and a boy who's three, and she's expecting again. My son's wife has one boy, two years old, and they are trying to have another. No luck yet. Ignacio's the only one who is still single."

They stood silent for a few minutes. *Doña* Cecilia's last statement seem to hang in the air between them. "But talking about children," she said, "how old is Laura?"

"She just turned sixteen."

"That's about what I calculated. But you must have been a child when she was born."

"Not really. I was twenty-two. I'm thirty-eight now."

"You don't look it, my dear. Why, putting you next to Ignacio, no one would think . . ."

Doña Cecilia let her sentence trail off, and the silence gathered around them once again. Eugenia leaned forward to smell one of the special light pink flowers with the dark edges.

"Wait here for just a minute," *doña* Cecilia said. She returned with a pair of garden clippers and reached for the rose Eugenia had been admiring.

"Oh, no," Eugenia protested, "please. I couldn't."

"Don't worry, my dear," *doña* Cecilia said as she clipped two blossoms, each one on a different stem of the large bush. "It actually helps to extend the blooming season when you cut some off. I'll put them in some water for now, then we can wrap them in a damp towel for you to take home."

A few minutes later, with the two flowers in a small clear vase on the patio table, the women sat down on the chairs next to it and warmed themselves in the spring sun. Then *doña* Cecilia reached out and caressed one of the roses.

"You know, Eugenia," she said softly, "this particular kind of rose is very special. It is absolutely beautiful in its prime. I have seen it attract bees and butterflies, almost in a frenzied kind of way. There is just something about it, something magnetic. But you know," she continued, her voice dropping even lower and hardening ever so slightly, "once it begins to wither, the bees lose interest very, very quickly."

Laura and the two Ignacios returned from the park laughing and joking, as if they had known each other all their lives. Eugenia was happy to see Laura in a good mood.

"I hardly have to ask if you had a good time," she said, putting her arm around her daughter's shoulders.

"We had fun," Ignacio's father said.

"Mamita," Laura said, "you should see the park. You wouldn't believe there's anything there, and all of a sudden, it just opens up right in front of you! And there's this beautiful fountain in the middle! And Ignacio and I were talking music, and . . ."

"I promise we'll come back another time," Ignacio said, looking at his watch. "Unfortunately I have to get back to the office. I'm already late, given all the paperwork I have to get off my desk today."

During the short ride back to *doña* Isabel's house, Laura kept up her enthusiastic chatter, asking Ignacio where the best neighborhood

music store was, discussing Chilean music with him. Ignacio recommended Víctor Jara, the singer-songwriter who had been killed
in the National Stadium after the coup.

"I think I'll go upstairs to my room and read for a while," Laura
said after they'd rung the bell and Rosa had opened the door. She
hugged Ignacio, a promising change from the stiff pecks she'd been
allowing him until that point, and disappeared into the house.
Eugenia turned to say good-bye.

"Thanks so much for that wonderful lunch. It was exactly what
we needed. It's been a long time since I've seen Laura in such a
good mood."

Ignacio took her two hands in his. "You, on the other hand,
have been rather quiet."

"Not really," Eugenia said, avoiding his eyes. "I've just been
enjoying listening to Laura."

Ignacio put a finger under her chin and brought her face up.
After meeting his gaze for a few seconds Eugenia moved away from
his touch, both uncomfortable and attracted by it.

"I'm not convinced," he said. "Ever since we came back from
the park, you've seemed a bit distant. Did something happen with
my mother?"

"Look, Ignacio, it's completely understandable. She's wondering
what you're doing bringing this woman and her nearly grown
daughter for lunch. I didn't realize you were the only unmarried
one of her three children."

"What did she say?"

"No, nothing. Don't worry. She was telling me about her
grandchildren. And you know how Chilean women are, they want
to keep their families close. She just wants the best for you; she
wants you to settle down."

Ignacio brought Eugenia into his arms and kissed her gently on
the lips. "And that's exactly why I went abroad to study and live

apart from her," he said softly. They stood together for a few more minutes, Ignacio's right hand cradling her head against his chest. Well, Eugenia thought, this time there was no connection to her testimony. But Manuel had been her only lover, and she had never really been good at reading the signs. He pulled away slowly.

"I'm sorry to bring up something that might be unpleasant," he said. "But it would be good for you to begin reclaiming your citizenship, and to start Laura's petition. I know it's early and you haven't decided how long you want to stay, but it won't hurt to get the process going, since it will take quite a while. I have the envelope in the car here with all the documentation you'll need, and I'll send Custodio tomorrow morning to take you down to the offices of the Investigative Police."

"Don't worry about it," Eugenia answered. "I think I need to start reorienting myself in the city. It's near a metro stop, isn't it?" At Ignacio's nod, she continued. "Then just give me the papers and I'll go on my own. I'll need to start going out by myself at some point, no?"

❧

Eugenia made her way through the crowd filling the metro station and found the exit, climbing the long escalator that rose slowly toward the street, passing right by the blind beggar who had managed to place himself strategically at the very top. Surely she was not the only person to ignore him, for the sound from his cup when he shook it was flat with the selfishness of that morning's rush-hour crowd. She emerged from the subway facing north, toward the Mapocho River. The Andes, still sporting a cover of winter snow, could be seen clearly to her right now that the most recent batch of spring drizzle had passed through.

She walked toward the west. In front of her stood the old Mapocho railroad station, its antique wrought-iron decorations standing out against the transparent blue sky. Then she turned right and crossed the bridge over the river, which was beginning to swell with the spring thaw. Almost immediately to her left she saw the old mansion, huge and past its prime, that now served as headquarters for the Investigative Police. She crossed the street, suddenly aware of a trembling in her knees. She passed through the small and ragged Plaza Neruda, named after Pablo Neruda, one of Chile's two Nobel Prize–winning poets. Given that Neruda had been a member of the Communist Party, she was not surprised that it had been left to decay under the dictatorship. She reached the corner where the entrance to the International Police section was located. A guard blocked her path, cradling a machine gun on his right forearm.

"Good morning, *señora*," he said. "Can I help you find what you need?"

She felt frozen in place, like a rabbit caught between the headlights of a truck, conscious of the sweating in her palms. "Good morning," she managed to answer. "Where would I recertify my Chilean citizenship?"

She thought she noticed a hardening along the guard's jaw. "You're already the fifth one this morning, *señora*," he replied, as if somehow this imposition was her fault. "It's the first window on your left as you enter the door right behind me."

She thanked the guard and walked in. Once her eyes grew accustomed to the dark inside the old mansion, she was able to see the window he had mentioned, where only two of the threatened five individuals were still waiting. She had all the needed documentation in the right order, so once she made it to the window the uniformed woman looked through the folder, then up at her, and nodded. "We will contact you in about four weeks," she said, already looking behind Eugenia.

"Excuse me, one more question," Eugenia ventured. The woman looked back at her. "Where would I go to apply for Chilean citizenship for my daughter? She's a Mexican citizen."

The woman's eyes rested briefly on her. "Down the hall to your left and follow the signs to the Naturalization Office," she said. "Be sure to take a number. Next!"

Eugenia turned to the left, and almost immediately saw the promised sign ahead of her at the other end of the large indoor courtyard. After taking a number from the small red dispenser, she sat back in her chair and began to relax, examining her surrroundings. It was clearly an aristocratic mansion, the kind that had been very stylish about a century before. Two floors of rooms opened out onto the central patio, each with its own hallways. There were staircases along the edges of the common space where she was sitting. It had probably been the Santiago home of an important landowning family, and when they had lived in it, the interior courtyard must have been full of geraniums, carnations, gardenias, and potted palms, with perhaps one or two honeysuckle bushes and even a rabbit hutch. All the rooms had high ceilings, and the doors that opened up into the center of the house were all double, with glass panels on the top half that could be opened separately in order to improve the ventilation.

The nineteenth-century ambiance quickly dissipated once she glanced at the windows of the various offices lining the courtyard, with their posters that proclaimed such slogans as: "The Investigative Police: Working to Preserve Your Security"; or "The Investigative Police: We Work So You Can Have Peace and Security in the New Chile." Men and women in grey suits moved quickly, their chins held up at purposeful, businesslike angles, from one office to the next. While there was clearly an effort to make it all look civilian and democratic, she thought, it was hard to get beyond the presence of the soldiers, stationed one to each door, along the circumference of the courtyard. Wearing helmets and holding automatic weapons, they stared directly in front with looks that were familiar. So much so, in fact, that suddenly she could not breathe.

She leaned back, trying to rest against the wooden chair. In an attempt to get her mind off the soldiers, she looked up toward the skylight that enclosed the courtyard from above. An attack of vertigo grabbed hold of her, and cold sweat gathered on her forehead and upper lip. The leaded glass in the skylight, she'd seen it somewhere before. And the shadows, shadows of bodies, their arms and legs spread out in all directions, woven together into human branches reflected through the glass, and from the rooms on the upper floor the screams of pain . . .

"*Señorita*? You all right?" An anxious brown face with high cheekbones, very close to hers, cut off her view of the skylight.

"Yes. Thank you. I'm fine."

"They just called your number, yes? Sixty-eight."

She walked into the office and found a man with kindhearted wrinkles around his eyes. When she realized she still couldn't talk in a normal voice, she simply handed him Laura's Mexican passport with its temporary residence visa. He looked it over silently for a few minutes.

"Laura Bronstein Aldunate." A smile played with the edges of his thick lips. "Excuse me, *señora*. Is she your daughter?" When Eugenia nodded, the smile spread across his face. "Please excuse my amusement. The name seems to be quite an unusual combination. In the fifteen years I've worked in this office I've never seen anything like it."

Inexplicably, his banter calmed Eugenia, and she answered with a smile of her own. "I understand," she said. "She's the product of a very different historical moment." But as she remembered, her eyes filled with tears. She was startled to see the beginnings of a humid empathy in the eyes of the man behind the desk. He was suddenly very busy, taking the forms out of his desk drawer, separating each page with a carbon, tapping it all against the desktop before putting it into his old typewriter. When he looked back up at her, he had regained the manner of a typical bureaucrat, even as a warm, sweet glimmer seemed to linger in his gaze.

"So you wish to apply for Chilean citizenship for your daughter."

"That's right, *señor*. We've always thought she was Chilean. After all, she was born in Santiago, even if it was the Mexican embassy."

"Yes, *señora*. That information is reproduced clearly in the passport."

He had cut in rapidly, interrupting her, almost as if he were afraid she would say too much. For a few moments the slow, methodical tapping of his fingers on the keys of the manual typewriter was interrupted only by his occasional routine question. Work? Family in Chile? Long-term plans? When he reached the end of the form, he pulled the three copies off the typewriter carriage with an exaggerated flourish and handed her one of the carbons.

"With this copy, *señora*, you must take Laura with you to the Foreign Relations Ministry and present a formal petition for citizenship, with two passport-size photos, plus Laura's own signature and fingerprints. Then you wait."

"How long do you think . . ."

"Impossible to say, it's totally unpredictable." He cut her off quickly, dismissing her with a single gesture of his right hand. Afterward he stood up, offering her the same hand in a more formal good-bye.

Eugenia stood also, and after shaking his hand she left quickly, picking up speed, passing through the main door, past the guard, then to her right along the edge of the squalid Plaza Neruda, and out to the main avenue. She did not slow down until she reached the metro.

⚙

His official telephone voice changed quickly once he heard her. "Eugenia? What is it? What happened?"

"I-i-i-t's . . . I j-j-ust . . ." She choked, and could not continue.

"Are you all right? Is Laura?"

"F-f-fine . . . I . . ."

"I'll be there in twenty minutes."

She was waiting outside the gate when he pulled up, bag over her shoulder. Her eyes filled with tears the minute she sat down next to him and, despite her best efforts, they began trickling down her cheeks. Motioning to Custodio to pull away, Ignacio put an arm around her. "Just drive along the Costanera," he said to the driver, "and take the road up the San Cristóbal hill."

Rather than ask her questions, Ignacio sat quietly, rubbing a hand gently along the nape of her neck. By the time the car had climbed the hill and was near the top of the paved road, she had managed to stop crying. After signaling to Custodio to wait for them in the parking lot, Ignacio got out of the car, came around the back, and opened the door on Eugenia's side. She took his offered hand and allowed him to help her out. He kept her hand in his, and they walked toward the patio of the new hotel that dominated the best view of the city.

"Would you like to sit and have some coffee?" he asked.

Eugenia shook her head. "Let's just walk out to the terrace," she said.

They stood at the edge of the viewing ledge. Letting go of her hand, Ignacio put an arm around her shoulders as they looked out over the city. It was later in the day, and the clarity of the morning had disappeared. Smog now covered the horizon in all directions.

The skyline had changed so much. The city had expanded both up and out, glass and steel skyscrapers now dominating the area east of downtown. Even further toward the mountains, large housing developments climbed into the foothills, disappearing behind the smoky curtain of pollution that hung down into the valley. She could still see the little cable cars that made their way slowly up and down, connecting the station at the edge of the Bellavista neighborhood below to the beginning of the pedestrian paths to their right. But the people riding them could no longer get that breathtaking view of the snow-capped peaks that had been there every morning as she was growing up. The memory of those mountains framed in the window of her childhood room when she woke up mixed now with the image of the bodies, also framed, arms and legs splayed, in the skylight above the patio of the Investigative Police.

"Can you tell me what happened?" Ignacio asked.

She felt new tears gathering in her eyes. "It was just that this morning . . . well, I took the metro down to the offices of the Investigative Police."

"Did they give you trouble? They shouldn't have. I made sure all the papers were in order, they should just have—"

"No, there was no problem. In fact the lady took my folder without even asking me any questions."

"Was it the office in charge of the citizenship applications? Did the guy give you a hard time about Laura? I can find out who he was."

"No, he was very nice. I just need to take Laura down to Foreign Relations, and then everything will follow its normal course."

"So what was the problem?" Ignacio was sounding increasingly confused.

"Well, I don't know exactly how to put it," she began. "Maybe it's just the stress I've been under, you know, coming back, Laura, my mother and everything . . ."

"Did anything happen at the police offices this morning to set it off?"

"I was just getting to that, it's just that now—well . . . I feel kind of embarrassed."

"You know you can tell me anything. And believe me, by this point, with all the stories I've heard from survivors, from the families of the disappeared . . . nothing you can say will shock me, you can be sure of that."

"Well. It was when I went back to talk to someone about Laura. You've been there, right? It's in the back of this old-style mansion. All the offices open up from the central patio. It looked so familiar, you know, so many of the old houses the wealthy families used to have in Santiago, that patio with the flowers, the skylight overhead. I don't know. Maybe it was the soldiers standing guard at the doors, with their helmets and guns. There was just a moment when I must have started hallucinating, I don't know, I looked up and—I swear, Ignacio, there were shadows of bodies reflected against the glass of the skylight, dead people, their arms and legs sort of intertwined, almost like a thicket of brambles. And then the screams—" She choked up, unable to continue.

His arm tightened around her, and he ran a hand through her hair. "Do you remember being held there?" he asked. After she shook her head, he continued. "Some people have come into the Commission and told stories like this. They go into a government building, and even though they've never been there before, they break into a cold sweat. Sometimes they hear screams of pain, sometimes through a set of French doors, or a skylight, like in your case, they can see dead bodies, or heads of bodies.

"The first time it happened, I chalked it up to psychological trauma. But after it happened a few more times, I started wondering. There isn't much about it in the mainstream psychology literature, that's for sure. Believe me, I checked. Then I interviewed the sister of a disappeared union leader who turned out to be one of these natural healers. You know, massage therapy, herbs, that kind of thing. And she told me that the body has a different way of storing memory than the brain. We're not conscious of it, she said, but bodies carry the memory of earlier wounds, and when something sets them off, a connection of some sort, suddenly they remember.

"At first it was all too New Age for me, you know? But I started to keep track. And when people told me stories like this, it turned out that they were themselves victims of torture. Their bodies were remembering. Something is still out there, lurking in the corners of this country. And it's you, people like you, who can tell."

He had brought her even closer as he talked. Now he placed a hand on the side of her face and brought her lips to his for a deep kiss, mouth open. She'd forgotten what it felt like, desire coming up through her belly, not able to get close enough, his young back and shoulders, hard thighs pressing, lifting her off the ground. Then the sound of the car horn.

"*Don* Ignacio!" Custodio's voice rang out. "An urgent call on the car phone!"

"I'm sorry. Still working." His voice was hoarse as he walked toward the car. She followed him and caught the tail end of his side of the conversation.

"No, I'm—there was an emergency with a witness, I . . . No, that's tomorrow afternoon. Yes. Probably not. I had to go out east to handle the situation, and now it doesn't make sense to . . . Oh, I'll be in very early tomorrow, no problem. Yes. There isn't that much more to prepare, I don't think. Okay. See you then."

"Well, I guess it's back to reality," she said after he hung up and they moved slightly away from the car.

"I'm not so sure about that," he answered. "What happened here seemed a lot more real to me than this phone call."

"That's not what I meant," she said. "It was nice of you to take care of me, to deal with your witness emergency so kindly."

"What was happening here was not about nice or kind," he said. "And I never handle my witness emergencies this way."

"But I *am* a witness. And there are a lot of emotions in your line of work."

"You're right," he said. "You are a witness, and a very important one at that. Next week we have your testimony before the Commission, and you'll be meeting *doña* Sara and *don* Samuel for the first time. Plus I know that Laura and her grandparents will need to meet, get to know each other. But once you and I are done with the Commission's work, once we're on the other side of this and things have settled down. We'll see."

✧

She felt it the minute she closed the gate behind her and approached the front door of her mother's house. Something had happened. *Doña* Isabel was sitting in the dining room drinking a cup of tea. As soon as she saw her daughter in the foyer, she stood up quickly. The heels of her shoes clicked loudly on the marble tiles as she rushed over and took Eugenia's hand.

"What is it, Mamita?" Eugenia's voice took on a concerned tone.

"Ay, *m'hijita*." Her mother looked down at their joined hands and shook her head. "I don't understand, I really don't."

"What are you talking about?"

"We were just sitting here, you know. I had just served us some tea. After all, we didn't know when you'd be back, I wasn't even sure when you'd gone out. In any case, we were just sitting here with Laurita, drinking tea. I'd just asked Rosa to bring us out some cake, you know, the special one I'd just made, and then . . ." She paused, seeming not to know what else to say.

"And then?"

"I honestly don't know what happened next, Chenyita. Suddenly Laura just stood up and ran out of the room. She ran up the stairs and slammed her door. I tried going up, Chenyita, knocking on the door, but she wouldn't answer."

Eugenia was already halfway up the stairs when her mother finished talking. She stood for a minute at the door to her daughter's room and listened. Silence.

"Laura?" She knocked gently. "Are you there? Are you all right?"

Silence. She tried again, knocking more loudly. "Laura?" She tried the door. It was locked. After standing there for a few minutes, she went back to her own room.

❦

Even over the sound of Neil Young in her earphones, Laura heard her mother's knock. She simply couldn't let her in. What would she tell her? That Grandma Isabel was a bitch? Even though it was true, and her mother kind of knew it, she just couldn't say it to her. So what could she do? She turned up the volume and listened to Neil sing "Crime in the City." She repeated it several times and thought back to what had happened at the table. After she'd told Grandma that something had come up and Mama had gone out to meet Ignacio, they'd decided to have some tea. At first she'd been really nice, offering her some of the cake from the day before. When she'd said yes, Grandma had tinkled that little bell. Laura couldn't get used to Grandma calling Rosa, or anyone, with a bell.

After Rosa went back into the kitchen, Grandma served them both pieces of cake. Laura took a bite of the luscious combination of crisp meringue and nutty lúcuma paste. Then Grandma started in on how happy she was that her daughter and granddaughter were back with her. At some point, she started harping on Laura's looks again. And all of a sudden she just laughed and said, you know, Laurita? If I hadn't driven to the airport with you and your mother, you a month old and your mama's breasts full of milk, I'd swear you were Rosa's daughter.

Laura stopped her Walkman and took out the Neil Young tape. She rummaged through her collection of tapes stored in the bottom drawer of the bureau and took out Silvio Rodríguez. Placing the new tape in her player, she cued up "I Give You a Song," the one she'd first heard at the Inti concert. "I give you a song when I open a door / And you appear from the shadows," Silvio began, accompanied only by his guitar. Laura thought back to Mexico City, to the nights when her mother's nightmares had first opened the door and her father had stepped out of the shadows. "I give you a song at daybreak / when I most need your light," Silvio continued. Would her father's memory ever give her light? "I give you a song when you appear / The mystery of love." Mystery, indeed. She wondered how Grandma's comment would have made Rosa feel. The worst part of it was that, in a way, she really did look more like Rosa. Toward the end of the chorus, Silvio added: "And if you don't appear, it doesn't matter." But it did.

✣

"There they are," Ignacio whispered as he and Eugenia turned the corner and headed toward the two-story stone building that housed the offices of the Truth Commission. Standing in front of the beveled glass doors at the top of a short staircase, framed against the smog-stained façade, Manuel's parents looked like tiny black bears. Their overcoats and broad-brimmed hats seem to melt into each other as in a watercolor, the edges bleeding into the surrounding background to create a furry splotch of ink.

They looked even smaller as Eugenia and Ignacio walked up the stairs to greet them. Eugenia had to bend just a little to accept the hug that *doña* Sara, ignoring the younger woman's outstretched hand, insisted on giving her. The smell of oranges was like a curtain going up on the past, and Eugenia could taste her own tears as she stepped back and found Manuel's intense stare looking back at her from this tiny woman's face.

"*Doña* Sara, *don* Samuel, this is Eugenia Aldunate." Ignacio was the only one who seemed able to speak, and his words sounded impossibly redundant. As they stood there, the drizzle turned into a steady rain. "There's still about an hour before our appointment," Ignacio continued, "and I see that none of us thought to bring an umbrella. There's a coffeehouse around the corner. Why don't we go warm up and get to know each other a bit?"

They walked down the stairs, Sara clutching Eugenia's hand. By the time they reached the coffeehouse, they were soaked, and they draped their wet coats on extra chairs. The smell of wet wool mixed with the aromas of baking bread and roasted espresso beans. Ignacio ordered espresso with milk and fresh rolls for everyone.

It was a small place with black and white tile floors and dark wooden chairs. Large antique lamps hung from the high ceilings. Many of the tables were empty now, the morning rush over; but the stale tobacco smell lingered just below the stronger scents emanating from the kitchen.

Ignacio's words were the only ones attempting to fill the stillness. He chattered on about current events, the difficulties of the new government, the military's 1980 Constitution. But soon he, too, fell quiet, his words punctured, one by one, on the pointed sharpness of the silence. *Doña* Sara reached again for Eugenia's hand.

"I can see why my son fell in love with you," she said, her voice ragged. "You are a beautiful woman."

Eugenia choked on the accustomed thank-you, shook her head, and fumbled through her purse for a tissue. She blew her nose, then wiped the wetness, along with most of the powder and blush, from her cheeks.

"Even lovelier without makeup," Sara continued. "Manuel hated the way the girls at his school put on makeup."

Samuel put a hand on his wife's arm. "Sarita," he said, "you know Manuel hated everything about the rich kids at his school. He didn't like being rich."

"The first time we met was at a demonstration," Eugenia said. "We argued at first."

Sara smiled. "He liked people who stood up for themselves. Especially women, I think."

"He really cared for my sister Irene, too," Eugenia said. "Irene is a very powerful and independent woman." Her voice broke.

"Perhaps we can continue this after the appointment," Ignacio intervened. "Eugenia, we went over your testimony in Boston; there won't be any surprises. But we just need the full story entered for the record, in the presence of the family members who brought the case." He scraped his chair back slightly. Sara raised her free hand.

"Just one moment, please," she said. "I need to make sure, before we go back there, that Eugenia understands something. *Hija*," she continued, squeezing the younger woman's hand, her voice shaking a little. "I must tell you that, several months before Manuel came to Santiago, I told him he was no longer welcome in my house. He had just been out all night, and I was angry. But that was the last time we ever really talked." She took a breath. "I never understood why he did what he did," she continued, "just as I never understood why my papa did what he did. With my papa, all I could see was how much it hurt my mama.

"That morning, after Manuel was out all night. I think that maybe I thought, if I put my foot down, perhaps he'll understand he can't treat his loved ones this way. If I show him this now, I can save others in his life some suffering. But that's not the way it turned out in the end, was it?" *Doña* Sara stopped a moment, and swallowed some cold espresso. "Every day that goes by . . . when I remember this, and regret it yet again, I say to myself, the memory and the guilt, is it all worthless? But finding you, being here with you today as you bear witness, knowing that Laura exists . . . well, I'm thinking that maybe there is still a use for it, all this pain."

They put their coats back on and walked out, a drizzle surrounding their heads in a light mist. They approached the Commission building and climbed the stone steps. Ignacio opened the door and led them upstairs into a large room with polished wood paneling, its high ceiling sending waves of cold air down onto their shoulders. Eugenia shivered.

"Please come in and sit down," Ignacio said, flipping a switch along the wall that illuminated just enough of the room to show a large mahogany desk and three chairs in front and one in back. He stepped behind the desk and pressed a button, and a young man in a grey suit materialized from a door camouflaged among the wooden paneling and stood next to him, pen poised above his stenographer's pad. Eugenia and Manuel's parents sat in the chairs provided, their coats still on to ward off the bone-chilling air of the room. The small gas-powered heater in the corner near the desk coughed and sputtered, almost as if it understood the impossibility of its task. When he spoke, Ignacio's voice had taken on the same official intonation Eugenia remembered from their conversation in her Boston apartment.

"As you know, Eugenia," he said, "even though we have a recording of your testimony in Boston that has already been transcribed and included in the official file for Manuel Bronstein Weisz, we still need for you to summarize, in your own words and in the presence of his relatives who have brought his case before the Commission, what happened to you and Manuel when you were arrested by the military police after the September 1973 coup."

Ignacio nodded to the stenographer, who looked expectantly at Eugenia. *Doña* Sara moved closer to her, the scraping of her chair echoing in the cold room, and took her hand. Eugenia cleared her throat.

"It was October 7, 1973," she began. "It was a clear and luminous morning, a bit chilly. A typical spring morning in Santiago."

VII

Belonging Out of Place

Sunday dawned clear and warm, and by the time Eugenia and Laura were in a taxi on the way to *doña* Sara and *don* Samuel's house, they felt comfortable without their sweaters. Getting out of her mother's house had probably also helped, Eugenia thought. The chill that had descended on them the day before, when she told *doña* Isabel that she and Laura had been invited to a barbecue at the Bronsteins', had been worthy of Antarctica.

Even *doña* Isabel knew that, sooner or later, Laura would need to meet her other grandparents. It was more a question of timing, and of the quickness with which they'd made the plans. "Couldn't you at least wait until after the New Year, Chenyita?" she'd suggested. "We can go down to the farm, spend the holidays. Laurita will love that."

Eugenia understood that her mother was still trying to win Laura over. A few weeks in the countryside might even inoculate Laura against the competing grandparents. But the harder *doña* Isabel tried, the more Laura retreated. And for some reason, her mother simply could not control her comments about Laura's looks. Even though Eugenia had been unable to find out what had happened the time that Laura had locked herself in her room, she suspected that it had something to do with her mother's obsession over who Laura might resemble. Since that moment, Eugenia's own relationship with her daughter had regressed once again to how it had been those last two weeks before they came to Chile, when Laura had simply retired to her room and locked the door, using her Walkman and her music to build a wall between them.

Thinking back on how little she had thought about Laura's feelings in her own eagerness to return to Chile, Eugenia had wondered if she should ask her mother to stop mentioning Laura's looks. Maybe then things would slowly improve. But the minute she considered it, she realized that the old dynamics with *doña* Isabel were still there, made worse by her own guilt at abandoning her mother. Eugenia knew she could not criticize or correct her.

After Eugenia had testified before the Commission and met Manuel's parents, it occurred to her that a connection with Sara and Samuel might help bring her daughter out of her shell. When she telephoned Ignacio to ask his advice, he immediately gave her the Bronsteins' phone number and urged her to call. "They're dying to meet Laura," he said. "But when I suggested to *doña* Sara that she give you a call, she refused. She felt that you needed time with your own mother, and that you'd be in touch when you were ready. She'll be thrilled to hear from you." Eugenia had called the very same day, and they had gotten an invitation to come for lunch the following Sunday.

Eugenia looked over at her daughter. She seemed almost glued to the opposite corner of the taxi's back seat, sitting as far away from her mother as she could. She was looking out the window. At least she hadn't brought along the dreaded Walkman.

"Are you looking forward to meeting them?" Eugenia asked. After glancing at her mother briefly, Laura shrugged her shoulders and continued looking out the window. "They're really thrilled we're coming," Eugenia continued. Laura rolled her eyes.

"You met them," she said. "Do they look like Papa?"

"Not really, now that you mention it. Neither of them has your papa's red hair, and they're both very short. But Grandma Sara's eyes have a look, when she stares at you very closely, that reminds me of him. And she smells of oranges, too."

The taxi continued up Apoquindo Avenue toward the *cordillera*. Eugenia could see that its majestic peaks were now stripped of snow as the spring thaw came to an end. When the avenue dead-ended at the old Dominican convent, its Sunday artisan fair overrun with bargain hunters, the driver turned right. There, at the corner of the first block, was the house that *doña* Sara had described. A small bungalow with large picture windows on all sides, it was surrounded by a stucco wall. The blood-red geraniums planted along its top matched the hue of the tile roof.

"Here it is, on your left." The cabdriver pulled up to the curb. Still surprised at how cheap cab fares were, Eugenia added a generous tip and they got out and walked up to the gate. The fragrance of barbecue, mixed with honeysuckle and orange blossoms, wafted in their direction.

The door flew open when Eugenia rang the bell. *Doña* Sara must have been waiting at the window. "It's so good to see you." *Doña* Sara gave Eugenia a tight hug, then turned to look at Laura. She reached out and took both of Laura's hands in hers.

"Laurita," she said. "Is it all right if I give you a hug?" At Laura's nod, she took the girl in her arms and held her for a long while. The difference in height was quite dramatic, Eugenia noticed. She wasn't sure if Laura's stiffness was due to her need to bend down, or simply to the situation in general.

Either way, Laura straightened up with difficulty at the end of the embrace.

"Well. Come in, come in." Sara led them back toward the middle of the house, to the indoor patio where Samuel was hovering over the grill. Struggling with two pairs of large tongs, he was attempting to adjust what looked like a small animal across the coals.

"Shmooti! Look, they're here!"

Samuel placed the tongs on a side table and wiped his hands on a towel, then walked toward them with his arms open.

"So this is Laurita," he beamed, gathering her up in another hug.

"*Don* Samuel," Eugenia said, "what are you cooking there? It looks like a small lamb, or maybe a goat . . ."

Samuel let go of Laura and smiled. "Yes, my dear, you're almost right. It's half a goat!" He chuckled at his own joke. "I lived in Argentina as a young man and learned to barbecue Argentine style. This is *cabrito*, or young goat. Since there are only four of us, I got only half. You are willing to try something a little strange, yes?" he added, turning back toward Laura once again. "At your age everyone has a good appetite."

At that point Sara came back out with some crackers and cheese, and a pitcher of red wine sangria. "No, it will be fine," she clucked at Eugenia's protest. "Laurita can drink it without a problem, it's mainly fruit and fruit juice anyway, and we'll eat something with it." They sat out in the patio. When the *cabrito* was ready, *doña* Sara served it with mashed potatoes and a salad of tomatoes and palm hearts. For dessert she brought out a plate full of snail-shaped pastries that gave off the fragrance of toasted cinnamon.

"These are my mother's *rugelach*," she said. "I haven't made them in years and I was never much good at baking, so you'll have to tell me if they are any good. But they were my mother's specialty, and Manuel's favorite . . ." *Doña* Sara caught herself, swallowing hard.

When the plate got around to her, Laura grabbed a cookie and took a huge bite. Luckily her daughter's sweet tooth was still in working order, Eugenia thought. But she was surprised at the enthusiasm of the comment that followed.

"Mmmm, *abuelita*, these are really good," Laura said. "They taste so great I can't believe you don't make them at least once a week. I can see why Papa loved them so much."

The bell at the gate chimed softly, and *don* Samuel got up to answer it. "That will be Tonia," he said. "We invited her over to have tea with us after lunch. Laurita," he added, putting out his hand, "I think you'll like Tonia. Come with me to the gate and meet her. We bring her back to your mama."

As Samuel and Laura went off to let Tonia in, Sara came over and sat next to Eugenia. "Thank you for bringing her to us today," she said. "You've done such a good job with her, she's absolutely beautiful."

"Ah! Finally I meet these two famous women!" The deep, booming voice belonged to a large woman with very broad shoulders. Her walnut-colored face was framed by delicate wisps of salt and pepper, timid refugees from the large black bun perched on the top of her head. Eugenia barely had the time to stand up before she felt herself disappear into Tonia's embrace.

"Let me see you," Tonia said, setting Eugenia free in a trail of burnt wood and rosemary. "You are just as I imagined," she continued. "But the most beautiful woman here is your daughter." Tonia turned to face Laura. "And, if truth be told, she looks more like the first Chileans than any of you." She laughed softly. "In fact, Laurita, you have just the kind of hair and complexion to show off what I brought for you." Reaching into a pocket in the apron she wore over her flowing skirt, she brought out a small cloth bag and shook its contents into her large palm. "*Copihues*," she said, holding out a pair of large, brilliant silver earrings for Laura to see. "Take them," she coaxed in answer to Laura's sharp intake of breath. "They're for you. Everyone says they're the Chilean national flower, and it seemed like a good way to welcome you home. But it's also true that *copihues* are a Mapuche flower, because they grow wild in our forests in the south, which is why they have been in our culture for hundreds of years. Go ahead, try them on. Look at yourself in the mirror."

Sara took Laura inside, and Samuel and Tonia sat with Eugenia as the fragrance of oranges grew more pungent in the afternoon sun.

"Tonia is from a small community south of Temuco," Samuel said. "But she spent years living in Sara's house when they were both girls."

"That was a long time ago," Tonia laughed, "before I finally accepted my place in life. I had to welcome my grandmother's spirit," she continued. "My grandma would not take no for an answer."

"For many years Tonia was a *machi*, a Mapuche healer," Samuel explained. "But after her son disappeared with the military coup, she came north. Sara's picture, she saw it in a magazine about the Committee and came to find us."

"Look, look!" Laura came running back for everyone to see. The large silver copihues hung, like upside-down tulips, from her earlobes. She had tucked her hair behind her ears to set them off, and the contrast between the shimmering patterns in the metal and the raven brilliance of her mane was breathtaking.

"They are absolutely gorgeous, *m'hijita*," Eugenia said. "Have you thanked Tonia?"

Tonia had stood when Laura returned to the patio and now took Laura's hands in hers.

"They were made for you," she said, and gathered Laura into her burnt-wood embrace.

"They're wonderful. Thank you so much," Laura answered, her voice muffled by the larger woman's biceps.

"You're welcome, little one," Tonia said, standing back and combing Laura's hair with the fingers of both hands. "Welcome home."

They sat out in the patio and Tonia prepared a gourd of *mate* tea for everyone to try. Laura liked the sweet, pungent, almost woodsy taste of the *mate*. Not since their lunch with Ignacio's parents had Eugenia seen her daughter so relaxed. But she was still surprised when Laura spoke up, putting her hand on Sara's arm.

"*Abuelita*, can I ask you something?"

"Of course, *m'hijita*, anything you want."

"Do you have a photograph of my papa?"

Eugenia shook her head in answer to the unspoken question in *doña* Sara's eyes. "I can't count the number of times I've regretted it," she said. "We never had the money for a camera."

Doña Sara stood up upon hearing Eugenia's answer and took Laura's hand, and they went into the house. Eugenia, Samuel, and Tonia sat in silence, watching the sun begin its late-afternoon descent.

"I think it'll take a while," *don* Samuel finally said, clearing his throat. "Sara made a book with all the photos when we packed up our house in Temuco."

When Sara and Laura returned, the sun had almost set, and they all scrabbled around for sweaters and shawls to fend off the evening chill. After a few moments they stood up to say good-bye. Grandmother and granddaughter shared an especially long hug as *don* Samuel went into the house to call a taxi. When the two women drew apart, Eugenia noticed that her daughter was holding a manila envelope against her chest.

"What did Grandma give you?" Eugenia asked when they were settled in the taxi and on their way back to her mother's house. Without a word, Laura passed the envelope to her mother.

Eugenia opened it to find a single eight-by-ten photograph. Although it was in black and white, there was no mistaking Manuel's hair and beard, his intense grey eyes. It looked like his last school picture, a school tie and V-neck sweater peeking out along the bottom.

Eugenia put the picture down on her lap and blinked back the sudden tears. It couldn't have been more than a year later that she'd met him, that same vulnerable intensity shining in his eyes, though his hair and beard had gotten longer and more ragged. For a moment she thought the longing that coursed through her would break her spine in two. She would soon learn that this was also the picture that *doña* Sara carried, pinned to her blouse, at every public gathering of the Committee of Relatives of the Detained and Disappeared.

❧

The phone rang the next morning during breakfast. "*Niña* Laura," Rosa said, peeking her head into the dining room. "It's for you. *Doña* Sara."

Laura hurried out into the hallway and picked up the receiver. "Hello?"

"Good morning, *m'hijita*. I hope I haven't called too early."

"No, Grandma. We just finished breakfast, and I'd been up for a while anyway."

"Good. Listen, Laurita, I have a favor to ask you. When I got down to the Committee's office this morning, I found a huge pile of new requests for documentation. They must have arrived on Friday, when I wasn't here. Me and Tonia, we just can't keep up by ourselves. I've called one of our members who has a son about your age, and I think he's going to help us after his school lets out at the end of the week. But I know it won't be enough. So . . . of course you'll have to ask your mother, but I was wondering if you might like to help us, too?"

"I'd love to, Grandma, and I'm pretty sure that Mama will say yes, but are you sure I can help? I'd just started tenth grade back in Boston, you know. I'm a year behind in school."

"Oh, don't worry, *hijita*, the work is not that complicated once you get the hang of it. And besides, from what I can see, you're a very intelligent young lady."

"Okay, Grandma. Do you want to wait on the line, or should I call you back after talking to my mother?"

"Just call me back, *hijita*. I'm sure your mama will say yes, but just call back and let me know when you're coming."

After she hung up the phone, Laura went bounding back into the dining room. "Mamita! Grandma Sara wants me to help out at the Committee! Can I? Please?"

Eugenia and *doña* Isabel looked up from their conversation. "What kind of help does she need?" Eugenia asked. "Did she explain on the phone?"

"They just got a lot of requests for documentation, and they need people to help because she and Tonia can't do it all themselves. She's going to ask another kid about my age whose mother works with them, but he won't get out of school until the end of this week."

"Is she sure that you and this other boy will be able to do the work she needs?"

"I asked her that already," Laura said, a hint of irritation in her voice. "She said she would teach me what to do."

Eugenia picked up her cup of coffee and brought it to her lips. "Then I'm sure it will be fine," she said after taking a sip. "And I think it's a great idea. It will help you make other friends and get out of the house."

"Are you sure it's all right, Chenyita?" *doña* Isabel asked. "The Committee is all the way downtown, isn't it, and Laura isn't familiar with the city. And I think the neighborhood around there has gotten pretty tough in the last years. I haven't been down there, but—"

"Don't worry, Mamita," Eugenia interrupted. "I'll go with her the first time, make sure everything's all right, help her find her way on the metro. It will do Laura good to start seeing other parts of the city."

An hour and a half later, after both mother and daughter had showered and dressed and they'd made a call to confirm arrangements with *doña* Sara, the two set off to the subway on their way to the Committee's offices.

⋯

"Laura! Laurita!" Eugenia called as she came down the stairs.

"I think she's in the backyard, Chenyita," *doña* Isabel called from the kitchen. "She's been out there for almost an hour helping Demetrio with that new jasmine vine, the one with those gorgeous yellow flowers that he's been trying to train up the side of the house. I don't know what's gotten into that child," she added as her daughter passed through the kitchen on her way outside. "She's spending so much time in the garden, and when she's not back there she's at the offices of that committee. I hardly see her, and—"

The rest of *doña* Isabel's sentence got lost in the slam of the screen door as Eugenia left the kitchen and walked down the back patio stairs. Laura was balancing precariously on the top of a stepladder, trying to loop the tallest branch of the vine over a hook that Demetrio had installed among the bricks halfway between the first and second floors of the house. Worried that startling her daughter in the middle of this task would be too dangerous, Eugenia waited until she was halfway down the ladder.

"Laurita. Have you packed your bag for our trip to the country? You know we leave tomorrow morning. From the look of your room you haven't picked what you're taking yet."

"Ay, Mamita." Laura struggled to keep the irritation out of her voice as she finished climbing down and stepped away from the ladder. Her hair was pulled back in a barrette, and the ubiquitous *copihues* danced back and forth against her tanned cheeks. "How hard will it be to throw a few things in a bag? How long are we staying, anyway?"

They had been fighting back and forth for several weeks. When *doña* Isabel suggested they spend the summer at the country house, Laura's reaction had been completely negative.

"I want to stay here," she insisted. "*Bobe* Sara and *tía* Tonia need me at the office." Eugenia had been startled by how quickly Laura had fit in at the Committee's offices, and her using the Yiddish word for "grandma" had also taken some getting used to. "Besides," Laura continued, "what is there to do out there? Here, I like to help Demetrio in the garden, and Joaquín and I go out for ice cream after we're done working at the Committee."

Laura had relented a bit when she learned that Irene was coming for the holidays, and that Sara and Samuel did not celebrate Christmas, so she would not be depriving them of a holiday celebration with her absence.

"Well, okay," she agreed. "But only for a few days."

Irene traveled almost directly from Boston to the country house, stopping in Santiago only overnight. That had been four days ago, and she'd been telephoning ever since to hurry them up. "The house is open and ready," she told Laura. "It's time to come down. You'll really like it." But Laura kept dragging her feet. She said good-bye at the Committee as if she was leaving for years, and Eugenia had caught her and Joaquín in the back room exchanging addresses. "We're gonna write every day, even if it has to be on toilet paper," she announced when Eugenia asked her about it. Then she'd gotten involved in Demetrio's jasmine project.

"*M'hijita*, with Irene there and everything, it makes sense to stay until after New Year's, don't you think?" Eugenia suggested.

"But Mamita, that's more than two weeks!" Laura wailed. "What will I do there?"

"Nobody will be back at the Committee until after the New Year, I can guarantee that. Besides, don't you want to spend some time with your aunt? She's really good on horseback, she can teach you a lot of things," Eugenia wheedled. "In fact, when we were growing up, there were days when she and Papa didn't come back until sundown. She can show you trails in the hills, places I've never been."

"Well . . . all right." Laura started toward the kitchen, then turned back. "So, how much should I pack? Can we do laundry there? Can I ride horseback in jeans and sneakers?"

Eugenia put her arm around her daughter's shoulders. "The servants will do the laundry. I don't think you need more than a week of clothes, and you can ride in jeans and sneakers. But it will get cold at night, so you'll need a sweater, and maybe a jacket or sweatshirt."

The two women banged the patio door, startling *doña* Isabel, and started up the stairs to Laura's bedroom.

⚬

"Am I glad I listened to Irene's warning and wrote down the directions she gave me over the phone," Eugenia said as she drove the rented car up to the large wooden gate that separated her family's property from the road. "Everything is so different."

"Mamita," Laura said impatiently from the front passenger seat, "I get it already. This must be the tenth time you've said the same thing."

It was true that she had been repeating herself since the moment they'd left the last small town on the way out to the farm. She'd seen, on the land itself, what Irene had said on the phone.

"You need to be ready for big changes," Irene had warned. "I know everyone says that the military gave the land back, and it's true, to some extent at least. But we only got back about half of what used to be our farm, and the rest went to the people who worked for us before. Everything's divided up now: there's a piece for Mamita, a piece for me, even a piece for you. They're all cultivated together, of course, but there are fences between them. Mama's just put in a small grove of fast-growing pines, for easy cash. The people who used to work for us, they're small businessmen now. A lot of them have planted pine trees too."

At least the man who came to open the gate looked familiar. When he approached the car and looked inside, his smile showed a gap where his two front teeth should have been.

"*Niña* Eugenia!" he marveled, "finally my eyes can see you again!"

She tried to remember who he was, and vaguely connected him to the family that had kept the horses, the Garcías. They had been the most loyal of all the workers, and had warned *doña* Isabel the day before the illegal takeover of the farm. But this couldn't be the patriarch from back then, who twenty years ago had already been at least fifty-five. His son?

"Inocencio?" she ventured. His smile widened, taking in all the folds and furrows of his weather-beaten cheeks. As he chattered on, giving her an update on all his relatives, explaining about his own family, his wife, four children, how he now had enough money to fix his teeth, she only partly understood his lisp. She focused on the piece of land that clearly belonged to him now, to the right of the dirt path that led up to her mother's country home. A late-model truck stood beside a newly painted residence that, she calculated, must have at least four bedrooms. The half-grown pine forest extending back from the house, as far as her eye could see, also belonged to him. Harvesting its ancestors had probably helped pay for all this prosperity.

"Well, *patrona*," he rasped finally, "welcome. You need any horses, you tell me, okay?"

She thanked him and said good-bye, off-balance with the contrast between his obsequiousness and his more modern capitalist ways.

"Mamita," Laura asked as they set off toward the house, "did you understand him?"

"Only partially," Eugenia said. "He has a country accent, and the missing front teeth didn't help."

"Oh, good. For a moment there I thought I'd just stopped understanding Spanish."

Irene was waiting for them when they pulled up. "Well, you made it in one piece," she said after hugging them both. "Did you have trouble finding the place?"

"Ay, Mamita," Laura said in mock dismay. "Don't repeat yourself yet again!"

"It's just that, since we left San Jacinto, I've been saying that I'm glad I wrote down your directions," Eugenia explained at Irene's quizzical look. "But the biggest shock was Inocencio García."

"Well, you recognized him, that's already pretty impressive," Irene laughed.

"What I just couldn't wrap my mind around was his kowtowing to me, calling me *patrona*, *niña* Eugenia, the whole thing, and then right behind him his large house, new truck, and pine forest!"

"Welcome to the new Chile, Chenyita," Irene answered. "María," she called, stepping back toward the house. "My sister and her daughter have arrived, and we need to get their bags to their rooms. Then," she added, looking at Eugenia, "maybe we can sit down and have a snack?" At Eugenia's nod, she called after María's disappearing back, "Just leave the bags in the rooms for now. We'll need you to serve the coffee, maybe some fried egg sandwiches. Has today's bread arrived? Did you check the hens to see if they laid this morning?" To María's muffled "*sí, señora*," Irene added, "I'll take care of setting the table. Just bring things out when you're done."

They sat down to frothy mugs of freshly boiled milk flavored with coffee. Country eggs sizzled inside fragrant rolls that tasted like they had just emerged from the oven. Even the orange juice was freshly squeezed. Sitting at the head of the table, her dark blond hair increasingly highlighted with modish streaks of white, her light brown eyes framed by discreet wrinkles, Irene looked the part of the grand country matriarch.

"Ayayay," Laura exclaimed, "I don't think I've ever tasted an egg quite like this."

"I'm not surprised, city girl," Irene teased. "It hasn't been an hour since María pulled them out from under our hens."

After they were done, Irene took them back to their rooms, making sure they had the towels and linens they needed, showing them where to hang their clothes and the extra blankets on the top shelves of the closets. At first, when Eugenia had seen the front of the house, it looked as if nothing had changed. But once inside, she realized something was different, although she wasn't exactly sure what. Then she began to notice subtle changes: a new window here, a different placement of a door there. Startled, she realized that the house had been redone, even as her mother had taken care to keep the same style and ambiance.

"It'll still get cold at night," Irene warned, "and we don't have heating in this old place."

"It's not as old as I remember it," Eugenia answered. "It's subtle, but Mama redid the house."

"That's true, *hermanita*, but we haven't put in central heating, and I don't think we ever will. So we'll just have to make do with blankets."

Not long after they were unpacked, the summer's buzzing afternoon heat settled down upon the house. After making sure there would be a mail pickup the next day, Laura retired to her room and closed the door. Irene and Eugenia retreated to the coolness of the living room, its thick curtains shut against the afternoon sun.

"What's up with her?" Irene asked once they had settled into the couch's thick cushions.

"I'm not entirely sure, but all signs are that she's found a boyfriend."

"Oh, really? That was quick!"

"His name is Joaquín. He's been working at the Committee since school let out for the summer, and she's been down there a lot, too, helping *doña* Sara."

"So that connection has worked out."

"Amazingly well, actually. Almost from the moment they laid eyes on each other."

"Well, that's good, isn't it? It's what you wanted."

"Absolutely. The problem is that it isn't working out so well with Mama."

"Oh? Not that I'm really that surprised."

"You know Mamita, you can probably write the script without my telling you a thing. But every word that comes out of her mouth, somehow it's always a judgment, a veiled criticism. Even before she speaks, I can see Laura tense up."

"You didn't think that had somehow changed, did you?"

"Well, I guess not. But it's just that in comparison to *doña* Sara and *don* Samuel . . . I don't know. They're so grateful to have Laura, that everything she does, everything she says . . . she can do no wrong in their eyes. And I think Mama's beginning to notice."

They were silent for a few minutes, relaxing into the quiet of the country afternoon.

"Maybe this is an opportunity for the two of them to get to know each other better," Irene suggested.

"Could be. We'll see what happens. By the way, when is Mamita expected?"

"Who knows. Too many things to close up at the house, leaving instructions for Demetrio, the usual. She called just before you got here. The car she hired had just pulled up."

❧

Doña Isabel made her entrance as they were sitting down to dinner. In addition to her three suitcases and several boxes of items for the kitchen, she brought two cases of wine.

"I think we should toast the fact we're all together," she said as she sat down. "I can't remember the last time I had both my daughters with me at the table, and I've never before had my granddaughter with me at my country house. So it calls for a celebration!"

Irene had prepared a chicken stew flavored with basil and rosemary picked fresh from the garden, and the thick flavors matched perfectly with the roundness of the Estate Reserve Merlot *doña* Isabel had chosen. It was the first time since she and Laura had arrived, Eugenia thought, that *doña* Isabel relaxed. After they finished off the peach cobbler María had baked, they settled back at the table with cups of sweet tea.

"Laurita," *doña* Isabel began after a short silence, "has your mother ever told you the story of the takeover of this estate?" When Laura shook her head, she continued: "Well, it was during the revolutionary years, you know, when Salvador Allende was president, and your mama and papa were students. Your mama and Aunt Irene were always worrying about me, and whether I'd be safe coming out here all by myself."

"Those were hard times, Mamita," Irene said. "Don't forget, you used to keep Papa's old hunting rifle by your bed at night. "

"That's right," *doña* Isabel said. "And it got especially difficult when that peasant group connected with the Revolutionary Left, your papa's organization, Laurita, began moving into this area. So in 1972, it must have been in late February, because it was so hot, they knocked on the door at three in the morning. They had decided to invade our farm. By dawn they'd covered the barns and gates with Revolutionary Left flags, plus handmade portraits of Che Guevara. And they had persuaded the servants and workers to join them!"

"What did you do, Mamita Isabel?" Laura asked excitedly. She had sat up straight as the story built to its climax.

"Well, *hijita*," her grandmother answered, basking in this new attention, "I'd always told my daughters that the servants were loyal. I was partly right! The Garcías—you remember Inocencio, don't you, Laurita? He's the one who opened the gate for you when you arrived. Well, Inocencio's father, who was in charge of the horses back then, heard the rumors. He told me the day before that a takeover was being planned. So I decided to leave before they arrived!"

"So the house was empty when they got here?" Laura asked.

"Exactly, *m'hijita*. It must have been quite a surprise! But I learned two important lessons. The first was that it's always better to know when you've lost and retreat gracefully. I should have done this more often in my life. The second was that you can't count on people all the time, no matter how loyal you think they are. After telling me about the takeover, the Garcías went right ahead and joined in, anyway!"

"Time for some cards!" Irene announced quickly, before the subject of loyalty could get out of hand. "How's your canasta game, Mamita? Why don't we teach Laura how to play! It's an old family tradition, Laurita, and your mama used to be a big champion."

"I haven't played in years," Eugenia protested, "I'm an easy mark now."

"Don't sell yourself short," Irene said. "Careful with her, Mamita, she's actually played pretty regularly with me over the years. Last time we played she beat me by a large margin!"

At first they played with the hands on the table so that Laura could get the hang of it. But after a few games, Laura decided she'd had enough and retired to her room.

"She's probably gone to write Joaquín another note," Eugenia whispered once she heard Laura's door close.

"She has a boyfriend already? She's taking after you, Chenyita," her mother said. By this point they were all just a bit tipsy on the second bottle of merlot. They played several more rounds of canasta, and *doña* Isabel kept winning.

"You're letting her win, Nenita," Eugenia accused finally, after their mother had beaten them three times.

"No, I'm not," Irene protested. "She's been practicing!"

Mama laughed with delight as she counted up the points and announced herself the winner of the fourth round. "What do you expect from a poor old woman whose daughters have left the country? What do I have except my canasta club? We've been playing three times a week for years. Too bad I didn't suggest we play for money," she chuckled, getting up from the table. "I've found I'm pretty good at making a little cash on the side. But I'm too tired now. You girls stay up if you want. I'm going to bed." She gave them each a kiss on the cheek and headed down the hallway, swaying slightly and humming to herself.

"Well, talk about surprises." Irene got up from the table and brought the wine bottle over to the couch. The two sisters sat by the fire and shared the last of the merlot between them. "Who would have guessed?"

"I know." Eugenia took a sip from her glass and giggled. "Mama was happy as a clam tonight. Maybe if we let her win at canasta, things will work out just fine."

⚬

The next morning Eugenia woke up early. The worst of the nightmares had not come back since she testified at the Commission with Sara and Samuel, and she had been sleeping much better. But that first night at the farm, she had been restless. She remembered dreaming about Ignacio. Every time they kissed in her dream, she woke up, then had a hard time getting back to sleep. He had promised to call once their work together was over, but perhaps he had thought better of it. She wondered now if he felt rejected by her on the San Cristóbal hill, after they'd kissed. When she woke up to see the beginnings of dawn through a crack in the curtains, she knew she would not be able to go back to sleep. So she decided to get up and take a walk.

Dressed in jeans and a jacket, she walked out the front of the house and down toward the main road, picking her way carefully among the ruts in the dirt. She could smell the sharp combination of pine needles and eucalyptus oil from the leaves under her feet. The sun was coming up over the mountains to the east and she stopped for a moment, noticing how the sunrise seemed to bounce against the dew that blanketed the ground right in front of her.

"Good morning, *patrona*. Up early this morning. Want a horse?"

She jumped. It was Inocencio. He was dressed in his work clothes, but the boots he had on were new and, from the look of them, probably custom-made.

"Good morning, Inocencio. You startled me! I didn't expect anyone up quite this early."

Inocencio's gaze focused on the loafers she was wearing.

"You want to ride, you need to wear boots. Those shoes come off at the first bump, believe me."

Eugenia brought the collar of her jacket up more tightly around her neck to ward off the cold. She didn't know why, but Inocencio was making her uncomfortable. Perhaps it was that he was standing just a bit closer than seemed proper. She moved back a couple of steps.

"You're right. These aren't the right shoes. But that's probably because I didn't plan to ride anyway."

"Why you up so early, then? Anything else I can do for you?"

"No, thank you. You're very kind." She turned to go.

"*Patrona.*"

She turned back to look at him.

"Why didn't you come back for so long? *La patrona* Irene, she's here every year, you can set your clock by her. But you . . ."

Eugenia focused on his face, trying to find some ulterior motive, but his eyes were as clear as the morning sky.

"I was in exile. After the military coup they picked me up and put me in jail. When they let me out I went straight to Mexico. I couldn't come back until the first democratic president was elected."

Inocencio stood in front of her, staring straight into her eyes. Eugenia felt increasingly uneasy. This was not the way country people had behaved when she was growing up. She held his gaze. Finally he looked down, but did not move away.

"That means you supported *el doctor* Allende," he said, his voice raw.

"Well, my boyfriend more than me. But the military picked us both up."

"*La señora* Chelita. We helped her, you know, when the young *barbudos* came. She didn't help you?"

"She didn't know where I was. When I finally got word out, Irene helped me leave the country." After another long silence, Eugenia turned to go.

"*Patrona.*"

She stopped again, but did not turn around.

"The *barbudos*, they helped us at first. At first we were glad that *doña* Chelita had left. But then . . ." Inocencio's voice got softer, the torn edges more pronounced. "Then, the *barbudos*, they got greedy. They wanted more and more land. Finally the soldiers came. They took some of the younger ones into the old house, in the back, where the old kitchen used to be. We could hear their screams for miles. Then the screams just stopped. We never saw them again." Inocencio turned then, and began walking away. His last words caught in the early morning breeze and came back to her, hovering in the air above her head. "I'm glad *doña* Chelita redid the house. It has fewer ghosts now."

⬥

In the week and a half before Christmas, Irene taught Laura how to ride horseback. The two went out every day and returned for a late lunch, with early summer dust and broad smiles on their faces. They'd sit together at the table, giggling. Eugenia was happy to see them getting along so well, glad that the distance between them that opened up during Laura's crisis in Boston seemed to be closing.

Doña Isabel was in her element at the farm, the grand matriarch, fixing large meals and baking treats daily in the old pot-bellied oven that had survived the reconstruction of the kitchen. In the afternoons they all retired to their rooms, and Laura wrote her daily missive to Joaquín that would go out in the next morning's mail. As Eugenia watched Laura bring the daily envelope, sealed, stamped and addressed, out of her room, she realized that her daughter had never written to her friend Marcie in Boston. Thinking back, she remembered that Laura had never written to her Mexican friend Cecilia, either. Gripped by guilt, she suddenly saw how both moves had forced her daughter to cut all previous ties.

Over dinner, as they slowly made their way through the first case of merlot, *doña* Isabel told stories of her childhood that even her daughters had never heard before. Laura was enthralled. As Eugenia sat back and listened, she was caught up in a modern-day Thousand and One Nights, with her mother a new Scheherazade spinning stories to save herself and her relationship to her only granddaughter.

On Christmas Eve, the roast turkey, mashed potatoes, and fresh asparagus from the garden were followed by an exquisite meringue cake. The glow of the fireplace provided both light and warmth as they exchanged gifts. When Laura opened the box from her grandmother, her reaction brought a satisfied smile to the older woman's face. Inside was the single, perfect string of pearls that *doña* Isabel wore every day. "It's only right that my only grand-daughter should begin wearing it," she said in answer to Laura's whispered thank-you. Though the old-world, classical style of the pearls did not completely match the large copihue earrings that hung constantly from Laura's ears, Eugenia knew it was the loving acceptance symbolized by the gift that mattered most.

Later that evening, after both grandmother and granddaughter had retired to their rooms, Irene and Eugenia sat by the fire.

"Well, that's the last bottle in the case," Irene said as she poured the remaining wine into their two glasses. "Lucky Mamita brought another one. It should last through New Year's."

"It seems almost too good to be true, don't you think?" Eugenia asked. "Mamita and Laura seem to be hitting it off so well after such a bad start. But I'm just waiting for the other shoe to drop."

Irene took another sip of the wine and settled back into the cushions of the couch. "You know what, Chenyita? I'm going to do something I rarely do, being the older sister and all." She raised her glass to her lips and drank a bit more wine. "Remember when we were arguing about what it was going to be like when the two of you came back? It seems you were right. Laura seems a lot happier here than she was in Boston."

"What a pity I don't have a tape recorder," Eugenia teased, giving her sister a mock slap on the arm. "This is probably the first and last time you'll ever admit to being wrong!"

"Well, you had your chance," Irene answered, laughing. "But seriously, she's learning to ride horseback very well. I think she's ready to come up into the hills with me. And Mama's happier than I've seen her in years." Irene finished her wine and set her glass down on the end table. "I never thought I'd say this, Chenyita. But maybe there's a form of payback here. After all we've been through, maybe it's time for our family to enjoy a bit of simple happiness."

❦

The phone rang the next day during lunch. María answered and came out to the table. "*Señora* Eugenia," she said. "It's for you. A *señor* Pérez?"

"Thank you, María." Eugenia got up from the table. "I'll take it in the bedroom."

"So, how's it going?" Ignacio asked once they heard María hang up the other extension.

"Surprisingly well. Irene, Mami, and Laura have been getting along famously. Mamita's been telling Laura stories from her childhood, and last night, during the exchange of gifts, she gave Laura her pearl necklace."

"I'm so glad to hear it. Do you think you'd be willing to leave Laura in your mother's and Irene's care for a few days?"

"Why?"

"Well, remember that I told you once we'd finished the work at the Commission, we'd see about us?"

"I didn't realize there was an us."

"That's the point, isn't it? To see if there is."

"And what do you suggest?"

"I could come pick you up. We could spend a few days on the road, just taking it easy. There are some beaches near your place, kind of rough and not that popular, that might be fun to explore this time of year. Just a vacation, some time together. No strings, no obligations."

"How long do you think we'll be? Would I be back for New Year's?"

"Hard to tell. Maybe we could leave that open?"

"I'll check. Could you call me back tomorrow?"

"All right. And Eugenia? Remember. No strings."

When Eugenia went back to the table, all eyes were on her.

"So?" Laura asked almost immediately.

"It was Ignacio," her mother answered.

"Well, duh. What's up?"

Eugenia took a sip of tea and looked around at the three other women at the table. "He invited me to spend a few days with him on the road, until New Year's give or take. I told him I needed to check with everybody before I answered."

"What do you think, Laurita?" Irene asked after a short silence.

Laura leaned back in her chair, her eyes on her mother, a smile spreading across her face. "What I think," she answered, "is, about time! What took this guy so long?"

Doña Isabel sat up straighter in her chair. "Laurita," she began, "are you suggesting . . ."

"Exactly. My mama's spent most of her good years taking care of me. She deserves a fling before she gets too old to enjoy it!"

Eugenia waited for her mother's shocked exclamation, and for Irene's and Laura's laughter, to die down before she answered. "Are you sure, Laurita?" she asked. "I could be gone for New Year's."

Laura smiled. She looked so much more at ease than she had a few weeks ago. "I'm sure," she answered. "In fact, me and Irene and Mamita Isabel can get drunk on the special cherry wine that's hidden away in the kitchen and I'll win at canasta. I've been practicing with María."

✧

Ignacio drove up two days later in a royal blue convertible with the top down. It felt easy and comfortable from the start, Eugenia thought, and so different from the chauffeur-driven black sedan with the car phone. They went south to Curicó and cut west through Hualañé to the coast at Bucalemu. With the sun low over the Pacific, its bright orange tones shimmering in the slate-blue swells right before they broke, froth-like, along the surf, they decided to find a place to stay. A tattered building hugged the beach, the remains of its originally salmon-colored paint faded to a mottled shade of rust. "*Pensión* Bucalemu," said the sign. "Breakfast Free. Dining Room open daily." Ignacio pulled into the empty parking lot.

"What do you think?" he asked.

"It looks pretty awful," Eugenia answered.

"Have you seen anything else? Do you want to get out and at least take a look?"

They got out and climbed the stairs to the porch, ringing the bell next to the door with peeling paint. Just as they were about to go back to the car, they heard a door close on the second floor and the muffled sound of feet on the stairs. A woman about Eugenia's age opened the door. Her tanned skin and green eyes sparkled, her hair streaked with white.

"Well, hello," she said, her lips spreading to show perfect white teeth. "I wasn't expecting anyone today." Her accent was hard to place, but it had traces of a European language, perhaps French or German. "Are you interested in a room?"

They looked at each other, not sure of what to say. "Well," Ignacio ventured, "at least something to eat. We saw the sign about your dining room."

The woman laughed softly. "Yes, that's an old sign. We used to have a dining room, with a cook and a waitress and everything. Business has been a little slow recently and I had to let them go last year. But wait," she continued, as they made moves to leave. "I could cook you up something. I was checking my traps earlier and found a couple of fresh *locos*. I also have some clams that a fisherman brought by earlier today and was about to make a soup. And there's always bread, and a bottle or two of red wine. You interested?"

"I think you had her at the word *locos*," Ignacio answered, putting his arm around Eugenia's shoulders. "It sounds great."

They watched the sunset from the picture windows in the dog-eared dining room. Angela kept up a conversation through the window that connected them to the kitchen. As they opened a first bottle of Cabernet, she headed off to the kitchen to begin preparing dinner, promising she would explain how she had ended up the owner of the *Pensión* Bucalemu.

"I'm a product of my time," she said, a stained white chef's apron tied around her waist. "I was one of those young rebels in the sixties. I was born on the German side of the Alsace border, but ran away from home and rode the trains to Paris. Then one day, during the student movement, you know, May 1968? I met this beautiful young Chilean boy and fell in love. We came back to Chile and spent that next summer surfing together along the coast here. In Pichilemu there was no one else back then."

She stopped talking for a moment to pay attention to her soup, beating the *locos* with a wide stick she took out of the cupboard. "You have to be very careful with these things," she explained. "If you don't beat them long enough before cooking, they get as tough as leather." She turned back to stir the soup once again, putting in some herbs and salt, then placed the *locos* in boiling water. The round, slightly tangy fragrance of seafood made their mouths water.

She took several tomatoes and a purple onion out of a large basket on the counter, then reached for some sprigs of cilantro to complete the ingredients for a tomato salad. "Anyway," she continued as she began slicing up the tomatoes and the onion, "we were very happy here. For several years we surfed most of the time, and worked in the tourist hotels during the summers. At the beginning of the seventies, you know, there were a lot of young people coming south, and times were good." She finished cutting the salad and reached up into one of the cupboards over the counter, bringing down a bottle of olive oil. After dribbling some of its contents across the top of the tomatoes and adding a pinch of sea salt from a bowl on the sideboard, she walked to the other side of the kitchen and opened a drawer. She rummaged around for a while among the various large kitchen utensils.

"Things changed in the spring of 1973," she said, her head still down, eyes staring into the drawer. "Why is it I can never find those damn salad tongs? I know they're here, in plain sight!" She reached a hand into the back and pulled out the offending item. The slam of the drawer was so loud that it made Eugenia jump.

"Damn onions," Angela muttered, swiping at her eyes. For a moment she busied herself tossing the salad, then drained the locos. "They still need to cool down a bit more," she said, coming back to retrieve her glass of wine. "And the soup needs another fifteen, maybe twenty minutes."

"So how'd you end up with the *pensión*?" Eugenia asked when Angela joined them.

For a moment Angela looked out at the shimmering remains of sunlight that were playing along the horizon, a bluish, then greyish reminder of where the sun had disappeared only a few minutes before. She stood up and went to the cabinet to retrieve a second bottle of Cabernet. She reached over and flicked on a lamp. The room glimmered, saffron-like. She took the corkscrew out of the pocket of her apron and opened the new bottle. Then she walked back and refilled their empty glasses.

"You have to understand that the coup wasn't the same here as it was in Santiago," she said, sitting down. "Why, if we'd actually counted up the members of all the political parties here, we wouldn't have used all the fingers on one hand." She stopped for a moment, and when she continued her voice was muddy and rutted. "But it didn't matter. They still rounded them up, all the young men with long hair."

By the time they finished dinner, they'd also polished off three bottles of Cabernet between them. There was something about Chilean wine, Eugenia thought dizzily, maybe especially the Cabernet. It made people feel like they'd known each other all their lives. Camilo, Angela's lover, had been picked up by the military police about a week after the coup, and even though she'd looked for him, gone to the local police outpost repeatedly over the next few weeks, he was never heard from again. The owner of the *Pensión* Bucalemu, a grizzled, long-haired man from further south, had also disappeared. In order to comfort his wife, for whom she had worked several summers, Angela moved into one of the upstairs rooms. People stopped traveling and business declined. One day in the early summer after the coup, when no one had appeared or even called to inquire about a room, the owner said she was leaving. I'm going back to my family in the north, she said. I just can't live here anymore. Some nights I hear him, or see his ghost in the moonlight that plays across the water. I can't stand it. The place is yours.

Of course they ended up spending the night. After Eugenia had hugged Angela, told her that she, too, had been arrested and her lover disappeared, they had cried together over the last remaining drops of wine. Then Angela had made up a room for them, fresh sheets on a double bed and a balcony overlooking the beach. By the time they'd brought up their bags and said good night, Eugenia felt like an entire layer of her skin had been pulled back, exposing nerve ends and raw flesh. She walked out on the balcony when Angela closed the door. A sliver of moon had risen, casting faint reflections across the dark water.

"If you want, I can sleep in the chair," he said. She could feel the light brushing of his breath along her ear. A tingle went down her back.

"I feel strange," she said, "and I don't think it's the wine."

"I know what you mean," he said, running a hand up and down her right arm, over the long sleeve she always wore. The tingle moved from her back to her shoulder in response. "It seems everywhere you go in this country, someone's got a story. And most of them won't get to the Commission. I didn't have the heart to suggest she report Camilo. And I suspect his family hasn't reported him, either."

She felt his lips touch the side of her neck, then move down to her shoulder. A burning feeling under her lungs made it hard to breathe. She turned and he kissed her full on the mouth, tasting of wine and cilantro. As he unbuttoned her blouse they moved back, away from the window and onto the bed.

He slowly peeled the blouse off her arms, and when he saw the purple marks there he ran a tender finger over them and kissed them, murmuring comfort. He took his time, lingering over each one. By the time he was done, she had melted, opening up to him completely.

When she awoke, the timid light of early morning was spreading across the recently abandoned pillow next to her head. He was standing out on the balcony, a jacket pulled on over his bare torso in an attempt to stave off the briny chill of the sea breeze.

"Did you sleep well?" she asked. He came back to her side, taking her in his arms. He smelled of salt and fish, with a lingering undercurrent of sex. As he began taking off his jacket, kissing her strong on the lips, she pulled back.

"Wait a minute," she said. "I'm not even awake yet. I need a cup of coffee."

He stood up and walked over to his bag lying open on the floor. Taking off his jacket, he put on a fresh shirt instead. He reached over and untangled his belt from among her clothes, threading it through the loops of his open jeans, then zipping and buckling them in place.

"I'm ready for the coffee, if that's what it will take," he said.

Eugenia felt a chill from the breeze and pulled the covers over her breasts. "I think we need to take it easy," she said.

"That's exactly what we're doing," he said. "We're not in any rush. A few days on the road, nothing to worry about."

"You know that's not what I mean," she said.

"But you also know that, ever since I held you in the armchair in your Boston apartment, there's been something between us."

"Maybe that's the problem. I'm not sure what happened in Boston."

"Come on, Eugenia, we were both there!"

"I know. But I'm not sure what it was, even though I felt it, you felt it and, to be honest, I've thought about it a lot since then."

"So have I."

"And since I got back, you've been the one person who understands. I don't have to explain anything to you. Like the time I went to police headquarters, and you knew just what I was talking about."

"So what's the problem, then?"

"Well, for one thing, when I went into exile you were just graduating from high school."

"What difference does that make? You're not going to start up with that age stuff, are you? I get enough of it every day without you starting on me! Besides, with the work I've done, the people I've met, the testimonies I've taken, I'm not just any old kid you picked up off the street!"

"True. Like I said, you're the only one who understands. But I wonder how much of it is just that. The first time we felt close, in Boston, was when I told you about Manuel. The time in Santiago, when we started kissing up on the Cerro San Cristóbal, you were consoling me after my hallucination at police headquarters. Last night, it was after Angela and I cried together."

"So?"

"I think we need to take it easy, figure out what's going on. I want to know how things feel when we're not dealing with torture or disappearance. Besides, in case you haven't yet done the math, I'm six years older than you."

"Age is not about math. And neither is love."

"I'd be careful about using that word. Things did not go well for me the last time I used it. Except I got Laura. And we can't forget about Laura."

After lingering over coffee and bread, they hugged Angela good-bye and headed north to the beach resort of Pichilemu. Walking along the gritty, mud-colored sand, watching the surfers in wet suits lining up to ride the curl, drinking second-rate beer in beachfront bars with diagonal cracks through the tiles on the floor, Eugenia felt the knots in her back loosen one by one. They were in no hurry. They stayed in another ragged hotel, the sheets smelling of brine, for three days. Their lovemaking was quiet and tender, sometimes mirthful, no longer the voracious hunger of the first time. At sunset they walked the beach and watched the sun sink piece by piece, first red, then pink, then gold, until all that remained was a silver afterthought across the horizon. On the fourth night, as they sat drinking glasses of homemade raspberry liqueur on the veranda of their favorite restaurant, Ignacio leaned back in his chair.

"I was thinking," he said, "that we might want to head further north tomorrow. We can spend New Year's at one of those quaint little places along the coast, and then we might drop by and visit my family. They're at the summer house in Algarrobo, near Valparaíso."

Eugenia sat up straighter and looked at him with some alarm. "Visit your family? Are you sure?"

"Look, we've been through this before. But now it's different. No, don't say anything. I heard you when you said we have to take things slowly. But even though I've lived independently since I was sixteen and I'm not like a lot of Chilean men who live at home until they marry, and don't even learn how to make a bed or boil water . . ."

"You do remember what happened last time, when we went for lunch. And now, we arrive together, obviously traveling together . . ."

"But that's exactly the point. They need to know what's happening in my life. They're my family."

"I don't think your mother's opinion will have changed in the meantime. She wants you close, you're the only unmarried son. I'm six years older than you, and besides, to be quite frank, I'm damaged goods!"

"Okay, look. Let's just see what happens. Let's head north, and we'll see how we feel after the New Year."

When they headed north toward San Antonio, they wore their bond comfortably, like an old shirt grown soft from washing. Walking, they sought each other out instinctively, shoulders touching, hand seeking hand. Sitting, for a meal or in the car, a free hand would find a shoulder or a knee. They laughed together easily, on the same breath, or finished the other's sentence. They spent New Year's Eve in a small fishing village, dancing and drinking cheap wine at a local bar. By then, nothing seemed more natural than the right turn Ignacio took, off the coastal road late in the afternoon of their sixth day together, following the arrow to Algarrobo.

The house was up among the rocks, a long set of stairs zig-zagging down from the veranda to the water's edge. Eugenia saw the family gathered on the porch from several blocks away, blotches of bright-colored summer clothes that hid and reappeared with each turn of the road. They arrived at the rear of the house, where a door to the kitchen stood open to allow in the early evening breeze. Four cars were already parked, two of them late-model station wagons suggesting the presence of children. They walked in, saying hello to the servants they met along the way.

"Hello!" Ignacio called as he got closer to the porch. "It's me! I brought Eugenia!"

Cecilia Letelier came out to greet them. She took Eugenia's hands between hers and gave her a quick peck on the cheek. "Why Eugenia," she said. "What a surprise. Traveling without your daughter, I see. So good to see you again." The stiffness of her voice belied her words. "Nachito," she said, turning to look at her son while still holding on to one of Eugenia's hands. "To what do we owe this unexpected pleasure? Can you stay a few days?" Without waiting for an answer, she led them out onto the porch. "Ignacio," she said, "look who's here."

Don Ignacio gave Eugenia a tight hug. "Eugenia, so good to see you. How's that lovely daughter of yours?"

"She's fine, *don* Ignacio," Eugenia said. "She's with my sister and my mother at our family's farm."

"And where is that, my dear?" *doña* Cecilia asked.

"South of here, a bit inland from the coast at Bucalemu, near San Jacinto."

"Yes, I know the area well, I have a dear childhood friend whose family has a place right near there. Why, after the agrarian reform, they—"

"Mamacita," Ignacio interrupted quickly. "We need to finish the introductions. Eugenia," he continued, taking her by the hand, "this is my sister Ceci, her husband Antonio, my brother Fermín, and his wife Soledad."

Eugenia made the rounds, shaking hands and receiving pecks on the cheek.

"We were just sitting down to have a pisco sour," *doña* Cecilia said after they had all settled back into the various pieces of wicker porch furniture. "Clemente!" she called toward the kitchen. "Bring out two more glasses for *el niño* Ignacio and his friend!"

They sat drinking pisco sours until the moon came up over the ocean, projecting its light in sheets across the surface of the water. As they continued to sit on the porch, the servants brought out a light supper of chicken and avocado sandwiches, followed by cups of consommé. Only when all the dishes were removed and snifters of cognac passed around did the family's attention turn fully to the new arrivals.

"Eugenia," Ceci said, "my mother had mentioned to me that you have a teenage daughter. You look so young, I can't imagine—"

"Ceci," Ignacio interrupted, "Eugenia's daughter Laura is sixteen, and she's a really lovely young lady. As you can imagine, it was really difficult bringing her up in exile. Eugenia has done a marvelous job, I have to say."

"Being in exile for such a long time must have been so hard," Ignacio's brother Fermín said after a short silence. "How did you—"

This time Ignacio's father interrupted. "You know what," he said. "Eugenia must be tired after a long day on the road. Perhaps we shouldn't go immediately to such heavy topics. We were hoping to see you again, Eugenia. We really enjoyed your visit when you had lunch with us in Santiago. But next time, you must bring Laura. Here in Algarrobo I can show her some wonderful places along the shore, in the crannies between the large boulders, where you can find the most beautiful shells."

"Papito," Ignacio said, "I didn't know you were still collecting shells. Why, the last time I looked in your study the shelves were absolutely crammed. Where are you putting the new ones?"

"Ay, Nachito, don't get me started," *doña* Cecilia complained, "I've been telling him that it's time to throw some of them out, but he's like a little boy when it comes to those things!"

Everyone laughed at that, and began teasing *don* Ignacio about his child-like attachment to collecting. The conversation then shifted to more mundane topics, and once the cognac was consumed and the moon moved further up in the sky, Ignacio's mother got up.

"I'll go make sure the rooms on the first floor have been prepared," she said. "I hope you don't mind sleeping in a twin bed, Eugenia. Unfortunately it's all we have left, with the house as full as it is. Luckily, with Ceci's nanny on vacation in her village in the south, there are two rooms open on the ground floor. Ignacio, do you know if Clemente got your suitcases out of the car?" After saying their good-nights, they followed her out into the hall.

"Ah, good, I see your bags are in the correct rooms and the beds have been made. You also have clean towels. Ignacio, can you show Eugenia where the bathroom is and how the shower works? Good. Well, I guess that's it then." She gave them both pecks on the cheek. "Welcome, Eugenia, it's good to see you again. I'm always happy when Nachito brings his friends to the house. Sleep well." Her summer sandals flopped briskly against her heels as she made her way up the stairs.

They stood alone in the hall for a few minutes. "You didn't have to defend me from your sister's comment," Eugenia said softly. "I can take care of myself."

"I know that. It's just that I don't understand why they have to harp on Laura, and on you looking so young all the time."

"I told you before we came about your mother's feelings. I'm not surprised that Ceci has been brought up to speed on it."

"Well, it's none of their business," Ignacio answered, taking Eugenia's hand and bringing her close, kissing her lightly on the lips. "Once everyone is in their rooms and a little time has passed, I'll come over," he whispered.

Eugenia pulled away and shook her head. "No, Ignacio. By bringing me here, I think you made it their business. And your mother made it perfectly clear that each of us was to sleep alone."

"Well, too bad."

"I prefer we not make a scene."

One last quick kiss on the mouth, and they closed the doors to their assigned rooms.

❧

Laura spent the first couple of mornings after her mother left strolling in the open-air patio in the middle of the large country house, drinking in the sun and the scent of wild roses, or sitting on a bench in one of the four covered passageways that framed the garden on all sides. She savored the snatches of conversation as her grandmother and aunt walked in and out. It was always around the noon hour that Grandma Isabel emerged from the kitchen, robe saturated with flour and the fragrances of promised treats. After planning the large afternoon meal, she would issue one last warning to María and Irene and walk back through the hall to take her daily shower. Once she had gotten out and dried herself, she signaled it was all right to enter by opening the door to her dressing room just a crack, but it was understood that only her daughter was allowed in. The lavender fragrance of her body powder and cologne mixed with the wild roses and the smell of fresh sun.

On the third day, Irene took Laura out horseback riding. They left early, packing a picnic lunch, and did not return until almost dinnertime. They galloped in the hills, along trails shaded by eucalyptus trees, their long, slim leaves redolent with spice under the horses' hooves. They ate lunch by the side of a gentle stream, its clear waters full of young trout. Later, when they stopped to rest in the tall, dry grasses higher up on the slopes looking out across the valley, Laura felt something stir deep within.

"I don't know what it is, *tía*," she said, "but I feel a bond with this land. I've never been here before, but it feels familiar."

"People say the blood speaks, Laurita. Maybe that's what it is. Your mama and I grew up with this land, coming every year. Maybe, somehow, that got passed down to you."

The feeling of rootedness stayed with her, even when they got back to the house and Grandma Isabel was fretting about being left alone for the whole day.

"I hope you don't pick up your aunt's old habits, Laurita," Grandma said at dinner. "When she was little and her papa was still around, the two of them went out almost every day. I never saw them."

"Well, Mamita," Irene teased. "Certain things must run in the blood."

That night, Laura had the dream for the first time. She was walking on the same trail where she'd galloped with her aunt. It started off as a warm, sunny day, but then a fog came down, thick as spoiled milk, turning everything a haggard shade of grey. As she struggled to find her way, a man loomed up from the shadows. He was not very tall, perhaps a head taller than she, and his clothes were a drab olive green. Blocking her way, he stared at her with large black eyes from under thick dark eyebrows that met in the middle. His eyes were so black, they had no pupils. As she tried to push past him on the path, he reached out a massive square paw and clutched her arm. "You've finally come back," he breathed, giving off a sour, humid smell. And she found she could not escape.

After that, every day she had a harder time getting out of bed. She was afraid to go to sleep at night, afraid the dream would come back. Listening to the comforting sound of Silvio on her Walkman, even cuddling Paco the pink porcupine, didn't push the dream out of her mind. She tried to write about it in her daily letter to Joaquín, but nothing sounded right. When her aunt took her out horseback riding again, she refused to go back to that trail.

❧

The convertible raced toward the north, hugging the two-lane highway between Valparaíso and Concón. It was about ten o'clock, and the sun was playing hide-and-seek with the morning fog that blanketed the cliffs along the ocean. Looking at the large rocks that jutted out, like elbows, into the sea, Eugenia wondered if one could build a small house on one of them. Pablo Neruda's house in Isla Negra was like that, a ship balanced on a large rock, closed and abandoned for nearly twenty years and only now opening back up. Even with the renovation in progress, sadness and loss still bubbled up from every corner, so thick you could hold them in your hand. Yesterday she and Ignacio, their arms around each other, had read people's messages, carved with love, desperation, or political orthodoxy, into the wooden fence that protected the house from the road.

Eugenia shivered in the wind that came over them now from the water, while Ignacio negotiated his sports car around the curves he'd known by heart since he was a teenager. She zipped up her jacket and looked over at him, his eyes behind sunglasses, his black hair ruffling about.

The morning had started auspiciously enough. They got up early and Ignacio announced that he was taking her up the coast to Concón, to a wonderful seaside restaurant where they had fresh *locos*. "I know they're your favorite," he said. Ignacio's mother had appeared, still in her bathrobe, her hair pulled back in a quick bun, and insisted they sit for a few minutes and drink a cup of coffee together.

"Tonight's going to be our last night here," Ignacio said as he finished off a second croissant. "Eugenia needs to get back to her family in the countryside and I have to finish up a couple of things at the Commission."

"But Nachito, you just arrived," *doña* Cecilia protested.

"Sorry, Mamacita, but you know that until all the work is finished at the Commission I can't control my time, even in the summer."

"Can you at least make it back next weekend? I've invited the Hiriart family, and María Paz was really looking forward to seeing you. Sorry to bore you with this, Eugenia, but María Paz and Ignacio have known each other since high school. They went out for a while before he left for Europe. Since he's been back I've always meant to . . . you know how these things are—"

"María Paz and I broke up before I left for Europe. There's a reason I didn't look her up when I got back, you know."

"I'm sorry, *hijito*, you never told me you'd parted on bad terms. It's just that with all that work you've had, first with the firm, then the Commission, you never seem to go out and enjoy yourself. You're not getting any younger, and I just thought . . ."

"María Paz's father was in charge of the detention camp near here."

"What?"

"Hundreds of people disappeared from there, Mama! And who knows how many more were strapped to metal bedframes and electrocuted within an inch of their lives!"

"Nachito, you know we don't agree with the things people did, but now that we have democracy back—"

"When did you ever stand up for anyone? Those criminals were in power seventeen years, and you looked the other way the whole time!"

"Did you break up with María Paz because of her father? It's not fair to blame her, you know, she—"

Ignacio's face had closed then, his cheeks crumpling inward. When he spoke again, his voice was low and gravelly. "Whose fault do you think it was, then? We're all to blame, Mama. Even those like me, who left the country instead of standing up to them." He got up from the chair and his napkin fell to the floor. "Eugenia," he said, bending to pick it up and tossing it on the table. "Are you ready to go? I'll meet you at the car in ten minutes. We can pack when we get back."

Since they'd started out in the car he hadn't said a thing. She'd heard him exchange a few more words with his mother when she was in the bathroom, but she couldn't make out what they were saying over the water as she brushed her teeth.

"How long till we get there?" She tried to make small talk. "Will we have time to walk on the beach first? Did you make a reservation?" she persisted. "I know it's not the weekend, but it is the summer."

"Just wait a little longer, okay?" His voice sounded torn. "I need a little more time."

They drove on in silence. Slowly the folds of fog began to move inland and the sea was revealed in all its majesty, waves sporting helmets of foam on their glimmering heads as they crashed among the rocks.

"It's not María Paz's fault, and it's definitely not yours," she finally said.

He banged his fist on the steering wheel and the car veered slightly toward the precipice. "I'm not asking for your absolution!"

"I'm sorry, Nachito. But at some level I think you are."

"How can you say that?"

"Your work with the Commission. Listening to everyone's stories, holding their hands, letting them cry on your shoulder. Sure, part of it is official. But now I see it's also personal."

They were coming to the outskirts of Concón, and Ignacio made a quick turn into a small parking lot next to a seaside walkway where couples were gathering for their morning stroll. They stood for a moment next to the wall overlooking the harbor. Then she took his hand and began walking, establishing distance between them and the others.

"So you think our whole relationship has been about my guilt," he said. She could barely hear his voice above the sounds of the waves and the gulls circling overhead.

"I didn't say that."

"What, then?"

"I'm not really sure. But remember what I said in Bucalemu? That I wanted to know how things felt when we're not dealing with torture or disappearance? I'm beginning to think we can never get there."

"Why not?"

"Because of who I am, mostly. But at some level, I also agree with your mother. You've become so consumed by the Commission, by human rights, it seems you can't allow yourself a normal life."

"Why are you defending her?"

"That's not the point."

"What is the point, then?"

"She's your mother, and she's no fool. Like I told you when we first arrived, by bringing me to their house, from our trip where we had so obviously been sleeping together, you fired the first shot. She needed to defend you from falling into my clutches."

"She's not entitled to decide what's right for me. Only I can do that."

"Maybe so. But you seem to need their approval. Otherwise, why did you bring me to their house?"

"Whose side are you on, anyway?"

She let go of his hand and stopped walking, leaning against the seawall. Seagulls glided by, and their caws seemed to be mocking her. When she looked down at her hands, she saw they were trembling. She had to force her voice out from behind the sudden swelling in her throat. "Your mother's entitled to think about what life should be like for you. She's entitled to want someone for you who's not six years older than you are, a returned exile with a subversive pedigree, and a single mother. And I think I agree with her. It's not right. I'm not right."

He had stopped next to her, and had been rubbing the toe of his shoe back and forth in the sand that was sprinkled among the stones of the walkway. He came closer and took her hand once more. "It felt awfully right in Pichilemu. Or what about Isla Negra?"

"True. The two of us alone. Walking along that scruffy beach with all those surfers. Or crying at Neruda's fence. But what about

Sundays, when it's time to take the kids to your mother's house? Or in the summer, when we argue over spending January at the beach or in the countryside? Or eating dinner at your sister's or mine's?"

He let go of her hand. "That's so trivial, it doesn't even deserve—"

"But Nachito, that's exactly why it does. When you're done at the Commission, you deserve a life where you can sometimes putter around in the everyday, talk about it, argue over it. You need to share that with someone who can laugh with your children in your parents' backyard and warn them not to hurt your mother's roses. That's not me."

She resisted the urge to take his hand again. She swallowed. A large weight pressed down on their shoulders. He rested both elbows on the seawall and gazed at the breakers below. She ran a hand over his forehead, pausing on the long strand that hung now, victim of the laws of gravity, halfway down his cheek. Then it blurred in her tears. When he looked up, he was crying too. And they finally had to drive on, through the curtain that descended now, murky and dank, across the summer sun.

⚑

Ignacio dropped Eugenia off at the farm shortly before midnight. They'd driven straight through from Concón, not even stopping for lunch, buying bad coffee and stale sandwiches at a convenience store next to the gas station. He called his mother from a phone booth, saying something had come up and they were not going back for their bags.

"She'll pack it up and send it to Santiago," he said. "Custodio will run it by your mother's house. I'll call and make sure that Rosa's there. It's mainly dirty clothes anyway."

Hair drooping over his ears and sad smudges under his eyes, he refused her offer to stay the night. Despite her stiffness, he gave her a tight hug and kissed her on the lips. Then he was off, the top to his convertible raised against the clouds of country dust. For a moment she just stood there, her lungs shut down by loss, watching the light of the full moon reflect silty and flat across the road. Then, forcing herself to breathe, she opened the front door.

Irene leaped up from the couch where she was still reading. Eugenia simply shook her head at her sister's startled question and walked back to her room.

"So it didn't look good last night," Irene said the next morning when the two sisters sat down for an early cup of coffee. "And it doesn't seem like you slept much, either."

"It's over." Eugenia blew her nose into the tissue she was carrying.

"Do you want to elaborate at all?"

"Ay, Irene, I should have known it from the start." She sipped her coffee for a minute, wiping her eyes with the frayed tissue. Irene went into the kitchen and brought out a fresh box, then refilled their mugs. Eugenia grabbed another tissue and blew her nose. "He said love wasn't about math, but six years is a lot, plus his mother . . . I did side with her, but what a bitch!"

"Whoa, Chenyita, that's a lot to take in all at once. Remember, I wasn't there."

"We made love the first night after we left, and the very next morning we had this argument, me saying I was older, him saying it wasn't about math. The idea of the trip—well, it felt so good when we were alone, in Pichilemu, walking on the beach. I guess I just relaxed, so I let him take me to his parents' house in Algarrobo."

"Oops."

"No kidding. I should have said no, but I guess at some level he really needed their approval, I could see that. Against my better judgment, I guess I hoped things had changed since the lunch in Santiago."

"You haven't told me about that one!"

"Until he phoned, you know, I honestly didn't think anything would come of it. But a couple of days after we arrived, he took me and Laura to his parents' house for lunch. His family is so like our family, Nenita! His dad is really sweet, he was so nice to Laura, but his mother kept harping about how young I looked to have a teenage daughter. And after lunch she took me out to her rose garden. I was admiring this one rose, so she clips two of them for me to take home. But at the same time, while she's being so nice, she goes on about how these roses are gorgeous in their prime and call so much attention to themselves, but once they begin to decline, no one cares about them anymore."

"Did you tell Ignacio about it?"

"It didn't seem right to go into detail at that point. But when we got to the beach house, it was clear she'd talked to his sister about me. Plus she knew we were together, and she made us sleep in separate rooms, twin beds. Then the last morning, before we went out, she got into this thing about some old girlfriend of his who was coming to visit next weekend. She did this whole song and dance about how he was getting older, didn't have a social life, that she was worried, and I'm sitting right there the whole time! But that wasn't the worst of it."

"What do you mean?"

"Turns out that the girlfriend's father had been in charge of a detention camp. When Ignacio found out, he broke up with her. His mother hadn't known about it. So it all came out, and he got going on how everyone is to blame for the dictatorship, even those like him who left the country. That's when we got in the car and drove north."

Eugenia took out a fresh tissue and wiped her eyes and cheeks. "Ay, Nenita, I just don't know anymore. In Boston, I longed to come back. I felt like such a foreigner there! Maybe that's why I jumped at the chance when the Commission brought me back to testify. I was hoping to come home. But now, I feel even more out of place. Will I ever be more than a survivor? Can I ever be more than a bad memory for people like Ignacio's parents?

"Maybe it's for the best. As much as it hurts now, it would have been worse if I had let myself get in deeper with him. I was up all night thinking about it. When we first made love in Bucalemu and had that argument about age, I said to him that I'd like to make sure we had something together that wasn't about human rights. Only last night did I see that, for him, these are beautiful but abstract concepts. I carry the damage on my own skin."

Eugenia began sobbing. Irene moved closer and took her sister in her arms. When Eugenia began to calm down, Irene took several tissues from the box, mopped her sister's cheeks, wiped her nose, and hugged her close once again. After a while Eugenia spoke, her voice little more than a whisper.

"I wanted to believe him when he said it wasn't about the math. My God, Nenita, I wanted to believe him so badly. Six years isn't that much, really. But when I did the math last night, it came out differently. For me it's a lifetime."

⋘⋙

It was late the next evening when *doña* Isabel made her statement, a bomb dropping, exploding in their midst. They were having dinner, three generations of women around the long table, Laura sporting her grandmother's pearl necklace as the gift that completed the circle. Sitting regally on one end, in a straight navy blue dress, no makeup, her hair pulled loosely into a knot on the crown of her head, *doña* Isabel looked absolutely majestic. The wavy wisps of silver that had fallen loose framed and decorated her face, matching the small pearls shimmering in her ears. The dense network of lines around her eyes made her look gentle, almost joyful, as if her life had left the marks of goodness in every crease.

Laura was telling her mother about her horseback outings with Irene. "You know, Mamita," she said, "I mentioned to *tía* Irene the other day how comfortable I feel here, and how things seem so familiar, even though this is my first time."

"That's wonderful," Eugenia said. "Before we came down from Boston, I told your aunt that I hoped you'd feel comfortable here. I knew leaving your friends was hard, but I was hoping you'd discover a new sense of belonging here."

"It's what I've been telling Laurita the past several days," Irene said. "The blood pulls."

Doña Isabel sat up straighter, and a single fierce line appeared between her eyebrows. "It's not only about blood," she said. "It's about commitment. About staying put. About being there when you're needed."

"What are you talking about?" Irene asked. "Mamita, all we're saying is that—"

"Ever since your papa left me, the two of you have been my only family. Where were you when I needed you most? For almost a year I thought one of you was dead. The other was driving cars, late at night after curfew, putting herself in danger, for what? To throw another subversive over an embassy wall? Then, for a few minutes on her way out of the country, I get to hold my only granddaughter. And finally, my other daughter leaves the country and only comes back for a month in the summer.

"It's been sixteen years, sixteen years alone, by myself. My friends asked me constantly, where are your daughters? They're surrounded by their families, their grandchildren. And I'm all alone. Every time I look at Laura now, I think, my God. It's been sixteen years. And where were you? I sometimes think that, maybe, it would have been better if you had died. At least then I could have shut the door and made my peace with it. And now, after all this time, you just waltz in and expect to pick up where you left off?"

For a moment, all movement stopped. Eugenia gasped. Laura stood up and almost took the tablecloth with her.

"*Abuelita* Isabel, how can you say that?"

Her grandmother waved a trembling hand. "*Niña*, I know it's harsh. I know your life hasn't been a bed of roses. But you must see it from my point of view. I feel like I buried my family twenty years ago. Do I go now and open up the grave, just because you decide you're ready to come back?"

Laura walked out. Her harsh sobs echoed off the walls as she ran down the passageway to her room. With the hard closing of her door the silence was complete. Eugenia felt frozen to her chair, her lips nailed shut.

"Mamita, how could you say that?" Irene asked.

"You, of all people, should know. Have you ever told your sister how we cried that day after you went to her room and found they'd been taken? Does she know how much you suffered after she disappeared? How can you take her side now?"

VIII

On the Other Side of Midnight

They left early the next morning, like refugees, bags packed quickly and carelessly, as silently as they could so no one would wake up. By mid-morning they were on the outskirts of Santiago.

"So what do we do now, call Ignacio?" Laura asked once they returned the rented car and paid the bill.

"I don't think so. I didn't have a chance to tell you before, but Ignacio and I had a fight. So we really can't call him."

"What happened?"

"It's kind of complicated, but let's just say that I didn't get along very well with his parents."

"What's up with all these old Chileans, anyway? Why do so many of them have a broomstick up their—"

"Laurita!" her mother interrupted quickly.

"Sorry, but it's true! The only ones I've met so far who are different are *tía* Irene, who doesn't count because she lives in Boston, *tía* Tonia, who's Mapuche, *Bobe* Sara . . . Wait! That's what we do! We call *Bobe* Sara!"

Over Eugenia's protests Laura went back into the rental car office and asked to borrow the phone. After first trying the offices of the Committee, she found Sara at home.

"*Bobe*? It's me, Laura. Yes, we're back in Santiago. Well actually, my mama and me, we came back by ourselves. No, there's nothing wrong. Well . . . actually, *Bobe,* we don't have a key to Grandma Isabel's house, and we were wondering . . . No, we just returned the rental car, we're downtown, and . . . Oh, *Bobe*, that's so sweet. We'll just take a taxi out, okay? Yes. And *Bobe*? Thanks so much. Kisses from both of us. Yeah. See you soon."

Sara was waiting by the gate when the taxi drove up. Once the driver brought the suitcases up to the front door and Eugenia paid him, they took their bags into the guest room.

"I'm sorry, darlings," Sara fussed, "but the house is small. Shmooti and I . . . well, we never expected to have a lot of guests. There are two beds, but you'll have to sleep together in the same room. And the guest bathroom, it doesn't have a shower. I guess we'll just have to share the one off the master bedroom, but I can get you fresh towels and—"

"*Bobe*." Laura put her arms around her grandmother. "Don't worry so much. You're a lifesaver."

By lunchtime they'd washed their clothes and made the beds. Samuel wanted to barbecue, so he and Laura went to the local butcher in search of some chicken or lamb.

"It better be juicy, *Zeyde* Shmooti," Laura said as they were heading out. "Can you tell at the store if it's gonna be juicy?"

"Shmooti always takes forever at the butcher," Sara said when they closed the door. "He has to catch up on the local gossip, argue over the fine points of each cut, you know. Let's go sit outside.

There's a nice cool breeze, and we can have some orangeade. I just made it fresh with oranges from the tree."

For a while they were busy setting up the chairs and table, trying to get the right angle so they could have both sun and shade. Sara poured them each a glass of the sweet liquid. It was delicious, Eugenia thought as they sat down and she took her first sip.

"So what happened, really?" Sara asked.

Eugenia took another sip of the orangeade. She put the glass down on the table, picked up a napkin and wiped her mouth. She looked down at her hands for a moment, rubbing the fingers of one along the top of the other, then rubbing her thumbs together. She crossed her hands between her thighs, interlacing the fingers.

"It's hard to talk about it," she finally said.

"I can understand that, *m'hija*, believe me."

"I know you can. I'm sure you can understand that my mama, well, what happened back then, you know, she hasn't been able to . . . she's still angry. But it isn't Laura's fault, and I—"

"You don't have to say anything else, really. I get the general idea. You can stay here as long as you want, you know."

"Thank you so much, *doña* Sara. But you understand that we'll have to get our own apartment, we can't be relying on you, and we'll have to find Laura a school for this March, if possible, and—"

"I can help with all that. I know some people who work at a good progressive school; it's quite near here. Nowadays it isn't easy to find openings at the private schools, but I'm sure they can help Laurita. Now I don't presume to know if Laura is baptized, but that doesn't matter at this school. It's often a problem at the private schools here, they're run by Catholic orders, you know. But don't worry about it anymore today, *hija*, let's just enjoy the afternoon."

"Thank you. One last thing before they come back. When we got in this morning, we were wondering who to call. It was Laura who immediately thought of you."

"Thank you, *hija*, for saying that. What a gift she is. I don't know exactly how to say this, but—I'm not sure, my dear, if your mother knows how lucky she really is."

As it turned out, *doña* Isabel did not feel lucky at all. The phone rang the next day, and it was Irene. Eugenia was the one to pick up.

"Chenyita?" Irene's voice was hard to distinguish through all the static. "Thank God I found you. Look, I'm calling from San Jacinto. When Mama found the two of you gone, she prohibited my using the phone at the house to call you. Then she went back in her room and hasn't come out since."

"She must be pretty mad."

"I think she's hurt more than mad. She wanted to apologize, she said, she knew she'd gotten carried away, but when she got up you were gone."

"I know she has a right to be mad at me. But not Laura. Why is it she's always there in the middle, taking the potshots meant for me? It's not fair."

"I know, sweetie. But families, you know . . . and ours especially, don't you think?"

"Well, look. For now, we're doing fine. So let's just wait a while, maybe when Mama gets back to Santiago. Maybe then she'll see things differently."

"Are you going to live with Manuel's parents?"

"No, *mi amor.* We'll find an apartment, a school for Laura. Once we're independent, maybe then it'll be easier to mend fences."

"Hopefully that will happen before February."

"How's that?"

"That's when I go back to MIT. My vacation only goes through the end of this month. And now that it's just me and Mamita, she's agreed to come back to Santiago by then."

"But Nenita, you and I have barely had any time alone."

"I know, sweetie, and especially now that so much is happening. But you know, my job . . . and besides, if I stay any longer, Amanda will . . ."

"You're right. Of course. By the beginning of next month I need to have Laura signed up for school, anyway, and we should be moved into our own place."

"So you've decided to stay for good?"

"Ay, Nenita, I don't even know what 'for good' means anymore. Laura seems so happy with Manuel's parents, and I just don't have the heart to suggest we move again. Yet I don't have a job here, and at some point I'll have to make a decision about Carmichael College. But we do need our own place. At least for now, until we can figure out what to do next."

✤

Over the next two weeks, Laura and Sara took a bus every morning to the Committee offices to help with filing and paperwork. When Samuel left for the bakery, Eugenia would leave with him and spend the morning looking for apartments. It was a bad time of year to look, since peak rental season was between September and November, for the next calendar year. Only small furnished apartments were still on the market, designed for single travelers, usually businessmen, on short trips to Santiago.

"You wouldn't believe the dives I'm seeing!" Eugenia exclaimed in the afternoons when they were all back at the house. "The kitchens haven't been used in years, maybe never! I think the knobs on the stoves are rusted in place by now!"

"You'll have more luck if you don't need a furnished place," Samuel suggested. "Perhaps you should buy some used furniture?"

"But *don* Samuel, we don't know yet what will happen in the long run. Laura isn't in school yet, I don't have a job. I'd rather wait before spending money on something like that."

"But Mamita," Laura protested, "we're staying, aren't we? You're not planning to take us back to Boston, are you?"

"*M'hijita*, we don't know yet, do we? I don't feel ready to make that kind of decision, things are still so unsettled."

"I don't want to move again," Laura said. "I don't feel unsettled. I'm just beginning to feel at home. And before, whenever I started to feel at home, you picked up and took us someplace else. I don't want that again."

The following week, with Sara's help, Laura and Eugenia got an interview at the local progressive school. They were lucky to get in before the end of January, when the school administration closed everything up for the February holiday. The principal was impressed at how bilingual Laura was, and marveled at what she called the multicultural sensibilities of Laura's family. These were code words for the unusual combination of last names. The Chilean obsession with last names didn't disappear, Eugenia realized, even in this supposedly freer milieu. It just got reinvented as multiculturalism. But then the principal lowered the boom.

"As you know we don't require a baptismal certificate," she explained, "but because we see ourselves as a service for our own citizens, we do require some proof of Chilean citizenship. There's no problem with that, is there?"

"Actually," Eugenia said, "Laura was born in the Mexican embassy on our way out of the country. She's always been a Mexican citizen. I put in an application for her Chilean citizenship months ago, but with the inevitable delays, plus the summer vacation, we haven't heard yet."

"But certainly you, *señora*. You're obviously a Chilean citizen."

"Yes, of course, but given my status as an exile I don't have a passport. Because I was classified as a political subversive, I was never able to update my old one. And all my papers are presently with the government as part of my petition for recertification."

After a short silence the principal sat back in her chair, running a hand through her carefully coifed blond mane. "Well," she said, "Laura can have a spot in our school for this coming March. But I'm afraid we need one of the two petitions to come through before she can formally attend. Perhaps you can see if one of them can be hurried along?" Then she stood up, signaling the end of the interview.

When they got back to the house Laura went straight to their room. She got out her Walkman, put in a tape, and lay down on the bed with her earphones on and Paco clutched to her chest. Though she did not lock the door, there was no use in trying to talk to her. Eugenia sat down with Samuel and Sara.

"You need help down at the Ministry," Samuel said. "One of the higher-ups, he goes to our temple. We'll talk to him."

"Thank you so much, *don* Samuel," Eugenia said. "I'm sure that will help. But I'm beginning to wonder about all this. I can't find an apartment. Laura can't go to school until one of us gets certified as Chilean. And here we are, in your house, imposing on your hospitality. It'll be coming up on a month pretty soon. It's getting toward the end of January, and school starts at the beginning of March. I'm not sure we're going to make it."

Sometime after midnight, Laura had the dream. It started off the same, on a warm, sunny day on the trail where she and *tía* Irene had gone horseback riding. A fog came down, and the same man loomed up from the shadows. He was dressed in olive green, and he reached out to grab her arm with his hairy paw. She refused to look in his eyes because she knew they had no pupils. But suddenly, from behind a tree, a young man with red hair and a beard jumped out and grabbed the man around his neck. Her papa. They struggled, and the man without pupils finally got loose and ran away. She reached out to her papa, but just as she thought she got hold of his hand, his image began to fade. No! She shouted, wanting him to come back. No!

At first Eugenia didn't know what had awakened her. It took her a heartbeat to realize where she was, still in the guest room in Sara and Samuel's house. It was pitch black, and then she heard Laura breathing, moaning. The small electric clock on the night table said three A.M.

"No, no . . . please . . . no . . ." She got up, afraid to turn on the light. Groping where she thought her daughter's bed began, she tried to find something, a leg, her head, gently trying to touch her awake. Then Laura's flailing arm scored a direct hit on her jaw.

"NO!" Laura roared.

Eugenia got up, first on her hands and knees, found the end of the floor and slowly stood up, running one hand along the wall searching for the light switch. She had to close her eyes against the first blaze of light. When she was able to open them back up, she saw her daughter sitting up in bed. The sweat had matted her hair down against her scalp. Her eyes were open, but she was not awake. As Eugenia approached, Laura moaned, then whined, then whispered "no, no, no . . ." She was still asleep. Her eyes, open still, had gone so black they had no pupils.

The dream came every night after that. It was always after midnight and went on for what seemed like hours. Eugenia did not try to wake Laura, but lay in bed listening to the moaning and roaring, then the descent into whines and finally whispers. All Laura ever said was no. In the mornings, when her increasingly sleep-deprived mother would ask her if she remembered anything, Laura said no. Their conversations fell into a pattern that repeated itself, like the dream, over and over.

"Are you sure?" Eugenia asked. "Maybe if you try to remember, if you tell someone, you'll begin to get to the other side."

"I never wake up," Laura answered, avoiding her mother's eyes. "How should I know what it is I'm dreaming?"

"I know what it's like, *m'hijita*. Remember? In Mexico, and again in Boston?"

"That was different."

"And why is that?"

"Because you were arrested and tortured, my papa disappeared. This is just a dream."

"But you don't know, do you, because you can't remember. And given how many nights it's come back, it's not just a dream. In Boston, when all the memories started flooding back, it helped to write in my journal. Do you want us to get you one? Or maybe a good therapist will help you sort it out. I could ask *Bobe* Sara—"

At that point Laura ended the conversation. As the February winds blew through the city, pushing the smog out over the surrounding mountains, an increasingly desperate Eugenia moved her bedding to the living room couch. "I have to get some sleep," she mumbled when Sara asked her if she was comfortable on that old thing.

✥

As the smudges under her eyes got darker, Laura still insisted on going to the Committee every day. The only person who understood her was Joaquín. At one o'clock every afternoon, through the rest of Joaquín's summer vacation, they took a break and went to a small park a block from the Committee's offices. They entered the café on the corner of the little plaza and asked for chicken-and-avocado sandwiches and fresh fruit juice. The owner, an older man with a large salt-and-pepper moustache, began to recognize them and even to have the bread toasting and the fruit in the blender when they arrived.

"Well, if it isn't the two young lovebirds," he chuckled when they appeared. "Your usual will be ready in a minute. The juice today is kiwi. Is that all right?" Every day it was a different fruit, and every day it was delicious, but he always asked just in case. He wrapped their sandwiches in wax paper, poured their juices into large paper cups, and always gave them a bit of extra change, shaking his head and smiling when Joaquín pointed his error out. "The difference is on the house," he always said. "See you tomorrow."

They sat on the same bench every day and talked music. After talking with Joaquín, Laura found she could listen to Inti-Illimani again. They both loved Inti, and he was almost as addicted to Silvio as she was. He also introduced her to other groups from the eighties, like Los Prisioneros. When their first album came out, he and his friends had really related to their name, Joaquín explained. People his age had always felt like they were in jail. Their parents had messed up the country with politics, and it was the kids who had to pay for Pinochet, with no money, no jobs, and the schools worse every year. Then they were the ones who had to put their lives on the line in the streets to bring the dictator down.

Even though she'd grown up in exile, Laura could see now she was part of this generation. She, too, felt like a prisoner: of her mother's past, her mother's desires, her mother's fears. And now a prisoner of her own dream. She liked their song "The Dance of the Surplus Ones," and the words of the chorus: "Join the dance of the surplus ones / No one is going to add to us / No one ever wanted to help us." She too felt like a surplus one. She often thought her mother would have been better off without her.

At the end of February, Joaquín was unusually silent as they sat on their bench and ate their lunch. They both knew that once he had to go back to school, they would only see each other on weekends. It hung in the air between them, thick as soup.

"You know," he finally said, "we'll still have Saturdays to ourselves." Laura didn't answer. "But maybe you should tell me now, while we still have a few days together," he continued. "At some point you're gonna have to tell somebody. And it might as well be me. You know I won't tell anybody else."

"I don't know what you're talking about," she mumbled, pulling at a stringy piece of chicken that peeked out from the side of her sandwich.

He took the sandwich out of her hand, wrapped it back up in its waxed paper covering, and placed it on the bench on her other side. He took both of her hands in his and pulled her close. He kissed her full on the mouth, more strongly than he ever had before, and one of his hands sought out her skin under her shirt, moving up and under her bra along her left side. When he let go she couldn't catch her breath.

"You know exactly what I'm talking about," he said, his own breath coming in short spurts. "There's no one else in this world I want to take care of except you. So you need to tell me why the bags under your eyes are getting bigger every day."

Joaquín stood up from the bench and, tugging on her hand, led them back into a part of the park that was protected from the street by a grove of mature oaks. There, among the trees, they found a patch of soft grass and lay down together. She told him about her dream, and how at first she couldn't escape from the man with the muddy eyes. When her papa came to save her, he always faded just as she reached for him. Every night, no matter how hard she tried, she couldn't hold on to her papa. She woke every morning exhausted from trying. He told her about his recurring dream, too, the headless man who was his papa and who stumbled around running into things because he did not have eyes to see. Neither had ever thought of telling their mothers, who lived trapped in their own grief and loss, about these dreams. In the tenderness of their joined lips they found they could escape together. With their fingers they learned to give each other pleasure.

✥

Sara and Eugenia were sitting on the couch that had become Eugenia's regular bed. The pillow and blankets were neatly tucked away in a corner. Although the school year had begun that week, there had been no word from Foreign Relations about either citizenship petition, so Laura still could not go to school. She insisted on going to the Committee every day and working on her own, staying until Joaquín came over after classes let out. Then the two of them spent the afternoon and early evening together, and Laura often did not come back until after dinner. When her mother asked where she had been or what she had done, she said she was tired and went to her room to listen to music. In the morning over breakfast she answered all questions with monosyllables, and she dreamed the same dream every night.

"I don't know what else to do," Eugenia said. "I've tried to persuade her to see a therapist, or even just to write in a journal, but every time I bring it up she cuts off the conversation. And the bags under her eyes are getting deeper and deeper, and she's spending more and more time with that boy Joaquín. Do you think they're doing drugs, or . . ."

"I wouldn't think they're doing drugs," Sara answered. "I know the boy's mother, and she is a caring and upright person. But Joaquín lost his father in the repression, too, you know, and his mother spent a good part of her life looking for him. So who knows how that affected the boy? Still, *hija*, and I don't mean to scare you with this, but perhaps our first concern should be whether or not they're having sex. After all, she's sixteen, you know, and he's seventeen. And they've been spending quite a bit of time together unsupervised."

"I've thought of that, too," Eugenia said, "but what can I do? If she won't even talk to me about her nightmare, what will she say if I ask about birth control?"

"Ay, *hija*," Sara said. "Being a parent is never easy. I remember how much I worried about Manuel when he rebelled, how powerless I felt. I'm sure your mama felt the same way."

"You're right," Eugenia said. "Now I can see my mother in a completely different light. But I'm worried sick. Every time Laura settles down somewhere, it seems I end up moving her again. Right now, with the uncertainty about school, who knows where we'll end up? I'm not sure how much more she can take. And she refuses to talk about anything with me. Do you think she could be in some kind of danger, and I would never know?"

"Maybe there's something else we can do," Sara said suddenly. "I was a couple of years younger than Laura when I had a horrible experience in school. It doesn't matter anymore what it was, but I felt like my world had broken in two. The only one who understood was Tonia. She was living with us at the time. I don't think I ever told her what happened. She just knew, somehow, what to do.

"This was before she became a *machi*. Later she could take a person's urine and read their whole story in it. It's like an X-ray of a person's life, she told me. But even then, when we were girls, she could see things that others couldn't. It's true that the coup turned her world inside out and she stopped working as a *machi*. But she really loves Laura and might be willing to help. There's no harm in asking, and Laura might feel more comfortable talking with her, as Tonia has a distance from Laura that neither you nor I have. I know she's going to be working at the Committee tomorrow.

If you go in the late afternoon, you can talk with her alone once Laura and Joaquín leave."

Tonia opened the door to the Committee's office before Eugenia knocked. This had happened several times before, that Tonia knew something before it had actually happened. When Eugenia had shared her surprise with Sara, the older woman smiled. "I know just how you feel," she said. "Even though I've known Tonia since we were ten years old, it still took some getting used to when we reconnected here in Santiago. But she's a *machi*, and they read the world differently."

Eugenia wondered now, as she entered the coolness of the old office and followed Tonia down the hall to the sitting room, if this ability to read the world had declined at all when the older woman had stopped practicing her craft. She didn't know much about what had happened to Tonia, just that it had something to do with the coup and her disappeared son. And now Eugenia was about to ask her to come out of retirement.

"Do you want some *mate*?" Tonia asked as she pointed to an armchair close to the open window. "I have some water on the stove." Eugenia nodded.

As she sat waiting for Tonia to return, she looked around the room. Through the door to her left she could see the main desk in the receiving area. Boxes of files were stacked everywhere. No matter how much work people did, they just kept piling up. And it would only get worse, now that the school year had started and Joaquín had gone back to classes.

"I put some sugar in when I pressed down the *mate* leaves, but let me know if it needs more." Tonia strode back into the room carrying two gourds, their silver inlays and silver sipping straws gleaming in the late-afternoon sun. She handed one to Eugenia, who sipped from it and nodded that the sweetness was fine. Tonia sat down in another chair facing Eugenia.

"Sara told me you needed my help," she said.

Eugenia took another long sip of *mate* before she answered. She'd learned over the past few months that the best way to deal with Tonia was to get straight to the point, but it still surprised her in a country where everyone else seemed to prefer an indirect approach.

"That's right, Tonia. It's Laurita. We're worried sick about her."

"What's wrong with that beautiful young girl of yours? She and Joaquín seem very happy working together." Since the beginning, when Tonia had given Laura the *copihue* earrings, the two had developed a deep mutual bond. Laura basked in the old woman's acceptance, and glowed when Tonia told her once that she looked like a Mapuche beauty queen.

"Well, I don't know what's wrong, and she refuses to talk about it."

"What worries you?"

"She's having nightmares. She insists she doesn't remember them when she wakes up, but from watching her I'd say it's the same one, or at least a similar one, every night. It's been going on for weeks, and she seems less and less willing to talk with me. There are huge circles under her eyes, and the only thing she looks forward to is seeing Joaquín. She's coming home late, and refuses to tell me where she's been. I just don't know what to do anymore, I . . ." Eugenia's voice broke.

"Well, *hija*, this way of acting, this rebellion, keeping secrets, many young people go through it, no? What makes you think it's more than this?"

"I know that rebellion is common at her age, and I remember doing a lot of things behind my mother's back, too. But Laura's been through a lot. She's worried we might have to go back to Boston, because we can't get her into school until her citizenship comes through, and I haven't been able to find work. She feels settled here, a lot more than I do, to be frank. And I'm worried that, with all this insecurity, she might do something truly irreversible, and because she won't talk to me, I won't be able to help her before it's too late."

"Like what, for example?"

"Take drugs . . . get pregnant . . . run away . . ."

Tonia stood up and went into the kitchen, returning with the kettle to refresh their *mate*.

"There really isn't much we can do to prevent this," she said. "It's the way of this generation. I see it around me everywhere. They're angry, they don't know what to believe in, and they think we let them down."

"But the nightmare, Tonia. It's taking so much out of her. How much more can her body resist?"

"Does she talk during her dreams? Can you understand what she says?"

"All she ever says when she's asleep is no, no, no. Which is pretty much all she says when she's awake these days. But one thing I can tell you is that her dreams seem to have a common structure. She starts out moaning, then she roars, then it goes back to moans, whines, and finally whispers."

Tonia sat forward in her chair. "Is there anything else you can tell me about the dreams?"

Eugenia thought for a moment. "No," she finally said. "I don't think so."

"Are you sure? Maybe something about how she looks?"

"Now that you mention it, her hair gets flat with sweat. And when I get close, *tía*, I can see her eyes are open. And the strangest thing, her eyes get so dark they have no pupils."

Eugenia didn't know exactly how to ask for help, and surprisingly Tonia stopped being direct. For a while both women hid behind the ritual of *mate*, Tonia offering more water and sugar, then quizzing Eugenia about the strength of the tea. Did it need more leaves?

"So *doña* Sara thought you might have some advice," Eugenia finally said.

"How so?"

"Well, she said you used to specialize in cases that were hard to understand."

"That was before. In my youth." Tonia stood up and walked to the window, staring at the street below. A silence settled over them, and Eugenia felt a chill go through her. She rubbed her hands up and down her arms in a vain effort to warm them.

"*Tía* Tonia, I know that you stopped working as a *machi* with the coup. *Doña* Sara told me."

Tonia's shoulders hunched forward. When she spoke, her voice sounded muffled. "That's why I can't help you."

"What?"

"I couldn't save my Renato. That's why I can't help you."

"But I don't understand, I—"

Tonia turned to face Eugenia. "*Kuku* Fresia, my grandmother, became a *machi* after she was hit by lightning as a child," she said. "But then Chilean soldiers burned down her village and turned her people's lives upside down. There was nothing she could do but bury them and walk on their bones, so she died of grief." Tonia walked over to Eugenia's chair and leaned down with her hands on the armrests, her face inches away. "When Chilean soldiers came to our village with the coup, *m'hijita*, there was nothing I could do but watch the young people die. For weeks I heard their spirits moan along the river." She stood up and turned around again, her back slightly stooped as she resumed staring out the window. "The broken gourd," she whispered. "My Renato . . . I couldn't read the signs."

Eugenia went to stand beside the older woman. The roar of rush-hour traffic rose up from the street. A man with an accordion and a trained monkey was setting up for business on the corner right below.

"*Tía*," Eugenia said, grabbing her arm. "Forgive me. But as one mother to another, I beg you. Please." The old woman refused to look up. Eugenia continued. "I know you love her, *tía*, and I'm not asking for much, not really. I'll even keep it a secret if you wish. But *doña* Sara said you could read a person's urine. No one else needs to know, especially not Laura. I can find a way to collect it at night, when she gets up to go to the bathroom. I have a special pan I just bought at the medical supply store, it'll fit under the toilet seat and she won't notice it in the dark. Just this once, please. I could never forgive myself if something happened and I hadn't . . ."

Tonia looked up at last, a glimmering mist in her honey-colored eyes. "I know what you mean," she sighed. "I didn't, and I haven't."

"Does this mean that you will—"

"Just this once. Put the pan in your bathroom tonight. In the hospitals they tell you to put the pee in the refrigerator after you collect it, but don't do this. I need it to be warm. Not warm from the body anymore, but just natural, at room temperature. I'll come by the house tomorrow morning. Once Laura arrives here I will say I have an errand, and I will come up to the house."

Eugenia let go of Tonia's arm and the two women stood there, next to the window, their eyes holding them together. For just a moment, in a lull of traffic and when the accordion grinder was taking a rest, a single swallow began chirping.

"Just put it in a clean glass jar," Tonia said, "so I can place it up against the light."

✧

The next morning broke cool and clear. Eugenia had been up most of the night, and as she stood at the window that looked out on the back patio of the house she could see the burnt tones of early fall spread across the *cordillera* to the east, gathering in the brown wrinkles of the valleys thirsting now for the first winter snows. Laura had been up at irregular intervals during the night. When Eugenia woke during one of her daughter's bouts with dreaming, she placed the pan in the toilet and waited for Laura's next trip to relieve herself. The girl had gone back to sleep again around five and Eugenia had crept into the bathroom, gathering the urine in a clean glass jar and placing it on the kitchen counter, washing and putting away the pan so that nothing looked out of the ordinary. Then she had wondered what to do with the jar sitting in the kitchen, and finally decided to take it out onto the patio and hide it in the corner right under the living room window so that it could not be seen from the house. When she'd come back inside and looked out to make sure it was well hidden, the glow of first light had caught her attention.

She heard movement, then water running off the master bedroom as Sara and Samuel began to stir, then to shower and dress. She wandered into the kitchen to put the coffee on. Samuel came out, as he did every morning, to put the bread he had brought from his bakery into the oven to warm.

"Ah, my dear, you are up early today," he said, giving her a peck on the cheek.

"Yes," Eugenia answered, not sure how much Sara had told him. "Laura's alarm is about to go off, so I thought I would get breakfast going."

By the time they'd finished breakfast and everyone was dressed and ready to go, it was nearly nine o'clock. At the last minute, Sara decided to go with Laura, and this delayed the departure even longer. Complaining that she was going to be late, Laura ushered her grandmother out the door to catch the bus.

Tonia rang the bell an hour and a half later. Eugenia let her in at the gate and took her along the side of the house, directly to the inside patio. "I have the jar out here," she said.

"It's good you kept it in the shade," Tonia said, picking it up. "Laurita seemed to be in a decent mood when she got to the office this morning, though I can see what you mean about the circles under her eyes."

Eugenia nodded. "Do you need anything else?" she asked.

Tonia shook her head. "Do you mind going back inside and waiting for me there? It's easier if I can do this by myself."

Eugenia headed for the door off the kitchen. "I'll heat up some water for tea," she said. She saw Tonia lift up the jar, the mid-morning light reflecting through the citron-yellow liquid. Then Tonia took off the top and smelled the contents. After placing the top back on, she put it up to the light again and moved the jar back and forth.

Eugenia had boiled water, prepared and drunk two cups of tea, and put another kettle on the stove by the time Tonia walked in. She looked up, worry lines etched along her mouth.

"That took longer than expected," she said. The kettle began to boil again. "Do you want a cup of tea?"

Tonia nodded, then emptied the urine into the sink, washing out the jar and the sink before she threw the jar into the garbage pail. Eugenia looked up from the teapot she was filling.

"What are you doing?"

"I've already read it, I know what it says, so I don't need to keep it around anymore."

"And what did it say?" Eugenia tried to clear her throat.

"The odor was quite strong," Tonia said. "But I'm not surprised. With all the death there's been in this country, most people's urine smells strong these days. But she's not pregnant, and she's not taking drugs." Her voice was almost too light.

"Did you see anything else?" Eugenia asked.

"Can I have some tea? Suddenly I feel really hungry. Do you have some bread?"

"*Tía* . . ."

The older woman ignored her, filling a cup with liquid from the teapot. She stirred in three teaspoons of sugar and took a sip. "The bread?" she asked.

Eugenia took out the remaining pieces of baguette from breakfast and put them on a plate. Then she opened the refrigerator door, took out some butter and jam, and placed all the items on the kitchen table. She brought out two breakfast plates, silverware and paper napkins, and set two places. Then she pulled out two of the chairs, sat in one, and offered the other to Tonia.

"What else did you see?" she asked.

Tonia sat down and began covering a slice of bread with jam. "It's really not that important," she said.

"What do you mean?"

"She's physically healthy, and as I said before, no drugs and no pregnancy. Now, when I moved the urine, it was sluggish and heavy. This is probably her tiredness, and the stress she's been under."

"It sounds like there's something else."

"Trust me, it's not important."

"What do you mean it's not important? Shouldn't I be the judge of that?"

Tonia took another bite of her bread, washed it down with tea, and looked up. When her eyes met Eugenia's, they had turned from honey to a silty shade of olive green.

"Believe me, *m'hijita*, some things are better left alone."

Eugenia sat up straighter in her chair, staring at Tonia. The older woman looked down again, stirring her tea and bringing the cup to her lips. Then she put the cup back on the saucer and picked up the paper napkin, folding it into thin strips, then unfolding it again. When she put it back down on the table, it looked like a tiny accordion. She refused to look up.

"I can't believe it," Eugenia said. "You're actually not going to tell me, are you?"

The older woman stood up and took her empty teacup to the sink. She rinsed it out and set it down inside the deep white cavity. "Sometimes," she breathed, "one moment, one thing said or not said, done or not done, it changes everything. And not always for the better."

"I can't believe it! You and *doña* Sara, more than ten years now, marching, demanding to know the truth about your children! Now you tell me some things are better left alone? I just don't get it! You must be joking; is this some kind of cruel joke? *Tía*, don't do this!"

Tonia stood looking into the sink for a good long while, almost as if she could find an answer beneath its porcelain surface. When she finally stood up straight and turned back around, her eyes were blazing.

"All right, then," she hissed. "I guess then you must know. Everybody must know everything now, truth and reconciliation and all that. I told Sara, I said, some of that truth is not going to be good. Truth is that way sometimes. It can hurt more than a lie. But I guess you must know, you insist on knowing it all.

"Her urine is very heavy and sluggish. It doesn't flow normally when I move the bottle, and there are small, dark pieces in it. These pieces tell me there is a man, but the heaviness and darkness say he is not a good man. There is a bad man in Laurita's past."

"But *tía*, how can that be? There haven't been many men in Laura's life, and they have all been good men—Manuel, Ignacio, *don* Samuel . . . wait a minute, what about Joaquín?"

"The man's presence in her urine is very large. It couldn't be someone she's only known for a short while. This man has been with her a long time, probably her whole life."

"That's impossible. Who could it be?"

Tonia came back and sat down at the table. She picked up the accordion napkin and began tearing it into thin strips.

"You know something else you're not telling me," Eugenia said. "Please, *tía*."

When Tonia looked up and met her eyes, Eugenia no longer saw any anger in them, but instead an immense sadness. "There is only one possible explanation," Tonia whispered, "especially when I put it together with the nightmares. Every night Laurita has a visitor. It's her father. But it's not Sara's son. No, it is an evil man, someone who has caused much death. He must have hurt you when you were in jail, and that's why Laura was born. He haunts Laura now, because she has lived a lie. She is not Manuel's child."

They entered suspended time, an empty place where nothing moved. The silence was so complete that the sounds of daily life began to trickle in through the windows, around the small cracks in the doors, through the curtains still drawn against curious eyes. The whoosh of a car passing on the street. The whistle of a vegetable vendor plying his trade on the sidewalk. A group of boys arguing over where they would play soccer. Even two birds fighting over a crust of stale bread on the patio. Sunny, lively sounds that bounced against the walls and, frightened by what they found, ricocheted out the way they had come in.

"No," Eugenia finally croaked. "This is the lie. You can't see something like that in urine. How can you say this to me?"

❦

Tonia sat with Eugenia for hours. Her strong hands rubbed along Eugenia's temples, massaging from the crown of her head down to the nape of her neck. Occasionally Eugenia would let out a sigh, sometimes a moan, but mainly she was silent. After Tonia had discovered a particularly tense mass along the side of her neck, Eugenia spoke.

"The math," she mumbled. "Why is it always the math?"

Tonia sat up a little taller, trying to see Eugenia's face. "What is this math?" she asked.

"All these years. I never did the math."

"I still don't understand."

"Laura was born on September 15, 1974."

"And?"

"And Manuel and I were arrested on October 7, 1973. The times I thought about it, well, between October 7 and September 15 there's more than nine months, but babies are late a lot. That's as far as I ever got. Or ever let myself get."

"I still don't understand."

"The problem is, *tía*, the coup was September 11, more than a year before Laura was born. No baby is three months late. Manuel was evicted from his last apartment less than a week before that, and with the small bed in the room we moved to, the horrible tension in the air even before the coup, we never had sex after that. So it was more than a year. You were right, *tía*," she trembled. "Truth isn't always good."

"Now it can no longer be good or not good," Tonia said. "Now it's just truth."

"But the rape . . . and *doña* Sara and *don* Samuel. They love Laura so much. She's given them a second chance. *Doña* Sara says she's like Manuel was with his Grandma Myriam and Grandpa David. The bond is closer than with parents, she says. Laura will lose that now, and so will *doña* Sara. And I'll lose them both. What am I going to do?"

"Do they have to know?"

"But you just said that now truth is truth! And besides, the dream. Don't you think that, at some level, Laura must already know? Plus my mother's constant comments about her looks, and how she doesn't resemble Manuel."

"Yes," Tonia said, "and maybe Sara knows, too, in her own way. But sometimes, *hija*, well . . . sometimes blood is not the only thing."

"Now *I* don't understand."

"Me and Sara, we're like sisters, we grew up together. We don't see each other for more than forty years. But when I walked up to the door of the Committee, and we stood face to face, we were sisters again. It's not always the blood. And I think that Sara will see this the same way, because Laura grew up as Manuel's child. She sees the love for her son in your daughter's eyes."

"But it's just not the same. We're talking about children now, mothers and children, Manuel and Sara, you and Renato, me and Laura. Sometimes it *is* about the blood. And what about Laura's dreams? The blood talks, Tonia."

"Not always with a single voice. Take me and Renato. He's not really my son, did you know that? My Florindo and I adopted him. But after he was killed, who died of grief? My Florindo, not his blood papa! Whose dreams did he haunt? His blood mama's? No! He haunted mine! He haunted me! No one else could help him cross the river of tears to his eternal rest. That's why I've worked with the Committee. Sometimes," and Tonia's voice became a breeze whispering through the room, "sometimes, it just goes beyond the ties of blood."

✧

They heard the gate clang shut, then a key in the front door. "Hallo! Anyone home?" It was Sara. She stopped short when she saw Tonia and Eugenia still on the couch, Eugenia's head in the other woman's lap, the curtains drawn against the early afternoon sun.

"I left Laura at the Committee offices," Sara said, a quizzical tone at the end of her sentence. After neither woman answered her, she continued: "Joaquín's mother came by to help with the accumulated files and said she'd stay and close up later on. Joaquín was going to meet her there anyway, and—" her voice faded out, and she just stood there. The silence deepened, until it seemed to echo off the walls.

"What is it?" Sara finally asked.

The room folded them into a hush soaked with the stillness of a graveyard. For a long time nothing moved. Then Tonia and Eugenia spoke together, syncopated stabs of sound.

"Laura—"

"Manuel, he's not—"

"The dreams—"

"Her father!"

Sara made it to an armchair. Silence again, drenched with dread. By the time she finally spoke the filtered light inside the room had gone flat. "Yes," she said. And after a long pause: "I think I knew. I think maybe I've known for quite a while."

"What are you going to do?" Tonia asked.

"Do? What is there to do? I'll tell Shmooti, of course. Though maybe he already knows. Sometimes he surprises me. And then Laura must know. In some deep place inside she probably already does. But we must tell her that it doesn't make any difference to us."

"But *doña* Sara," Eugenia began.

The older woman raised a hand. "No, *hija*, "she said, standing up from the chair. "There's been enough loss already, enough mourning. Tonia, remember the last time the curtains were closed like this? It was when Manuel was confirmed dead. That's when we found out about you, *hija*, and we started looking for you. Shmooti and I spent three months, do you remember, Tonia? Three months with the curtains drawn, sitting shivah, Jewish mourning. We had so many people to mourn, you see. His parents, my parents, Manuel. We were surrounded by loss, by death. But enough is enough."

She began pacing then, and as she moved around her voice got softer, then stronger, depending on the way she turned, wave after murmuring wave, a current that wandered through the room punctuated by pauses.

"I told you, my dear, when you first came to stay here, that your mama didn't know how lucky she was. When Manuel was little, I was so tangled up in the web of my own fears that I don't think I ever listened to him, not really. And then he left for Santiago.

"And the thing is, I never saw this, never got a chance to figure it out, while he was still alive. The times Shmooti and I have said, why couldn't we have a second chance, if only just to say we're sorry. But that's the irony of it. If he hadn't disappeared, if he hadn't forced us, finally, to come look for him, I don't think I would have ever understood any of this.

"That's how it is, raising children. Most of what you need to know, you find out when it's too late. That's the way things work out most of the time. That's why your mama's so lucky, because she got a second chance. But so did we, with you, with Laurita.

"Tonia knows this, too. We've met children through the Committee of Relatives, most of them around Laura's age, like Joaquín, who never knew their papas. Often their mothers were so sad, so traumatized, that they hardly ever spoke to their children about them. Blood of their blood, and they can't remember. But it's different with the two of you. Even though Laura never saw a picture of him, somehow, growing up, she still was able to paint one in her heart.

"I would rather have Laura than a granddaughter who is my own blood but has no idea who my son was. Even Joaquín, with the photograph of his father pinned to his mother's blouse every day of his life, doesn't have a clear picture of what his papa was like. You and Laura have my son's likeness engraved in your hearts."

◆

When Laura got home it was already dark. She could feel the change in the air inside the house, and goosebumps prickled right under the skin of her arms in response. Her mother and grandmother were sitting together at the kitchen table, and they jumped just a bit, startled, when she walked in. Her grandma stood and came around the table, hugging her just a little too tightly.

"What is it, *Bobe*?" she asked, hoping that Joaquín's smell was not too obvious on her neck.

"*Hijita*," *doña* Sara answered, "you know how much we love you."

This sounded serious. Had they discovered that she and Joaquín were . . . and then her mother stood up, too, and came around the table and hugged her too tightly.

"What's going on?" Laura asked in alarm.

"Well, we've been worried . . ."

"And it seemed that—"

"So we asked Tonia—"

"And she read your urine, and . . ."

Laura raised a hand against the sudden avalanche of words. "Wait a minute," she said. And then the words sunk in. They'd taken a sample of her urine and Tonia'd read it. Were they afraid she was pregnant? Did they not understand that she and Joaquín . . . and what business did they have! "You took a sample of my urine without my permission?"

"Well, it's just that—"

"We were so worried . . . your nightmares and everything, so we—"

"How dare you?"

"Laurita, wait," her mother said. "It's important that you know what we found. It may be that you already suspect this, with your dream coming every night, but your father is not—"

"I may not be eighteen yet, but I'm entitled to my privacy! Even if you were wondering about me and Joaquín, you can't just . . . What did you just say?"

"Laurita," her mother said very softly, taking her hand. "What Tonia found is that your father is not Manuel. And I'm afraid it's true. It was one of the guards. All these years and I . . ."

Laura gasped, running from the kitchen into the bedroom. She slammed the door, and Eugenia heard the loud click as her daughter locked herself in. First Eugenia knocked, and then Sara, but all they heard was crying. After a long while, when there was silence, they tried knocking again. But still there was no answer.

Eugenia and Sara went around to the patio and found the window open. When they looked in, they saw the bedroom was empty. Eugenia climbed in through the window and unlocked the bedroom door, letting Sara in. When they opened the closet, they found one of the small duffle bags gone, along with some of Laura's clothes. The finality of it only sank in when Eugenia realized, looking at her daughter's bed, that the Walkman and Paco the velvet porcupine were also gone.

✂

The phone rang later that evening, and Sara picked it up.

"Hello? *Doña* Sara?"

"Yes?"

"It's Marcela, Joaquín's mother. *Doña* Sara, before you say anything, I just want you to know that Laura is here, and she's safe."

"Thank God."

"*Doña* Sara, I don't know what happened, but she arrived with her bag about an hour ago. She was crying, and refused to tell me what was wrong. I told her she could stay with us. I set up a bed for her in my room."

"Ay, *hija*, you don't know what a huge weight you just lifted from my shoulders. I need to tell Eugenia right away. Could you just wait a moment? I'll be right back, I—"

"Wait. I really need to get off. I left her with Joaquín at the kitchen table, drinking some *mate*, but of course I didn't tell her I was calling."

"All right. I'll talk with Eugenia tonight, and at some point tomorrow we'll give you a call. And thank you again, Marcela. You really saved our lives."

Eugenia called the next day around lunchtime. "Marcela," she said when she heard the other woman's voice on the phone, "this is Eugenia. Is this a good time?"

"Hi, Eugenia. Yes, we can talk now. Joaquín is in school and Laura left this morning for the Committee. I encouraged her to keep up a routine, to get her mind off whatever has been happening."

"I wanted to thank you. You don't know how much it means—"

"Actually, I think I do." Marcela's voice sounded choppy. "You and I both know how it feels when someone we love . . ." Eugenia heard a cough.

"Yes," she said. "Has she told you anything?"

"Only that she can't go back to *doña* Sara's. I'm sure she's said more to Joaquín, but neither of them is talking to me."

"I'm not surprised. Marcela, we don't know each other very well, so forgive me if I'm completely out of line here, but . . ."

"She's not Manuel's daughter, is she." Eugenia tried to answer, but all that came out was a hack. "I bet *doña* Sara wasn't entirely surprised, either, was she? Don't worry, you don't have to answer.

Eugenia, it's just that, in the Committee . . . over the last fifteen years . . . Let's just say that this is not the first time I've known about a case like this. We've seen so many things, you know. And yet, when it comes to our own families . . ."

For a while the rough syncopation of their breath was the only evidence that they were still connected. Marcela recovered first.

"*Doña* Sara already knows this," she said. "But all this truth . . . at first, I thought I would get some relief from knowing. But instead . . . Eugenia," she continued, "just leave her here with us for a while. I'll keep her focused on her daily routine, let the two kids talk things out between them. I'll keep track of what they're doing, I'm sure you know what I mean. You and I both know that our mothers couldn't stop us, either, but I'll make sure they're protected. And then we'll see."

✠

For several weeks after she arrived at Joaquín's house, Laura did not dream. Then one night, when the rains had let up briefly and a full moon had risen, clear and bright, above the city, the man in olive garb returned. They were no longer on the path in the woods but in Santiago, in a park she did not know. He reached out a hairy paw and grabbed her arm, and he smelled of mold. But she didn't struggle, there was no point. When she stood still and looked at him, for the first time his eyes were not muddy and she could see his pupils. With a start, she realized they were her eyes.

She startled awake, but everything was quiet. The light of the full moon still slanted in through the small space between the curtains. She could hear Marcela's regular breathing in the bed across the room, so she hadn't cried out during the dream. She felt the tears on her cheeks. She groped for her Walkman on the floor next to the bed and cued Prince's "When Doves Cry." Then she reached for Paco and cuddled him close. She knew she would not sleep again that night.

✿

The early April rains fell hard, bringing the oak leaves down with them. After several weeks trying to decide what to do, Eugenia decided to move back into her mother's house. Since the confrontation at the end of the summer, *doña* Isabel had remained reclusive, staying in her room, asking that her lunch and dinner be brought to her there. Irene had extended her vacation through the middle of February and asked for a family leave through the end of March. But she finally had to go back to work.

"It's like after Papa left, Chenyita," her sister told her on the phone when she called to say good-bye. "The falling out with you, with Laurita . . . I think something just snapped. I really don't feel comfortable leaving her alone."

"Don't worry, Nenita," Eugenia answered. "With Laura gone, it's better for me to move back in anyway."

"I feel so terrible, leaving you in the lurch this way, Mamita depressed, Laurita not talking to you. But I don't have a choice now, unless I quit my job."

"Nonsense, Nenita. With all you've done for me, for all of us, over the years . . ."

"And Amanda. She's been so understanding, but when I talked to her last night she was crying."

"Don't worry. Maybe if I'm in the house, taking care of things, it'll be easier for me and Mamita to mend fences. Besides, what else do I have to do except to wait things out? I've sent Laura several cards saying I'm sorry, and Marcela says she reads them, but she doesn't answer me. And she won't respond to Sara, either."

"Do you think you'll come back to Boston at some point?"

"I have no idea."

"If you do, you know you can stay with us as long as you want."

"Yes, *mi amor*, I know that. And give Amanda my love, okay?"

So over *doña* Sara's protests, Eugenia packed her bags. "It's really for the best," she insisted. "Marcela keeps saying things will get better, and I want to believe her. But I can't just sit here in your house waiting for my daughter to be willing to talk to me. Besides, Irene finally had to go back to Boston and, in her present condition, my mother can't be left alone with the servants."

April blended into May, and then the early June snows fell on the *cordillera*. Every morning that dawned clear after a heavy rain, the massive mountains covered with white, was like a miracle. After consulting with Rosa about the day's meal plan and meeting with Demetrio to discuss the garden, Eugenia took a walk down by the Mapocho River. As she measured the arrival of winter in the swelling of the current, she thought about Laura. The loss of Manuel was overwhelming, Eugenia realized, severing all kin connections with the people who had most accepted her in Chile. Did Laura now see herself as a constant reminder to her mother of the pain and torture she had suffered? Would she ever be able to forgive Eugenia for the lies they had lived? *Doña* Sara insisted on seeing the future with optimistic eyes. "At some point, *hijita*," she told Eugenia on her weekly visits to their house, "Laura will realize that, having lost Manuel so painfully herself, she shares even more with us, not less, than before."

As Eugenia grieved the loss of her daughter, her mother seemed to revive. She asked for the newspaper every now and then, and began to complain when the toast was burnt. One morning, Eugenia heard her mother in the shower.

"Chenyita!" her mother called, shortly after the water had been turned off. "Can you come in here? These towels look like they haven't been changed in months!"

Eugenia read in the living room most days, taking breaks to walk by the river or in the park, and at least once a week she wrote a short letter to Irene, bringing her up to date on their mother's condition and the lack of progress with Laura. *Doña* Isabel still spent the morning in her room, having breakfast in bed and not getting up until the early afternoon. But she and Eugenia began to dine together under Rosa's watchful eye. There was a caution to their interactions now, both women still nursing the torn ligaments of their mutual hurt. But occasionally, especially after a glass of wine, the beginnings of a playful tenderness would emerge in a gesture, a hand resting briefly on a forearm, a quick kiss, like a butterfly's wings, on the forehead.

The phone rang one morning as Eugenia was finishing her coffee. She knew Rosa was upstairs serving her mother's breakfast, so she got up to take the call.

"Hello? Ewegeenea Aldunate, please?" The pronunciation, it had to be from the United States.

"Yes. This is she."

"Ms. Aldunate. This is the Dean's Office at Carmichael College. Please wait on the line for Dean Henderson." A short pause, then a deep female voice.

"Ms. Aldunate, I'm so glad I caught you."

"Hello, Dean Henderson, how are you?"

"I'm fine, thank you. Ms. Aldunate, I'm calling because we haven't heard from you about your plans. The end of your leave is coming up now in mid-August, and we were wondering if you were meaning to return."

"Oh my God. I'm so sorry. It's just that there have been several emergencies here over the past several months, and my mother's been ill."

"I'm sorry to hear that. It sounds like your return to Chile has been stressful. But I'm afraid that I must have an answer from you by the end of next month. I can actually extend your leave one more semester, but to do so I need to have firm assurances from you that you will be back by the end of next January. Otherwise, I'm afraid I will need your letter of resignation."

"My goodness. I had no idea. I'm sorry. It's just that . . . I don't feel prepared to decide, now, I . . ."

"I completely understand. Look, would it help if I extended the deadline until the end of August? You would have one more semester in any case, and quite frankly, I don't think we could find anyone to replace you."

"Oh, Dean Henderson, that would be wonderful. I promise I will be back in touch with you by the end of August. Thank you so much."

❧

They were sitting at their favorite café, inside now in the middle of the cold winter rain, drinking coffee and milk and sharing a hot ham-and-cheese croissant. The flaky dough, crispy from the oven, melted in Laura's mouth and she chewed on the ham, savoring the contrast of salty and semi-sweet flavors. As usual, Joaquín had picked her up at the Committee right after school. They left the office now before four, since that was when *doña* Sara usually arrived.

"At some point you're gonna have to stop running from them," Joaquín said, his voice muffled slightly behind his portion of the croissant. It was the first time he'd brought it up so openly, and he was probably right. She knew that deep down. But she just wasn't ready.

"Maybe," she said. "But you don't know how it feels. I just can't. Not yet."

"It's been more than three months. Don't get me wrong. I love living with you, and I know my mama loves you, too, but—"

She put her mug down hard. "Look. No one knows me the way you do, and you're the only one I really trust. But believe me, this one you just can't understand!"

"Why not?"

"Come *on*! That's such a stupid question! Shall we review the story? My mama and I grow up alone, in exile. Every time I feel I have a home, she pulls out the rug from under my feet. The one thing I can hold on to is that my papa was a wonderful man, who cared about the poor, and she loved him so much. Remembering him hurts, but somehow, between the nightmares and the crying, I manage to put together a picture of him.

"And then, from one day to the next, it turns out he never was my papa in the first place! And the people I've grown to love most in the world, my *Bobe* and *Zeyde*, aren't even related to me anymore! And now, every time I look in the mirror, I see my mama's rapist! Let me see. Did I forget anything?"

With that last remark, Laura stood up from the table, over-turning her mug. The coffee and milk spread across the surface and began dripping down from the opposite corner onto the black and white checks of the tile floor. Joaquin reached across for the napkins and tried to soak up the liquid still on the table. Laura sat back down, crying quietly. The owner arrived with a mop and pail and cloth and, after cleaning up the mess, took the now-empty mug back behind the counter. Joaquín slid his chair over next to hers. She buried her face in his shoulder, sobbing.

"You're right," he said after her sobs had quieted a bit. "I can repeat your words, I now know them by heart. But I can't really understand." He ran his hand over her thick mane, smoothing the edges back into place. "Still," he said, "I've listened. And well . . . maybe in some ways, you aren't as unique as you think." She pulled away at that, but he continued.

"Of course it's different for me. I didn't wake up one day and find that my papa wasn't my papa. But my whole life, Laurita, growing up . . . I felt that my mama cared more about the picture pinned to her blouse than she did about me, flesh and blood, living and breathing right in front of her. When you used to tell me about your mama's nightmares, how you felt like *her* mother, comforting her, I knew exactly what you meant, because the same thing happened to me. At the same time, I envied you. I've never told you this. I felt your mama told you more about your papa—yes, the man you grew up knowing as your papa—than my mother ever told me about mine. Strange, isn't it? Turns out he might not have really been your biological father, but in some ways you still know him a lot better than I'll ever know mine."

The owner came back with another mug of coffee and milk and set it on the table, waving off Joaquín's attempts to pay for it. Laura took a couple of shaky sips.

"I used to be so angry at her," Joaquín continued. "A couple of years ago, I had a pretty rocky time. I was cutting school, drinking with some guys from the neighborhood. Smoked a lot of pot, sniffed some stuff, was getting pretty close to the edge. I'd been to the Committee a couple of times, just to see what all the fuss was about. And then I ran into you."

He moved his chair closer again. She sat stiffly, but didn't move away. "At first I only came back to see you," he whispered. "But I began to see the same story in those files, day after day. Mine. Yours. All of ours. We all hurt, yet we're all to blame. But it's not our fault."

Slowly her stiffness lessened. After a while she put her head back on his shoulder. They sat in the half-light of the lamps that hung over the counter. The rain still fell, at first in loud sheets on the metal roof of the café, then letting up until only a light spattering could be heard above them. When it finally stopped, she sat up. Her voice was crumpled, like a piece of cloth kept too long, folded, in the drawer.

"So what can we do now?" she asked.

IX

A Velvet Porcupine in the Suitcase

For weeks after Dean Henderson's call, Eugenia paced her room at night. With the electric heater turned off, in the early hours of the morning, she could see her breath. Sometimes, when the grey and orange of winter dawn mixed with the swirls of mist emerging from her mouth, she'd catch a glimpse of Manuel's face. What was he trying to tell her? Every night, his face seemed further away.

She was less and less able to call up his memory, his black tobacco and orange smell, the soft roughness of his beard. Every time he appeared before her, he was more faded, less defined. She struggled to regain his contours, the warm longing in the middle of her chest. Where was he going, disappearing yet again before her eyes?

The math. Why hadn't she done the math? His elusive presence berated her from a distance. What was it about being the heroic widow, the sacrificial mother, that she hadn't done the math? How could you, his faded image seemed to ask. How could you hurt Laura this way?

What choice did I have, she yelled back inside her head. They all admired your sacrifice, even if I didn't know why it mattered. So what else did I have? You had your life, his shadow said. And even if she wasn't mine, you had Laura. The daughter of a rapist and a killer, she answered, and I was her mother. What did that make me?

One morning, when the light broke slate-grey against a curtain of smog, she felt rather than saw the beginnings of an answer. Not doing the math had allowed her to avoid coming to terms. Would she now have to pay the price of not raising Laura honestly, by losing her entirely?

The insomnia faded, and at night she relived old nightmares. At first they were the same as always, faceless figures inflicting dark pain and nameless terrors. But then they changed. She began to see the torture room, to smell the dank mold in the corners. She was once again lying on the metal bedframe, wires wrapped around her arms to increase the power of the electricity. She tried to wake up, but the charge coursed through her, burning all the way up to her shoulders.

Every morning she woke exhausted, yet driven to write everything down. There were three men she began to recognize in her dreams, mainly by sound since they would hood her before taking her into the torture cell. She wrote about the texture of their voices, the smell of their sweat, how they sometimes laughed among themselves or commented on the latest soccer scores. And then the explosions of pointed light behind her hood when they turned on the juice, how she thought her neck would snap in two.

One night she dreamed she was in her cell. Shivering under a thin blanket, she felt the spikes of the straw mattress gouging her side. The door opened and at first she thought they'd come to take her to the "power plant," as they sometimes called it. But there was only one man, and he didn't put a hood on her. Talking to her in a soft, oily voice, he lifted the blanket and pulled up her gown. When he was done, she almost wished for the electricity. After that he came many times, a short man with a single brow across his forehead and eyes so dark they had no pupils.

Three men, one torture room, countless electric charges. Countless rapes, one cell, one rapist. Finally she could do the math.

When she woke the next morning, she realized she'd run out of room in her last notebook and would have to go out to buy a new one. Still in her pajamas, she stepped into the closet to grab some clothes to wear and her foot bumped against something soft that had been pushed to the back. It was her bag from the trip with Ignacio, and it still had the dirty clothes in it. She took out one of her blouses, the one whose sleeves he had peeled off her arms when they first made love in Bucalemu. It had been the first time since Manuel that sex had been connected to love in her life. Eugenia sat down on the bed for a moment, forcing herself to breathe through the familiar burning of grief in her chest. Then she pulled on a pair of jeans and a sweater, emptied the bag into her hamper, and walked out to the corner bookstore.

The first thing she did when she got back was to write down her dream from the night before, including the image of Laura's father. Then she began thinking about the dirty clothes at the back of her closet. Ignacio had fallen in love with the suffering victim. Had she been unable to accept this, his adoration of her as an icon? Or had she been afraid that, in accepting his love, she would have had to reveal herself to him? Would he have left her then, repulsed by the truth of her past?

She started writing in a new notebook from the pack she'd just bought at the store. In large capital letters, on the front page, she wrote the title: "MATH LESSONS." Her testimony before the Commission had been about Manuel, but this was different. She knew, as she turned the page to begin her text, that the dreams and scribblings she had been gathering over the past several weeks would be its core. Now, she struggled for words to frame the introduction.

"There are so many more of us," she began. "We have not been executed, and we have not disappeared. We have dedicated our lives to the memories of those who have. But by spending so much time with the dead, we have deeply hurt our loved ones still alive. This is my story," she continued, "of the hurt I have suffered, but also the damage I inflicted on my daughter. I could not face the truth of my own suffering. I could not tell her the truth of her own origin. And now it may be too late."

Eugenia put down her pen. Was it too late? Suddenly she was filled with the need to talk to Laura. She looked across the room at the clock on her nightstand. Ten-thirty in the morning. She was probably getting ready to leave for her work at the Committee, and then it would be nearly an hour before she arrived. Eugenia decided to take a shower, get dressed, and drink some coffee. By the time she was done, Laura would have arrived at the office.

When she called, it was slightly before noon. Tonia answered the phone.

"Tonia? This is Eugenia. How have you been?"

"Eugenia, it's good to hear you. I'm fine. How is your mother?"

"Much better, thank you. She and I are getting along much better. But you, as much as anyone, understand how long these things take."

"You're right, *hija*. But it's funny you should bring this up now. I've barely seen you over the last months, and I know how difficult this time has been for you. But I wanted to tell you that, sometimes, healing comes in unexpected ways."

"How so?"

"Well, as it turns out, after I read Laura's urine, I realized that there were things I could do to be useful, if only I could stop feeling sorry for myself. So I've started taking on clients again."

"That's wonderful, *tía*! I'm so happy to hear it, even if I can't say I'm happy about the consequences of that first reading."

"I know, *hija*, and that reminds me. Laura is here. I'll tell her it's you."

"Hello?" Even though she had tried to prepare herself while she waited for Laura to pick up the phone, Eugenia still felt out of breath, and at a loss for words.

"Laurita," she managed. "It's me."

A short silence. Then: "I know. Tonia told me."

"Thank you for picking up the phone. Laurita, I need to see you. I have a lot to tell you."

"About what?"

"I've been doing a lot of thinking, a lot of writing. I've remembered things I had blocked out. Most of all, I want to tell you I'm sorry."

A much longer silence, punctuated by short, jerky breaths. When Laura spoke, her voice was raspy. "You've said that before, that you're sorry. You've told me the same thing in those little cards you send. What else is there to talk about?"

"*M'hijita*, please. I've remembered now, details of my torture, things I'd completely blocked out, I . . ."

"And this is good news?!" Laura's voice exploded, forcing Eugenia to move her receiver away from her ear. "You think this is good? That you can finally remember my real father? Is this why you want to see me? Isn't it enough that I see his face every morning when I look in the mirror?"

A sharp crack, followed by a dial tone, and Laura had hung up. Eugenia tried calling back. The busy signal told her Laura had left the phone off the hook.

❧

When Rosa ducked her head into the dining room after the phone rang the next morning, Eugenia allowed herself the wild hope that it was Laura.

"*Doña* Eugenia," Rosa said, "it's *don* Ignacio Pérez on the phone."

"Hello?" Her voice felt like thick pudding in her throat.

"It's been a long time." He waited for an answer, and when none came, he continued. "You may not want to talk to me, but please. Just listen for a moment." A short pause, and when she didn't hang up: "I'm sure you remember what happened when you visited the office of the Investigative Police. At first, after we'd discussed your experience, I didn't think any more about it. But about two months ago, I began to wonder. Something just kept gnawing away at the back of my head.

"To make a long story short, Eugenia, we investigated the history of the building. And you were right. It wasn't one of the larger, more notorious torture centers. But for about ten years it was a way station for people being transferred from the provinces to the larger concentration camps. Thousands of people, many of them later disappeared, moved through there." He stopped for a moment. "Are you still there?" he asked.

"Yes." It sounded like a croak.

"We're putting a plaque on the front of the building, part of an effort the Commission is involved in as we tie up the loose ends of our work. The inauguration ceremony is two weeks from tomorrow. Do you think you could say a few words? We'd be honored."

"Yes," she said, her voice clearer.

The day of the ceremony was cold and rainy, so they decided to hold it in the large room where Eugenia had sat that day nine months before. The area had been cleared for the occasion, and along one wall, facing the lines of chairs, was a small podium with a microphone. Ignacio approached it first. He was dressed formally, the long strand of hair in its usual place over his right eye. Eugenia now noticed a streak of grey in it. Perhaps he would not be hounded quite as much about his youthful appearance, she thought.

"I am very glad to see all of you today," he began. "Some of you know me, but I also see a number of new faces, for which I'm glad. My name is Ignacio Pérez Letelier, and I am one of the lawyers of the Commission on Truth and Reconciliation. As we wind down the period of our investigation, we have taken it upon ourselves to leave an additional record of the events that have hurt our country over the past twenty years." He paused, looking down at his notes.

"As many of you know, our mission has been limited by the political situation in Chile. Officially, we could not listen to the people who, while still alive, have been irreparably damaged by the repression. All the tortured, those who lost loved ones and spent their lives looking for them, the children of the disappeared, the abandoned." He stopped briefly. "These people have not had the opportunity to speak publicly, on the record, about their experiences.

"This has not changed, but we may have found a way to open the door just a crack. A number of the places where people were tortured were also stopping-off places for those who, in the end, were executed or disappeared. Not because of the torture, but because of the deaths and disappearances, these places are a part of our purview. As a first step toward recognizing all those who have worked with us, helped us confirm the fate of their loved ones even as they themselves cannot be properly heard, we are attempting to mark these sites in some way.

"This office of the Investigative Police is one such place. For ten years it served as an intermediate stop on the caravans of death that traveled through our country. So today we place a plaque at the doors of this building, and even though we can't stand in front of it for our ceremony because of the rain, we want to recognize the person who made this possible. If it hadn't been for her, we would never have known the history of this building. If it hadn't been for her, who survived torture and intense suffering at the hands of the military police, we would have never been able to confirm the details of the disappearance of the first victim of repression whose case was brought before us.

"It is therefore not only my pleasure, but my distinct honor, to introduce to you Eugenia Aldunate Valenzuela."

As Eugenia stood up, she was surprised to hear loud applause. Her knees felt weak as she approached the podium, especially since Ignacio's use of both her paternal and maternal last names in his introduction had emphasized to her the importance and formality of the occasion. But his tight hug held her up until the weakness passed. "Thank you," he whispered in her ear before rejoining the audience. She placed her notes, hands slightly shaky, on the lectern and looked up at the people sitting in the audience.

The first row had been reserved for her invited guests. In the middle, right in front of her, sat *doña* Sara and *don* Samuel. Next to him, on his left, sat Tonia, Laura, Joaquín, and Marcela. She was glad to see that Tonia had been able to persuade Laura to come. After their phone conversation, she hadn't had the courage to try and invite her daughter personally, but perhaps what she said today would help in some way. And maybe, someday, she would share with her daughter the testimony she was still writing.

It was the first time she had seen Laura since she'd run away. She looked older, the cut of her jaw more prominent, her hair gathered up into a twist held in place by a large clip. Tonia's *copihue* earrings still hung prominently from her ears. She was holding Tonia's and Joaquín's hands. On *doña* Sara's other side sat *doña* Isabel, and the seat next to her had now been occupied by Ignacio.

Eugenia's gaze rose up to take in the rest of the audience, every seat in the room occupied. Among them she saw the long manes and handlebar moustaches, now dappled with grey, of the Revolutionary Left. She was glad they were there for Manuel.

"Thank you so much for coming today to help mark this place and its history," she began. "I am very grateful to the Commission, and especially to Ignacio Pérez, for the work they have done in confirming the fate of my beloved *compañero* Manuel Bronstein. I am also extremely grateful to his parents, *doña* Sara Weisz and *don* Samuel Bronstein, whom I never had the opportunity to meet before I returned to Chile last year." She was interrupted by more applause.

"But I would be terribly remiss if I didn't also recognize other loved ones, people whose support and—I must say it—suffering, have accompanied me throughout my years. My mother, here with us today, has suffered immeasurably because of the events that shattered my life. I have never really told her how grateful I am for her love, and how sorry for the pain I've caused. My sister, who despite her own loss got me out of prison and into exile, has been my guardian angel throughout the last twenty years. But most important, I wish to recognize my daughter Laura, also here today." Eugenia stopped for a moment, swallowing several times.

"As many children of disappeared, tortured, or traumatized parents must know, being the daughter of such a victim is not easy. Inevitably the surviving parent's needs come first, because she is too damaged to do what normal parents do, which is to put the needs of their children above their own. In the case of my daughter, to this has been added a recent discovery that has, I think, made many things difficult to repair—and to forgive." Her voice broke. She took several sips of water before she was able to continue.

"This is not meant as a plea for reconciliation, whether at the level of the individual or the society. It is instead a reminder that truth does not, in and of itself, bring reconciliation. As a very wise and dear friend said to me one day," she looked up to meet Tonia's eyes, "once something is known, it becomes truth and nothing more.

"As we begin to learn this truth, as we begin to live with the consequences of this truth, whether measured in plaques or in shattered lives, I hope we can learn to take responsibility for it. Not only so that, to use an already overused phrase, it should never happen again. But also in our attempts to account for the damage, hurt, and pain that, even as victims, we could not prevent ourselves from inflicting on those we love."

For a split second all Eugenia heard was silence. Then thunderous applause as those present rose to their feet. She moved back toward the audience but hesitated in front of the first row. Through the mist that gathered before her, she tried to decide where to sit. Laura and Tonia stood together and, taking her hands, led her back to an empty seat that miraculously opened up between them.

❧

When the mail arrived early the next afternoon, there was an official envelope addressed to Eugenia Aldunate Valenzuela and Laura Bronstein Aldunate. Embossed in the upper left-hand corner was the seal of the Ministry of Foreign Relations. Eugenia opened the envelope with shaky fingers and found a single, heavy sheet of paper, the same seal at the top, and the stamped signature of the Minister at the bottom. "Dear *Señora* Aldunate," she read. "Your two petitions, for your own recertification of citizenship and for your daughter's recognition of citizenship, have been approved. You can pick up your papers at our downtown office, on Moneda two blocks from the Presidential Palace. Our hours are nine to one, and again from three to seven in the afternoon." Eugenia looked at her watch. If she left now, she would miss the rush hour and get there in plenty of time.

Putting on a jacket, she walked out to Providencia, down the stairs at the Pedro de Valdivia station, and took the metro to the Moneda stop. By four o'clock she was in the correct line at the Ministry, and an hour later she had collected all the necessary papers, as well as the instructions on how to get her and Laura's identification cards.

As she emerged from the building with all the materials in two manila envelopes, it suddenly occurred to her that she might still catch Laura at the Committee offices if she swung by on her way home. Now that they had both been accepted as Chilean citizens, it was probably the best chance she would have to bring up the topic of the future with her daughter. And with Dean Henderson's deadline a little over a week away, she had the future on her mind.

Tonia opened the door before Eugenia had a chance to knock.

"Ay, *tía*, no matter how many times you do that, it still scares the living daylights out of me," Eugenia complained, giving the other woman a tight hug.

"I just knew it was you," Tonia laughed, "so why wait?" She drew back a bit, putting her hands on both of Eugenia's cheeks. "I'm so glad you came by, because it gives me the chance to tell you how beautiful the ceremony was yesterday. But this is not the reason you're here, is it?"

"No, it's not," Eugenia said. "I'm here because earlier today I got some good news. Laura's and my petitions for Chilean citizenship have been accepted, and I'm on my way back from the Ministry. I decided to stop by and, if she's still here, I can give her the papers."

"That's excellent news," Tonia said. "Come in and sit down. I'll call Laura. She's still in the back doing some filing."

As she settled into an armchair in the sitting room, Eugenia remembered the last time she had sat in the same chair. It had been nearly four months earlier, when she had come to ask Tonia to read Laura's urine. It felt more like four years.

"Mama?" Laura walked into the room. Eugenia stood, and the women kissed awkwardly before retreating to separate armchairs. Laura's hair was gathered in a single ponytail, the ubiquitous *copihues* glimmering in her ears. A light coat of dust, probably from the filing she was doing, covered the front of her brightly colored hand-knit sweater. Eugenia was once again impressed by how mature her daughter seemed.

"So Tonia said our petitions were accepted by Foreign Relations," Laura said after a short silence.

"That's right, *hija*. Your documents are all in here," Eugenia said, waving one of the manila envelopes in the air. "The only thing you still need to do is get your identity card, and there's a page of instructions in the packet. I already read mine and it's pretty easy, all you need is a couple of small photographs and the fee, which I'll be happy to pay for."

Laura came over and took the envelope from her mother's hand. "Thanks," she said. "I'm making a bit of money here now, but it's not a lot." She sat back down and opened the envelope, nodding as she went through the contents. "Laura Bronstein Aldunate," she said. "Shouldn't we change that now to Laura Aldunate Aldunate? I think that's what happens with children who don't know who their fathers are." Her voice was firm, and she looked over at her mother with steady eyes.

Eugenia was silent for a moment. Of course. It hadn't even occurred to her, but Laura was right to ask. Did they need to go through the whole process again? "I don't know," she said.

"You don't know what? If that's what is done for children without fathers? Of if that's what we should do now?" Laura's voice and expression remained calm.

"Legally, I guess you're right. But I'm wondering about *doña* Sara and *don* Samuel. How they would feel about a name change."

"Is it really up to them?"

"You're right, *hija*. But when we found out about your father, even before we told you, *doña* Sara said that, for them, it changed nothing. They still felt that Manuel's memory was embedded in your heart."

A curtain seemed to fall over Laura's eyes, and she put down the documents on the side table next to her chair. When she passed a hand over her forehead, the fingers were trembling slightly.

"Well," Eugenia said, "I expect that you could petition for a name change at a later point if you wanted to. I could ask Ignacio if you'd like, I'm sure he can find out if he doesn't already know."

Laura sat bent over, elbows on knees. "I'll think about it," she said.

"*Hija*," Eugenia ventured after another silence. "There's another reason I came by to talk to you. Now that we're both citizens, it seemed like a good time to think about our future plans. You now have the documentation you need to go back to school."

Laura looked at the envelope sitting on the side table. She folded her hands in her lap, and her right thumb began to rub back and forth across the top of her left hand. Then she unfolded her hands, picked up the envelope and held it upright on her knees, as if the name on the front contained an answer to the question in the air between them.

"Joaquín has only one more year in high school," she said finally. "We've been talking about getting our own apartment after he graduates. By then I'll be eighteen and legally independent. He wants to study Law, and if he scores highly enough on his aptitude test—"

"But Laurita," Eugenia interrupted gently. "What about you? You need to think about graduating from high school. I'd hate for you to have to repeat yet another year."

Laura's voice was steady but sharp. "I will not live apart from Joaquín."

"But *hija*, you're not even seventeen!"

"I don't care. You're right that I need to go back to school, and I will. But I will not live apart from him. I want to go to a school near where we will live."

Eugenia wasn't sure what she had been expecting, but it was not what her daughter said. As she got back on the subway on her way out to her mother's house, she wondered what to do next. Laura's "we," she realized, no longer included her.

She thought of her mother, just now coming out of her depression. Since they'd gotten home yesterday after the ceremony, she had seemed so happy. She thanked Eugenia, over and over, for what she had said. She thought about Ignacio looking so much older, and the physical response she still felt when he hugged her after her presentation. And then there was the matter of her job in Boston.

That evening, after lingering over dinner with her mother and celebrating her newly recovered citizenship, she returned to her room. She took a shawl from the chair near the desk, wrapped it around her shoulders, and carried her second mug of coffee out onto the balcony. It was about ten o'clock, and stars glimmered in the clear late-August night. Off to one side she could see the Southern Cross, its glow dimmed by the lights from the city's multiplying buildings. Yet there it stubbornly remained, shimmering softly through the flashing of Santiago's night sky. Memories were like that, too, Eugenia thought. Even as everything changed around them, they shimmered on.

Before she came back to Chile, her memories had rooted her to the past, surrounding her in nostalgia and desire. She'd hoped that Laura, too, would feel connected, that they'd build a life together in the land where they were born. But now that she knew the truth, she had no idea what came next. With her citizenship she might now be able to find work, but she knew that other *retornados*, those who like her had returned from exile, were having a hard time. Did she go back to Boston, to her fragile university position, and take up where she'd left off? After talking to Laura earlier in the day, she knew that if she did, she would return alone. And then there was the question of her mother.

Eugenia thought of Ignacio, and the attraction that was still present between them at the ceremony the day before. The connection to Manuel, to human rights, had been the origin of a deep mutual passion. She remembered when he'd kissed her scars before they made love for the first time. But was she more than a vehicle for his redemption? And his connection to his family, so like all the other elite Chilean families she had known. She could never play the role of wife and mother they expected. In fact, she couldn't play any of the roles Chilean society offered her. Returned exile. Redeemed subversive. Wise matron of memory. Her roots that had so powerfully beckoned to her in exile now tied her up, drawing her down into a dark, subterranean place she did not recognize as her native land. Even at the farm, when she had run into Inocencio García early that first morning. Her mere presence had called up his ghosts too.

She went back into her room, sat down at the desk, and took out the new notebook with its half-completed essay "Math Lessons." She wrote through the night. The next morning before breakfast, her eyes bleary from lack of sleep, she realized she was done.

She took a day to rest, and another to read her essay over slowly, stopping every now and then to savor the texture and color of the voice she saw reflected there. She thought back to the Guatemalan student who had come to her office a year and a half before. Now, she realized, she could easily answer the young woman's questions. Not that she'd been entirely wrong before. But personal experience meant nothing until you could look it straight in the eye.

She couldn't continue to do this, and certainly not write about it, or tell her students about it, if she remained in Chile. There was no work for her here, especially without the credentials that would establish her as an authority in the eyes of others. And as she had learned from her encounter with Ignacio's family and with Inocencio at the farm, most Chileans did not want to confront the past openly.

She called Carmichael College the next morning. "Dean Henderson," she said after her call had been put through. "It's been very hard for me to reach a decision. Still, today I feel confident in saying that I wish to come back to the college and resume my teaching position. I can write the letter today and send it to you by courier service if you wish."

"Professor Aldunate. Thanks so much for calling. And I'm so glad to know that you will be rejoining the faculty. Just send the letter to me by certified mail, even if it takes a few extra days. That will be fine."

"Thank you, Dean Henderson. There is, however, one more thing I wanted to ask you."

"About taking an extra semester's leave, I expect. As we already discussed last time, that will be just fine, as long as you return in time for the spring semester. Please include a sentence to this effect in your letter."

"Thank you, I did want to confirm that as well. But my question was actually a different one. Dean Henderson, I would be very interested in applying to change my position from permanent adjunct faculty to tenure-track."

"Oh. Well, in order to do this, you would have to have a Ph.D."

"I'm aware of that, Dean Henderson. Given my teaching experience and my years as a professional journalist, I would presume that if I wrote and submitted an acceptable dissertation, it would be enough?"

"I expect so, Professor Aldunate, although I would have to confirm this with the relevant individuals on our faculty. I must ask you, however, whether this is a precondition for your return."

"Oh, no, not at all. But I would like to know soon, since, if the answer is positive, I would like to use the next six months to make as much progress on a dissertation as possible."

"I see. Well, then, I guess everything is settled. I will get back to you as soon as possible with the answer to your additional question."

A week later, Eugenia received a phone call confirming that, with an acceptable dissertation submitted in crosscultural reporting, she would be awarded a Ph.D. and a tenure-track position. She knew that her testimony, polished now, was already crosscultural; but for the whole of the work to be considered an acceptable dissertation in journalism, it would have to include different points of view. So for the next several months, with the collaboration of Tonia and *doña* Sara, she gathered stories of repression in three cultural registers: her own, *doña* Sara and *don* Samuel's, and finally Tonia's. As she had learned over the previous months, there were many stories out there, including Angela's and Inocencio's, that were still hidden and crying out to be told. Perhaps with time she would come back and record more.

They carried out the interviews at the office of the Committee, and as Laura became aware of them, she offered to transcribe the tapes. She was back in school now, and the lack of new requests for documentation had begun to lighten the workload. On weekends she would sit and listen. Eugenia was pleased to see that, one day, while Tonia was talking, Laura sat next to *doña* Sara and held her hand.

Eugenia struggled with the careful transcripts her daughter prepared. Which should go first? Which last? She decided to place them in rough chronological order, though her own story ended up sprinkled throughout. And she concluded with Tonia's.

⸻

I've told you before, *m'hija*, that the blood doesn't always speak with one voice. Sara and I became sisters not because we were born in the same family, but because I didn't want to be a *machi*. I got sick when I was six years old, chills rattling through my body so strong my mother tied me up in a goatskin so I wouldn't hurt myself. Still I snaked across the floor, and once I got so close to the fire in the hearth that the tail hairs attached to the hide caught fire and my mama had to beat me with a broom to put it out.

We tried everything, all kinds of cures. Though it thundered in my head and swords of light exploded behind my eyes, the white-coated doctor in the hospital just shook his head. "There's nothing wrong with her," he said; "it's in her mind." So my mama took me to the local *machi*, an old man who smelled of smoke and spoke like a rock cracking in two. He read my pee as if it were a book. "It's an ancient spirit," he said. "A fiery lightning *machi* who died of grief after the Great War." My mother's fingers turned to claws upon my arm. "Oh no," she breathed. "It's Grandma Fresia."

Once we knew that *Kuku* Fresia's spirit had staked her claim inside my head, Mama sent me away. That's when Sara and I became sisters. But with time, as our bodies began to change, *Kuku* tracked me down. I dreamed again, stinging whirlwinds that made my body ache all day when I woke up. Then the fevers came and I shrank to the size of a small child.

They finally took me home, wrapped in a blanket in the back of a hired truck. *Don* David put me on his lap to cross the lake in my father's small boat, shielding me from the cold wind in the hollow of his arms. Once on shore, he carried me up the hill to my family's house. "There's nothing more we can do," he explained when Mama opened the door. "It's much too strong." That very night Mama took me, still wrapped in the blanket, to the *machi's* house.

They said I roared at first, because *Kuku* Fresia was so angry. I don't remember exactly, but I know that after a trance my throat was sore, and sometimes my whole body ached with bruises from how hard they'd had to hold me down. I recall images, fields covered with human bones, all mixed together, and mine among them. My ancestors' bones called out to me from underfoot, begging me to tread gently.

With time, the flood of energy *Kuku* unleashed became a river whose might flowed in a clear direction. The old man taught me herbs and cures and I spent days in the swamp, learning to unlock the power hidden in each nook and plant. With my large hands I wheedled music from sick people's bones and foretold the future in the crackle of their joints. But my dreams kept taunting me, their meanings hanging just beyond my fingers' reach. All the old man could say was that dreams didn't offer themselves willingly. You had to unlock them, coax them out, reach down and remove the kernel they contained.

One day Mama came to get me. "There's a man," she said. "He saw you picking plants inside the swamp, so he knows what you are. But still he wants you badly enough that he brought a horse." That night I dreamt a tranquil lake, large and clear and deep, and its waters washed the soreness from my heart. When I awoke, I gathered my few things and my new drum and climbed the hill toward my parents' house. At the top I saw a man astride a horse, his eyes two pools of liquid peace. He stopped right by my side and stretched one arm out toward me. Without a word, I took it and swung up behind him, arms around my Florindo's waist as we galloped off.

At first the people in his community were afraid. That changed one soft spring night when a desperate mother brought me her child, a baby with large almond eyes too big in a wizened face. The baby's urine spoke to me clear as a newborn stream, and with a mixture of four plants picked at the break of day, then crushed into a brew forced down the throat, he was cured in three days. As news spread, people began lining up every day along our walk.

One morning, before the earliest riser had staked a claim outside my door, a small gurgle called me out from beside the hearth. The almond-eyed baby was lying there, in a basket crib covered with vines of red and white *copihue* woven through its edges, upside-down waxy blossoms moving gently in the dawn-swept mist. His eyes were still too large for his small face, and as they looked at me they said, "You saved me, so now I'm yours." We called him Renato, which means "reborn."

I'd never seen my Florindo so playful. He'd lie on the floor for hours letting Renato pull his hair, his ears, his nose, with pure pleasure on his face. As soon as Renato could walk, Florindo began taking him to the fields and teaching him to plant potatoes and take care of the sheep. They became inseparable. I was worried, though, especially when Renato neared his sixth year with us. What if *Kuku* or one of her companions decided to find new living quarters? Florindo only laughed. "Don't worry, Tonia," he said. "Natito doesn't share your blood. *Kuku* and her friends can't get a piece of him. Besides, his feet are planted firmly on the ground." And with time, it seemed that Florindo had been right.

When the wildflowers bloomed in the spring of Renato's twentieth year, everything changed. I couldn't remember when government offices had opened on time before, sour-faced old hags at the typewriters suddenly replaced by smiling young things who wanted to help. By the next year, the poor in the countryside got tired of waiting and just started walking onto the farms. Renato took part in one takeover, on a large estate just down the road with a fancy wooden fence and a grove of eucalyptus trees. Every time he stopped by to see me and drink a gourd of *mate,* his too-big almond eyes shone bright with hope.

After one of these visits, when Renato came to help Florindo with the busiest part of the harvest, I first had the dream. A broad river flowed quietly toward the sea, and its waters were so clear that I could see the rainbow-colored fish swimming peacefully near the sandy bottom. I was so happy looking at them play, chasing each other around the rocks that made eddies in the current, that I didn't see the darkening clouds over the mountains. Suddenly, as if from nowhere, huge coughing birds the color of sludge, with tentacles covering their heads, swooped down upon us. Their bellies opened up and an army of toads and spiders crawled out, covering the green pastures as far as the eye could see. Everything turned brown in their wake and began to die. The dream started to come more and more often, until it felt like I was having it every night. I woke up screaming, covered with sweat, my Florindo holding me in his arms.

At first Florindo only chuckled as he rubbed my back and wiped the sweat from between my eyebrows. "Don't worry," he said. "It's about the wheat spiders that come with the harvest. I know you're really scared of them, Tonia, but it's all right. I've filled the drainage ditch around the house with enough water that they'll drown before they make it in." He changed his mind when the harvest was done and the dream kept coming back. "It must mean something else," he muttered. But neither of us could fathom what that was.

The winter began badly, the ground deeply frozen before the July rains, which then ran off because they couldn't penetrate the ice. The river swelled, a dark and murky current rushing by our house. My herbs and plants went under, and I had to make do with those I'd dried the year before. Renato came by late or not at all. When he did appear, drinking his gourd of *mate* and warming his hands by the fire in the hearth, there were deep circles under his eyes. When I asked him what was wrong, he looked up at me, his gaze as murky as the river. Then he cradled the gourd between his hands like a newborn puppy, staring down into its depths as if the answer to my question were lurking there. "I think we've lost," he whispered. "The tide is turning. The big fish, I can see it in the way they move. They're getting ready to swim back up the river."

When the moon began to wane in the night sky, the rains stopped and the days dawned frigid cold. One morning, as I tried to warm myself by a sputtering fire with no dry firewood to feed it, a harsh, repeating cough grabbed my attention. I rushed to the door and flung it open, not even able to finish my thought that someone was really sick, and what could I do with only dried herbs, before I saw them. Huge olive-colored birds coughed their way down from the sky, massive propellers churning tentacle-like at the top, and landed in the meadow of Renato's agrarian reform center. As I ran toward them, their bellies opened wide, and toad-colored soldiers came flowing out like insects, fanning out across the meadows with their guns raised. Renato had been right. Their time was up.

Years later, people who worked there after the great estate was returned to its previous owner said they heard ghosts in that room on the second floor of the boss's house, the one where the soldiers tortured the peasants. I think they were telling the truth, because what they described is what I heard that morning, clear and frigid as a glacier, when the helicopter birds came tearing down into our lives. The blows and moans, followed by screams, echoed for miles around. They took the leaders and tied them by their waists, then dangled them from the leg of an olive-colored monster bird and flew them out over the swollen river, dipping them in until they could breathe no more. Some died from lack of air, and I saw their souls steam up out of their bodies before setting out along the river of tears. It was not their time to die, which is why they returned to the place where they had passed, condemned forever to repeat the suffering that went on that day. They are the ghosts who scream on moonlit nights.

Luckily, Renato was not among them. He escaped, along with two or three others, and even when they took the dogs and hunted for them that first night they found nothing. I didn't know where he was, but I beat my drum hard for the first time in many weeks, hoping that somehow I could persuade *Kuku* to help him hide. The following night I dreamed him on the far side of the river, cutting a quiet midnight path toward the hills that hug the coast. The smoking fire in the hearth bid him farewell.

Florindo and I stayed close to home. Even if they had no money, people still needed healing, more now than before. But as I cut and ground and mixed my herbs, I knew there was nothing in my swamp or in my hands to heal lives broken by the olive-colored scourge. *Kuku* had been powerless, too, the first time the toad-colored plague came down upon our lives. Now it was my turn to add my generation's bones to the pile upon which others had to tread.

One night, as I was covering embers in the hearth for the next day's fire, I heard a scratch at the door. "Natito," I breathed. Renato was so skinny that his shirt hung like a cape upon his back. Pieces of shoe dangled from his feet. The dirt was caked on every part of him that showed. I uncovered the embers and placed on them the driest log I had, then ran to wake Florindo. Together we filled a metal tub with hot water. After putting a pot of soup to warm, I left to find an egg or two under my large red hen, while Florindo helped Natito into the tub and washed his back, murmuring over each bruise, then drying him in the warmth of the hearth.

Once he had clean clothes on plus Florindo's best boots, had eaten a few bites of egg and drunk some warm soup, Natito looked up. I could almost see the bones beneath the skin along his cheeks. His voice was like the whisper of a quiet breeze at dawn. "They're closing in," he said. "They're not more than a step or two behind. I can't stay the night, but maybe if you wake me in an hour or two . . ."

I sat for a long time, watching him by the fire's eerie glow. A gust of wind startled him awake, and he sat up. "Some *mate*?" I asked. He nodded. The kettle must have still been warm, or else it had less water than I thought, because it boiled while I was still pressing the *mate* leaves into the bottom of the gourd. I took it from the fire to let it cool a bit. "It's no good if it boils," I said. But he was in a hurry, and afraid, and somehow I believed it had cooled enough. But I was wrong. As I poured, the gourd broke clean in two.

On countless days and nights since then, I've wondered what I could have done. The gourd had broken, that was clear, a jagged gash next to my hearth, at the very center of our world. What did it mean? The mate leaves had dribbled out with the water, no pattern left to read. Renato knew. "Mama Tonia, I can't wait," he said. He hugged me quickly and ran out.

Could I have hid him in the back, behind the bales of hay? Or maybe in the swamp between the reeds, among those crannies only *machis* know? My mind moved slow, too slow. And then the drumming steps beside the house, a blow, breath rushing out, a shot. Through a crack in the door I saw Renato's spirit steam up into the sky, toward the shore, seeking the river of tears. They took his body, dragged it up the path toward the road. But I knew his spirit would be back. It hadn't been his time to die.

I took some comfort in the fact his soul was near, but though I told Florindo, it was no use. He couldn't hear. I dreamed Natito every night. "He passed right by two hours ago," I'd say. But Florindo just sat by the fire, each day a little thinner, a bit more stooped. I knew exactly what was happening, although I sneaked a bit of urine to be sure. He was dying of a broken heart. Not even *machis* have a cure for that.

Those were the darkest months, when fear and grief sank into all the corners of the house. People stopped coming, because they knew a house like that can hold no cures. The clouds and fog hung low, close to the roof, an endless dusk. I dreamed Renato constantly. Then finally, one night, he came to me the way he'd been before the olive-colored scourge. His almond eyes shone large and bright. "Papa Floro is ready," he said. "His time has come, and you must help him reach the other side."

When I awoke, my Florindo was already getting cold. I closed his eyes, washed him, and put on his newest clothes. I wrapped him in a woven blanket and carried him up the path. He'd shrunk so small from grief, he weighed less than a baby calf. By the time I got to the cemetery, the word had spread, and neighbors flocked to help me dig the grave. People say that weeping is a woman's job, and that our sobs push our loved ones down the river of tears and into the next world. If that's true, Florindo must have made it all the way in just one night. When dawn broke the next day, I sat by the hearth and resolved that I, too, would die of grief.

But Renato wouldn't let me. He came to me each night in dreams. "Sit up, Mama Tonia," he'd say, and shake me by the arm. "You can't give up just yet. Papa Floro's fine, just fine. But I can't stay with him, you know, until the circle closes for me, too. I need your help."

What could I do? I chose not to have children because I didn't want them to suffer as I did when I became a *machi*. I'd dreamed a combination of plants that, if you crushed them and mixed them in a paste, they closed your womb. But it had done no good. Natito was beyond the ties of blood. How could I help him rest in peace?

When the new moon was rising in the summer sky, a young Mapuche girl from the city knocked at my door. Her hair was short, and she wore jeans and a sweater. But she stood respectfully until I asked her in.

"*Señora* Antonia," she said after we sat down. "I'm with the new Mapuche organization, in Temuco. Some of our brothers and sisters who worked to help the poor under the previous government disappeared and are still missing. Our group helps their families request investigations through the Catholic Church in Santiago. I believe that one of them, Renato Painemal, was your son?"

I searched for words and found none. She took a magazine from her bag. "This magazine is called *Solidarity*," she said, "and it's put out by the Catholic Church. The story on the cover is about a mass grave of peasants that was just found near a mine in Lonquén. It's only the beginning, because we must learn what has happened to all the disappeared. The relatives must know the truth."

I took the magazine from her hands. I struggled to read the words, rusty from lack of practice. Then I turned the pages, looking at the pictures. Suddenly my eyes locked on a woman, her mouth open as if yelling, with a photograph hanging like a necklace on her chest. I knew her, but I couldn't place her.

"Who is she?" I asked.

"She's Sara Weisz de Bronstein, one of the founders of the Committee of Relatives of the Detained and Disappeared."

"Who is the young man in the picture around her neck?"

"It's her son, *doña* Antonia. All members of the Committee carry pictures of their disappeared loved ones."

"Is there somewhere I can find her?"

"The organization has an office in Santiago, in the Archdiocese. It's easy to find. We can help you buy a ticket."

I was on the next bus. The next morning, bleary from lack of sleep and disoriented from the traffic, smog, and noise, I somehow made it to the center of town. Asking almost everyone I saw, my rumpled, strange appearance reflected in their eyes, I finally found the street and the large old house. Opening the door, I ran up the stairs to the second floor and saw a brass sign with the Committee's name on it. I knocked, and Sara opened the door. She didn't recognize me.

"Yes?"

"Sara Weisz?" Her eyes darkened with surprise, and fear.

"Who wants to know?"

"Sara, it's me, Antonia Painemal. Tonia. Remember me?" First a blank look, then a flood of memory in the shape of tears.

"Tonia? From Temuco?"

"Sara, I saw you in this magazine." I held it up. "The picture, it's your son, isn't it? I lost my Renato, too. Remember when you were hurting? Back when we were girls? And I would rub your back to help you sleep? Sara, I need your help now. Please. I must help my Renato rest in peace."

She hugged me then. Her hands felt good along my back.

❧

Eugenia got up early and took a shower. By the time she got dressed and collected all her toiletries from the bathroom, the sun was just beginning to redden the sky. She stood out on the balcony for a moment. Along the street below, a solitary garbage truck had begun its rounds, metallic crushing noises punctuated every now and then by the human yet unintelligible shouts of the workers. She stepped back into her room and, as she finished the last of her packing, thought back to the events of the past weeks.

At first she thought she might persuade her mother to come back to Boston with her. As her own plans had developed, Eugenia was on the phone several times with Irene. Her sister's warm voice helped calm the storm of uncertainty that surrounded her. Now that Laura would no longer be with her, Irene and Amanda had suggested, and there was no need to live in a good school district, there was plenty of room in their big house for both Eugenia and *doña* Isabel. The third floor, used mainly for storage, had its own bathroom and a separate staircase that led outside. It could be refurbished into a small apartment, and if *doña* Isabel joined them the two bedrooms up there would provide a measure of privacy. At first *doña* Isabel seemed to like the idea of living with her two daughters. But then she backed away. She was not ready to move to a different country, she said.

Eugenia had been saddened by her mother's decision. After the public apology she had offered her at the dedication ceremony, they had become much closer over the past couple of months. Going back to seeing her mother once a year, only on vacations, was not going to be easy. But going back to Irene and to Boston, to what would now be a tenure-track position, was exciting. And Irene had suggested that, with the powerful stories it contained, there might be publishers interested in reading her manuscript.

Eugenia suspected that her mother's change of heart had something to do with Laura. As she transcribed the tapes for her mother's dissertation, Laura also began coming over for tea. At first it was only occasionally, but then it had become a regular Friday-afternoon event. She came over in her uniform, straight from the school near Joaquín and Marcela's apartment. She was doing fine, she reported, though it was hard to make up a whole year in six months.

One Friday, Eugenia and Laura went walking next to the Mapocho River, the late-afternoon sunlight on their faces as they turned west toward downtown. At one point Eugenia tried to explain why she was leaving. Laura waved the subject off and took her mother's hand in hers. They sat down on a bench near a bridge, their hands still locked together. Listening to Laura talk about her plans, Eugenia began to understand. Displaced by exile, Eugenia had longed for home, but her daughter had grown up with no roots to call her own. Now, surrounded by family and enveloped in Joaquín's love, Laura belonged. By returning to the United States, Eugenia realized, she might finally set her daughter free.

As the date of Eugenia's departure approached, Laura offered to come and spend the last weekend with her and *doña* Isabel. They took walks in the afternoons and played canasta late into the night. It had been hard to let her leave the day before, but she needed to get back and study for a big test.

"Promise me something, Mamita," she said as she gave her mother a final hug good-bye. "When you finish packing the big bag you have in your closet, but not before, take a look in the left-hand corner."

With difficulty she had followed her daughter's instructions. Now, as the rising sun lit the room in shades of gold, she was done. Reaching along the left-hand side of the suitcase, underneath her carefully stacked slacks and under her softest, most worn-in jeans, she found, cuddled in a corner, Paco the velvet porcupine. An envelope was tied around his neck with a pink ribbon. Inside she found a note written in her daughter's bold, loping hand. "He's always protected me and kept me safe," it read. "Now he can do the same for you. Love, LBA."

Swiping at her eyes with both hands, Eugenia stepped out onto the balcony once again. She took a deep breath. The sun was struggling to be seen behind the thick bank of clouds that blocked her view of the mountains to the east. She thought about her mother, *doña* Sara, Tonia. The trauma of losing their children had marked their lives every day. Even Irene, who did not have children of her own, still carried the scar of losing Gabriela. Having finally made peace with her mother, Eugenia could see how lucky they were to have a second chance. But for a moment she felt envious. With Laura staying in Chile, *doña* Isabel and *doña* Sara would have the Friday teas and the Sunday barbecues that would now be lost to her despite the annual family reunions. This, she realized, was the enduring wound of exile, a gash between herself and her family that no amount of time or healing would ever entirely repair.

She watched as the sun finally won its battle with the clouds, and only timid wisps of cotton remained along the edges of a deep blue sky. The day promised a transparent clarity that spoke of jasmine blossoms. Walking back into the room, she closed the suitcase.

"Rosa," she called. "Can you phone a taxi, please? I think I'm ready to go to the airport."

Acknowledgments

It's been nine years since I resolved to take my passion for fiction writing seriously and signed up for my first summer writing festival at the University of Iowa. For the following four summers, I was blessed by the mentorship of Lan Samantha Chang, who helped me remember that I did know how to read and write fiction; Rick Hillis, who suggested that I was perhaps writing a novel rather than short stories; and Lon Otto, who first provided me with what he called "the novelist's toolkit," and then had the courage and clarity to tell me when I needed to stop taking courses and just write. The fifth summer of my journey, with a completed novel manuscript in hand, I attended a master class at the Nebraska Writers' Conference taught by Curtis Sittenfeld, where in addition to her excellent advice I benefited from the comments of my classmates Judy Crotchett, Dan Gearino, Peter Obourn, Luan Pitsch, and Lee Parks. Curtis has been more than a teacher. Her ongoing mentorship, encouragement, and sage advice have been invaluable.

Curtis also introduced me to my agent, Lisa Grubka, who from the beginning saw what my novel could become. Her sharp and well-focused feedback, unflagging enthusiasm, and ongoing encouragement made it possible for me to continue through several revisions. Lisa's foresight and deep insight were also responsible for matching me up with Jessica Case, my editor at Pegasus Books, whose wise line edits and great sense of humor have been a real gift. Thanks are also due to the foreign rights team at Foundry, and everyone at Pegasus for their faith in this novel.

Family and friends, too, have been crucial to my ability to transform earlier drafts into a novel. My husband, Steve J. Stern, an expert on memory in Chile, read various versions, not only with enthusiastic and loving support, but also with the sharp eye of the historian. My sister, Ignacia Schweda, and her husband, Robert Schweda, provided astute and honest feedback from the point of view of the lay reader. My parents Ignacia and Richard Mallon shared their deep and multigenerational experience with Chilean culture. My sons Ramón and Isaiah Stern have supported me throughout, and Isaiah read an earlier draft and gave me welcome comments. I am also extremely lucky to count as friends many enthusiastic readers who provided support and help along the way, including Ana Mariella Bacigalupo, Marjorie Becker, Sue Elias, Nan Enstad, Linda Newman, and Lou Roberts. I am also deeply indebted to my Chilean family, to the Reuque Paillalef family, and to the families of the Mapuche community of Nicolás Ailío for welcoming me into their homes and hearts during my many trips back and forth between Chile and the United States since the mid-1990s.

Born in Santiago, Chile, **FLORENCIA MALLON** grew up in Latin America and the United States. She received her B.A. from Harvard University and her Ph.D. fromYale University. She has taught Latin American history at the University of Wisconsin-Madison since 1982, and in 2006 was named the Julieta Kirkwood Professor of History. She is currently Chair of the History Department. A prize-winning historian, she received the Bryce Wood Award for Best Book in Latin American Studies for *Peasant and Nation: The Making of Postcolonial Mexico and Peru* (1995); and the Bolton-Johnson Prize for the Best Book in Latin American History for *Courage Tastes of Blood: The Mapuche Indigenous Community of Nicolás Ailío and the Chilean State, 1906-2000* (2006). She is the recipient of several national fellowships, including a John Simon Guggenheim Fellowship, an NEH Fellowship, and a Fulbright Faculty Research Abroad Fellowship. She is one of the founding editors of Duke University Press's Book Series on "Narrating Native Histories."

Florencia Mallon lives in Madison, WI, with her husband of more than thirty years, fellow historian Steve J. Stern. They have two sons. This is her first novel.